THE
BANDIT

one day, the devil met an angel...

B.B. REID

Rogena Mitchell-Jones, Literary Editor
Ami Hadley, Proofreader
RMJ-Manuscript Service LLC
www.rogenamitchell.com

Cover Design by Amanda Simpson of Pixel Mischief Design
Paperback Formatting by Elaine York, Allusion Graphics,
LLC/Publishing & Book Formatting
www.allusiongraphics.com

DEDICATION
To all the Daddy's girls.

Mian's name is pronounced My-an.

PROLOGUE

Once a Daddy's girl...

MIAN

"I'M GOING TO prison, Mian."

I can't remember a time I ever hated my father. Not even when I grew breasts and noticed boys. But when he uttered those fateful words...

I raged inside.

Theo Ross was a notorious thief and playboy, but he was also my father. My fist struck the table, and I turned my glare on full force. "You *cannot* give up this easily. I'm not."

Eyes greener than the amazon stared back at me. I had my father's eyes. Maybe that's why I could read them so well when no one else could. I recognized remorse in the depth of his striking gaze, but I also saw pity. He thought I was naive. A clueless girl with my head stuck in the clouds.

But I wasn't naive.

My father just didn't know me anymore.

After Mom had died, the only thing that mattered to him was the next job. He'd say it was all for me, but after so many years, I knew better.

I couldn't keep my mother, and now I knew I couldn't keep my father, either.

"I can't be there for you anymore." He reached across the table and enveloped my hands. I couldn't stand to see the defeat in his eyes anymore so I fixated on the slight tremble of his large hands. It was the only sign that he was far from calm. My father was best at concealing his emotions and thoughts so he'd give nothing away. In his line of work, the ability to master it meant life or death. No one had ever been able to read him except Mom and me. "I regret that the most. I just want you to know that."

Should I remind him that he hasn't been *there for me* since Mom died? For months at a time, he pushed me away so he could chase riches. Or maybe it was the other way around...

"We still have a chance."

He shook his head in defeat, so I closed my eyes to block the sight. My father had always been a man larger than life, but I was not seeing that man today.

The guards.

The walls surrounding him.

The bars that would imprison him.

It weakened him.

"No, baby girl. It's over. It's time I paid back what I've taken."

"Why are you giving up? You can't leave me!" He hung his head, and I could see the slight tremble of his shoulders. When he finally lifted his head, he seemed to have regained himself.

"I'm sorry I have to leave you, but I'm not sorry for what I've done." His lack of remorse made me flinch, but he didn't notice. "I'll never be sorry for taking care of you the best way I could. I love you, Mian. Never doubt that."

The shield I carried cracked. "Mom loved me too, but she left, and now you're going away, too. I'll be alone."

"You won't be alone. Your Aunt Gretchen and Uncle Ben will take care of you. They're family."

I bit the inside of my cheek. He wouldn't listen if I reminded him of the truth. He'd assume it was my emotions speaking. My aunt and uncle were evil, vicious people who hated kids, hated me and hated my dad even more. They never approved of how my father made his money. They were God-fearing church folk who stayed true to their hypocritical faith.

Daddy may be a criminal, but he always took care of me, and he had loved Mom fiercely. "It won't be the same," I answered instead. I was never comfortable speaking badly about anyone—even if it were true.

He used his thumb to wipe away a tear. "You're going to live a better life than I did, Mian. Your mother would be so proud of the young woman you're becoming."

"But who will read me a bedtime story?" I sniffled and hoped my attempt at a joke would win him over.

He chuckled and flashed the smile that used to make my mom sway on her feet, once upon a time. "Nice try, Mian. I haven't read you a bedtime story since you were ten years old."

Just before Mom died.

I was sixteen years old now, and despite his absence in my life for the last six years, my birthday was one day he refused to miss. A late breakfast visit to Tabitha's Frozen Treats was our tradition that had remained unbroken. Until now.

We both shared the first laugh for either of us since he was arrested. My father had lived lawlessly since he was nineteen, but this time, he'd gotten caught.

"Daddy, can I ask you something?"

"Anything."

"Why do they think you killed Uncle Art?"

Daddy killing my godfather should never have been a possibility. They had been best friends and partners for almost twenty-four years. I've even heard the story of how they met.

Daddy saved Uncle Art.

My father may not have been perfect, but he was loyal. Killing him didn't make sense.

"I—I'm not sure I should answer that."

What?

"Don't you think I need to know?"

"No, baby girl. I don't."

"Why not?" I barked and drew the attention of the couple sitting at the next table. "Was it money? Is that why you killed him?"

Normally, he would berate me for the disrespect, but he only sighed. "If anyone deserves a chance to go to college and have a better life, it's you. Money shouldn't stand in the way of that."

"Dad, I would never have wanted you to sacrifice your freedom or *kill your friend* for me."

Something in Daddy's eyes changed, and when he spoke, I didn't recognize him. "Art wasn't my friend. I learned that the hard way and I dealt with it," he claimed icily.

"Why would you say that?"

He shook his head. "You aren't to blame for my decisions. I don't regret it and neither will you."

"That's not an answer."

"Maybe not. But it's the only one I can offer you."

"Well, it's too late. I already regret it, and I already feel responsible. What if they give you life? You won't be there to see me graduate. You won't walk me down the aisle. You won't meet your grandchildren. You're not supposed to be in here. You're supposed to be free." I dropped the broken shield, and for the second time since they took him away, I cried.

He tried to offer a smile and failed, but just like the fighter he is, he tried again. This time, his full lips lifted into an easy smile.

I only wished it had reached his eyes.

CHAPTER 1

Some mistakes aren't worth the lesson.

MIAN

ONE YEAR LATER

I TOOK ONE last pass at my hair with the flat iron and topped my primping off with a single coating of strawberry lip-gloss. After careful inspection for my best friend's benefit, I swapped making kissy faces at the mirror for a nice eye roll.

"I can't believe you're really going to go out with him," Erin squealed. She's been my best friend since the sandbox and claims she's Marilyn Monroe reincarnated.

"What's not to believe?" I faked being insulted since the truth was more likely to lead to an argument and an hour of "I don't get you, Mian."

The truth? I was already rethinking this date.

"Because this isn't like you. He's a senior..." She then emphasized, "...in *college*," as if I wasn't already aware.

"We're just going to grab dinner and catch a movie. We're not getting hitched."

"He's the quarterback at Weston and his family's loaded and powerful." There was peaceful silence, but I didn't bask. My count made it to five. "You should let him fuck you." She then dramatically groaned to make her frustration obvious. "I don't even know why you're hanging on to your v-card." Her face twisted, and for a second, I thought I was the one trying to sell my body for mediocre fame. "I know you're a romantic or whatever, but the *one* probably won't come around for another ten years or so. You might as well give it up now so you're already experienced if he does."

I stared until she turned away to fix her already perfect hair in the mirror. I tried but couldn't think of a response that wouldn't end our twelve-year friendship. Erin had always been reckless and self-destructive, and sometimes, I believed corrupting me was her one true goal in life.

"I'm not holding on to anything," I corrected. "I'm just not willing to jump into bed with any willing guy."

"*Guys*, Mian." And then she elaborated. "You're hot which means they're *all* willing."

"That doesn't mean I have to be."

"Ugh. You're so stuck up," she whined. "So, what are you going to wear?"

I nodded to the jeans and blouse I had thrown on top of my bed and took one last look in the mirror. I was happy to skirt that 'stuck-up' comment. My father always taught me to make smart choices in life despite his. Erin didn't know my father's hopes were all I had of what he had left behind. Making them a reality was the only way I felt close to him.

"No, you are not wearing that. That's not even sexy!" The red was about as racy and sexy as I was willing to go. I wasn't committed to this date, but I was willing to play the part to get her off my back.

"I'm not planning to jump into bed with him."

"But that doesn't mean you don't have to play the part," she argued. Erin and I may not stay on the same page, but we somehow read each other well.

"What part is that, Erin?" I couldn't keep the bite out of my tone if I tried. We were polar opposites. Our friendship didn't make sense, but it held on.

"The part that says, 'I'm not a total bore.' You used to be spontaneous and sexy. Ever since your father got knocked, it's like you lost your sense of humor. Life is still worth living, you know?" I watched her pick up the snow globe my father gave me on the first anniversary of my mother's death when I was too afraid to admit how much I missed her. She carelessly shook it and then turned her nose up at it as if it wasn't the most important something to me.

"Are you saying I'm suicidal?"

Her tone lacked contrition as she twisted her lips and asked, "Are you?"

I tried to keep my emotions detached, but it was hard pretending Erin wasn't right. I was different. My mother's death and my father's arrest had stripped away pieces of me until only the necessities remained.

I was walking and talking, breath and flesh. Nothing more.

"You know, I think my aunt and uncle will be back soon." I wanted her gone, and it seemed she couldn't care less what her words did to me as she unbuttoned her blouse until her breasts were nearly popping out of her shirt. I could swear her nipples were playing peek-a-boo with her collar.

"Suit yourself." She shrugged. "But at least take my advice and sex it up a little. You want him to come back for more, not over the hills looking for better. You never know how many other girls are waiting and willing to take your spot." With a wink and a flounce, she was gone.

I unlocked my jaw and blew out a breath to calm down, and then spent the next half hour pissed off at her anyway. My mother's death and my father's incarceration may have fucked me up, but I was far from dead.

I still wasn't dressed when the doorbell interrupted my brooding. I quickly dug around in my closet and pulled out the skimpiest dress I could find, and thanks to my aunt and uncle's rules, still happened to be dinner and movie appropriate. Their religious views prohibited me from wearing anything that didn't pass the fingertips. I was just grateful I didn't get stoned for flashing an ankle. I shrugged into the dress and took one last look at myself in the mirror. The dress was made of dark brown and navy sweater material that hugged my petite frame, emphasizing the little roundabouts I passed off as curves.

Okay, not curves.

What I had was more like an angle.

I tried not to stress too much over my physical appearance. I was more fond of the perception of beauty rather than the way things really are. I could make the world whatever I wanted it to be on a piece of paper. It was the art of my own mind that inspired and drove me.

Who needed looks when you have that kind of power?

When the doorbell rang again, I rushed downstairs and snatched open the front door. My heart was pounding while my date, Aaron Staten, son of Senator Henry Staten, appeared collected on the other side of the threshold.

"For a second, I thought I was being stood up," he greeted and laughed nervously.

"Sorry. I didn't hear the bell," I lied. I didn't want to give the impression I was trying too hard. He already had the upper hand being older and popular.

His gaze trailed over my body, and he took his time appraising me. It made me even more anxious to get this night over with—I couldn't care less if he appreciated how I looked.

"You look beautiful."

I nodded and offered a polite smile. It was more than what I expected, but maybe he felt obligated to compliment me. It would have been awkward not to after blatantly checking me out. I took in his blue collared shirt and freshly laundered jeans and said, "You look even cleaner yourself."

"Thanks. I shaved," he said. I tried not to look surprised since I hadn't even noticed. I didn't really think he had facial hair to begin with to make shaving necessary, but I appreciated the gesture nonetheless. "Shall we go?"

"Yes. I'm starving." I stepped out and locked up.

"Actually, I was thinking we could hit up my frat brother's party tonight. He's turning the big two-one."

My brain was screaming abort while he smiled obliviously. Partying with a bunch of college kids with someone I barely knew wasn't smart, but I didn't know how to decline without appearing lame. Erin would have jumped at the chance.

I nodded and followed him to his car.

This was my chance to prove Erin wrong, blow some steam, and forget that today was exactly one year since my father told me goodbye. I hadn't seen him in a year since he was found guilty. He forbade me to visit, and I couldn't find it in me to disobey him after the unexpected rejection.

Fuck him.

"YOU LOOK NERVOUS," Aaron stated as we parked.

"I'm not nervous, but I am having second thoughts," I admitted. When we arrived on the outskirts of campus, the two-story frat house painted blue, gray, and white with Greek letters prominently displayed was crawling with people. Music poured from the speakers inside the house, turning this side of campus into a nightclub. It took five minutes, and by that time, I was really having second thoughts. Drunken guys lingered around even drunker, half-dressed girls who made me feel severely overdressed in my sweater dress and boots. It was freaking January, yet most of them strutted in miniskirts and crop tops.

"Why? You're here with me. It's the safest place in the world." I ignored Aaron's attempt at being charming. He hadn't noticed since his attention was now on a freakishly tall, thin guy with shaggy brown hair. He held a red solo cup as he called out Aaron's name repeatedly while stumbling in a drunken stupor across bodies littering the yard.

"What's up, man? I see you brought food to a dinner party," he remarked as his eyes devoured me. My skin felt like it was being attacked by a million tiny bugs.

"We're on a date," Aaron answered, making his gaze shift.

"So, you brought her here?" I guess his brain wasn't completely fried if he had more date etiquette than his friend did.

"Yeah, she didn't mind." His tone suggested he wouldn't care either way if I wanted to be here. "What are you drinking?"

"A little of everything. You and your lady should grab a cup." He tried to appear suave, but he was too drunk to sound like anything but stupid. Inside, there was a makeshift bar littered with open bottles and discarded cups. "Mian, you drinking?"

Common sense told me to decline, but the need to self-destruct won. I took the cup he offered and took a healthy swig. If I were going to get through this 'date,' I'd need alcohol. It wasn't my first rodeo, so I figured I could handle myself if I needed.

Unfortunately, my weak bladder was near bursting after my third cup and a few dances.

I shifted away from Aaron's exploring hands and shouted over the music, "I need to pee!" I got a few dirty looks from girls of the slut persuasion, but I was too wasted to care. Aaron chuckled and took my cup. I stumbled up the stairs, and after nearly falling in a closet and walking in on a couple going at it, I finally found a toilet.

I was already peeing as soon as my bum met the cold seat and was relieved I'd worn a dress. I had no idea how much time had passed, but a knock on the door jarred me awake. I realized I must have dozed off so I quickly cleaned up and opened the door. Aaron stood on the other side, leaning against the jamb and wearing a cute grin.

He may have annoyed me at the start of the date, but the booze definitely warmed me up to him. I hooked my arms around his neck and fell into his muscular body. He was hard in all the right places, and then I blushed when I realized that *all* of him was hard. He lifted and carried me away before I could kiss him. Maybe I was in rougher shape than I thought. Maybe I turned him off. Maybe...

I felt a pillow like softness beneath me and lazily looked around. We were in someone's bedroom. Before I could question anything, he fell on top of me and moved between my legs.

I let him kiss me knowing if I were sober, there was no chance I would have allowed it. He gently ran his hands down my sides but then grew too bold too quickly and began to push my dress up. The drunk induced fog cleared and I pushed at his chest. My heart stopped when I felt his grip tighten on my waist as I struggled to escape from under him. I was ready to scream when his lips finally lifted from my neck. He stared down at me as he took deep breaths in and out. He looked like he was considering something in his head.

Finally, he stood, and I watched as he adjusted himself in his jeans. He looked pissed, but then his expression changed to boredom. "I should take you home. I'll be downstairs."

And then he was gone.

I was relieved as I tugged my dress back into place and ran my fingers through my hair. I should have stayed true to my initial decision about him. His willingness to continue our 'date' ended now that it was clear my virginity wasn't on the table.

Well, fuck him very much.

I stomped downstairs, feeling a lot more sober than I had coming up only to see him holding another solo cup and talking up some blonde.

Of course.

Why not go blonde, right?

The girl who presently had his attention looked like a guaranteed fuck. If I had my own way home, I would have left him to it, but instead, I awkwardly ended their verbal fuck fest by clearing my throat.

Her smiled dropped, and his gaze barely skimmed my forehead before he turned back to the blonde and whispered something in her ear. Whatever he said caused her to giggle outrageously. I'd been with him for all of two hours and not once found him that funny.

"I guess I'll be in the car then." I didn't wait around for a response and made my way through the dancing crowd. After checking my phone, I realized I only had thirty minutes until my aunt and uncle would be home. I was prepared to extend my curfew by an hour as part of my rebellion, but now that the rush was gone, I wasn't as willing to give my Aunt Gretchen an excuse to go off on one of her religious tangents.

I found Aaron's Mustang and tried the door, but it was locked. Fifteen minutes later, he sauntered from the house swinging his keys and whistling. He still held his cup as he unlocked the door and sat inside.

"Would you mind?" I gestured to the cup. There was no way I'd trust him or anyone to drink and drive with me as a passenger. "I'm not comfortable with you *literally* drinking and driving."

"Oh. Shit. I forgot I still had this. Drink it for me, will you? I probably shouldn't have anymore." I gazed at him suspiciously as he added, "If I go back inside, it will be another fifteen minutes before I make it back out. Your curfew is at midnight, right?"

He had a good point, but I couldn't outright ignore the alarms going off in my mind. It went against everything my parents managed to teach me before they were both stolen from me. "You didn't spike it or anything, did you?"

"Why would I do something like that?" he asked while staring ahead. His jaw tightened as he quickly pulled away from the curb. Maybe I insulted him. Before I could apologize, he barked, "Hurry up. We can't have this in the car."

"Just toss it out the window."

"It's a college party. Cops are always nearby. I don't want to get pulled over for littering and have them figure out it was alcohol. My dad will kill me." Right then, we passed a cruiser waiting along the darkened part of the street. I snatched the cup and quickly downed the contents. I had to lean my head back when I felt the alcohol heat my blood and fuddle my brain.

The last thing I remember was Aaron glancing my way, sporting an accomplished grin and lust in his eyes.

CHAPTER 2

Promises are made to be broken.

MIAN

EIGHTEEN MONTHS LATER

"MIAN, WE HAVE to let you go. This isn't working out."

I turned my face just in time to save myself from his smelly spittle. Jerry had a disgusting habit of spraying his words all over his victim's face. The sweat sticking to my face from my two-mile run and his saliva was a deadly concoction I wanted no part of. Everyone knew to give Jerry wide berth when he was speaking to avoid being assaulted by his fishy saliva. I, however, made it my mission to kiss Jerry's ass as much as possible. Shifts were hard to come by at the small diner.

"Mian? Did you hear me?" I was too busy holding my breath to avoid as much of his to hear anything he'd said. Seriously, how can his breath always smell like fish when he never actually ate any? According to him, he wasn't a fan.

"Are you breaking up with me?" It was a weak shot at humor, but that was because I refused to use tears. It seemed my desperate attempt to make it to work by running two miles had proven fruitless. I pulled my white dress shirt from my sweaty skin and smiled, but it was weak.

I couldn't lose this job.

This was my fifth job in less than six months.

"I'm sorry, Mian. You've only been here five weeks and have repeatedly been late or have failed to show up at all."

"Jerry, please don't do this. I'll work an extra shift for free tonight, just please don't fire me. I can't lose this job. I have Caylen." I was counting on tonight's tips just to make it through another week.

"I've tried to be sympathetic to your situation, but it's gotten out of hand. There are many other people who need to work as well. People who can show up for their shifts."

He walked away, but I couldn't let it end there. I'd beg. I had no options, and no options meant no pride. I pleaded with the manager and made every promise possible that I knew I couldn't keep until he lost any show of sympathy and forcefully showed me, with his hand on my arm, to the door.

The sound of the restaurant door slamming behind me as I stood on the street echoed ominously around me. This waitressing gig was my only source of income, and now it was gone. I balled my fist and entertained the idea of shattering the front window. If I could afford the hospital bill after I broke my hand, I might have tried. I knew it wasn't Jerry's fault I lost my job. It wasn't anyone's fault that I was the world's biggest fuck-up.

When it became clear Jerry wouldn't offer me another chance, I started down the street. It was nearly a hundred degrees outside since we were in the middle of summer. The heat made me consider the impossible, but then a cool breeze swept by, and I decided to outrun the sun was best left to the professionals.

My walk gave me plenty of time to agonize over what awaited me when I made it home. Maybe the sun would take pity on me, and I'd go up in flames.

Chicago moved around me, completely oblivious to my own world crashing around me yet again. I needed a distraction. My fingers itched for my pencil and pad. I could create another world with the stroke of my hand and get lost within it.

And by lost, I meant *hide*.

The hustle and bustle of the city used to excite me but now it only made me miss home.

But home wasn't home anymore—not without my father.

He used to bring me to the city, and we'd visit our favorite ice cream shop and goof around for hours, sometimes days, during the summer. Of course, that was all before my mother died and he decided he preferred to avoid me.

I relocated permanently when my aunt and uncle kicked me out after graduation. I spent the first half of my summer pretending to wait for my first semester of college. That lasted until my aunt walked in on me stepping out of the shower and caught a front row view of the invasion in my belly.

I was thrown out on my ass that very day, and the next thirteen months became a constant battle for survival.

I wanted to hate my aunt and uncle more than I already did, but that would mean denying my pregnancy hadn't been my fault.

And Aaron's.

When I tried to come clean about what resulted after that night, he pretended we were strangers. Aaron's denial was the final turning point down a path different from the one my father paved for me. Daddy's dream that I'd go to college died by my hands. My aunt and uncle helped long before I'd gotten pregnant. The money my father hid from my aunt and uncle had only lasted me a year before it ran dry. While my father entrusted his brother to me because he had no choice, he still took measures to protect me from them. When I was kicked out, I used the funds he set aside to get by. Unfortunately, it hadn't been enough. Turns out, my aunt and uncle's hospitality came with a hefty price tag, which cut into the money he was able to leave me.

I stretched every penny and saved, but none of it mattered in the end.

Daddy had been sentenced to twenty-five years in maximum security. His sentence killed our hope of being reunited sooner than later. I remember watching my father when the verdict was delivered and later when he was sentenced. He never reacted. He sat there unmoving and unsurprised.

He'd lied to me.

He knew he wasn't going to get off. He played me to lessen the pain only to amplify it the day he was taken away in cuffs for the final time.

Our first and only visit occurred two and a half years ago. That was when he forbade me to come back.

"I don't want you to come back. Not for me."

"Why wouldn't I come see you? You're my dad. You're all I have."

"You have so much time left. I don't. I want you to use your time to make something better. This is it for me. Your

future is the only thing I can make right. And that means I can't be a part of it anymore."

I can still feel the heat from the tears I shed over him, the hurt in my heart, and the emptiness I was left with when he turned his back on me for the last time.

After five minutes of struggling through the June heat, I reached the quarter-mile mark of my journey...the bus stop. Behind me, I could hear the rumble from the exhausted bus engine approach. My feet stopped moving, and I watched it roll to a stop. The hiss of the brakes engaging and then the door swinging open, greeted me.

Fuck it.

Weakly, I ascended the few steps and reached inside my bag to pay. My tattered wallet was already open and staring back at me was an empty pocket.

The driver became impatient and grumbled, "It's two bucks to ride, miss."

I nodded.

Embarrassed and worn, I wordlessly stepped down. Bus rides were a luxury best reserved for when time wasn't on my side. I figured we'd eat more often if I didn't make city transportation another monthly reason to struggle.

Yesterday, when I was in danger of missing my shift, I had no choice but to catch the bus.

And so went the only two bucks I had to spare. I didn't always end a shift with a pocket full of cash. Yesterday's tips had been spent on groceries and supplies for the week and the two measly bucks I had before my shift was spent to save a job I no longer had.

If today had gone as planned, there would have been no sun, and I wouldn't have needed to be saved by a bus. I would have walked through a dangerous city at night with a pocket full of cash I made from tips, and everything would have been okay.

But today wasn't a day for plans.

I survived the rest of the trek to the subsidized apartment building I called home. My clothes stuck to my skin as I entered the run down building. As much as I dreaded facing the music, I wanted out of them more.

After I had been evicted from the decent apartment I rented while pregnant, I was forced to lower my living standards. The payments became too hard to make each month, and the manager was no longer willing to offer extensions without him getting blown on occasion. After I had refused him, the smell of piss stained hallways and the drug addicts that decorated them became my new reality.

I held my breath and waded through the living dead looking for their next hit and made my way to the stairs.

I hated the stairs as much as I hated the building.

It wasn't the way a few of the boards were missing or how the ones still intact creaked. It was the constant groping and pinching I had to endure from the addicts and the dealers that chose to make the hallways their storefront.

The elevator was no longer an option.

The steel doors that were designed to keep people from falling to their death when closed were left open when it broke down, and the owners didn't find it necessary to have it rectified.

"You're home early." I trudged into my third-floor apartment and found, Anna, my friend and neighbor, waiting on my tattered couch.

"Uh, yeah. I kind of got fired," I confessed and toed off my shoes.

"Oh, no! It's totally my fault!" She hopped up from the couch with her hands covering her mouth. "I'm so sorry I was late!"

"It's not your fault, Anna. You're just a kid." Anna was seventeen years old and the most genuine person I'd ever known. After she Caylen, she volunteered to babysit for free, which I readily agreed but under the condition that I pay her anyway. So far, I'd been able to hold up my end of the bargain—until tonight.

"Yeah, but so are you," she countered.

"I'm a nineteen-year-old single mother. I'm not a kid anymore."

She fell silent as her face lost its normal perky hue. I kicked myself and stumbled to apologize just when her eyes brightened again. "Hey, I have a thought! In a few months, he should start walking."

"Yeah?"

"Well, you'll have a better chance of keeping up with him. My mom had me when she was only sixteen. She says she was lucky she was young enough to keep up with me after my father up and died and left her with a kid he forced her to keep in the first place."

I waited for the explosion of anger and hurt that never came. "She really said that?"

She shrugged and didn't appear bothered, which only broke my heart for her more. "Why wouldn't she? It's true." Her gaze lifted from her feet and met mine. "It's okay really," she assured. She laughed, but even a deaf person could tell it was forced. "I'm used to being repeatedly told how I'm a burden who ruined her perfect body."

I wasn't a violent person. I preferred avoiding people who upset or hurt me, but her mother made me want my first taste of blood. Anna's father died in a car accident when she was six. A drunk driver t-boned his car, killing him instantly. Since then, she's been under the sole care of her irresponsible mother. Her father and mother's families had long written them off thanks to Brandi.

When I moved in seven months ago, we formed an instant bond. Our friendship never felt forced because we had more in common than I'd ever had with anyone, including Erin. She'd still been around until Caylen was born and then decided a baby in the mix would cramp *her* style. I haven't heard from her since, and even after twelve years of friendship, I didn't feel any love lost.

Anna's eyes were clouded, and as someone who shared her pain, I knew all too well the dark place she was headed. "Where is Brandi, anyway?"

She rolled her eyes, and my shoulders relaxed. Anger was sometimes less dangerous than sadness. "Off with her latest boyfriend." She huffed. "She is so selfish! She was the reason I was late to babysit Caylen, you know?"

"It's okay, Anna. That job wasn't going anywhere anyway."

She frowned. "What are you going to do for money?"

I shrugged as if I wasn't breaking into tiny irreparable pieces. "I'll do what I've always done. I'll find another one."

She appeared thoughtful. "Until then, don't worry about paying me. I'll still babysit for you when you need to look for work."

I sighed and felt at least one of my burdens disappear. "You're an angel, you know that? I promise to pay you as soon as I can."

"It's no problem. I love Caylen." I nodded. "And he loves you, Mian." I nodded again. "It will get better." I didn't react that time. She'd said the same thing each time I lost a gig or the lights were turned off. I just wasn't sure I believed her anymore.

The sudden intrusion of Caylen's cries filtered from the only bedroom in the apartment, which we shared. "I have to get that."

We laughed and ignored the heaviness in the room. After seeing Anna out, I made my way to the bedroom. Across the room, in the crib I had found for a bargain, was the reason I even still tried.

I smiled when I saw that he had managed to kick off his blanket and continue to throw a tantrum fit for an eight-month-old. I scooped him up and cradled his warm body against my chest. He no longer screamed, but his fussing went on as he tried to eat his fist.

"I'll guess you're hungry, huh, little guy?" I left our bedroom and entered the kitchen. I hadn't had the chance to prep his bottles before leaving for work, so I made quick work of it one-handed while attempting to soothe him. After popping the bottle in the microwave, I took stock of what we had and calculated we had enough food and diapers to survive another week. Whatever I did, I had to move fast. Time moved fast when you didn't want it to.

Tomorrow, I'd search the papers and every square inch of the city by foot if I had to.

There were thousands of restaurants in the city.

One of them had to be hiring.

I WAS STILL jobless after a week of scouring as many places as I could, as often as I could. I even took Caylen with me on the cooler days to search for work. I was now down to the last of our food with no money and no solutions.

"Mian?"

I recognized the voice and groaned. Joseph 'Joey' Jones was my second-floor neighbor. He lived here with his mom since he was seventeen and still in high school. He also had an unfailing crush on Anna and begged me to talk him up to her every time we ran into each other. The one time I asked, Anna had made it clear she wasn't interested. "Not my type and never will be," is what she said. I pushed through the fronts doors and quickened my pace when the sound of his footsteps grew closer.

"Hey, wait up!"

I could hear him breathing now so I turned and forced a smile. "Hey, Joey. What's up?"

"Damn, girl. I had to run after you. Did you not hear me?"

"Nope."

"Oh, that's cool. So where are you headed?"

I shrugged. "Nowhere special." I attempted casual but his bushy eyebrows bunched together under his backward red cap. I could even see the riots of dark curls peeking out from under it.

"Why so secretive?" He chuckled and stuffed his hands in the pockets of his cargo shorts. I've known Joey since the first day I moved in, and he had offered to help me unload my meager belongings. He's always been nice and helpful and even chauffeured Caylen and me around in his beat up old Chevrolet when the weather was too bad to trek it. I had no real reason not to trust him.

It's just that trusting people with your secrets made you vulnerable, and I'd had enough of that already.

"I lost my job," I offered. "I'm hunting for a new one." I left out the part about me being destitute and almost out of food.

"With Caylen?" He nodded to him strapped to my chest. The carrier had been a godsend in the form of a hand-me-down I graciously accepted from Tara who lived on the first floor. She had seen me struggling to carry Caylen and two handfuls of groceries one day and had helped me carry them. After thanking her for the help, she'd reappeared at my door with the carrier. Turns out, she had a two-year-old son who'd outgrown it. I turned it down, feeling wrong for taking from a stranger until she patted her arm where her birth control was planted and reassured me she had no plans of having another one.

"Anna's working today."

"Right." He looked from me to the baby and then met my gaze again. "I could watch him if you want."

I hesitated because I didn't want to hurt his feelings. Joey's maturity level wasn't quite there for me to trust him with my baby. "That's okay. I'm just filling out applications today."

It was a lie I was hoping he didn't see through. I was actually heading to one of the only payphones that probably still existed. I had scraped up change in a few junk drawers and planned to use it to call the last two people I ever wanted to ask for help.

"Oh, okay then." I nodded and turned away. "Before you go..."

Damn it.

"Yes?" I really wanted to get this phone call over with before I backed out altogether. Joey was threatening that.

"Have you talked to Anna lately?"

"What do you mean?"

"About me."

"Joey..."

"I know what you're going to say, but maybe she's changed her mind!"

"Why don't you just talk to her yourself?"

"Because..."

"Because what?"

"Because she's beautiful," he answered softly. His eyes shone with admiration, making me wonder just how deep his crush actually went.

"And you have trouble talking to beautiful girls?"

I wondered what that meant for me since he talked to me just fine. I wasn't conceited, but I never considered myself unattractive either. Feeling self-conscious, I ran my fingers through my hair in a subtle attempt to improve my appearance. I suppose it's what I got for letting stress make me not care what I looked like.

His laugh broke through my self-loathing, and I cut him with my glare. "Of course not or else I wouldn't be able to talk to you either." I actually blushed, but then remembered this wasn't about me. "It's just that I see her as someone I want to..." He blushed.

"Have sex with?"

He flinched at the bite in my tone. "No! More than that. I just don't know how to explain what Anna means to me."

Oh, jeez. He was in love with her!

It was sweet yet incredibly tragic since I knew without a doubt that Anna would never feel the same.

"Joey?"

"Yeah?"

"If it's meant to be, it will be." Jeez, that was lame but what else could I say?

He nodded and studied his feet. I expected him to argue or to launch into one of his many crazy schemes he came up with to make Anna love him, but instead, he turned with shoulders low and walked back into the building.

I stared at the door and considered going after him but what good would it do? Lying to him wouldn't help him either.

"And the award for World's Biggest Asshole goes to Mian Ross," I mumbled.

"THIS IS THE Ross residence." Hearing my aunt's nasal voice made me consider hanging up, but then, my baby boy cooed and wriggled against me with his adoring and trusting eyes staring up at me. He didn't deserve to suffer because of my pride, so I took a deep breath.

"Aunt Gretchen, how are you?"

"Who is speaking?" The temperature drop in her tone told me she knew exactly who was speaking.

"It's Mian."

"Mian. Hmmm. I hope you're well," she answered. I could almost hear her derisive snort. "Why are you calling?"

"I—we... need your help."

"Mian, really—"

"Please, Aunt Gretchen. I lost my job, and I'm out of money. If not for me then could you consider your great nephew?"

"I'm sorry, Mian. We gave you a chance but you chose to be just like your father. You chose to sin over God, so now you have to pay your penance. Please don't call us again." The line died. The only family I had left and the only way for my son or me to eat tonight had tossed me away like trash for the second time.

When I discovered I was pregnant, I was devastated and afraid. I managed to hide my pregnancy for five months. Despite my aunt's religious beliefs and how far along I was, she demanded that I get an abortion.

"You're to get an abortion and do it quietly."

"Aunt Gretchen, I can't. How could you ask me to? I thought—"

"You are not going to shame me in front of the church. Cleanse yourself of this sin or get out of my house."

I'd been on my own ever since.

Counting out the change I had left, I realized I had enough to make one more phone call. I had to make it count.

I picked up the receiver and hoped my memory didn't fail me now. I'd dialed it so many times in the past only to hang up that I knew it wouldn't.

"Hello?"

"It's Mian." I decided to cut to the chase. My own aunt didn't offer me the courtesy of recognition. I had no reason to believe *he* would.

He exhaled heavily into the phone while I held my own breath. "What do you want?"

"I'm sure you know what I want, or I wouldn't be calling. Believe me when I say, I want nothing else from you."

"So you think you'd just pin a baby on me to get paid?"

"You and I both know that's not what this is about. I lost everything because of you."

"I don't know what you're talking about."

"You *raped* me. Or don't you remember? You should. I was the one drugged out of my mind while you had all the fun."

"What are you going on about?" He'd snapped. Indifference was replaced with anger, and for the first time since I told him about Caylen, he reacted. "You know what? It doesn't matter. Because no one would believe you."

"Are you sure about that? Caylen—that's his name by the way–is your son. Whether you want to believe that or not, all it will take is a simple DNA test to prove."

"Yeah? And how do you think you could get me to do that? Tell the police? My father will bury you."

"You underestimate the way the justice system works these days. It's no longer politicians who rule the world. It's social media. It's drama. It's scandal. All I have to do is point, and you lose."

"You're out of your mind."

"That's where you've got it twisted. I'm a mother trying to feed her child—a child that you wronged the moment you stuck your dick in me *without my permission*."

"You're bluffing."

"Am I?"

"Even if you aren't, you'd have a tough time proving the son of a senator raped *you*." I imagined his face twisting with disgust as if *I* were the one drugging and raping.

"Maybe not. And it may be that the age of consent in Illinois is seventeen... but we both know the twenty-one-year-old son of a senator impregnating an underage nobody, whose father is in prison for murder, and who also accuses him of rape, will *destroy* your father's career when this goes public. And it *will* go public, Aaron."

Silence.

It stretched on for so long that I thought maybe I had finally won.

But I was wrong.

The line had died and with it, my last lifeline.

Did I have the strength to withstand such scandal? He was right when he threatened that his father would bury me. And what about my father? Did he even know about Caylen? Only Anna knew of how he came to be. I couldn't even trust Erin with the truth. Did I want my father to find out from behind prison walls that his daughter had been raped?

I stared down at Caylen lying still against my chest. His eyes were closed and his breathing deep. It was trust that I'd take care of him and protect him while he slept. My shoulders shook as I mentally collapsed, but when he shifted and scrunched his face at being disturbed, I remembered he still needed me to fight.

Back at our apartment, I laid Caylen down for his nap and only when I put a safe distance between us did I allow myself to cry. All the normal feelings of despair and desperation that usually followed loss of hope spilled from me as I sunk to the floor.

How could I fool myself into thinking I could do this? I couldn't take care of myself. It was selfish of me to bring such an innocent life into my fucked up world. Despite his conception, Caylen had become the light in my world—the one thing I had to hold onto since my mother died and my father's incarceration.

I loved him more than I thought loving someone could be possible.

What if that meant setting him free?

I cried until I had nothing left. I cried for my parents. I cried for my innocence. And then I cried for my son, who would undoubtedly suffer unless I did the only thing that was left for me to do.

When the last tear fell, I rose up.

I only ever allowed a certain amount of time to feel sorry for myself before I let it go. Sorrow and tears wouldn't feed my son. I made a bottle for Caylen to have when he woke and then sat down on my lumpy sofa in my box-sized living room and studied the fading paint. The only thing I had to decorate the wall was a family portrait of my father, mother, and me in front of our house. It was one of the few things I had salvaged from our home before it was seized by the bank.

I was still staring at the portrait when a single thump startled me followed by the wall vibrating from the force. The thump quickly became a hard rhythm and then the unmistakable sound of a male groan in the throes of passion filtered through the thin wall. If Brandi's latest boy toy woke up my son, I'd scratch her fucking eyes out.

The sound of their fucking increased to the point of obscenity. I surged to my feet, intent on putting a stop to their good time, when the frame suddenly plummeted to the floor. I stared at the spot on the wall where the frame had been. Brandi and her guest never stopped fucking on the other side of the wall but I no longer cared.

The answer to my problem had revealed itself.

It meant a promise had to be broken.

CHAPTER 3

...always a Daddy's girl.

MIAN

"WHO ARE YOU here to visit?"

"My father."

"I need a name, miss."

"Oh, right. Theodore Ross." The lobby officer started tapping at her keyboard.

Please be on there.

Two and half years ago, my father forbade me to return. I assumed that meant he'd take my name from his list of approved visitors, so I was here solely on the chance that he hadn't.

"Ok, Miss Ross. I need a valid form of identification..." I hid

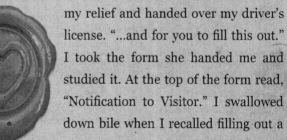

my relief and handed over my driver's license. "...and for you to fill this out." I took the form she handed me and studied it. At the top of the form read, "Notification to Visitor." I swallowed down bile when I recalled filling out a similar form before his trial. Even though he'd left me on his list after all this time, he could still deny my visit.

I quickly filled out the form and returned it to the officer. She then returned my ID and instructed me to wait. Thirty minutes later, I was shown to security, and my relief returned full force, but on its heel was anxiety. I hadn't seen him in almost three years.

Would he look the same?

Sound the same?

Would he even be happy to see me?

He accepted my visit so maybe there was a chance he missed me as much as I missed him. I floated through security and rode with an elevator full of visitors and two security guards to the eighth floor.

My hands were sweating so I ran them down my jeans and gave myself a pep talk. He was my father. Despite what he'd done and how far he'd pushed me away since Mom died, he would always be my father. Neither of us could change that.

Finding a seat was easy since the visiting room was mostly empty. Today was the start of the Fourth of July weekend. Incarcerated loved ones were forgotten about for summer beach fun.

I took a seat furthest away from the ears of the guards and waited with my gaze fixed on the table. The volume in the room rose as the inmates were released. I could hear tearful greetings and kisses being exchanged. I held my breath through it all.

"Hey, baby girl."

I worried for nothing. His voice hadn't changed a bit. I felt him standing by my side. I wanted to jump into his arms and beg him to come home, but I was too afraid of the answer.

"Hi, Daddy," I whispered my greeting to the table.

"I'd believe that if you actually looked at me."

Shit.

Here goes.

I tore my gaze from the table. The first thing I noticed was his chest. It was bigger than I remembered. The next were his shoulders. They were broader than I remembered. It was obvious he spent his time packing on muscle.

My gaze continued their journey until I was staring into eyes so identical to mine.

They were greener than I remember.

"Hi, Daddy."

"That's much better." He opened his arms, and I leaped from the chair and launched myself into his arms.

I wasn't going to cry.

Crying was for pussies.

I shoved my face in his chest and bawled like a baby.

"I've missed you too, baby girl." He held me for as long as he could until a guard ordered us to break apart.

He squeezed me once and then moved away.

I've missed his hugs.

We took our seats and just stared at one another until we burst into laughter. "You look good," I remarked. He did look good. I wasn't sure what I expected, but it didn't appear he was suffering.

He ignored the compliment and studied me. "You don't."

"How perceptive, Father."

He wasn't amused. "Mian."

"You're a grandfather."

The atmosphere around us changed with the simple flip of a switch. He blinked and sat back. Then his hand shot up, and

he ran it down his face. "No. No. No. No," he chanted. "Mian—"
His voice caught.

"I'm sorry, Daddy."

His eyes glistened with unshed tears. "How did this happen? This is not what I wanted for you."

"It doesn't matter now. He's here, and we need your help."

"He? You have a son?"

"Yes. His name is Caylen Theo Ross."

My father's lips trembled. He tried to smile and failed. "Do you have a picture?"

I flinched. "No. I'm sorry. I didn't think—I mean I wasn't sure—"

"It's okay," he cut in. "Next time."

No, it wasn't okay. I didn't have many photos of Caylen, but he deserved to have one. "Yes, next time."

"Is he why you're here? When was he born?"

"October 30th." Confusion twisted his features. "What's wrong?"

"That was almost nine months ago. Why am I just now finding out?"

"You forbade me to contact or visit you, remember? I'm only here now because I have no choice."

"Ben should have told me. Is he here with you?" His tone was frigid now. "I'd like to speak with him."

"Daddy... Uncle Ben and Aunt Gretchen kicked me out before Caylen was born. I haven't seen them in over a year."

He leaned forward and growled, "What?"

Oh, God. I took a deep breath to prepare myself for the shit storm. "Aunt Gretchen wanted me to terminate. It was too late, so I refused, and they kicked me out."

I watched his fists curl around the edge of the table. His knuckles were white and his face was red fury. "I gave those motherfuckers every dime I had to look after you. I'll kill them."

"Daddy..." I looked around nervously. I was sure threats like that wouldn't be taken lightly in prison.

"Son of a bitch." He snatched his hands away from the table and ran his fingers through his hair. "I should have never trusted them with you. I had no choice baby girl, you have to understand."

"I know, Daddy. It's water under the bridge now."

"The hell it is."

"Please, calm down."

"How can I calm down? You've been on your own for over a year, and I had no idea. Are you doing okay?"

"No, Daddy. I'm—we're—not. I have no money, and we're almost out of food."

He frowned. "What about the money I left for you?" My father had built up savings in my name in the event I ever needed it. When he got knocked, the savings had accumulated to twenty grand.

"It's gone."

"How could it be gone?"

"I had no medical insurance for Caylen's doctor's visits. Our expenses were too much even when I held a job. I had no friends or family to babysit so I could work. There was just so much, and I couldn't get ahead. I'm sorry. I—"

"No, baby girl. Stop it. I know you did the best you could."

"But we're going to starve," I cried.

"You won't let that happen."

I sat up straighter to appear strong. Here comes the hard part. "No, I won't and you won't either."

"Mian... I have no money. I gave everything I had to your aunt and uncle in order to convince them to take care of you. I—"

"I know that, but there's another way."

"How? Anything."

"Your last job. I want to know who you were going to hit and for how much."

"What?"

"I'm going to finish what you started."

"No, baby girl. Anything but that."

"It's not up to you anymore. If I can't do this job, then there's nothing left but shaking my ass or selling it. Take your pick, but I will *not* let my son starve."

His shoulders slumped. Maybe I won. "I didn't want this for you."

"I know, but someone switched the cards when we weren't looking, and I was dealt a different hand."

"It's dangerous. He'll kill you if you're caught."

I smiled despite the warning. I knew the way my father's mind worked. He couldn't convince himself not to give in so he'd try to scare me out of it first. I was winning.

"Then I won't get caught."

"No, Mian. You don't understand," he stressed.

"Then *make me* understand," I countered.

"The mark... it was Art."

My mouth opened, but nothing came out. My mind raced too quickly to piece together a complete thought.

How could this be?

Daddy may have gone down for Art's murder, but a part of me had never believed he actually did it. When Bea named him as the person who shot Art in the heart, I still didn't believe it.

43

Now my father was telling me...

"You did it, didn't you?" He had never fully admitted it before. He allowed me to believe that something had gone horribly wrong, and he was left holding the blame.

His eyes were sad and full of remorse. "That's between me and the dead."

"You don't think I deserve to know why you threw away your freedom and ruined my life to kill your best friend?" As soon as the words were out, I wished I could swallow them whole. I watched my strong father flinch. His eyes flashed with the hurt that I had caused.

"I am sorry, Mian."

I hung my head because I couldn't take the look on his face anymore. "I shouldn't have said that," I whispered to my lap.

"Four years ago, Art got this big client. Powerful. Word spread quietly among their inner circle and business for Art was booming. He was bringing in more money than ever."

"Who was this client?"

"Too dangerous."

"Daddy..."

"No. The client's name is not relevant to the job, and I don't want you mixed up in a politician's dirty business. It's never pretty."

I knew the Knights did more than just grand theft. Business with politicians pretty much confirmed that their business got a lot dirtier than what met the eye.

"So, why bring him up?"

"I know you've been Crecia."

I blinked. "I didn't know you knew," I admitted guiltily. My father avoided me, and I kept secrets. We both had reasons to feel guilty.

"Art rarely kept things from me."

Then why kill him?

"Oh."

"Anyway, after Art started bringing in truckloads of money. He said he wanted a bigger home, hoping it would persuade Bea to give him more sons. He had it built and moved his family."

"Where is this house?"

"Bea loved Crecia so he compromised and had the house built on the secluded land."

Where the buses didn't run, and I couldn't walk to...

Great.

"I need the address." He recited the address without hesitation, and I committed it to memory. "How much?"

"Sorry?"

"How much were you going after?"

He hesitated, and I could see his mind working. "What makes you think any money would still be there?"

"There may not be any, but there's got to be something valuable."

He must have sensed my desperation. His head tilted and his eyes narrowed. "When are you going to make the hit?"

"Tomorrow."

He bent low and hissed, "Are you out of your mind? It's too risky. You have no skill and no plan to pull off a job this soon. You're going to get yourself killed!"

"Art is *dead*."

"But his son is *not*."

I sucked in air and slammed back against the chair. This wasn't news to me. It wasn't what sent me reeling. It was the sudden return of emotions and memories that washed away denial and the carefully sealed compartments in which I had locked away everything Angel Knight. I had not allowed myself to think about him or even speak his name in almost three years.

With five words, my father pressed the button that released the past. Maybe even permanently. The last time had nearly destroyed me.

"Are you sure you're going to be able to do this?"

I held my stomach to calm the flutters. "Positive."

"If something happens to you—"

"I can do this," I reassured. "I'm my father's kid, you know."

He had searched my gaze before he answered. "Yeah, I know, baby girl. That's what scares me."

I LEFT THE building feeling lighter than I had going in. When visiting hours were close to ending, and I still hadn't managed to assuage my father's worry, I did the unthinkable and appealed to his guilt.

"I thought going to prison and leaving me alone was the worst you could ever do to me but it's not... Letting your grandson and I starve is far more fucked up."

My stomach turned because, even though I was sorry I spoke then, I was even sorrier they were true.

I got what I wanted.

The combination and location of the safe.

The money my father had been after would be long gone after three years, but maybe it's been replaced with more. I have no idea the condition Art left his only son when he died. Did he take over the business? Did he leave him an inheritance?

The estate my father described might not even be owned by the Knights. What if Bea or Angel sold?

I had no choice but to risk it all to gain in return, so I shook off what ifs and plotted my next step.

"Hey, how did it go?" Joey stood next to his car and pocketed his phone he was just thumbing through.

"Better than expected."

He grinned and bounced on his toes. "So, did you ask him?"

"No, sorry. Must have forgot." Joey wanted me to ask my father if he ever caught two buff dudes getting it on. There was no way in hell I would ask my father that. Not that he would discuss it with me anyway, but I agreed for the sake of getting a ride.

"But you were in there for over an hour!"

"We had a lot of catching up to do since it's been two and a half years."

"Right. Forgot." We hopped in, and he cranked up the car. "So where to, Miss?" He tipped his cap and made a goofy face.

"Actually, I need a favor that doesn't involve you driving me, but does involve your car..."

"Name it."

CHAPTER 4

Some ghosts are just memories.

ANGEL

"WHEN ARE YOU coming home? I need to get my dick wet."

I laughed into the phone, not at all surprised at the topic my right hand chose after two weeks of no contact. Lucas Devlin was the male equivalent of a nympho. If it was hot, tight, and wet, he fucked it.

"Why do I need to be home for that? You need me to hold your hand or some shit?"

He snorted and said, "It was a separate question and statement. I just thought I'd save time by getting it all out at once."

"I'm flying in tonight. I had to tie up some loose ends and knock a few heads together." That was putting it mildly, actually. The blood I spilled on this job wouldn't be easily washed away.

"We should do something tonight. Z misses you."

"It's true, sunshine!" His shout came from the background rather than another phone line, telling me they were together.

A groan escaped me. If the two of them spent the last week together, I knew I was walking into more bullshit than I cared to handle. Lucas Devlin and Zachariah Ellis were runaways who escaped the system together at the age of fifteen and thirteen. They managed to evade getting caught for six months when my father found them robbing a married couple for their money with stolen guns and no bullets. He admired their brass balls, as he put it, so he hired them. Despite my father's reservations involving me in the business so soon, the minute the three of us were put in one room, we became inseparable. We stole together, killed together, and even fucked together. The first time someone called us The Three Musketeers, Z literally tried to stick his foot down their throat.

We're brothers. Simple as that.

"What have you two been up to?"

"Nothing much. Getting shit-faced and fucking," he answered bluntly. Lucas was usually nonchalant about anything that didn't directly involve killing and getting paid.

I shook my head, feeling like the cock blocker in a nontraditional sense. I was the leader, but with it came feeling I wasn't just their friend but their father too. This was all after pops died of course. He had been as much a father to them as he had been to me and his death gave us a common goal.

Each of us wanted the man who killed him dead.

Three years after my father was murdered and my rage was just as strong as the day I received the phone call. My day of birth had taken on a new meaning.

"Angel, you there?"

I sprinted away from the dark reaches of my mind and tucked away the memory of my father's murder where it belonged. "You two act like horny thirteen-year-olds."

"But possess the stamina and finesse of a man at least twice that."

"You're twenty-seven, genius."

"Precisely," he retorted. "Chicks dig me."

"Whatever. I'm out. I'll see you tonight." I ended the call and rubbed my aching shoulder. This job hadn't been an easy one, but then they never really were. My list of reaps was growing ever long, but what else was I supposed to do when they resisted?

The job is the only priority. You must be willing to finish it by any means necessary. That includes killing. Are you ready for this life, son?

Arturo Knight was a known and feared heist lord, and when the occasion called for it, and the money was right, he was a hitman. He gained his wealth by taking what didn't belong to him. I was only sixteen when my father realized my interest in what he did for a living was more than just innocent curiosity, so he decided to bring me in. Doing the job was the only lesson he had seen necessary to teach me.

You're a Knight. Killing and taking shit that doesn't belong to you will come naturally.

But I never got to prove to my father that I could be more than his shadow because Theo Ross, the man I called godfather, had betrayed my father.

I considered myself a patient man. There was a spot high on my list of reaps reserved for him, and I was willing to wait twenty-two and a half years to put him in his grave right alongside my father. Justice wasn't complete until it was dealt by my hand.

With the help of Lucas and Z, I took over the business. One by one, I gained the trust of my father's clientele after some of their enemies disappeared, and I fattened the lining of their pockets pro-bono. It took more time and resources than I cared to sacrifice, but eventually, I had them on board. I wasn't a man to take no for an answer and had no qualms manipulating people in my favor. Most might say I was controlling and obsessive, but then most people didn't grow up with a father like mine. He would have expected nothing less.

As my father predicted, I had a talent for taking what I wanted and killing when I had to was simply exercise. I was even bringing in more cash than my father had ever seen. Even though I kept Lucas and Z on board, I still took some jobs alone and cut them in on the profit from those jobs. They never asked questions because they already knew the answers. I trusted Lucas and Z with my life, but my father trusted Theo with his and ended up trusting the wrong man.

I packed up my duffle and called a car before making my way to the elevator. I stood in place, waiting for the elevator to arrive, and thinking that maybe I needed a fuck to release the tension I felt in my shoulders. When the elevator doors opened, I froze in place. Inside stood a woman small in stature with dark hair and pouty pink lips. Her beauty was painfully familiar along with her wide, emerald eyes that stared back at me. I was gazing upon a ghost.

My ghost.

Mian.

Innocent, sweet, vulnerable Mian.

But then my ghost batted her lashes and licked her lips invitingly and I knew this woman wasn't Mian. There was nothing innocent about this woman who maintained eye contact as she extended her arm and pressed the button to stop the doors when they began to close. I'd been staring too long, and now she thought I was interested, and I admitted to myself I had been until I realized she wasn't who I wanted.

She wasn't the sixteen-year-old girl I used to lust after.

Reluctantly, I stepped inside and moved to the far corner, furthest away from her. When the doors shut and the elevator began to descend, she angled her body sideways, facing me just enough to display her breasts in the low cut top.

I pinned her with my cold gaze. "Look, I know what you're aiming for, and I'm not fucking interested."

She had the decency to look embarrassed and mumbled an apology as she faced forward once again. I could have laughed at the irony. I was thinking about getting laid only moments before the opportunity presented itself but lost interest when I realized it wouldn't be some doe-eyed kid I shouldn't even be thinking about.

When the elevator arrived at the lobby, the woman practically ran out with her tail between her legs. I stepped out after her and took in my surroundings. I had enemies that would take any opportunity to kill me, even in a crowded hotel.

"Mr. Knight, good evening. I hope you enjoyed your stay," the front desk attendant greeted. I checked out and found a car waiting for me when I stepped outside. With a nod to the driver, I hopped in the back, but as soon as my ass touched the seat, my phone rang.

"Z, what's up?"

"Someone's in your house."

CHAPTER 5

Fair exchange is no robbery.

MIAN

THE CYLINDER TURNED. The sound of the lock disengaging was music to my ears. Smiling, I pocketed the tension wrench I had borrowed from Joey.

The double doors stood at least seven feet tall and were made of dark wood with several rows of panels from top to bottom. The elegant knobs looked as if they were dipped in a pot of gold. I pushed open the heavy door and stepped inside.

Whoa.

The vast entrance alone was a statement of Arturo Knight's wealth. Above hung two candle chandeliers with dangling crystals to dazzle. The tiled floor was made of marble, and the two staircases flanked the entrance leading up the second-floor balcony. A black metal railing made of intricate designs protected it. The Knights were loaded in an obvious way.

The sudden and frantic beeping of the watch I also borrowed from Joey interrupted my inspection.

Seven minutes.

I reset the timer and made my way up the curved stairs to my right. It was just two days before the fourth. If I were lucky, Bea would be on vacation. So, for the last sixteen hours I watched.

No one came. No one went.

It wasn't until night had fallen that I made my move.

My father berated me for not planning and called me an amateur for taking too many risks. But our survival was threatened by time I didn't have. How could he judge me anyway? My father had defied odds on a regular basis, and because of him, following in his footsteps became inevitable. Even though he expected more of me, it never stopped him from sharing his secrets when I was a kid. But it was always about the job. Never about his marks.

It was the same each time.

He'd teach me the trade and then would warn me not to get any ideas.

"You're going to college, baby girl. One day you'll be an accountant. You'll be a square, unlike your old man, but what's important is that you'll be better than me. Promise me, Mian."

"I promise, Daddy."

This job had been different because it was personal. When the police questioned why he killed his best friend, he said Art had taken something from him. That night, he was only supposed to take back what was his, but instead, my godfather was murdered.

Now it was up to me to finish what he had started.

He never explained what it was, but I assumed it was money. Why else would he go along with my plan to finish the job?

My father was a good man.

He loved us.

He'd want Caylen to have all that he deserved and so I exploited that to break through his reservations.

The greatest challenge was believing the money my father was after was even still there.

But that was what plan B was for.

Down a short hall off the east wing, I found a small balcony at the end and two doors. Taking the one on the left first, I pushed inside and found a guest room. Across the hall was the same deal.

I moved back down the short hall and turned left down another hall—this one shorter but wider. At the very end were double doors. I walked through them and found another bedroom. This one was at least twice the size of the others and dominating the center was an enormous bed. The headboard was painted black and reached high over the wide mattress. The silk sheets were also black, adding to the intimidation. It wasn't exactly a woman's touch.

A shiver passed through me, but then something caught my eye.

Against my better judgment, I moved to the foot of the bed for a closer look and found a dark gray tie curled on the bedding. I picked it up before I could rethink and wondered about the man it belonged to.

After twenty-three years of friendship, Art betrayed my father, and my father killed him. Maybe there was a clue hidden somewhere in this castle that would tell me why.

My stolen watch beeped, breaking my train of thought.

Seven minutes.

I was wasting time.

I looked around the room for something valuable. There was too much space to decorate every inch. Art and Bea must have thought the same and chose to keep it simple. A loveseat faced the bed, aligned directly with the center.

I wonder...

A few years ago, Erin was curious about threesomes so she convinced me to watch a video with her. The first two videos were nothing special. I forced myself through them since Erin thought they were hot. But then we stumbled upon one that I'd never forgotten. For his anniversary, a woman gifted her husband his fantasy—to watch her with another man. I watched him watch his best friend and wife make love from a love seat very much like this.

Would Art enjoy seeing his wife make love to another man? Or maybe he just liked to watch her...

Beep beep! Beep beep! Beep beep!

Getting caught in a fantasy allowed another seven minutes to pass by. I tore my gaze away from the love seat and reset my watch. I looked around and finally found what I was looking for. There were two doors adjacent to the bed. The door on the far left was open so I could clearly see it was a bathroom. The other was closed. I quickly moved toward it and pushed open the door.

Bingo.

This time, I didn't waste time admiring the grandeur. I ventured deeper inside the closet with my eye on the island at the center. I ripped open the first drawer. Inside were an array of watches and rings.

Jackpot.

Snatching up the watch with the most bling, I stuffed it in my pocket, shoved the drawer closed, and ran from the room.

The safe my father was after three years ago is hidden behind a painting in the second-floor study. At the time, I didn't think the hiding spot was very original, but now I just found it convenient.

The main hallway curved past the balcony and led to the west wing. Off to the right was another short hallway that led to the study. The doors were locked when I twisted the doorknob, so I fished the torque and tension wrench from my back pocket and knelt. After much poking and prodding, I felt the pins give.

My watch went off again and the end of another seven minutes broke through my victory.

Shit.

The doors to the study matched the front doors but weren't as heavy. When I walked through them, I was half expecting the ghost of Arturo Knight to be waiting on the other side, but all I found was a massive desk in front of oversized windows. Parallel to the desk was a brown leather couch that spanned the length of the desk. On the left wall, a bookcase was built into the length of the wall, and on the opposite wall were paintings decorating the space.

Thinking I'd miscounted, I counted the frames again and found six, perfectly spaced paintings. Daddy had said there would only be five. The paintings were large and probably weighed at least half my body weight.

I slumped against the door.

My father had been right.

I had no skill to move on a job like this without a plan. Naively, I'd given myself ten minutes to get in and out. Thirty minutes had gone by, and I was no closer to getting in that safe than I was when I started.

I straightened from the door and moved until I was standing in front of the first painting of a man I didn't recognize. The hook holding up the painting was too high for me to reach. I moved to the second and then the third and so on until I came to the fifth painting. The familiar features of a man I hadn't seen in years were captured with skillful accuracy.

Arturo Knight.

A chill passed through me at the same time the watch beeped again. I reset it and frantically searched for leverage and found a single seat chair decorating the corner to my right. The elegantly carved legs and back and a decorated cushion of the chair weren't meant to be besmirched as a ladder, but it would have to do. I dragged it to the painting of my dead godfather and planted my dirty, torn chucks on the cushion. Stretching to the tips of my toes, my fingers were able to reach the top of the frame where the hook sunk in.

Lifting the heavy painting was harder than I originally judged but with a grunt and sheer will power, I removed it.

Holding it, however, while I stared at the empty space was impossible. The painting slipped from my fingers and crashed to the wooden floor.

There was no safe.

Or at least there had been.

I ran shaking fingers over the obvious patch in the wall in disbelief. It had been my only chance. Leaning forward, I touched my sweaty forehead to the lump in the wall and rolled my head back and forth.

Three years...

I waited too long.

I wasn't sure how long I'd stayed in that position until my watch beeped again. Slowly, I lifted my head from the wall and stepped down.

I should have left. Instead, I reset my watch and then stared down at the painting of my godfather. The piece didn't seem to suffer any trauma from the fall.

Art stared back at me with an expression carved in stone. He might have been a ruthless criminal, but he had always been good to me. After five generations of bandits, it ended with him.

"It's all over, godfather."

His dark brown eyes stared back at me almost as if he were challenging my claim. I suppose a man like him would defy anything that wasn't to his liking.

Just like your son.

His *son.*

Arturo Knight was as powerful as he was dangerous but his son...

My legs trembled.

...his son was a dark replica of the man my father murdered.

Their legacy wouldn't have died with Arturo.

Angel would never let it.

"Oh, God." My gaze was pulled away from the painting until it found another. The last one in succession.

The *sixth.*

The floodgates opened.

So many memories I couldn't keep suppressed any longer drowned me. The same man trapped in the painting stood between those gates with his arms outstretched and his strong hands holding them open.

Keeping them open.

My body jerked, and I found myself clutching the back of the chair and dragging it over.

It had to be.

I launched myself on top of the chair, and with strength I hadn't possessed before, I lifted the painting. Staring back at me was black metal about a foot wide and high. A keypad was centered to the right of the handle.

After setting the painting down and recalling the combination from memory, I said a quick prayer for it to work. I reopened my eyes and positioned my index to key in the first number.

That's when I heard it.

The faraway sound of a door closing.

I was no longer in this house alone. Art may have been dead, but Angel was not, and the reality of how much trouble I was in slammed against my chest from the inside.

It was too late to pretend I wasn't here.

So, I did the next best thing.

Slipping from the study, I ran to the main hallway and stayed close to the wall. There were three bedrooms I could hide in on the east wing but the balcony poised over the foyer would expose me. I should have been running for the exit, but even a rookie such as me knew it was the most likely avenue to get caught.

With careful steps, I slid along the wall, deeper into the west wing. Another set of doors like the master suite on the east wing was up ahead.

Fuck it.

I threw open the door and slipped inside. Looking around, it appeared to be just another guest room. This room, however, had small pieces of life to it, though not as much as the master suite.

This must have been Angel's room...

"I'll take the west wing," I heard a hard voice call out.

Shit! Shit! Shit!

I was trapped, and from context, I gathered he wasn't alone. I didn't recognize the voice, which meant my childhood crush turned worst nightmare wasn't the one hunting me. Standing in the middle of the bedroom, I knew the owner of the voice would catch me at any moment.

Hide.

I analyzed each potential hiding spot and acknowledged each as worse than the last...

Heavy footsteps drew closer.

Time had run out.

Since the closet was the likeliest place a person would hide, I chose the bed and wiggled my way under it with little effort. I guess being petite had its advantages after all.

Breathing became impossible when the shadow of the person's feet stopped outside the door.

Maybe he could smell fear...

I wanted to shut my eyes, but I was more afraid of not knowing when my doom would happen.

The bedroom door opened.

The boots stepped inside.

I was no longer alone.

He waited, and I prayed.

Suddenly, his feet turned. He headed toward the closet. I listened as the door was snatched open and items were tossed aside as he tried to uncover my hiding spot. When it was clear no one hid among the cargo and dark jeans Angel had favored when we were kids, he moved to the bathroom. Finding nothing, he made his way to the side of the bed and stopped.

I closed my eyes for self-preservation, but it was too late. The stranger's voice disrupted the silence.

"Come out. Come out. Wherever you are."

I didn't come out.

After a moment, his heavy footsteps plagued my ears once again. He must have discarded the possibility that an intruder would hide under the bed since most people stopped thinking it was a good hiding place after age ten.

I cracked my eyes open and stared at the open doorway. He stood in it, and I could tell his back was turned to the room. The door slowly closed and only then did I breathe again.

Until the unthinkable happened.

Beep beep! Beep beep! Beep Beep!

I froze, but it didn't matter.

Two seconds later, my hiding spot was missing its key element when the mattress and support were ripped from above me and effortlessly tossed away.

I looked up into the startling silver eyes of the devil's envoy.

"Hello, pretty girl."

"SHOULD WE FUCK her up or keep her on ice?"

God, I was straining so hard that I wasn't entirely sure exploding wasn't the next step. I've been trying to make sense of the one-sided conversation since I was tossed over the broad shoulder of a man I hadn't seen enter the room and was carted downstairs.

The one that found me had suffered a pretty hard blow to the kneecap so I could escape what was left of the bed.

Unfortunately, he'd managed to recover before I could escape...

"Give it up, girl. I'm bigger than you."

I ignored his leering face and looked for an avenue of escape.

"Stronger than you."

I scoffed and considered jumping from the window. Could I get it open in time?

"Faster."

Guess not.

With no other option, I got into a fighting stance and prayed the meager training Angel gave me—one of the few things he did right—paid off. "So try me, bitch."

The sudden glint in his silver eyes was my only warning a second before he launched.

Throwing myself out of the way just in time, I scrambled to put distance between us. He stood where I once was, and I moved closer to the door.

I expected anger and insults. The pretty man dressed in blue jeans and a fitted white tee stared back at me with interest. He certainly didn't look the type to storm castles and scare little girls from under their beds.

Figuratively speaking, of course, since I did break in.

"Why are you just standing there?"

He reached into his pocket and pulled out his phone. His attention was no longer invested in me.

"Because you already lost." The whisper came from behind, so close it tickled the hairs on my neck.

I'd forgotten he wasn't alone.

Goose bumps spread from my neck to my fingers, and the voice materialized in front of me in the shape of a man. His blonde and black hair was pulled carelessly into a bun. His green eyes twinkled as he smiled. "Hi, there."

I was lifted in the air before I could react and tossed over his shoulder. I jerked into action and pounded against his back, but I might have been throwing feather punches because he didn't break stride or even indicate he was in pain as he carried me from the suite to the staircase and down.

I could feel the presence of the other man following, but then his voice speaking curtly into the phone confirmed he'd followed.

"It's a chick, man. Yeah... she's alone."

Man Bun never took his eyes off me and with half a grin on his pretty face, he looked too friendly for what was happening here.

I sat on the marble floor of the entrance where he ordered me after I had socked him and sat crossed legged as he instructed. He stood in front of me with his hands shoved in his pockets, but something told me not to misjudge his easy stance. He could probably slit my throat before I untucked a leg.

The other one brooded a few feet away with his phone plastered to his ear. He wasn't as friendly as his partner was, but he hadn't hurt me either. I sat as still as I could and listened in on his side of the conversation but understood nothing. They either spoke in code or didn't believe in complete sentences.

The defined muscles in his arms, powerful back and broad shoulders straining against the thin shirt he wore told me where he spent much of his time. I wondered if he was one of those guys who were all muscle and not much else. His dusty colored hair was messy in a fashionable way. Maybe he'd just rolled out of bed with someone who couldn't keep her fingers from running through it. I knew I wouldn't.

"You look like you have a question," Man Bun commented. His lazy grin grew into a full-fledged smile when my gaze jerked from his partner. It was obvious I'd been caught ogling. I ignored his comment and his smugness and let my gaze fall to his chest. A pristine white button-up covered the area, but it didn't hide the muscles bunched beneath them. He wasn't as strongly built as his friend was, but he was no less impressive. The black jeans he wore emphasized his muscular legs and fit him like a glove but not tight enough to make me question how much air he was getting down there. Black suspenders hung from his jeans, giving him the appearance of a rugged geek. On his feet were black Nike high-tops.

My perusal traveled back up and found he was no longer watching me. His attention was on his friend's conversation and a deep frown obscured his soft features. Instead of investigating his change in mood, I studied his hair. His dark roots faded into the blonde highlights before disappearing behind his skull and into whatever tie he used to hold the strands together.

He had a playfulness about him that made me wary. He probably knew exactly how attractive he was and how much power he could wield with his assets.

My gaze pinpointed the spot where my fist had connected with Man Bun's jaw as soon as he released me. A bruise was beginning to form, and I smiled at my handiwork. His partner's slight limp as he paced told me he still felt my kick to his kneecap. It was too bad it didn't shatter.

I bet they wouldn't be writing home about the hundred-pound girl who kicked their asses anytime soon. They hadn't seemed to be in any rush to hurt me. I even hurled insults as I was carried down, but they never reacted.

"What the FUCK do you mean *let her go*?" The angry outburst from the brooding one caught my attention. His was already fixed on me. His disdain for me was obvious, so I made sure to return the gesture. "Why?" he growled into the receiver. He listened and then scrubbed his hand down his face. "Fuck. Fine."

I made sure to look real smug about that. He caught my smug look and expressed with his eye and the curl of his lip exactly how much he wanted to murder me. When he started toward me swiftly, my smile dropped, and I scooted back on my bum.

"It's for you." He extended the phone, but it might as well have been a bomb.

"Um..."

"Take it," he demanded through clenched teeth.

"Why?"

He snatched the phone back and stabbed the screen. "You're on speaker," he informed. There was nothing but silence while my heart pounded in my chest.

"Tsk. Tsk."

So much for lucky breaks.

"Ever the disobedient one..." I felt my blood drain when I recognized the refined voice. It was deeper now–stronger. "Even when you're in my house *uninvited*."

"You have something that belongs to me."

"You expect me to believe that?"

I shrugged to hide the tremble, but then remembered he couldn't see me. "Believe what you want."

"There are consequences to bad decisions."

"I'm sure I don't know what you mean."

"But your father would, wouldn't he?"

I sucked in a breath and tried to talk myself out of being afraid. There was no way he could know my father had anything to do with this. "My father is none of your concern."

"Wasn't it your father who sent you?" I didn't answer that. I wouldn't. "If you won't answer, maybe I should ask him myself."

"No!" His silence shattered my armor. "My father didn't send me." My voice begged him to believe me. It was only half the truth. If he had a choice, I wouldn't be here, but I gave him none.

I waited, but only silence followed. I looked to his two henchmen who listened to our exchange with curiosity and confusion etched on their perfect faces.

"I'll see you soon." He didn't say more. The line disconnected, and I was left feeling as if fainting would erase everything that just happened.

CHAPTER 6

Devil, meet angel.

ANGEL

NINE YEARS AGO

"ANGEL."

The commanding gruff of my godfather's voice pulled me away from the video game. Lucas and Z were sleeping off last night's job, so this was all I had to occupy my time. His tall, muscular frame filled my bedroom doorway. It was actually my second bedroom in my home away from home where I spent my summers away from the nauseating boredom of the countryside.

I paused the game and threw down the controller. I had been in a bad mood since my father, once again, denied my request to initiate me. "What's up, Unc'?"

 I was actually surprised he was here since my father left for one of his safe houses an hour ago. They rarely made moves without each other.

His face cracked into a wide smile. "I want you to meet my pride and joy."

I didn't get it, and I'm sure my face said as much because he stepped aside after a beat. Brown hair and pale skin came into view, and I realized that his pride and joy was a girl.

My first thought was that she was pretty.

And then, I noticed how soft she looked.

Fuck me, but she was *tiny*.

Standing next to her father, she looked completely breakable. Except she stared back at me as if it were the last thing she would ever do.

Mine.

My body jerked and it completely ruined me when she did the same. Her father was still talking, oblivious to what was happening between us.

The territorial feelings were foreign but the powerful urging to do something about them was winning me over.

"Baby girl, this is the son I'll never have." Theo's boast regained my attention.

"She's yours?" I already knew that, but I needed to hear him say it.

"She's mine," he answered with pride.

I couldn't tear my gaze away from her even when I felt him watching me. Theo was as sharp and as dangerous as my father was. If I didn't turn it down, he would notice and lock his daughter away in the tallest tower in the furthest land because he was a smart man.

"What's her name?" I sounded hostile even to my own ears, which is how I ended up stunned speechless when she answered instead of her father. It had nothing to do with the sweet, soft sound of her voice.

Nothing.

"Mian." There was defiance in her tone. I used it with my father whenever he was around. "And you can ask me."

I drank up the sound of her voice and reveled in it. My lips even twitched trying to fight a laugh when her shoulders squared. She was trying to prove how tough she was, but all I saw was someone pretending not to be affected. She was giving everything away just by standing there, and if she licked her lips one more time...

"She's feisty like her mother. I'm going to have my hands full when she's a teen."

The wind had been knocked out me. I resisted bending over to allay the pain in my gut. I mentally swore and kicked myself.

I was lusting after a *baby*.

I just assumed she was small for her age with soft features but sixteen like me. *I should have fucking known.*

Theo was still rambling on. I only managed to catch the tail end of it. "...and so I'll need you to look after her until your father and I return."

I hadn't hesitated nor did I miss a beat. I wanted time alone with her. Even if knew I couldn't do anything about it. I needed to know if this was real or imagined. "How long?"

"Until Sunday."

Two days.

I'd have two days alone with her.

"It's going to cost you."

He chuckled and crossed his arms over his thick chest. I wanted muscles like his one day. Maybe even better. "I'd be disappointed if it didn't. How much?"

I shook my head. I had enough money. More than any sixteen-year-old I knew, but I had yet to earn it. "I want you to talk to my dad." I glanced at Mian. She was looking around my room as if she had landed in a foreign land.

"About?"

"I want in." I wasn't sure how much I could reveal around her. Theo had never brought her around before. I'd always thought Theo being a father was a rumor. Similar to the rumor that she never came around because his late wife had forbidden him from exposing their precious daughter to his dangerous lifestyle.

He grunted. "Impossible." His answer was quick, making me wonder if he already knew what I would ask. "He doesn't want you in."

"Then make him want me in."

"You're his son. He'll want what's best for you."

"I know what's best for me."

"You're sixteen. You don't know shit," he spat. Theo had never been one to sugarcoat something already covered in shit.

"I know you're going after whoever's stealing your jobs."

Theo swore and muttered something about needing soundproof walls.

"You shouldn't know about that."

"But I do." He tried to stare me down. Two years ago, it might have worked, but I wanted this.

My father was a notorious criminal.

A bad man.

And I admired him.

Even without my father's blessing, I'd follow in his footsteps.

"Fuck." He glanced down at Mian apologetically, but she pretended she wasn't listening. "I'll talk to him, but I do not promise anything."

"I wasn't asking for promises."

"You're a smart kid." He shook his head with pity. "You could do better."

"It doesn't mean anything if it's not what you want." I cut my eye at Mian when I felt her watching me again. Her pink lips were slightly parted. Theo didn't respond. He turned to his daughter and lowered his tall frame to his haunches. Her gaze reluctantly shifted from me to her father.

"You good here?"

"She'll be fine," I dictated.

Her body stiffened, the only thing moving were her flaring nostrils.

It seems she hated being spoken for. I smiled for her father's benefit and wondered why I'd done it. Was it because I didn't want to give her a chance to say no? I'd been in their presence together for less than ten minutes and already knew he indulged his daughter. Spoiled was written all over her.

"Well, I guess it's settled," he said clearly amused. He stood to his full height and ruffled her hair. I waited for her to complain and fuss over her hair like chicks do, but she only smiled up at her father and offered a fist bump when he set it up.

Yeah, definitely a daddy's girl.

Theo left, and for the first time, I was alone with her. The air felt thinner, and the walls closed in making the room appear smaller. I felt as if I were being strangled by the need to be even closer.

I bet she's just a baby, perv.

"Tell me how old you are."

"That's a rude question." The way she scolded me, she might have been twice my age.

"Like you care." Was there anything typical about this girl? "How old?" I repeated.

"Ten."

"Bull. Shit."

"Well, I am." She stepped around me and looked at the wall above my headboard. I had posters of buxom beauties stashed on almost every inch of the space.

What could I say? I'm a breast man.

"Did you feel they were all necessary?" Her back was turned, but it didn't matter. I could hear the disapproval in her tone.

"You can never have too many breasts."

"As someone who will one day possess them, I beg to differ."

I closed my eyes, but it only made the visual even more lucid. She was just a little girl, and I was six fucking years older than she was. Neither one of us was even legally able to consent to sex, but it didn't erase the vision of her older with soft, perky Ds.

"Are you even listening?"

"Sorry?"

She sighed. "I said I'm hungry."

"The kitchen is downstairs." I retook my spot in my gaming chair and picked up the game controller. I needed the distraction that came with violence since I was crushing on a girl who was practically a toddler.

"This is your house."

"I'm sure you don't need help finding the kitchen," I answered without taking my eyes from the video game.

She didn't move. I had a feeling she was expecting me to jump and see to her needs. When it became clear I wouldn't, she huffed and stomped from my bedroom. I paused the game when I couldn't hear her footsteps anymore and hung my head.

It took less than five minutes of having her out of my sight for me to run after her.

I found her in the kitchen staring into the refrigerator with her nose turned up. I was light on my feet so I was floored when I entered, and she turned her head.

"Don't you have anything besides sandwich meat and Gatorade?"

"You vegetarian?"

"No, but there's nothing I want in here."

"Pick something." I waited to see if she would obey. She slammed the door closed and planted her hands on her nonexistent hips.

Cute.

"Didn't you hear me?"

I leaned against the doorjamb and crossed my arms. "If you're going to be a brat then I guess you aren't hungry."

She put her back against the door. Maybe so I could watch her lick her lips. She was even prettier angry.

Ten. She's fucking ten.

"Are you always so mean?"

"Are you always so spoiled?"

"I'm not spoiled. I'm hungry."

"What did you have in mind?" Why was I asking?

She didn't even think about. "Frozen yogurt."

"That's not food."

"Daddy and I passed a shop on the way here." Her eyes brightened, and she completely ignored my comment. "It's just around the corner."

"You're not leaving." Theo's orders to keep her safe meant not letting her out of my sight. It was one hell of a convenience because I had no intention of doing so until her father came back and took her from me.

"Not by myself. Daddy says I have to stay with you no matter what. So will you take me?"

"No." I stood up straight and walked away before she had a chance to convince me. I didn't trust her.

Not.

One.

Bit.

I heard her small footsteps running after me and picked up my pace. It was official. I ran from a little girl.

"Why not?" Her yelling amused me.

"Because I said so."

"So? That's not good enough. I want to go."

"I'm not your father, kid."

"No, you're not because you're an asshole! My dad gives me whatever I want," she taunted.

I stopped climbing. She wasn't expecting it, so when her body collided hard with my back, she was gone in an instant. Her fear-filled gasp struck a chord in my heart so that the beat quickened. Pivoting on my feet, I caught her shirt in my fist just in time. Her body leaned at an angle.

Shit. She would have gone head first, and her father would have killed me.

I pulled her up until she was standing upright and released her when I trusted she was steady on her feet. Only then did I start to breathe again.

"I'm going to tell my dad you pushed me." She stuck her little nose in the air and dared me not to beg for mercy.

My eyes narrowed into slits. *I save this little cunt's life, and she threatens me?* "Then maybe I should push you so your father won't know what a liar his precious daughter is."

Grabbing her shirt again, I push my fist into her flat chest until she's leaning over again. Her shriek is followed by teardrops spilling from emerald pools. I release my pinky from my fist to taunt her.

"I'm sorry!" Terror has stricken her smooth, pale face.

"No. You're not." I set her upright again and push her against the wall. "But you will be if you threaten me again."

Leaving her standing there looking too afraid to breathe, I lock myself in my bedroom.

I shouldn't have been trusted with her.

HER FATHER DIDN'T show up that Sunday. Two days turned into an entire summer with us at each other's throats. I began to think Theo had forgotten about his daughter altogether when he finally showed up at the end of summer. But he came with news neither of us was willing to accept.

"Daddy, what do you mean I have to stay here? For how long?" Her tone wasn't one she should be using with her father, but he indulged her anyway.

"For a while."

"But what about school?"

"You're going to transfer to a school here in Chicago."

I looked at my father who watched Theo's daughter with a small grin. He was amused by her bratty behavior, but I knew he wouldn't accept the same for me.

"Dad?"

"Yeah, son?"

"I'm not sure what's going on..."

His grin dropped and his gaze hardened. "You wanted a slice of the pie. This is your way in."

"What about Mom?"

"While I'm alive, your mother doesn't make the decisions when it comes to you... or her," he answered frigidly. I simply nodded because I knew my acceptance was all he expected. He was good to my mother and me. He even loved us, though some would disagree. His hard exterior was sometimes hard to turn off because of the hazards of his job.

"Daddy, I don't want to stay here with him. He's mean."

Her father's gaze flitted to mine. I expected anger but instead, got sympathy. Perhaps her father wasn't as oblivious to her spoiled behavior as I thought. "Are you sure it's not because he doesn't let you have your way?"

"I'm not staying here with him. I'll run away."

"Excuse me?"

She either missed the hard edge his tone took or didn't care. "You heard me."

I looked at my father who didn't seem to find her brattiness cute anymore. Instead, he watched Theo to see what he would do. Meekness wasn't something my father aspired to have or even understood. If Theo didn't correct her behavior, I knew my father would. I stood back to watch it all unfold and even fought a smile.

"I will not explain myself to you but *you*, little girl, will do as I say." She opened her mouth to argue, but Theo's hands flew to his belt. He unbuckled it with sure fingers and whipped it through the loops until it was free. Folding it, he stared down at his defiant daughter who looked as if she'd found her senses. "Are we clear?"

Rather than answer, she turned and walked away. I could see she was crushed and just a little bit fearful. I tried to put myself in her shoes and knew I wouldn't have reacted any less defiant. She'd only lost her mother four months ago, and now she was being uprooted from the only home she had known.

Just before she passed me, she stopped and stared at me directly. There was nothing in her eyes. They were blank from defeat.

"I hate you."

Soundlessly, she left the kitchen, and I couldn't help but think I would have hated me, too.

I glanced at Theo. He stared after her—his stance was relaxed now. I think we were all relieved that she hadn't fought him. He didn't want to hurt her any more than she wanted to be hurt.

My father cleared his throat in a subtle command for my attention. I gave it to him. He stood and closed the distance between us. His strong grip seized my shoulder. "Don't fuck this up, son. This is the only chance you're getting."

CHAPTER 7

A missing legacy.

ANGEL

PRESENT

I MADE LUCAS set Mian free because while I had a secret fetish for self-torment, I knew I wasn't ready to see her again. Hours later, her presence lingered in my father's home. I swore I could smell her scent. The possibility raised the hairs on my skin.

Lucas said he found her in my old bedroom hiding under the bed of all places. The knowledge that she hadn't changed pleased me when it shouldn't have. She was impulsive and challenging. Perversely, I liked that she still had fight left in her.

I looked forward to breaking her spirit.

Instead of my old bedroom where Lucas had found her, instinct led me to my father's study in the west wing.

The door was left cracked, something I would never do, so I pushed it open and took in the havoc

she wreaked. The desk and bookshelf had been left untouched. My inspection of the room shifted to my right where six generations of bandits were displayed proudly.

The last two in the lineup were missing from their rightful place. The safe hidden behind my own portrait had been discovered and left exposed.

Son of a bitch...

My glare shifted to the floor where a toppled chair lay among the discarded portraits. I was impressed that she even managed to lift them considering I could bench press her body weight easily.

Curiosity morphed into desperation. With quick, angry steps, I stalked to the safe and punched in the numbers. The sole content of the safe was detrimental to the prosperity of the Knights. There was no way she could have gotten inside without the code. It was only ever known by a Knight, but I needed to see for myself that I hadn't just ruined my family by letting her go. The keypad beeped and flashed green after I entered in the combination. The lock disengaged. I yanked on the handle and shoved my entire forearm inside the metal box.

Empty.

She got me.

She *fucking* got me.

Fortunately, for me, she had no idea who she was fucking with. My lips spread wide, and my cock hardened from the promise of the great pleasure I'd get by teaching her.

Mian.

Sweet Mian.

I'm going to destroy that little girl.

"YOU LOOK LIKE shit." Lucas walked into my father's study where he found me the next morning. I'd been too eager to plot my little bandit's demise to sleep. "What the hell was last night about?"

I watched him get comfortable on my father's couch while I sat on the other side of his desk. I took over the study after he died, but it still felt like his. The study, the house, the business. The only part I felt was truly mine was my reputation. I earned that shit.

Too fucking bad my father would never know how ruthless his only heir had become. Maybe even more than he had ever been.

Lucas stared while I clicked at the mouse and brought up a game of solitaire. I usually plotted best when I indulged in the game. "What would that be?"

"I'll see you soon," he mimicked. "Are we terrorizing kids now?"

"She's not a kid anymore." No one recognized that irritatingly, dick-hardening fact more than I did.

"Then why else would you let her go?"

"I want to play with her a little."

His teeth clicked. "Didn't your mother ever tell you not to play with your food?"

I cut my eyes at him and saw his smirk. "I'm going to savor this then."

He chewed the corner of his lip in silence. I could tell he was thinking, and Lucas thinking was never a good thing since he was intuitive as fuck. "I think it was obvious last night that you two know each other. Did something more happen between you two?"

I paused the card game and turned to bring him into focus. "No."

What I left unsaid was the fact that she'd been too young for *something* to happen. We lived together for five years but in that time, she turned my world upside down.

Nothing and no one tortured me more than Mian.

Not all the shit I stole or the lives I took.

Not the money or power.

None of it compared to little Mian Ross.

She would grow older. Her body would change. The sound of her voice would change. Hell, even the look in her eyes...

She became bolder with her crush, making my grip on morality slip.

I've wanted to fuck her spoiled ass six ways to Sunday since she was fourteen. I was young too and still much too old for her. Not to mention self-destructive and out of control.

But not so out of control I'd cross a line that I couldn't uncross. Especially, behind bars, which was where I would have belonged if I did all the things that crossed my mind when she tempted. Oh, how she had tempted...

"How do you know her?"

"She's Theo's kid."

His eyes flashed hatred when I mentioned my father's killer. "Bullshit." I shook my head and waited. He sat up and beat his fist against his chest. "Why the fuck would you let her go?"

"I told you."

"You didn't think she would be useful to us now? I don't feel like playing. I *feel* like making Theo suffer."

"And he will. They both will."

"How, man? She's gone."

"You escorted her home last night?" He nodded slowly. I could see the wheels in his head already turning. "We make a move when it's the right time, not before. She can't hide and she sure as fuck can't run."

He shook his head, but I could see his muscles relax one by one. "I didn't know Theo had a kid."

"I first met her when I was sixteen and she was ten. Her mom had just died that same year, and Theo didn't want the burden of facing his daughter."

Lucas swore.

"So where did that fit you?"

"I'd been asking for an in and my father finally gave me one. My first job was a fucking babysitting gig. He moved me into the brownstone against my mother's wishes and left her alone out there in the country."

"Is that why Z and I couldn't come around anymore?"

I nodded. "My orders were to keep her protected but mostly isolated. Her mother never wanted her involved in his other life. I guess it was his way of keeping his promise to her."

"Damn. Why didn't you at least say something?"

"We both know my father. One fuck up and that was it. I wasn't taking chances."

"When was the last time you saw her?"

I swallowed back pain. "Three years ago. It was a couple of months before her father murdered mine."

On my fucking birthday.

"Shit," he mumbled.

I decided not to share that our brief separation was mostly due to what an asshole I had been to her. We had a falling out after I stomped all over her feelings for good. I could still remember the look on her face when I walked away...

"So, you haven't seen or spoken to her since then?"

I shook my head. "I called so she could wish me a happy birthday." His eyebrows bunched, and I could tell he was about to dig deeper in shit I didn't care to share so I quickly changed the subject.

"The book is gone."

"Gone? What do you mean gone?" Alarm and disbelief wiped away any confusion he'd had about my past.

I shrugged as if she hadn't run away with the past, present, and future of the Knights. "She got in the safe."

"Fuck!" He rubbed at his forehead and pulled his phone from his pocket. "I have a man on her. He can grab her and have her here in less than two hours."

"No."

"No? What do you mean *no*?"

"I mean we do this my way." *As we always do.*

He stared at me for a beat before exploding. "Are you fucking serious right now?"

"Deadly."

"She could—"

"I want her to make her next move, and we're going to be there when she does. Even if her father didn't send her, which I highly doubt, I don't think she's working alone."

"She could be."

I shook my head sharply. "She had information that only a Knight should know. She's not a fucking Knight."

"Your father is dead. Who else could it have been?"

"Theo."

"You said only a Knight—"

"My father trusted Theo with more than just his life. It was a mistake that cost him his life."

A mistake I had no intention of repeating.

I saw Lucas flinch and knew he knew exactly what I left unsaid.

I didn't have the patience to assuage his feelings or sense of security regarding our friendship right now. He was my brother. I'd die for him but not by his hand. Not like my father.

He trusted the wrong man.

History would not repeat itself.

He sighed and locked his gaze with mine. "So, this is your plan?"

"We make her think she's safe and then we take it all away."

"What about her father?"

"He's in prison. He can't protect her." He'd already done a shit job at it anyway if he was behind last night.

"Do you think she knows why Theo killed pops?"

"Her presence here last night gave me a pretty good clue."

Lucas's nostrils flared. "Art's death by Theo's hand never added up. When we take her, I have no intention of letting her keep secrets," he warned. I stroked the light scruff on my chin and considered his threat.

He wanted Theo dead.

I wanted him to suffer.

My father taught me that gratification was appreciated more when taken slowly.

"Trust me, brother. Theo's kid won't be taking anything to her grave but her corpse."

He still didn't look convinced, and I was quickly losing my patience. Mian had no power over me anymore. "You two have history. You practically raised her. You think you can put her down when it's time?"

"There's nothing left protecting her except for mercy, and I have none when it comes to her."

Lucas's lips twisted. "Are you're sure nothing happened between you two?"

"She was a fucking kid."

"She still is." His grin was slow. "Then again with that body, I'm not so sure."

The appreciation in his gaze twisted my gut, and I didn't like it one bit.

"You saying you want to fuck her?" A switch flipped in my brain giving me the okay to kill this motherfucker if he tried.

"I know at least one of us in this room does, and it's not just me," he shot back. "You want her so bad, brother—you're practically shaking with it. It's been three years since you've seen her. That's some serious backed up tension. When the two of you are finally in the same room again, you just might spontaneously combust."

"Are you done yet?"

"You may kill her, but that doesn't mean you can't have fun with her first."

"She couldn't handle me."

"That's because you remember a kid. I," he pointed to his chest, "saw a woman."

"I don't want her."

Lie.

"Maaaan," he drawled. "Who are you trying to fool? Yourself or me? Because you'd have better luck fooling me than yourself."

"Is there a point to this conversation?"

"No point. I just need to know when and where you need me."

"I have a flight to Florida in a couple of hours. While I'm gone, I want you to get this place ready so we can extend an invitation this time."

"YOUR STEPSON, MR. CASTRO." I glared at their butler nearly cracking my molars to keep from correcting him. Marrying my mother after my father's death didn't make Victor my stepfather, it made him an opportunist.

And a dead one as soon as my mother came to her senses.

"Angeles?" My father's childhood friend and bookkeeper pulled me into a hug as soon as I was within arm's reach. I allowed the embrace, but I refused to return it. Victor was Cuban with average height, receding hair line, and a bushy grey mustache. "I wasn't expecting you."

"Is it going to be a problem?"

I was pissed when he married my mother, but that was nothing compared to the storm I brought down on him when I learned he was moving her all the way out to Florida.

Away from the life she had with my father.

Away from *me*.

He chuckled and patted me on the back even when his eyes didn't share his amusement. "You, my son, are very much like your father."

Unfortunately, for him, it was true.

Unfortunately, for me, my high was blown as soon as my flight touched down, so I wasn't equipped to be pleasant. My habit of using weed to mellow me started after meeting Lucas and Z. They introduced me, and I never looked back.

I haven't talked to her since she snuck away and married this prick.

I missed her.

However, loyalty to my father's memory wouldn't allow me to forgive her. If he were alive, Victor would never have had a chance with my mother, and my father would have killed him for even thinking so. Victor exploited her vulnerability, and now she believed she loved him.

Despite what would have been, I respected my mother's wishes, as my father would have wanted, and left him breathing.

"Your mother was beginning to think you'd forgotten about her. She never stops worrying, you know?" I followed him onto the terrace where he had come from. On the table where he sat was a crime novel beside a bowl of grapes.

"I see you are enjoying retirement."

"Forced retirement," he reminded with a smile.

"You married my mother."

"Son—"

"No." I shook my head and stared at the waves crashing in the distant. "I don't want to hear it."

"Very well." We sat in silence. Victor plucked a few grapes from the bowl while I tried to get my temper under control.

"Where is she?" I asked when the urge to kill him wasn't as strong.

"Having tea with a friend. She'll be sad she missed you." I didn't miss the fact that he didn't offer to notify her of my presence.

"Doesn't matter. I'm here to see you."

His bushy eyebrows reached for his receding hairline. "What do I owe the pleasure of your visit?" He plucked another grape from the bowl.

"The book is gone."

The book was many things.

It was a black book of clients who paid us to give them what they didn't earn or make their problems disappear. It was a contact list of people paid off to keep their mouth shut and look the other way. It was also a history book of every job taken, tracing back six generations. It was a legacy inherited by every generation of Bandit, and it incriminated not only the Knights but also everyone we serviced, fucked over or used. It was insurance for our clients but also blackmail to keep them in line.

His hand froze from tossing a grape in his mouth. "How could it be gone?"

"We underestimated Theo's reach. He sent his kid."

"Mian?"

"Does he have a bastard I don't know about?"

He ignored my snarky question and leaned back. "When?"

"Last night. Lucas and Z caught her hiding in my father's estate. She said she was after something that belongs to her father."

"Where is she now?"

"Not important." I didn't trust Victor with the information. "We let her go."

"Why?"

"I never considered her knowing about the book. She had nothing on her when we released her."

"So she has a partner."

"I'm sure of it."

"She needs to be disposed of. What are you planning to do about it?"

"We watch her, for now, to see where she goes and who she knows."

"She may have already sold it. What about this partner?"

"They have to meet again to either sell or collect. I don't give a shit, but I want them both."

"It's not a fail-safe plan." His lazy regard for my abilities pissed me off, but I kept silent. "Your father wouldn't like you being this stupid."

My fingers gripped the arm of the chair to keep from doing the same to his neck. I watched as he arrogantly picked another grape from the stem and popped it in his mouth. I didn't like him talking about my father after he decided to fuck and marry his wife.

I would say that our rocky association was a love lost since he'd been my father's oldest friend, but I never felt close to him even when I was just a kid. Theo had been the one who was like a second father to me.

It was all so fucked up.

"My father would want me to be smart. This isn't some random person off the street or even a rival. She was family."

"And now she's just the daughter of your father's murderer. Don't forget that."

"I haven't," I pushed through clenched teeth.

"We'll see."

Fucking A...

I'm going to kill this prick.

"Once she makes a move, I will take her. Not. Before." I leaned forward and locked gazes. "And I won't hesitate."

"Good." He chomped on another grape. I considered filling his airway with the entire bowl and watching him choke to death.

"I came here because I need information, some kind of leverage over her. I was hoping you might have something. I can see that I'm wasting my time." I stood to leave.

"Wait." I ignored him and moved for the exit. "Son."

I froze and counted to five so I wouldn't remind him that while he may have married my mom, I would never be his son. I'd seen what having a father like Victor would eventually do. Eliana Castro was a gold digging bitch with scales like her father. Not only that. Once upon a time, Victor entertained the idea of me marrying his daughter. My father refused the idea of an arranged marriage, which put an invisible strain on their relationship.

"I was out of line. Your father would be proud of you."

I wasn't surprised by his quickness to apologize. Victor had always gone out of his way to stay in my good graces, even if it meant ignoring his own daughter.

Victor looked up expectantly. He waited for me to accept his apology.

Not going to happen.

"I didn't come here to talk about my father." I'd never be comfortable with a man who would sleep with his friend's wife before his body was even cold in the ground.

"I'm sorry for that, too." An uncomfortable silence followed another apology I wouldn't accept. "Look, Ross's kid needs to be dealt with. If she was after anything, it would have to be the book."

It didn't add up.

None of it did.

"How would she know the combination to the safe?"

"Your father trusted Theo—more than anyone." He grunted. My gaze narrowed on his face. Was the resentment I just witnessed real or imagined? The hard glint in his eyes was gone as quickly as it appeared.

"And?"

"And it's possible Theo relayed this information to his daughter."

"For what reason?" I grilled even though I'd already considered the possibility. "He's locked up, and Mian is no thief."

"Are you sure about that? She got into your father's estate, didn't she? He'd obviously taught her enough. He could have groomed her just as your father intended to groom you."

"Impossible. The last thing Theo wanted was for his kid to follow in his footsteps. He did everything he could to keep her interest at bay."

"Impressionists are good at making you see only what you wish, too."

The wheels controlling reason turned furiously. My mind raced to find another explanation. "It doesn't make sense."

"It doesn't always have to make sense to be the truth. Your father was powerful, but he was also feared. That book— your family's legacy— was the key to Chicago. He owned it, possessed it, and controlled it. Whoever controls it, takes the city... and any city of their choosing."

"She's not some aspiring crime lord."

"But what she needs is money, I imagine. She's a young, single mother in a dangerous city. With her father's guidance, she could sell it to the right buyer. I didn't hear anything after that.

She's a young, single mother...

Single mother...

Mother...

Mian had a kid?

Rage, pain, and jealousy—each fighting for dominance.

She had a fucking kid.

Even when jealousy still questioned how it could even be possible, my conscience had already accepted the fault.

I. Let. Her. Go.

When her father murdered mine, I made myself forget her. I beat my heart black and blue until I was convinced she had never been.

I'd known she'd always choose him over me, so I made her pay for her father's betrayal by forgetting.

"How old is the kid?" I choked. It was clear he had been keeping tabs.

"Not even a year old. The kid's date of birth escapes me." He fluttered his fingers as if it was of little importance. Perhaps to a man who'd never fantasized about the day he'd own her mind, body, and soul, it was a blip.

But to a man who possessed those thoughts every single day for six fucking years...

I was nothing other than tormented.

Was she married?

Were they a happy fucking family?

No.

She was too young.

Damn it. She was *mine*.

"Use the boy."

I blinked to clear the fog telling me to murder. "Come again?"

"Her son. Use him."

I felt like I was being strangled. If it showed, he didn't let on. He continued to talk and eat those damn grapes.

"You saying I should hurt her kid?" I'd much rather hurt the prick who fathered him.

"You don't have to."

If you can't.

It was the real meaning he'd left unsaid.

Son of a bitch.

"Maybe I just need to make her think I will."

CHAPTER 8

Pretty girls shouldn't starve.

MIAN

"SO HE JUST let you go?"

Anna showed up to see if I needed her to babysit about ten minutes after I rolled out of bed. If I hadn't been so afraid of who might have been standing on the other side of the door, I would have cried at her thoughtfulness. Last night hadn't gone as planned.

Scratch that.

Last night, I'd made the second biggest mistake of my life.

"He let me go," I confirmed. When Anna noticed how spooked I was when I opened the door, the confession of my first and last job poured out of me.

She didn't sound as if she believed I had gained my freedom so easily. She wasn't the only one who found it strange. I was just glad I didn't have to add paranoid to my list of faults. It would have gone right under moronic.

"What do you think he meant by *seeing you soon*? I mean it's so spooky. Do you think he'll come after you?"

"I don't know." He's stayed away all this time. A part of me was hoping last night wouldn't change that. The other part—the moronic one—was curious. It's been three years since I've seen him. What kind of man was he now?

His errand boy insisted on seeing me home safely. So, not only did Angel have reason to come after me, he now had access to me. During the ride back to the city, I just knew he was taking me somewhere private to dump my body after silencing me forever. But then he asked for my address and actually drove me home.

"But what if he *does*?" Anna whispered as if Angel could hear her. "Maybe you should call the cops. He basically threatened you, right?"

"He's not going to kill me. He's probably just blowing smoke." No matter what our fathers did to each other, we were the innocent bystanders. Surely, he knew that?

Maybe he did before you broke into his house and stole from him.

My worry shifted to the expensive watch burning a hole in my hoodie. There was no way Z missed the watch when he searched me. He had to know I lifted it yet he let me get away with it.

"But didn't you say your father killed his? What if he wants revenge?"

"He would have come looking for it long before I broke into his father's home." After his father was dead and mine was imprisoned for it, he'd forgotten all about the stupid kid with a crush.

"Just be careful. You're the only friend I've got," she pouted.

"I promise. I don't plan on ever seeing Angel Knight again, and there's nothing he can do to change that."

She laughed, making her eyes bright again. "Well, good. Just as long as we're clear on that."

I stared at Caylen sleeping on a blanket a few feet away but felt her watching me. "What?"

"How did you get all the way out there anyway?"

"Borrowed a car."

"Whose?"

"Joey's."

She groaned probably guessing what that meant. "Mian," she whined.

"I'm sorry, but I promised him."

"I'm still not interested."

I smiled sheepishly. "He just asked for me to talk you into catching a movie with him."

"Mian!"

"Honestly, I don't see what the big deal is. Joey's sweet."

"Yeah, you'd think so because he doesn't drool all over you."

"Please? Would you just consider it? One date. That's it. You'll never know for sure until you give it a try."

"Oh, I'm pretty sure. Joey doesn't do it for me. He doesn't give me butterflies. There's no electricity."

"Ok. I need to confiscate your library card. You really need to cut down on the corny romance novels."

"You should give it a try. You never know until you give it a try," she mimicked. She made a face, and I laughed.

"Tell you what... you go on one date with him, and I'll read one of your embarrassing obsessions." She seemed to mull it over but didn't seem convinced. "Ok, I'll suffer through two books, and I'll even discuss them with you."

"Deal."

MY NAILS BIT into my palm, and I welcomed the pain. I read Jerry's sign a second time. He was the neighborhood pawnbroker, sometimes loan shark, and it appeared he'd chosen to indulge in the holiday festivities.

I walked away with the watch tucked securely in the pocket of my baggiest jeans. I knew better than to flash or flaunt a watch this expensive-looking around here. I wiped away the tear that escaped and kept my head low.

I had about a day's worth of food and supplies. Jerry wouldn't be back for two days.

I could already hear my son's cries when his tummy yearned for food that wouldn't come.

I had to do something.

Jerry's shop was just around the corner, so I was back at my building in no time. I started up the steps when I heard the husky voice call out. "Hey, cutie pie."

Looking up, I spotted Brandi, Anna's mom, stepping out of a car that looked more expensive than the building we lived in. She was a statuesque blonde bombshell who left every man's tongue wagging who lived in Mercy Homes. Shaking my head, I took in her skimpy attire. The high heels she strutted in looked like stilts, and I wondered how she balanced in those things.

"Hey, Brandi."

"Why the down face?" She frowned and lifted my chin. "Have you been crying?" I nodded because what was the point in lying? "Come with me and tell Brandi all about it."

I ignored the screaming pleas for common sense and followed her into the building up death-defying stairs to her apartment door. I glanced guiltily at my own door knowing Anna was inside watching Caylen and waiting for my return with a pocket full of cash.

Guilt washed over me.

Brandi was a single mom who knew what it was like to be a teenage single mother. Talking to her about my woes made more sense. Anna was my dearest friend, but she wouldn't understand. Not like Brandi.

She flipped open the dingy white door to the fridge and bent over. "Want a beer?" she called over her shoulder.

"It's ten in the morning." Plucking a bottle from the fridge, she slammed it closed and grabbed a bottle opener from the top. I watched as she turned to lean against the door and popped the top from the bottle. Defiantly, she stared me down and took an unladylike swig.

"Get your panties out of your snatch."

"Maybe I should just go." Her crudeness made my stomach turn. I started for the door.

"I know how you can solve your money troubles." My hand paused above the doorknob. "A girl as pretty as you shouldn't have to starve. You certainly have the body to make sure that never happens."

I dropped my hand and turned to face her. My eyes narrowed, and she smirked in return. "What are you talking about?"

"How many dead-end jobs will you have to lose or pointless interviews will you go to for you to realize that doing the right thing doesn't pay?"

"Anna told you?"

"These walls are thin, girl. There are so secrets in a dump like this."

"So, what would you suggest?" I wouldn't take any advice Brandi dished seriously. I was merely curious. According to Anna, she brought home enough cash to move them out of this place, but her mother preferred spending her earnings on expensive shoes and trips out of town.

"Using what you got to get what you need."

"My wits?"

She snorted. "Your wits are going to starve you, girl... Unless you add a little something on the side." Her eyes raked my body making me shift uncomfortably.

"I'm not having sex for money." Despite what I said to my father, I knew I could never do that. Selling my body to feed Caylen would mean nothing if I couldn't look him in the eye every day.

Her trilling laugh broke the tension. "I wasn't suggesting you *fuck* for the money." I cringed. Brandi could be harsh and crude. "Leave that to the big girls. If it wasn't for that cute little boy, I wouldn't believe you even knew what sex was." She laughed again.

I gritted my teeth to keep from cursing her out. "So, what were you suggesting?" I managed to keep my tone even to mask my irritation.

"You dance for it."

"Dance?" Understanding dawned. "You mean strip?"

She shrugged and set the bottle down. As she strutted forward in her stems, I watched her warily. "Yeah, honey. I mean strip for it. You take your clothes off, I *guarantee* they will pay."

I shook my head and took a step back. "I'm not doing that."

"You don't have a choice."

"Excuse me?"

"How are you going to put food on the table? Even if you get another dead-end job, the money is not as quick, or even as good, as taking your clothes off."

She closed the distance between us and reached around. When I felt my hair shift, I realized she'd grabbed my ponytail. With a tug, the band slipped from the strands and tumbled free. "You're so pretty."

"It doesn't change the fact that I won't do it."

"It's not so bad. I bet you'd be really good at it. You're young. Your body is still tight. The men will cream their pants and give up their entire paycheck just to get a peek at you."

Another denial was poised to spew from my lips, but nothing came out. Why was I hesitating?

"I—I don't even know how."

Her fingers tugged at the button my shirt until it slipped free. "I could teach you."

Taking a deep breath and holding it, I considered her offer.

Would it really be so bad?

"Mian?"

I jerked free. The spell Brandi cast was broken by the interruption. She didn't appear bothered when our heads turned toward the front door.

Anna.

"Oh. Hey."

"What are you doing here?" She held Caylen, his back to her chest, as she stood in the door I hadn't heard open. Caylen's blue eyes found me, and I felt a stab in my gut when he smiled wide. The sound of his happy giggles tore me apart.

Could I really do this to him?

Could I really afford not to?

"I was just—"

"We were having girl talk," Brandi interrupted in a dismissive tone. When Anna ignored her and started to question me, Brandi cut her off. "Here." She reached inside her bra and pulled out a bill that was damp with her sweat.

Ew.

"I need cigarettes."

"I'm watching Caylen," Anna replied.

"His mother is home now." She thrust the bill at her and glared until Anna reluctantly accepted it.

"It's okay. I got him." I was more than ready for this to be over and was sort of grateful to Brandi for sparing me from Anna's questions. I took Caylen from her arms, flashed a fake smile, and escaped.

CHAPTER 9

*Keep your friends close
and your enemies closer.*

ANGEL

I RETURNED TO Chicago. I wasn't ready to deal with my mother's emotions, so I slipped out of Florida without seeing her. Since I wasn't ready to forgive her, I had to stay away. My father would haunt me if I abandoned her completely, so instead of doing my duties to her myself, I had Lucas and Z check on her regularly. From their reports, she was doing well. I told myself it was all that mattered.

For now.

"Say that again?" Lucas called to run down Mian's activity in the few hours I had been gone.

"Bruce says she went to some pawn shop on Trent but didn't go in."

"Hm. Where did she go after?"

"Back to Mercy Homes. Some babe got out of a Jag, and they went in together. She hasn't moved since."

"Check the place out and let me

know what you find." I ended the call and looked down at the brunette with her head in my lap. "Stop."

She released my dick from her lips with a wet pop. "What's that, baby?"

I stood up causing her to fall on her thong-clad ass. "Move." She pouted and stared up at me with hungry eyes. She wasn't doing it for me, and I had a pretty good idea why. "Get out."

I disappeared into the bathroom and hoped she'd be gone by the time I was done. Turning on the shower, I stepped inside the glass walls and gripped my dick.

Christie's lips weren't the lips I needed to have wrapped around me.

They weren't small and soft.

They didn't tremble with fear or curl with disdain when I was near.

They didn't moisten from the tip of her tongue sweeping over them after she'd bitten into the skin...

My grip slid from the base to the tip of my dick. A grunt forced through my lips and was lost within the sound of water rushing from above.

Closing my eyes, I pumped again.

It wasn't wise.

It meant letting her in my head.

Giving her control she didn't know she had.

But the feeling was too good not chase.

My hand moved faster, racing for the finish.

Goddamn.

I needed...

Her.

"Fuck!" I bit my bottom lip the way she would when she

was turned on but needed to hide it and came. I was getting restless thinking about having Mian under my power again.

I slipped out early the next morning and made my way to the prison. I may have given into my dick last night, but I wouldn't be ruled by it. Moving through the crowd of people rushing in to visit their loved ones, I found an empty locker and stored my phone, wallet, and keys. I checked in with the lobby officer and then waited for the clearance to go through security like many times before.

After waiting for half an hour, we were allowed into the visitation hall. Despite the crowd, it didn't take long to find the man I came to see. When he spotted me, I nodded and took a seat.

Jonny was a reckless druggie who specialized in grand theft auto when he was on the outside. He was also as sneaky as they come which is why I hired him to get close to his roommate whom I had a deep interest in.

"Hey, man! How are you?"

"What do you have for me?" As usual, I skipped the pleasantries and jumped right into business, but Jonny always insisted on being friendly.

"You're still an ill-tempered son of a bitch, eh?"

"Jonny..."

"Right. Remember, I told you he never gets visitors?" He took a look around and leaned in. "Well, three days ago he gets a visit."

"From who?"

"He said it was his daughter. I never even knew he had a kid since he never mentioned it before."

"Did he say why she was here?"

"Said she was in a bad situation and needed money."

"What else?"

"I couldn't get much out of him, but he did say something about a book."

"A book..."

"Yeah. He said if he could get to it and sell it, then his daughter and grandson could survive."

I wanted nothing more than to hurl the plastic chair across the room.

Mian Ross was not just a gifted liar. She was fucked, too.

CHAPTER 10

Sex pays the bills...
unless you're bad at it.

MIAN

I STARED UP at the flashing sign lit in a perception of gold. The lettering mirrored the popular casino in Vegas. Taking a deep breath, I wobbled inside Caesar's Palace on a pair of Brandi's stilts.

Was I really going to do this?

A couple of shots of whiskey and a bag of Brandi's tricks ensured I would. I even allowed Brandi to babysit because I couldn't admit to my best friend that I'd fallen so far that I'd resort to taking my clothes off for a stack of dollar bills.

The first thing I noticed when I walked inside was the thick cloud of smoke. The second was the earsplitting volume of the music and some rapper's claim that all he wants for his birthday is a big booty hoe.

I wobbled forward until a burly bouncer with midnight skin, a bald head, and a face tattoo smashed his

hand into my chest. I careened backward and braced myself for the fall, but a hard warm wall behind me broke my fall. I peeked over my shoulder and found another beefcake standing with his arms crossed.

"Pay the cover."

"But I...I'm... I—"

"Look, I don't care how fine you are. You don't get in without paying the cover." He held out a beefy hand with his palm up.

"I'm not here to, ummm..."

His bushy eyebrows furrowed. "You here to see Caesar?"

Too ashamed to speak the words, I nodded.

My stomach pitched and turned when he took his time looking me over. Something like approval shone in his eyes, but then his hand lifted from his side to finger the black belt on Brandi's trench coat I was wearing. I shrunk back.

He snorted then laughed when he noticed my reaction. "Girl, you ain't here to see no Caesar." Beefcake number two joined in on the amusement.

"Yes, I am. Are you going to let me in or not?"

"Sure. Sure. I got to see this. Follow me." With a lift of his chin to his partner, he turned and disappeared into the dark and the smoke. I struggled to keep up. Thankfully, the neon lettering on the back of his shirt guided me through the crowd. It was the fourth of July, and it seemed as if all of Chicago had chosen this place to celebrate. I could smell the booze, sweat, and sex, but was too afraid I'd turn and run if I peeked. When he finally stopped, I noticed it was in front of a purple door with a gold handle. Gold lettering spelled out Caesar's Throne. Apparently, the sleaze of this place was hidden in plain sight.

Beefcake One knocked three times and then waited dutifully to be permitted entrance.

"I'm busy," a gruff voice on the other side called.

"Boss, I got a hot one for you."

There was a pause and then a shuffling followed by heavy footsteps. The door suddenly flew open, and the first thing I noticed was the red silk shirt and chest hair peeking out from underneath. He wasn't very tall or muscular, so he didn't intimidate me like Angel's goonies had. Black slacks covered his legs and were tailored nicely to fit over black wingtips with gold tips. I lifted my gaze to his face and found him checking me out much like I had been doing to him but with a lot of lust. His dark hair was slick from grease and pulled back away from his face. He didn't look a day over thirty, and I had to admit he had appeal.

If you were into the mobster type.

"What's your name?" He never took his eyes from my legs when he finally spoke.

"Mian."

"Not very sexy." I bit back a smart retort and waited. His gaze finally met mine, and I found his eyes were as dark as his hair. "You don't talk much. I like that." He turned into the room and held the door open. "Get in here," he roughly ordered.

I shuffled inside when I should have strutted and was just thankful his back was turned. The door closed making the music muffled and leaving only the rapid thump of my heart. Feeling a presence behind me, I peeked over my shoulder to see that Beefcake had followed us in with a leer.

"Out, Jones."

I sent Beefcake Jones a smug smile and watched him mutter with his massive shoulders slumped as he left the room.

When the door closed a second time, I became painfully aware that I was alone with a man I didn't know.

"So, you want to dance for Caesar?"

Confused, I looked around before answering. "You're not Caesar?"

"I am."

Apparently, his ego was as flamboyant as this club and his gold-tipped shoes. I tried to think of what to say or do next, but instead, I fidgeted and tried to recall Brandi's version of a pep talk before I abandoned what was left of my virtue behind along with my son.

"I know I said I liked that you didn't talk much, but this is an interview. If you have nothing to say, then let's get down to business. Lose the coat." My hands flew up to the belt. "No, girl. Do it slowly."

He extended his hand to the left and pressed a button I didn't see. A rhythmic beat I didn't recognize filled the room. I stood frozen trying to recall the moves Brandi showed me hours before. The singer took over now. The beat just background noise now. I instantly recognized the sexy, harmonious croon of Beyoncé singing about rolling up a partition.

"Any day now."

I jumped into action and lifted my foot to take an exaggerated step forward.

But something went wrong.

Horribly wrong.

The heel beneath me wiggled causing me to collapse and tumble forward.

Shit.

CHAPTER 11

She's no damsel.

ANGEL

"RUN THAT BY me again?"

"She went into Caesar's wearing a black trench coat and red heels, Boss."

"How long?"

"Ten minutes."

"Report to me the *second* she leaves." My keys bit the inside of my palm as I tore through my father's house for the garage with Lucas and Z on my heels. We had been going over our plans for Mian when Lucas got the call. He listened as the caller spoke while I sat frozen. Instinct, perhaps, had warned me that Mian was the cause of the call. When he wordlessly handed me the phone, my suspicions were confirmed.

I knew Caesar's. Lucas, Z, and I used to sneak in when we were kids to get an eye full. A blue-eyed, buxom beauty named Candy introduced me to

the pleasure of blowjobs. My classmates who I had fucked on a regular basis were always too prude or scared to take the step.

"What's the plan again?" Z questioned rhetorically. I could hear the amusement in his tone after Lucas finished explaining what had sent me into a rage.

What was the plan?

I wasn't ready to take her yet.

She hadn't made her move.

Caesar was a businessman, and a greedy one, but he wasn't interested in anything that didn't have to do with tits and ass. Not to mention his strip club was a front for something much more lucrative.

Selling pussy.

Any girl that worked for him sold their pussy whether they wanted to or not. It was a condition for a job at the Palace.

Mian risking her life to rob me started to make sense. She was never the type to use her body for gain. With my family's secrets to sell, she would be free of Caesar.

How far down exactly had Mian spiraled?

I considered for the first time that I no longer knew anything about the girl I practically raised.

"He's got a point," Lucas said, siding with Z. I came to a stop at the entrance of the garage and faced them. "We still don't know who her buyer is, and I'm not convinced it's her pimp."

My rage was clouding my judgment, so much so that I wanted to smash Lucas's face in. And for what? To defend her honor? It was clear she had none from the moment she welcomed the first John between her legs.

"Besides..." Z smirked when I glared. "She's your target, not your damsel."

CHAPTER 12

Pick on someone your own size.

MIAN

EIGHT YEARS AGO

MY SCRAPED HANDS rested loosely against my sides as I limped home.

No.

Not home.

It was just the place my father dumped me so he could rob and chase riches around the world with Uncle Art. Some days, I questioned why I still loved him despite his need to keep distance between us. I had been reduced from being his favorite person to spend time with to an obligation he checked in on whenever he remembered I hadn't died with Mom.

I dug out my keyring when I reached the brownstone. The rough material of my shorts rubbed against my sore hands, and I hissed from the sting. My knees were just as bad and so was my busted lip from hitting the ground when I fell.

I turned the key in the lock and pushed to open the door, but it didn't give. I twisted the knob again but the door refused to budge, and I realized the top lock must have been turned. Disgust made me forget my scraped hands and knees.

He was in there.

With a girl.

He always locked the top lock to keep me out when he was entertaining someone.

Yuck.

Except, *not* yuck.

Angel Knight was hot—a fact that couldn't be denied. Not even by me. I just could never figure out why the thought of him with girls made my stomach turn. Sighing, I took a seat on the stoop and waited for him to finish. An hour later, the door opened and out stepped a leggy blonde with a satisfied smile. I turned my head when I saw her lean in for a goodbye kiss and cringed when I heard their lips meet.

A deep groan came from beyond the door, and the kiss went on.

After three minutes of nonstop lip locking, I decided I'd had enough.

I coughed and coughed again until I was pretending to have a choking fit finally gaining their attention.

"Calm down, kiddie tits. We're done." I heard his laugh just before he disappeared back inside without me seeing him.

I glared at the blonde as she practically skipped down the sidewalk. I shot up with a huff but then winced when my knees reminded me of my injuries.

After walking inside, I came to a dead stop when I found him standing there waiting for me with a bored look.

"What?"

"What happened to your lip?" His tone matched his face until his gaze trailed down and stopped at my scraped up knees. "Jeez, did you fall?" Dark brown eyes watched me curiously.

"You can say that." I avoided his gaze and limped around him. There was a first aid kit in the bathroom that I desperately needed.

"Bullshit. You got beat up, didn't you?" I heard his mocking laugh. It was closer than it should have been since I walked away, which meant he had followed me. "What's her name?"

I stopped at the top of the stairs and whirled around to face him. "Jesse Newman. And *she* isn't a girl."

The smile dropped from his face quicker than it appeared. "Say what?"

"He's even meaner than *you*. I hate him."

I hate you.

"You're fucking with me, right?"

"Nope." I turned and limped the rest of the way to the bathroom. I could see from my peripheral that he was still standing at the top of the stairs. Stupidly, I met his gaze. He definitely wasn't laughing anymore.

I WALKED THROUGH the front doors the next morning dreading school. Last night, I bandaged my palms and knees and treated my busted lip as best as I could and forced myself through my homework assignments. I hadn't heard a peep from Angel after I told him I was beaten by a boy. Was he upset that he wasn't the only one getting a kick out of making me miserable?

Angel never did seem like the sharing type.

I found the object of my thoughts standing at the bottom of the stoop, dressed in a white muscle shirt, black shorts, and a frown. "Took you long enough."

Was he actually waiting for me?

"Are you waiting for me?" My brain screamed for me to move, but my feet refused the command.

"What was your first clue?" He tilted his head as if he really expected an answer.

"Why?"

"I'm walking you to school."

"Why?"

"That the only question you know?"

"Okay... what for?"

"Just come on," he bit out showing his impatience. Five quick steps later, I was standing beside him. Rolling my eyes didn't make me feel any better, so I looked up with a quirk of my eyebrow—*God, he was tall*—and waited. He started walking, and I followed. We made the fifteen-minute walk in ten with his long strides and me practically running to keep up.

He had never walked me to school before even though he was supposed to be protecting me. It was no secret that we couldn't stand each other, so we limited the time we spent together. He taunted me occasionally, and I tattled to my dad to get him trouble. That was the extent of our interactions.

The schoolyard was already busy with kids rushing from cars and school buses to hurry inside the building. Some loitered around with the intention of skipping as soon as the teachers and their parent's backs were turned. Jesse Newman would be one of them.

Maybe he would be waiting around for a second helping of his foot in my ass. I tried to fight back, but he was just too big, and the other kids just egged him on. I didn't even have Erin around to help, not that she would have. She would have been even more scared than I had been. Jesse decided to turn his bullying on me when I stopped him from kicking the shit out of some kid who had run off as soon as Jesse's back was turned.

Big mistake there.

With no one left to punch, he'd socked me a good one and called me a nosy cunt. Some kids laughed and egged him on while others stood around too afraid to say something or even call for help. I fell when his fist connected with my lip. When I got back up to face him, someone from behind pushed me, and I fell forward. It was how I got my scrapes.

Mr. Phillips, my math teacher, finally noticed the commotion and hurried over. Jesse and his posse wasted no time kicking rocks. I didn't want a repeat the next day so when my teacher questioned me, I told him I'd fallen and limped home before he could ask any more questions.

"Do you see him?"

My head flew up to meet Angel's hard gaze. "See who?"

"Jesse," he answered through clenched teeth.

Naively, I scanned the crowd until my gaze fell on the blond hair and pudgy face of Jesse Newman. Angel followed my gaze, and a split second later, he was moving in his direction.

Oh.

I ran to keep up even though I knew I wouldn't be able to stop him. Jesse and two of his goonies were standing on the side of the building, away from the crowd and teachers, while they pushed around the same boy from yesterday. I guess he liked to get a head start on his quota for the day.

He was wearing his signature faded blue hoodie that he never took off, even in the heat—even if it made him smell rank. I don't think he even knew what deodorant was. Rumor was his parents were not only poor but also abusive. He probably used his size over his classmates to make himself feel better about it and stole lunch money to eat.

After yesterday, though, it was hard to sympathize with him.

"You Newman?" Angel demanded when we were close enough

"Who wants to know?" Jesse mouthed. That was before he looked up. I took great pleasure in watching his eyes bug out of his head. "Do I know you?"

"Do you want to know me?"

"I—" He looked around and shuffled his feet. His two friends, carrot top and shaggy, had already put space between them and Jesse. The kid they were pushing around looked up in awe from the ground. "I don't think so."

He looked ready to piss his pants, and Angel hadn't done anything other than stand there.

"But you know her, right?" It wasn't until Jesse's accusing blue eyes landed on me that I realized he was referring to me.

"N—no."

Liar!

Angel pointed to my busted lip. "Hm," he said in that way that let me know shit just hit the fan. "So, this isn't your handiwork?"

"I never touched her! I swear!"

"Funny. She says you did."

"She—she's lying!"

"Say what?" Angel took a menacing step forward. "Let me hear that again? She's...?" He waited.

Tears gave Jesse's eyes a glossy sheen.

Jesse Newman was actually crying.

I grinned.

"Tell you what. I'll give you a chance to apologize."

Jesse didn't hesitate. His head whipped toward me. "S—sorry."

Angel shook his head and smiled. "I don't accept that kind of apology." His tone never lost its calm, but I could hear the sinister edge beneath it.

"What do you mean then?"

"You're going to let her return the favor."

What?

"B—but—but—but—but... I can't let a *girl* hit me!"

Angel's fine shoulders lifted in a careless shrug. "Okay then." I watched his powerful hand as he balled it into a fist and took another step forward.

"Wait!"

"What? You don't want a girl to hit you, right?"

"Please, sir."

"Ah... I see. It's not fun when they're bigger and stronger than you, is it?" Stupidly, Jesse shook his head. "So, what will it be?"

He looked between Angel and me weighing his options. I knew what he decided when he sniffled, and his body slackened. "Okay."

"Okay...?"

He quickly pointed a chubby finger at me. "She can do it."

Angel's grin was slow and scary. "Good. Because she's not going to stop until *I'm* satisfied." Jesse gasped and looked ready to bolt, but Angel was no longer paying attention to him. He was staring at me now. "Do your worst, kid."

"Um."

His stare went from hard to impatient. "It's not an option."

It was then I realized that I was just as much a pawn in Angel's game as he was. If I refused him, Angel would likely pummel him, which wouldn't fare well for Jesse. Angel would leave permanent damage. Beating up Jesse in front of his friends would be doing him a favor.

After stealing another glance at Angel, I squared my shoulders and tried to look tough. Jesse didn't look particularly worried about me. His terrified gaze was still locked on Angel.

I swung, landing my first punch on his arm. I stepped back, hoping it was over. Jesse didn't move, but his face said he hoped it was over, too.

I should have known better.

"Again."

I didn't hesitate this time. I punched his shoulder, this time, harder. I could tell he felt it this time when he winced.

"Again."

I chose his chest. Rearing back, I put my weight behind it this time. This time, I was rewarded with a low *oomph.*

Angel didn't need to direct my next hit. The rush I felt spurred me. I delivered blows, again and again, choosing tender spots, and giving it all I got until he was on the ground trying to escape the pain and humiliation.

My arm was too tired to continue, my breath was coming in and out hard and fast, and I had built up a nice sweat. Feeling good, I looked behind me, hoping to see approval but found his expression impassive as if I'd just completed a crossword puzzle rather than beating the shit out of my bully.

"Are you satisfied?"

He smirked and shook his head slowly.

Jesse was crying now, and my guess was he'd seen Angel's answer, too. What more did he want? I glanced at Jesse's friends and wondered if they stuck around out of loyalty or fear, and then I wondered which one pushed me yesterday.

"Class is starting—"

"You came home bleeding yesterday," he interrupted.

"Yeah?"

"I don't see blood on him."

My stomach turned. I was the one assaulted, but Angel was the one out for blood. What if I couldn't make him bleed? Would Angel do the deed himself?

I searched Jesse's face for his most vulnerable spot and then swung my leg over Jesse's prone body. I cocked back my elbow and let my fist fly. He screamed and clutched his nose but then screamed louder and removed his hands. His nose and upper lip were now covered in red.

I did it.

I didn't mean to smile, but it felt good.

I actually made someone bleed.

If I wasn't careful, I could become addicted.

"What is going on here?" My victorious moment was shattered by the shrill outrage of the intruder. Mrs. Rogers, my English teacher, stood a few feet away sporting a scowl. Her crooked red glasses, red lipstick, and dull brown hair pulled into a hideous undo did nothing to help her appeal. "Jesse? Why are you on the ground? Oh, my God! You're bleeding!" That's when she noticed me. Fist balled and standing over him. "Miss Ross, in the principal's office now! Mr. Newman, we need to get you—"

"She's not going anywhere but to class. Do what you want with him." I looked back in time to see Angel flick his hand to Jesse.

"Excuse me? Who are you and why are you on school property?"

"I'm with her." He moved closer behind me until I could feel the heat from his body and smell his body wash.

He said he was with me.

Angel Knight is with *me*.

Why did that send tingles up my spine and unleash butterflies in my stomach?

"I don't care who you're with, young man. She is going to the principal's office, and you will leave school property before I have you arrested."

"Call them. We'll do it from Principal Field's office."

He knew the name of my principal?

Sweeping out his arm, he sent her a smug smile. "Shall we?"

She stomped away in her ugly brown heels with Jesse in hand but not before demanding I follow. I did because, Angel or no Angel, I was in trouble that Angel couldn't fix. He couldn't very well demand I beat up a teacher or even the principal to make a statement.

We were shown inside the principal's office after Jesse was escorted to the nurse's office. I could feel Angel at my side the entire time.

"Mr. Fields, I have Mian Ross with me, and her *friend*."

But he wasn't my friend. He was my babysitter.

It didn't escape my notice that he didn't bother to correct her.

"Mrs. Rogers, what is this about?" Mr. Fields demanded impatiently. His sharp gaze landed on me and then slid up to Angel, and I could have sworn I saw him pale.

Glancing up, I searched Angel's face but his gaze gave nothing away. He looked bored again.

"I found Miss Ross outside *beating up* Jesse Newman while *he*," she thumbed in Angel's direction, "watched. He says he's *with her*." I could hear the disgust in her voice. Oh, God. Did she get the wrong idea? Did she think Angel was my *boyfriend*? That would be insane since he's seven years older than I am. He was turning eighteen next month, which would legally make him an adult even though he never acted the part.

"I think we should suspend her and ban him from school grounds—."

Mr. Fields held up his hand, silencing her tirade. "I will handle this from here, Mrs. Rogers. Please return to your classroom."

"But—"

"Now, Mrs. Rogers." His tone was much harsher this time. Mrs. Rogers huffed, and stormed away, leaving a cloud of stale perfume and hair spray.

Once she was gone, Mr. Fields sat back, but he wasn't paying attention to me. He and Angel were having a silent argument, and I was invited.

"What are you doing on my school grounds, Knight?"

Wait... They knew each other?

"Why was she attacked on your school grounds, Fields?"

Whoa.

Angel's voice sent a chill down my spine. I shivered when the temperature in the room seemed to drop below zero. Mr. Fields appeared flustered despite it.

"I wasn't aware of an altercation involving her had taken place."

"It wasn't an altercation. She was beat down. End of story."

"Like I said—"

"I heard you the first time," Angel cut in. "But her father didn't pay you twenty grand so you could sit on your ass and not know shit. Someone had to be held accountable. You're lucky it wasn't you."

Twenty grand?

Oh, crap.

I wasn't even aware my father had that type of cash.

"Now just a minute, young man—"

"We're done here. Mian is going to class, and you aren't going to do shit but ensure this doesn't happen again." I watched, entranced, as Angel dominated a man at least three times his age. I felt heat on my cheeks and in my belly and didn't understand how it got there.

"I won't take orders from a child!" For the first time since we arrived, I saw Angel react, as infinitesimally as it was. His jaw ticked.

"I can call my father if you like?" Angel's voice was calm and low despite the muscles working in his jaw.

"No. That won't be necessary. I'll take care of it."

"I'm sure you will." Without looking at me, he said, "Go to class, Mian." I wasn't sure why, but I hesitated until his head turned and repeated the demand with just his cold gaze.

I left the office and dragged my feet down the hall. I'd just turned the corner when I heard the familiar fearful cry of one Jesse Newman. Peeking around the white brick wall, I saw Jesse was trapped between Angel's tall frame and the wall. He was bent low so that he could talk in Jesse's ear. I strained to hear, but he spoke too low. A second later the hairs on my skin rose, and I realized I was being watched.

Jesse was gone, and Angel stood alone.

"Class," he ordered before disappearing through the school doors.

CHAPTER 13

A stolen son.

MIAN

PRESENT

"THIS IS A fine watch. Yes, indeed. I can tell a pretty penny was paid for this. Not a crack or scratch on the bezel. Eighteen-karat gold. Stainless steel..."

He continued to appraise the watch while Caylen slept in my arms. My patience was running low, waiting for the guy to finish eye fucking the watch and pay me.

We were hungry.

After leaving Caesar's last night, I went home to more bad news. Not only did Caesar deny me a job, but Caylen had also caught a bug. This was the most peaceful he's slept since last

night when I arrived at Brandi's to hear him screaming away his poor lungs. I'd heard him from the stairs since the walls were thin, and the few moments it had taken before Brandi opened the door with him struggling in her arms were the scariest. I took him away from her and checked him over for injuries while she looked on nonchalantly. I rushed back to my place before she could ask how the audition went.

Anna had still been out on her date with Joey, so I hoped that meant it went well.

"I can give you six hundred for it," the shop owner grunted. I pushed aside my woes and glared at the shriveled up man with a receding hairline.

"That's an eight-thousand-dollar watch. Six hundred isn't even ten percent."

"I'm trying to run a business here."

"And I'm trying to survive." I had no money and no insurance to pay for a doctor's visit for Caylen. It broke me each time he'd fret and cry. I knew he was suffering and there was nothing I could do about it.

"Fine. Eight hundred."

"One thousand or no watch."

He continued to try to talk me down, but I refused every offer until he finally said, "Nine hundred. I can't do more than that, and no one else will give you nearly as much."

"Sold."

I took the money and hurried from the shop just as Caylen began to stir. The pawnshop was only a few blocks away, but the neighborhood wasn't safe to walk with a pocket full of cash.

Desperate to get home, I hurried around the first corner and bumped into a wall with arms that saved me from a painful fall. "I'm sorry," I said when I was steady on my feet. "I'm not usually so clumsy." I checked to make sure Caylen was still asleep and then looked up at the stranger who saved me from a broken ass. Instinctively, I took a step back. His unfamiliar face was harsh and angry. "Uhhh... sorry again."

I sidestepped him when he didn't move, but another stranger stepped forward to obviously block me. Panic kicked in so I looked around the secluded street, but there were no bystanders around since the city was still recovering from the fourth. There were two black beamers sitting on the curb. I squinted hoping to see someone sitting inside, but the windows were tinted pitch black.

The engines were running, but the lights were off.

"Mian Ross?"

Cold dread crept up my spine.

He knew me.

"Yes?"

He didn't bother to answer. His creepy gaze rose over my head, and suddenly, I felt hands wrap around my biceps. My heart thumped fast and hard until it fell at my feet. I fought as hard as I could with Caylen strapped to my chest. He had woken up when I started to struggle and sent a cry into the air.

That's when the unthinkable happened.

My worst fucking nightmare.

The guy I'd run into unclipped the carrier and ripped him away.

"No!" My scream ripped from my gut. I kicked and fought as he handed Caylen to a man who stepped from one of the waiting cars. He was carried further and further away even as I fought and screamed. Tears stung my eyes and clouded my vision until I could no longer see what was happening.

I heard a car door open and close and then the unmistakable sound of it driving away. It sucked what was left of my self-preservation.

"Ahhhh!" My scream was a cry for war. The first act to saving my son. I bit into the hand of my captor until I tasted blood when he tried to silence me with his hand over my mouth. The metallic tang of his blood on my tongue only fueled me. He cursed from the pain and dropped me. I would have ran, but the man who started all of this quickly grabbed me.

"The easier you make this for us, the sooner you get your son back." Mention of my son had me slacking in his grip. I studied his face but had no recognition of who this man was— who so coldly took my son—who he could even be.

"Who are you?" I thought they were merely trying to rob me but why take my son for nine hundred bucks? They could have easily overpowered me and taken the money, which told me they weren't mere street thugs.

"I don't matter. There's someone who would like to speak with you." It was then I noticed the lit cell phone he now held in his hand. I glared at the screen and saw that the phone call had already been going for two minutes. Whoever was on the other line had heard everything. With shaking hands, I took it and waited.

"Hello, Mian."

I might have died when I heard his voice. I could no longer feel my limbs, and I wasn't sure I was even still breathing until I whispered his name. "Angel?"

"It sounded like you put up quite a fight." Pissed off, I wondered if he were actually praising me until he said, "That was stupid."

"You did this? Where are they taking my son?"

"They are bringing him to me as I requested."

"Excuse me?"

"Fair exchange isn't robbery. You have something that belongs to me, and now I have something that belongs to you."

"I'll fucking kill you. Do you understand that? Give me back my son!"

"In due time. First, I want to play."

"My son has nothing to do with whatever sick game you think this is."

His chuckle was deeper and smoother than I remembered. "So what's his name?"

"Excuse me?" I gasped and struggled to control my breathing, but it was impossible as I replayed the image of my son being taken.

"You risked a lot for him. Surely, he has a name."

"His name is Caylen, and I would risk *everything* for him."

The silence was brief and then he coldly uttered, "Well, then *Caylen* will be waiting for you at my father's home. You have two hours." I realized a moment too late that he had hung up, so I looked around for answers.

I was alone.

CHAPTER 14

The supreme art of war is to subdue the enemy without fighting. — Sun Tzu

ANGEL

I HUNG UP and closed my eyes tight. Catching her unguarded gave me some of the sweet satisfaction I had yearned for, but I wouldn't be completely satisfied until I had her helpless and at my mercy.

She would learn quickly that I had none when it came to her. Not anymore. Leaving her alone these past three years had been mercy enough until she made the first move that put us at war.

I was the Bandit and the Knight.

The position came to each new generation when the last son stepped down or died. Protecting our legacy meant protecting the family and it was now my duty. I would fulfill that duty by imprisoning her under my control.

Completely.

I could have easily taken her when I had her son stolen from her arms, but what fun would that had been? She needed to suffer in the worst way—a way that only a mother could, and while my actions sealed my fate and my spot in hell, I welcomed the rush I felt knowing I'd have her soon.

"Do you think she will come?" Lucas, breaking the silence and stole me from the dark and back to reality.

"What other choice does she have? We have her kid." Each time I was forced to acknowledge that Mian spread her legs for some faceless man was like a knife stabbing deep. The wound felt akin to betrayal. It was jealousy of another man taking what could never be mine. Secretly, I added the pain she caused to her list of grievances and promised to make her pay.

"She could go to the police. You haven't paid off every cop in the city. So what then?"

"She's a smart girl. She'll know going to the police is a risk."

Lucas decided to push. "But?"

His paranoia wasn't unwarranted. Lucas didn't know Mian. I knew her all too well. "She's pigheaded like her father. She thinks she's a fighter." I could get lost in memories of just how pigheaded my little bandit could be. Back then, I enjoyed pushing her. It was like luring a fish out of water and watching it squirm.

I would show I was merciful by letting her drown in her illusion of safety before doing it all over again.

"So how will we persuade her?"

Mian's love was possessive. I've seen it in how she mourned her mother and loved her father, despite him being undeserving. Fear would make her seek help, but instinct would drive her here instead. She's a mother. "He's all the persuasion she needs."

"My murder *vitae* doesn't include children." He looked visibly sick. Silently, I shared his sentiment. Of all the bad shit

I'd done, stealing a kid was the most fucked up. I told myself it was for the greater good of my family, but what honor can be found among thieves?

"I'll handle the kid if it comes to that."

He tilted his head thoughtfully. "And her?"

I held his gaze and spoke only when I trusted my voice would give no reason for doubt. "I vowed on my father's grave that she'll suffer."

Just hours before Mian had waved the red flag, I visited my father's grave for the first time since he was put there.

It seemed fate wasn't on her side.

The doubt in Lucas's eyes slowly faded away. He then scratched his chin and looked beyond my shoulder as if recalling something important. "She's pretty scrappy," he finally said and then chuckled at the memory. "It may not be as easy as manhandling her into doing what we want."

"Hence, the kid. We beat her if we have to, but use the kid to persuade her before it comes to that." A familiar glimmer brightened by the second. Lucas was nothing if not daring. He got off on pushing limits, same as I.

"And if we could persuade her another way?" I glanced across the room where Z dwelled in a corner. He had been quiet until now.

The three of us had shared more women than either of us could count. When one of us was through, if she proved tempting enough, she would find herself in the next brother's bed. However, Mian was still alive so we could bring her pain, not pleasure. "Fucking her won't be on the agenda even if she wants it."

And with one or all of us *persuading* her, there was no doubt she'd want it.

I felt my cock harden and swiftly tent the sweatpants I'd slept in. Of all the women I've sampled and devoured, Mian was the only one to make me feel anxious like a horny teen again. She made me vulnerable.

And for that, I *had* to destroy her.

I was thankful for the desk hiding my erection even if I failed to hide my irritation. Lucas was smirking when he said, "We want to know if she means something to you."

"She's revenge. She's the daughter of the man who murdered my father." I glanced back and forth between the only two men who could challenge me and live to do it again. "Pure and fucking simple."

He waited a beat before saying, "How many times do you think you'll need to say that before you start believing it?"

"What else does she need to be?" I questioned coldly.

"For your sake, we hope you never find out," Lucas answered smoothly. My gaze shifted to Z, and I braced for his two cents, but he remained quiet. He looked as if he was concentrating with a deep frown wrinkling the space between his eyebrows.

When he noticed my attention, his expression slackened into impassiveness. "What are we supposed to do with the kid while we torture his mother?" His swift change in subject wasn't expected, but I welcomed the opportunity to end the interrogation. "We're not nannies and hiring one is risky. It could backfire on us."

His argument wasn't one that I hadn't considered before. Outside of Lucas and Z, there wasn't anyone I trusted. After my father's death, I was firmly against letting anyone else close. Lucas and Z were left in charge of the men we pay to get their hands dirty—dirt such as kidnapping a baby in broad daylight. Even then, we kept only a few on the books because I trusted no one who hadn't bled for me or with me.

"I've got it covered."

"How?"

"Milly." She was my parent's part-time maid and had been on vacation the night Mian broke in. Whenever she wasn't cleaning, a silent alarm that rerouted the signal to me instead of the police was activated. Mian had mistaken good luck for fate's worst hand.

"The maid? You think we should trust her?"

"My father trusted her to clean his home, which meant he was paying her more than a maid's salary to keep her mouth shut." Lucas and Z didn't look convinced, and frankly, I wasn't either. My father's death had proven that he wasn't very adept at trusting the right people. "We use her if we're in over our heads. Not before."

Collectively, they nodded. Caring for a baby while I tortured Mian for information and paid Theo back for his death by breaking his precious daughter wasn't ideal, but my choices were as limited as Mian's days.

I checked my watched and realized only twenty minutes had passed since we took Mian's son. If she were smart, she would be on her way by now. There was only one thing left to do.

I snatched up my phone and placed a call to a man who would ensure Mian would obey and come quietly. She lived in one of the most dangerous areas in Chicago, and it just so happened that I had the district's commander in my pocket as well as the city's Chief of Police. I should have had eyes on her a long time ago.

But you wouldn't have just stopped there...

The sour voice of the police commander's voice chased away destructive thoughts. "Mr. Knight, to what do I owe—"

"Cut the bullshit. Who do you have on rotation tonight?" He immediately ticked off a list of names. Most of district seven was in my pocket, but there were a few straight shooters. When he coughed and mentioned one overzealous cop who thought himself a detective and had been a thorn in my side for years, I cut him off. "Give Office Garrett the rest of the night off."

"Is there any reason why you're making such an impossible request? He'll ask questions."

"Do you think I give a fuck? Garrett is your problem. Handle him, or I'll handle you both." I gave him a detailed description of her even though I haven't seen her in three years. I'd rehearsed every line and plane of her body over the years when my infatuation wouldn't allow me to forget she ever existed. I could have found her but forcing myself not to was tantamount to sanity. "If she comes, show her the door. Got it?"

"May I ask why she would come here?"

"I don't pay you to question me. I pay you to do what the fuck I say." I hung up and rubbed my temples. A strong drink might have done a better job alleviating the headache, but if I overindulged, I wouldn't have been on guard for when she arrived.

"Thomas is beginning to ask too many questions," Z remarked. "Are you sure we're paying him enough?"

"We're paying him all he's going to get. Any more and he'll be more beneficial to me dead." The ice around my heart made me sit back with my eyes closed.

When had I become this ruthless?

"She's left the city."

My eyes cracked open to see Lucas's phone lit in his hand and Z's steady gaze watching me. "Are you ready for this?"

Since I first laid eyes on her.

When the men arrived with the kid, Lucas and Z disappeared to handle it. I could hear his cries no matter how much distance I put between us. I wondered if he cried for her or if he could sense the danger he was in.

I found myself standing in the doorway of the prison I'd made just for her. To the naked eye, it was a normal guest room, but to Mian, it would be so much more. The large bed rested against the far wall where two tall windows flanked the bed. The sills were wide enough to properly seat two people. The bed's honeycomb headboard was adorned with black leather cuffs that stood out against the gold finish. They were attached to the head and footboard, and I knew Mian would question their presence when she saw them.

Had they been used on someone?

Would I use them on her?

I knew the way Mian's mind worked better than she did.

Since she wouldn't be a guest in the traditional sense, the bed was left bare. My mother preferred zoned temperature control since she chilled easier than Dad and me. The temperature in her prison had been lowered to sixty degrees.

I smiled and pictured her face the moment she realized there was no surviving this. Everything she'd encountered during her time here was designed to overwhelm her. Comfort was the last thing she'd be afforded. This wasn't the worst I could do to her. How far I went would depend on her.

My father's lessons didn't include how to toss a ball or catch fish.

His lessons taught me how to be cruel without lifting a finger.

This was one of many reasons I was grateful for his lessons. Putting my finger on any part of Mian's body would land us both in fucked up territory. That's where Lucas and Z unknowingly came in. I'd lied to them earlier. If I ever found myself unable to resist her, I planned to unleash them on her. They'd willingly perform when I couldn't, and I would no longer want her after they had her.

She wasn't like the women we share. Once they were through with her, she would finally lose her hold on me.

I was counting on it.

CHAPTER 15

Behind enemy lines.

MIAN

I SEARCHED THROUGH the cheap plastic phone and found nothing. No contacts. No messages. Only one phone call had ever been placed. It must have been one of those throwaways I've seen my dad use.

Call the police...

After quickly dialing the three digits, I placed the phone to my ear and waited for the automatic connection. "Nine-one-one. What is your emergency?"

"Please, my son—" I didn't get the chance to say more. The phone disappeared from my ear, and I lost my grip. I spun around and found another hulking body standing over me. This gooney was just as large as the last. His sharp jaws, amber eyes, and shoulder length blond hair was almost Nordic.

"No police," he grunted with an American accent.

My body swayed and threatened to hit the concrete. Fear for my son replaced desperation at the knowledge I was being watched. Why hadn't Angel just taken me when he had the chance? What game was he playing?

"Will you take me to him?"

He shook his head. "Not my orders."

Before I could argue or scream as I should have, he disappeared with the throwaway. Fifteen minutes later, I hailed a cab.

"Where to?" the cabbie impatiently demanded. He was already eager to get to his next fare. I recited the address I was grateful to have committed to memory. He turned around and stared with a knowing gaze. Under normal circumstances, I could never afford this type of fair. I reeked of poverty. "It's going to be two hours because of traffic."

I swallowed my scream of frustration. I had already lost too much time finding a cab. Art's home was hidden deep in the rich suburbs of Illinois where buses didn't venture because everyone drove foreign cars—not to mention the only thing out there were rich families who lived miles apart.

The cabbie wasn't done trying to dissuade me. "It's going to be expensive."

Slowly, I pulled the cash I had made from the pawn and with shaking hands, slapped it against the window dividing us. "This is nine hundred dollars. It's all yours if you can get there sooner."

Wordlessly, he turned back and gunned the engine. My head rested against the backrest of the cab. My innocent baby had fallen into the hands of a monster. And the boy who protected me for six years and taught me how to throw a punch was that monster.

After my mom had died, my father's light and zest for living never returned. Gone were the days when he taught me how to make the best of life even during sad times. His lessons had become nothing but a myriad of harsh realities and truths.

But there was one lesson I'd never forget...

One day, someone is going to cause you pain. When that day comes, you show them what hell feels like.

Before Mom had died, my father would always promise he'd be there to fight all of my battles. When she was gone, I stubbornly never let that part of him go. Even when he did.

Angel was sickened by the hold my father had on me.

He knew how much my father's absence hurt me. I knew how much he hurt me. My father *knew,* too. He just hadn't cared.

"We're here, Miss." I jerked upright and looked out the cab windshield. The beautiful monstrosity was even bigger in daylight. It wasn't the only difference. The stone wall that surrounded the acres was now adorned with a metal gate. On the left pillar was a keypad. I was running out of time and was unsure of how to get inside. He never mentioned a code. Had it been in the phone?

Frantically, I looked at the time on the dash.

I'm out of time.

Just as I felt the first tremble of grief, the metal gates slowly opened inward, clearing a path.

Sagging against the dingy seats, I simply breathed. The cab drove through the gates, and when the car stopped once again, I took the wad of cash I promised and handed it to the driver.

I was gutted when he accepted the money without remorse. He was grossly overpaid, but the gleam in his eyes told me he didn't care that I was back at square one. I had no money to feed us if we made it out of this alive. Caylen needed a doctor, and now I didn't even have the cash to pay for the visit. Our future wasn't looking any brighter than our present.

Not for the first time, I considered giving him up if I wanted him to survive. I needed his survival more than my own.

The taxi took off as soon as I shut the door, and I wished for the world to stop, even if only for a moment.

I climbed the familiar steps lined with fresh flowers and thick, green bushes. I didn't have time to admire the landscape when I was here three nights ago, but the beauty was more than I expected from ruthless men. I waited for a beat in front of the gargantuan doors.

The closest house was miles away. *Help* was miles away. Could I really do this?

At some point, while I stood there deliberating, the right door opened. A woman dressed in an ugly, navy dress stood in the doorway with a sour expression. I would need an ally if escape was necessary. Could she be it? I searched her face for signs of kindness.

"Mr. Knight has been expecting you. I presume you are Ms. Ross?"

Nope. Not friendly.

"I presume I am," I answered with mock propriety. Angel had waged a war when he took my son. Anyone he associated with was the enemy. I guess that included the help.

She lifted her nose higher in the air and stepped away to clear a path inside without losing her pinched expression.

"He awaits you in the common room."

"Oh, does he? Tell him I await him here, and I'd like him to bring my son who he kidnapped. I *presume* you know about that?" She pinned me with a stare unbecoming of hired help and walked off without offering a response. She had to be an employee. I saw none of Angel's features in her, and Angel didn't strike me as the type to prefer women twice his age. She was either loyal to a fault, or he paid his help well not to ask questions.

While she was gone, I admired the opulence a second time. Everything was grander in the light of day. I was almost sure the entry was larger than my entire apartment. I used to think my humble home was the stuff of dreams, a castle in its own right, but then the fairy tale ended, and I was left in rags.

It was obvious that Angel hadn't suffered from the loss of his father. Why Angel would go through so much trouble because of a stolen watch? He even let me go...

I'll see you soon.

He *warned* me.

He told me this would come, and I chose not to believe him. I chose to live in the past and ignore the man he was today. I couldn't give him the watch back since I sold it and now I didn't even have the money. Would he consider other options for restitution?

Goose bumps spread over my skin.

Angel had been terrifyingly crafty for his age. How much worse could he do as a man?

The possibilities were enough to give me nightmares. The watch I'd stolen was just one of many. I was surprised he even noticed it was gone. Despite all he had, he chose to use an innocent child—*my* child—as his pawn. It was beyond cruel. And it will kill him.

Angel Knight was undoubtedly a dead man and this nightmare wouldn't end until I saw that he truly was.

"Mian."

Every part of me froze.

The voice that arrested me was deep and commanding and did as designed.

It stole my obedience.

I turned and was slut struck by the sight of his large body dominating the open space.

He seemed taller. He was *definitely* bigger, and...

Oh god...

Sexier than he was three years ago.

His hair was shorter and looked much fuller now. The low trimmed beard framing the bottom of his face was new and promised a nice tickle to whatever lucky girl's thighs he stuck his face between.

"You made it on time. I'm impressed. I was beginning to think maybe sending your son to you one piece at a time would do the trick."

His sick threat freed me from the brief lapse in sanity his face and body had caused. The only part of me that mattered broke at the thought of my son being hurt.

"Where is he?" I was forced to speak through clenched teeth.

"In due time."

"I want him now, or I swear to God—"

"Be careful what promises you make."

"I will find a way to kill you," I finished anyway.

"No, you won't." His confidence was nauseating. "Because if you fail, you die and you're afraid to die."

"I'm not afraid to die," I lied.

"Maybe not. But you're afraid of what will happen to your son if you die. Your mother is dead. Your father is locked up.

Your only known family wants nothing to do with you...." He paused, waiting for me to react. After my aunt and uncle had refused to help me for the sake of my son, they became nothing to me just as I had always been to them. "I think you'll cooperate," he finished when I didn't react.

"I hate you." The declaration seemed childish in the face of evil. Angel had been guarded when we were kids, but this was more. Something had cut out his heart and locked away his soul just to take over his body.

"As opposed to what? Loving me?"

The thought of loving someone as cold and cruel as he was made me wish I'd puke on his expensive shoes, so I chose not to respond.

We both knew the truth. It first happened when I was twelve. He'd been eighteen at the time. It was impossible for either of us not to see. Since then it was promised that he'd do whatever it took to push me away and make sure it stayed buried.

But it never did.

Our years together had been ritualized. Some days, he'd treat me as if I were an infestation he couldn't get rid of. He would barely muster the kindness to extend a hello or at the very least respond to one. He'd go out of his way to avoid me even though we both knew it would never do any good. Other days, when tip-toeing around each other hurt too much, he'd let me in. This was usually during the summers when we were stuck alone together all day for two months. He'd teach me how much fun trouble could be. Sometimes, I even pretended to like those movies filled with testosterone and bullets so he'd let me be alone with him in a dark room.

And then it always happened.

I'd get too close, and he'd pull away.

"You could make this all go away." The cold calculation in his tone scared away our memories.

"How?"

"Give me back my property."

"I can't do that."

His jaw tightened. "And why is that?"

I was tempted to gulp like some cheesy cartoon. "Because I sold it."

HIS FINGERS PINCHED my skin as he dragged me deeper inside. I wrestled to get away, but it did no good as he manhandled me upstairs. He didn't stop until we were in front of his father's office. Flinging open the door, he pulled me inside an empty room and used his free hand to slam the door shut. But even trapped, his hand clutching my arm failed to let go.

"Explain."

"I think I was pretty clear."

His hand tightened, causing me to wince. I could tell by the muscles working his jaw that he was grinding his teeth. "Who was the buyer?"

"So you can steal his family and threaten him, too? No chance."

Surprisingly, he let me go and stalked across the room. When he rounded the desk, he planted himself behind it and glared. "I'm just going to jump right in and remind you that I have your son and now I have you," he boasted. "I'm willing to use your son to get what belongs to me. How hard I push depends on you. If you want to continue this game, know that I don't intend to play fair."

I pretended to think it over first. "Nice speech, but you forget I know you and I'm not afraid of you."

He tipped his lips, smiling lazy, and said, "You still thinking that?"

"It's not something I doubt."

"Your mouth hasn't changed."

"So your pretty pink lips say."

His frown deepened. "Come again?"

Shit.

I didn't mean to repeat his words from years ago, but the heated whisper in which he spoke them were engraved in my memory.

"Nothing. Uh... It's nothing."

His stare grew more intense by the second and then suddenly he was a blank canvas again. "Who was your buyer? Don't make me ask again."

"There's nothing you can do that will make me give up an innocent man."

"Innocent?" His eyes blackened and narrowed as he stood up and planted his fist on the desk. "You think he's innocent? What do you think he plans to do with it?"

The door bursting open interrupted my chance to answer. The two heartthrobs from the other night sauntered in.

Man Bun spotted me first. "Hey, you made it!" His grin was bright and honest as if he believed I accepted an invitation to a dinner party instead of rescuing my son. Under normal circumstances, I would have admired the two dimples residing in his perfect cheeks. His bone structure made me itch to sketch him.

The broody one acknowledged me with a head nod and a passing glance. His chosen trick of distraction was his open shirt displaying his bare chest. He wore dress pants, thank fuck. I might have had a stroke if they had been missing, too.

I had literally been handed every woman's wet dream on a silver platter. I was alone in a room with three of the world's finest specimen of men, and I wasn't even enjoying it.

"Are we all good here?" Broody questioned. He was eyeing me as if I were the one who couldn't be trusted.

"We are. Our guest was getting ready to tell me who she sold my property to."

"I was not."

"Are you stupid or just ready to die?" The growl that came from Angel's brooding companion was as real as if he were actually a predator of the jungle. I wasn't expecting it, so I froze just as an easy prey would. I should have faced him off. Give him the confrontation he so clearly craved. But instead, my gaze shifted to Angel, who passively stood by, fully prepared to let this man bulldoze over me. He clearly had no intention of stepping in if this got ugly.

Give 'em hell then.

Resigned to fight my own battles, I took as many steps necessary until only an inch separated my nose from Broody's chest. Convincing fearlessness required I tilt my head enough to kill him with just a look.

Sadly, he didn't die. He smirked and then amped up his glare to rival my own.

"It's true, I've made a lot of stupid mistakes in my life, *but,*" I popped my lips for emphasis, "I'm willing to bet nada plus zilch doesn't equal the same for both of us. So, tell me. How many bullies will it take to screw in *your* light bulb?"

He didn't answer me, but his lips did the same twitchy thing Angel's did when he was amused but preferred to hide it. "I see we have our work cut out for us," he answered. His gaze never left mine, but I had a feeling he wasn't speaking to *me*. Angel grunted, confirming my suspicion. Seriously, what was up with these men and their aggressive—albeit panty melting—sounds that really meant nothing?

Broody's gaze dipped as he rubbed his chin. "I never minded a little hard work, Sprite."

My body jerked at his use of the nickname Angel christened me with when we were kids. Well... *I* was a kid. He was legally a grown man for most of it, which was also why he'd always been so far out of reach...

I turned to face the culprit.

I didn't feel his friend's hot gaze on my body.

It did nothing for me.

Nothing.

"How much did you tell them about me?"

"Everything." I turned his answer over in my head. He definitely didn't sound apologetic.

"Don't you think that was private and unnecessary?" Only he had ever called me that and it was from an easier time that seemed so far away from where we were now.

"Don't think of it as gossip, little one." Man Bun had been content to keep silent, but it appeared he had found his voice. Maybe it got lost in those deep dimples... My gaze shifted to him. His perch against the door was to no doubt keep me from getting to the other side. "Think of it as..." His lips stretched. Those damn dimples deepened. "...therapy."

"How would Angel talking about me be therapy for him?'

"Wouldn't you like to know?" Broody teased.

My shoulders squared, ready to fight again. "Isn't that why I asked?" He opened his mouth ready to growl some more when Angel stepped in.

"Enough!"

Angel rose from his desk and moved close enough to grip my arm. He pulled me away, and when he stepped between us, I stared at his back in disbelief. My view of his friend's bare chest was now obstructed, but this view was much better. Until he turned and forced me under the full force of Angel's glare.

What's wrong, pumpkin? You seem tense?

His gaze narrowed as if he read my mind. "Give me a name, and I'll release your son."

For some reason, I looked at Man Bun for reassurance, but he was an expert at giving nothing away. I turned back to Angel whose attention had never left my face.

"And what about me? We're a package deal."

The bastard smirked. "How else do you think I got you here?"

"You son of a—"

"A name, Mian. This deal has an expiration date."

The name of the pawnshop owner slipped from my lips. I panicked, and now I had condemned an innocent man. It was too easy. Did that make me a monster, too? I had just signed an innocent man's death certificate. That guilt tripled when a conniving grin spread his lips.

"Thank you, Mian." He dismissed me as he turned to face Man Bun, giving me an unobstructed view of Broody, who was already barking orders through his phone. "Z, please show her where she'll be staying."

"Staying? Why would I be staying? We had a deal." God, I sounded like some cheesy action movie actress but what else was I supposed to say? I had been played.

"And I'll honor it after I know this is legit." I was then forcibly removed from the room. I screamed until we reached my cell. I was expecting a dungeon or at least a basement. I should have known that would have been much too simple for him. Instead of a damp, dark room with concrete floors and blood on the walls, I was led inside a plush bedroom suite that looked far too comfortable for its purpose.

I spun around and found Man Bun, whose name I now knew was Z, attempting to leave. "Hey!" I shouted. He turned and lifted an eyebrow but offered nothing more. This was the time for me to beg and plead and offer money I didn't have. "What's your name?"

He smiled.

I tried not to melt.

"Z."

"No." His confusion was evident in his frown. "Your *real* name. The name your mother gave you."

For the first time since meeting him, he didn't appear friendly. His face had turned to stone, and his gaze was glacial as he glared across the space separating us. "Zachariah."

I nodded because the name fit, and then I did something stupid.

"Is she dead?"

"I don't know where she is." He turned, stepped on the other side of the portal, and tossed over his shoulder, "And I don't care."

The door slammed shut and shook the frame. I heard the sound of the lock turning before I could even contemplate running. The final click might as well have been the sound of my freedom being discarded.

I was officially Angel's prisoner.

Along with his two friends who I would bet had just as many demons.

I was outnumbered and outmuscled which meant I would have to use my wits to get out of this unscathed. I slowly took in my surroundings but found nothing that could be used as a weapon. The bedroom had all of the basic furniture—a dresser, nightstand, chair, and an enormously wide bed. There was nothing to indicate that anyone had ever lived here before me. I studied the bed and panic seized my lungs in a tight fist.

What stopped me wasn't the missing pillows or sheets to cover the mattress.

Handcuffs.

He had freaking handcuffs!

I charged forward until my knees touched the side of the bed. I inspected the cuffs hanging from the gold painted iron. The design was simple—elegant even—and even though I wasn't an expert, instinct told me these weren't from a gag gift collection.

My attention slid to the footboard and just as I suspected, there hung the same style of cuffs.

Could I hide them?

I looked around the room for a potential hiding spot until

I discarded the idea entirely. A man as resourceful as Angel would only find more.

Or worse.

He'd use something else. Something less gentle.

Like rope.

I took a deep breath and released. It wasn't steady, but I was no longer on the verge of fainting either. Maybe these were left over from a previous lover. Maybe he had only left them to get under my skin.

Mission accomplished.

Slowly, I backed away from the bed until my back rested against a wall. Something dug into my hip so I spun and realized it wasn't a wall but a door. Pushing it open, I discovered the en suite.

It was small yet still five-star worthy. There was a glass-enclosed shower with stream jets completing a full three sixty. The stone tile complemented the wooden floor, and beside the shower was a garden tub that I ached to take advantage of.

Reluctantly, I turned away and did my business while promising that one day I'd have something like this to call my own. The design of the faucet was contemporary like the rest of the bath. I didn't have long to admire the sleek design when the water turned scalding hot. I yanked my hands from under the running water.

What the hell?

I turned the fancy knob and shut the water off and reached for a towel only to find there weren't any available. Seriously? I couldn't even get a hand towel? I fought an eye roll and realized this must be part of his game. The same as the sheets.

Angel thought he'd humble me by making me beg for sheets and towels.

As fucking if.

If he wanted me on my knees, he had to do better than that.

I wiped my hands down the front of my jeans and left the fancy bathroom. When I looked up, I found the woman who had let me in earlier, waiting. "Can I help you?"

"Mr. Knight has requested your presence at dinner tonight."

"Has he?" I looked her up and down and noticed she held a black box in her hand. "Could you please tell Mr. Knight that I am requesting he go fuck himself?" I batted my eyelashes sweetly.

"This evening's dinner attire has been selected." Her face never once lost its pinch as she passed me and primly lowered the box on the bed.

My lips curled. She might as well have been offering me a neatly wrapped infectious disease. I inspected it as much as I could from the other side of the room. Unless we were having dinner in a swimming pool, there was no way anything I'd fit into could be inside. I was small, but not so small that clothing my size would fit inside the box that wasn't even big enough to fit more than a single shoe.

"What's in there?"

"I told you. This is your dinner attire. You are instructed to wear them and nothing else."

Her answer pretty much sealed my fate. There was no way I was wearing what was or *wasn't* in that box.

I was here against my will and didn't exactly bring my very meager wardrobe to choose from. Wisely, she left before I could interrogate her.

My gaze landed on the laminated black box just as the sound of the door locking echoed in the room.

Could I truly be intrigued or just plain stupid?

I tried to tell myself it didn't matter what was in the box. I wasn't going to dinner. I damn sure wouldn't entertain whatever bullshit game Angel was intent on playing. I was only here to find my son, get the hell out of dodge, and make sure Angel Knight was sent somewhere that would guarantee he'd be ass fucked every single day until his number was up.

But... My feet moved forward, the plush carpeting keeping my movement silent. I would feel guiltless if my brain wasn't screaming that I was a fool.

Curiosity killed the cat.

Curiosity killed the cat.

Ten hesitant steps and I was running my fingertips over the smooth, flat surface before lifting the top. Transfixed by the beauty of the contents, yet confused how this could be considered dinner attire, I lifted the string of pearls and silver mask with black beading and a small feather adorned on the right corner.

Where the hell was the rest?

CHAPTER 16

Hate isn't always black and white.

ANGEL

"I GOT A look at the kid when Vincent brought him in. He's not looking too well." I turned to the sound of Lucas's voice. I'd been staring at the ceiling holding my second drink when Lucas and Z interrupted the little slice of peace I had found. When Z left with Mian, I had her kid brought to me. The first thing I noticed was that he didn't have his mother's eyes.

"Yeah, I noticed. You think he's sick?"

"Sickly. It looks more serious than just a cold."

"Fuck." I weighed my options. None of them allowed letting the kid die if it didn't serve me.

"It's like I said," Lucas voiced, "I can't have a kid's life on my conscience."

"We'll ask his mother. Maybe there's some medication he needs."

"I saw the apartment they are living in. If it's medication he needs, he isn't getting it. There wasn't even food in the cupboards. She's either destitute or strung out."

"When did you do this?"

"When she was shaking and fucking for money. I figured you'd be curious."

I tossed back the rest of my drink and reached for the bottle. She was in my house looking for something to sell. The Knight's black book could gain her unlimited supply of drugs if she sold it to the right people. Her father may not have wanted his lifestyle for her, but it didn't stop him from sharing trade secrets from time to time. When we were kids, she was the only person who understood my frustration at my father's insistence to keep me tucked safely away. Her desire for the life wasn't nearly as strong as mine was, but still, she understood. "So did you find drugs?"

"None. The place was clean, but there wasn't much to begin with."

"So she's broke. How the fuck could that be? Theo had money, and despite his shitty parenting, he loved that girl. He would have left her every dime he had."

"Unless she got crazy and burnt it all."

I shook my hand without wasting time considering it. "She's smarter than that."

"Not from the looks of it."

I cut my eyes at him in warning. Lucas's eyebrows reached for his hairline. I fucked up and revealed too much. Defending her against my brothers would be painting my hand red in front of an audience.

I reached for the blunt sitting in the nearby ashtray and lit up. If I couldn't focus, then I needed to forget. Getting fucked up was the quickest route to forgetting. Lucas, Z, and I dabbled as kids until it progressed into a regular thing. My father had never approved of my habit and always swore it would eventually lead to stronger avenues of escape.

We sat in silence as we passed the blunt amongst ourselves until we smoked it down to a roach. "Be careful with this girl. She affects you even when she isn't in the goddamn room."

"She's nothing."

"Don't lie to your brothers."

"Then I'll make her nothing," I growled. Just like that, they blew my high and frustration returned full force. "This is more than just recovering the book. This is retribution. If Theo Ross can't pay for my father's death, then his daughter will."

I felt the conviction in my threat which scared me most of all. My desire to possess this girl was a sin, and now it threatened my future and my brothers' trust. Wanting her was undoubtedly the cruelest wrong I'd ever done.

I listened absently as a phone rang and Lucas impatiently answered. He swore and then ended the call.

"What was that about?" Z questioned.

The frustration in Lucas's eyes warned me before he even spoke. "They finished tossing the shop."

"And?"

"They found nothing, and the owner is insisting he knows nothing about a book."

"What else did he say?"

"He says the only thing that was sold to him this morning was a watch. They checked his sale's receipts. It checked out."

"Could be a cover up," Z remarked.

"How much did he pay her?" I questioned.

"Nine hundred."

Z blew air from his lungs. I ignored him and said, "Which

means the watch was likely worth thousands. If she had a watch like that, why would she need to rob me?"

"It was one of your fathers." I was surprised to find the answer to my rhetorical questions had come from Z.

"I thought you said you searched her?"

He shrugged. "I did. I saw the watch."

"And you let her keep it?"

He shrugged again, and if I hadn't just drunk and smoked my fill, I would have shot him, but my reflexes would have been too slow.

Then again, I too was once a victim of Mian's innocence.

"I think we should pay our bandit's conspirator a visit before dinner."

I STEPPED OUT of the shower, free of another man's blood. He had screamed, and begged, and insisted. I hadn't found the book, which freed the merciful part of me to believe him.

So, instead of killing him or taking his hand, I sent his livelihood and hard work up in flames.

No one could say I wasn't a merciful man.

Padding over to my closet, my mind wandered to my little prisoner. She had been mine to protect, and now she'd become mine to do with whatever the fuck I wanted. It was long overdue. And now our fathers' weren't around to protect *us* from each other.

Dinner was already waiting when I entered the dining room. Lucas and Z sat at the table with tense expressions while Milly waited behind my chair ready to serve my every whim.

That should have been Mian's place.

Fuck.

"Where is she?" I knew as soon as I walked in that Mian was the cause of the tension. Her absence likely had something to do with it.

"Miss Ross has declined your invitation to dinner and has chosen to remain in her room."

"Is that right?" Milly nodded and looked like she had more to say. "What else did she say to you?"

"Not to me," she corrected. Her face reddened, and her expression tightened further, if possible. "She instructed me to tell you that she'd rather starve and imagine you choking on your food."

"And?"

"And..." Her lips pressed tighter, if possible. "...if that didn't work to die anyway."

I felt the smile on my lips that had nothing to do with humor. "It seems our guest needs a lesson in manners. Milly, you're dismissed until I say otherwise. Your payment is waiting on the table by the door."

She didn't even blink, which is why I paid her a hefty salary, and she immediately replied, "Have a good night, Mr. Knight." I waited until I was sure she had left before standing up. "What are you going to do?" Z questioned.

"I'm going to incentivize our guest."

"Maybe I should go."

"Why?"

"Because you're not ready to be alone with her. You know it as well as we do. Isn't that why we're here?"

"He's right," Lucas chimed in. "If we let you near her in

your current state of mind, she'll be ass up with you balls deep, and our dinner will get cold."

"Fine. But I want her at this table in ten minutes, or I'll do it myself."

A chuckle came from Z's direction. "You're a cranky bitch when you're horny." He took off with Lucas on his heels. I threw back the glass of wine that had been sitting in front of me and counted slowly in my head.

CHAPTER 17

Well, it's not a pumpkin.

MIAN

"KNOCK, KNOCK. YOUR carriage awaits."

I looked around for a weapon, but it was too late. They were already through the door and quickly closing the distance between us. "Beavis and Butthead." I flashed a mocking smile. "I would say it's nice to see you again, but my mom insisted that it's rude to lie. What brings you to my humble abode?"

Broody's face gave nothing away, but Z grinned and said, "Our princess has ice in her heart."

"As far as you're concerned, you would only be so lucky."

"Well, I guess I should look forward to *feeling you* out." His

 smile was easy, his voice was like liquid honey, and I had the feeling it was just a mask until his lids lowered and his gaze warmed about a hundred degrees. The way he watched me didn't feel like a game. It felt like I was being seduced. Of course, I'd only ever had sex once,

and the choice hadn't been mine. If I couldn't recognize a predator, how would I know if I were being seduced by one?

"Mian?" He grinned knowingly.

"Don't count on it," I snapped to cover up my curiosity.

"Mian." This time, it was Broody who snapped, so my attention thankfully shifted away from heat to the frigid gaze of his companion.

"How may I help you...?" I realized I still hadn't learned his name and left him to fill in the blanks. He didn't.

"You declined his dinner invitation."

"And?"

"It wasn't a request." What was up with these men thinking I would jump simply because they commanded it?

"Sure sounded like one to me. Angel requested that I share a meal with him and I declined."

I crossed my arms and waited for him to force me or threaten to hurt me if I didn't please his precious boss. He did neither.

"Eight minutes."

"Sorry?"

"You have less than eight minutes until Angel comes after you and you don't want that."

An innocent but totally fake smile spread across my face as I tilted my head playfully. "I don't?"

"No, Mian. You don't. You want your son safe, and you want him to free you both."

"And having dinner will make that happen? What about the buyer?"

They both tensed. What was so special about that watch? If I had known it would cause me this much trouble, I would have demanded more money. "One step at a time."

"Which would be?"

"Believing that we are sparing you and your son a night of suffering."

My heart threatened to break through my chest while my arms uncrossed and weakly fell to my sides. "Why should I trust you?"

"I'm not asking for your trust. I'm asking for your obedience."

"People don't normally *ask* for obedience."

"I'm not most people."

"Yeah, only the psychotic ones steal a child from their mother's arms."

He snorted. He *actually* snorted. "It's not as if you made it hard."

"Excuse me?"

"You were alone and unprotected with a baby in a bad neighborhood. It could have been someone with nothing to lose. They would have killed you and the kid right there on the sidewalk for the lint in your pockets."

His words clenched my gut in a fist and twisted. What he said was true. I made a bad choice—a few of them—and now I would pay the consequences. While it is no excuse or invitation to kidnap my child, I was forced to admit where I'd gone wrong.

"So, you're saying I'm a bad mother?"

He rolled his eyes. "I'm saying you're stupid."

One moment there's distance between us, and the next we're standing toe to toe. My chin was up, and his head lowered until we were glaring at each other. I'm not winning, but I'm not losing either... until something passes between us and suddenly has me feeling that I'm in over my head. Before

I can retreat, he's gripping my arms and pulling me closer into his hot chest.

"You have something you want to say to me?" The closeness soaks me in his warmth and scent. Not to mention his *mouth*. His breath is sweet, and his lips are perfectly kissable. That couldn't be. Evil men weren't supposed to look and sound, and—Oh, God, he pulled me closer—*feel* so sexy.

I needed a distraction and quick. His body was screwing up the signals my brain was sending to the rest of my body.

"What's your name?"

"What?" The bewildered look on his face said I was crazy. I was crazy, but crazy was all I had to protect me.

"I'm going to kill you the first chance I get. I prefer to know who I'm killing just in case hell asks questions at the gate."

He smirked. I didn't expect that. "Lucas."

"Hi, Lucas. Did your mother or your father give you your name?"

His hands tightened around my arms. Oh, boy. Did talk of Mommy and Daddy piss him off? Z, who watched us with a bored expression, had a similar reaction when I questioned him about his mother.

"I wouldn't know because I don't know them."

So, they were both orphaned... "Don't know them or don't remember them?"

"Does it matter?"

"I think it does to you."

He studied me for a moment, and I wondered if he was actually considering it until I felt my body jerk. I looked down to see the button of my jeans undone. They were covering my lower body... and then they weren't. I was staring at them lying twisted around my ankles when I felt the same being done to my shirt. The cool air touched my naked skin once my shirt was gone, and it woke me the fuck up. I bucked, but strong arms swiftly closed around me from behind.

"We have six minutes," I heard Z say—no *breathe*—against my neck. Jesus, when did he even move?

"Let me go!" His hand shot up and muffled the sound of my scream.

"You do not want him to come in here. We're doing you a favor, Sprite."

"Don't call me that!" I spoke into his hand, which muffled my voice.

"Not now, Sprite. We're trying to get you out of your clothes."

"Stop. Please!" More muffling. It was Lucas and Z who tore my clothes from my body, but it was Aaron's smile I saw the moment he knew he had won. I didn't realize I was crying until my tears were being wiped away by a gentle finger.

"Shhh," Lucas demanded.

"We're not going to hurt you," Z softly assured.

But I knew the warning behind it that went unspoken. They weren't going to hurt me if I didn't make them. Men like them don't stay alive doing what they do without taking a few first.

"Stop," I tried again to no avail. They had already taken so much, a part of me wanted to just hand them the rest.

But I wasn't my father, and I wasn't my mother. I wasn't going to give up on my son and leave him behind to their mercy.

"Your panties and bra are next," Lucas announced.

"Can you accept what is expected, or do we need to proceed?" Z questioned. I didn't want to bare my body for them, but they were giving me a choice to endure their hands or be free of them. Feeling numb, I nodded.

"Good girl. We'll wait outside."

I wanted to tell them there was no need. I saw the contents of the box and knew Angel intended to parade me, naked, in front of his friends and company.

They moved to the door and just before the door closed, I heard, "The clock is ticking, Mian Ross."

Z.

"You have four minutes."

Lucas.

I wanted to rage and tell them where they could stick their clock and do with their dinner, but I didn't. I sunk down on the bare mattress and pulled the box closer to me. If they were warning me not to tempt Angel, then maybe, I should do exactly that. Maybe it was time I get my head in the game and play it better than the men who started it.

CHAPTER 18

Outnumbered but not outsmarted.

ANGEL

THE WINE GLASS I'd refilled was poised below my lips, and I had to anchor my feet to the floor when she appeared nine minutes and forty-three seconds later. The moment my gaze found her may have been the first time I ever lost at my own game.

She was naked except for a silver mask and the pearls around the tempting column of her neck. I wanted her like this—vulnerable and humiliated. From the rigid way she held her body as she entered the dining room, I could tell I got my wish.

I just wasn't expecting a rock hard dick for my trouble. Z cleared his throat when my staring bordered on embarrassing. Lucas was too busy staring at her ass to notice the tension.

Fuck me, but she was gorgeous. Everything about her was small from her pouty lips to the tiny pink toes resting on the marble floors. I could probably wrap my hands around her waist and have my fingers overlap. Her tits were small making her dusky pink nipples seem larger than normal. They looked slightly reddened, which made me wonder if she nursed the baby. Her stomach was still as taut as I remembered it, but I could also see the faint evidence of a few stretch marks on her otherwise unmarred skin. The marks didn't detract from her beauty. It only made me hungrier... and curious.

What would it be like to breed Mian Ross?

"Our food will get cold if you two continue to eye fuck each other," Z broke in. He sounded bored, but the bulge in his pants suggested otherwise. When he took his place at the table, I turned my attention back to Mian.

"Sit."

"Why?"

"Because I have three simple rules and doing as I say is number one."

Her eyes narrowed. "And the others?"

"Don't test me." I paused until I could feel her anticipation and fear. "And don't lie to me." One of the benefits of her naked state was the ability to see her entire body flush and tremble. There was nothing for her to hide behind.

"If you think—"

"I don't think, Mian. I command."

"Command your puppets. Do not command me. My father—"

"Is in prison," I reminded. She used to wield her father's influence over mine when we were kids when she couldn't get her way. When she batted those lashes at her father or even at me, I was reminded that she was my ticket into the business.

"And yours is dead," she countered, snapping me back to the present. I was out of my chair and moving down the long dining table, but I wasn't quick enough. She lunged forward and grabbed a knife from the place setting that was meant for her. My jaw clenched. Milly didn't have the foresight not to give Mian a knife. I doubted Mian had found an ally in the stubborn woman so easily. "Stay the fuck away from me, or I will gut you."

Lucas had never moved from his place behind her. He moved closer, but she didn't seem to notice, so I planted my feet and crossed my arms. I could feel a smile trying to break free, and just for the hell of it, I let it free. He was almost on her. I just had to keep her attention on me, which had never been hard whenever we were in the same room together.

"Don't believe me?" she sneered.

"Oh, I believe you, which is why Lucas here is going to stop you." I nodded, and he effortlessly grabbed her around the waist, pulling her naked body into him at the same time, grabbing her wrist and tightening his grip until she cried out and dropped the knife.

"Easy does it," he cooed in her ear. He gently lowered her into her seat and pushed the chair in. He leaned down and whispered in her ear low enough to keep it between them. Whatever he'd said caused her mouth to part and her eyes to lose focus and glisten. I kept my expression blank and made a mental note to ask him what he'd said to her later.

Z looked from me to her and said, "Now can we eat dinner?"

"Fuck you."

Z's smile was wide, but his eyes had darkened as he leaned forward to rest his forearms on the table and trap Mian with his gaze. "Maybe you will."

She sneered at him. "God, you're delusional if you think I'll touch you."

"That's enough," I ordered before he could continue their game. Z wouldn't hesitate to scare her for his own amusement, and for some reason, that bothered me even though I needed her to be scared and helpless.

"Sure thing, boss." He nodded and dove into his food. Mian just stared back at me.

"Eat."

"I said I wasn't hungry."

"And I said to eat."

"I don't trust you."

"I don't give a fuck. Eat before I have Lucas *shove* the food down your throat."

"It would be good practice, sweetheart." Even though I told them they wouldn't touch her, it didn't stop them from taunting her with the promise of sex. She shot Lucas a murderous glare and then picked up her fork. There was a moment of hesitation, and I was pretty sure we were all holding our breath to see what she would do with it. When she smirked and stabbed her fork in her salad, I knew she played us. She tested us to see if she could evoke the same fear as we forced from her.

She had no fucking idea.

Z had already completely wiped his plate and dug in the dishes placed in the middle for seconds when I finally relaxed enough to eat. I had taken no more than a bite of the chicken when a cry rang out.

"Oh, my God." She stood up, her chair scraping the floors, and toppling in her haste. "Where is he?" she growled but didn't wait around for an answer. She took off in the direction of his cries. I set down my fork and nodded to Z since he was the quickest, and he gave chase.

I could hear her screaming her son's name, and then, suddenly, her screams stopped. Mian was sharp-tongued and spoiled, but I never expected her to have any true fight in her. When she was brought back, he pushed her in my direction but stayed close behind her.

"Do you hear your son crying for you?" I asked unnecessarily as I rose to my feet. I wanted to torture her in the only way that would allow me without touching her. I could barely restrain myself being in the same room with her.

I expected tears. I expected begging. She exploded. "All of this... for a fucking watch?" Her scream echoed around us while her son's cries grew louder in the distance. "I knew you were an asshole, but I never took you for a materialistic asshole." She shook her head in disgust. "It will take some time, but I'll pay you back somehow. I swear."

I would have snorted at the fact that she thought I was doing this to be an asshole. My father's murder had made me much worse, and she was about to find out how much.

"Your story checked out. The unlucky bastard who bought my father's watch was very adamant it was his only business with you. Unfortunately, you and I both know it's not a fucking watch I'm after."

"Then what you're after has nothing to do with me because... I... don't... have it!"

I stalked her and then grabbed her shoulder and forced her over the table before pulling my gun and pressing it against her skull. She wiggled her tight little ass against my dick, and I knew she felt what she had done to me when she gasped. "No more lies. Where's the fucking book?"

Her back stiffened. It wasn't the reaction of someone who didn't know of my family's legacy and prosperity of our fortune. But then she blurted, "Oh, God. That's even *worse*. You're after a *book*?"

"You're a terrible fucking liar, Mian." I slid the hammer back and smiled when she trembled at the sound of the click. "What are you willing to do to have your son back?"

She turned her head just enough for me to see the fire in her eyes. "Kill you. That's what I'm willing to do." *Damn, that just made me harder.* "I don't have this book you're looking for so you should just kill me now because *I* won't hesitate." She pressed her head back against the gun, and I was tempted—so fucking tempted—to just blow her brains out and be done with it.

"I would never make dying easy for you," I assured. My free hand slid to my mother's pearls around her neck. I tugged the necklace until it bit into her skin just enough to scare her. "You should know better than that."

There was a large bead of sweat that rolled from the top of her spine to the middle. Leaning forward, I licked up the droplet and felt her full-body shiver. She tasted salty and sweet.

"What are you doing?" She wiggled to free herself.

"Tasting you." That earned me another shiver.

"Why?" she yelled. I didn't answer because I didn't know why. I heard her long exhale and pulled the necklace tighter until her air supply was cut off. She began to struggle in earnest. All her struggling did was to make my dick even harder, and that's when the lightbulb lit.

I knew exactly how to be the monster Mian Ross could fear.

I handed the gun to Z and grabbed her wrists. Stretching

them in front of her, I put all of my weight on her back and ground my hips against her bare ass.

"Let me go," she gasped when she finished sucking in air.

"Why would I do that?" I whispered in her ear. "You've been begging for my dick inside you since you were fourteen..." I transferred her wrists into one hand and used my right to trail down her side. "...you're legal now."

"I don't want this," she cried.

I kicked her legs apart. "Then tell me what I want to know."

"I can't!"

"Sure you can." Kissing her shoulder, I freed one hand to unzip my pants and free my dick.

"Angel, please." She was trembling uncontrollably now, and her fierceness had been replaced my timidity. "I really don't know anything."

"Sure you do." I pressed against her and felt the tight entrance to her sex part. I could feel my restraint slipping. I only wanted to scare her into talking, but now that I felt her, I wasn't sure how I could stop. "After I'm done with you, Lucas and Z will have a turn." I pushed my hips against her to taunt her when a sorrow-filled cry shook me to my core.

I tore away from her.

Lucas, who had been lazily watching us, sat up.

I heard Z curse behind me.

We each have tortured many men for information in painful, unimaginable ways. We were immune to begging, cries, and screams.

But *never* have we ever heard anything like this.

I'D GONE TOO far.

Shame, disgust, and anger all took turns fucking me up. I never wanted to rape her. A part of me hoped she'd see past my game and challenge me as she always had. I felt sick to my stomach for the first time since I took over after my father had died. I made her think I would rape her before killing her and when I'd gone too far, snapping my control, and turning the game into reality, I released a demon inside her, and she passed out to escape it.

I had Z carry her unconscious body back to her room while I locked myself in my office to think. Something had happened to her. I was more sure of it than I was of my next breath.

"She's tougher than you thought," Z laughed and bit into a roll from dinner. His stomach was a bottomless pit. He never stopped eating. "You underestimated her."

"We can break her," I said unconvincingly.

"It sounds as if we already did," Lucas pointed out. His eyes were closed as he rested his head against the back of the couch. "She sounded pretty broken to me."

I could still hear her broken cry an hour later.

"What were you thinking?" Lucas questioned. "Fucking her isn't part of the plan, remember?"

"Not if she wants it," I reminded and felt my stomach turn. Taking pussy that hadn't been offered to me wasn't my cup of tea.

"That much was clear," he remarked. I detected the jealousy in his tone. I didn't miss the heated glances throughout dinner.

I couldn't keep my eyes off her body either, and even now, I was still seeing her. I remembered the ramrod position of her spine, her hardened nipples, and the distrustful glances she kept gifting me as she picked over her food. She'd barely eaten a quarter of her food, and I too exhausted, decided if she chose to starve herself, I wouldn't care. I'd never get my book, but she'd never save her son either.

From the state we found them in, it might have been safer for them both to be with us. They were barely surviving with no money, no food, and no security. The report my team gave told me she'd just left a pawnshop when I gave the command to take her. It must have been where she'd gotten money to get here, and now I knew what she'd sold to get it.

Mian was a smart girl. If she stole the book, then she knew its value, which meant she was either more desperate for money than we'd thought or... she was telling the truth and sold a fucking watch instead of my family's legacy.

"We're in this together," Lucas growled. I looked away from nothing in particular and found them watching me with hard gazes. "Whatever you're thinking, we need to know."

"You went inside your head again," Z clarified.

"She should be awake by now." I pushed my chair back and rose to my feet, and they followed as I made my way to her room.

"You sure you want to do this?" Z questioned. "Remember why we're here."

Because I can't have her.

"I'm sure," I answered. She must have heard us coming because a tiny squeak penetrated through the bedroom. I could hear her shuffling. To hide? To find a weapon?

I fingered the key from my suit pants and unlocked the

door. There was no sign of her when the door opened, so I cautiously stepped inside. "Are you really hiding when there's nowhere to go?"

"Maybe I'm just waiting for you to make a wrong move," she countered through the darkness.

"There's nothing here you can use to take out all three of us." I took another step inside.

"Just your own stupidity. With the three of you put together, I might as well be armed with an atomic bomb."

"Fuck this," I heard behind me. The light flickered on, and my eyes immediately found her sitting in the far corner with her knees to her chest. I instantly noticed the absence of the mask and necklace. She was completely naked without them since Z had taken her clothes. Finally, our gazes clashed and she smirked with triumph.

"Three bad men scared of one little girl."

I decided not to play her games. I came here for one thing, and I am going to get it. "Come here."

"And if I don't, you'll beat me." She rolled her eyes, and I would have believed she wasn't afraid if her body hadn't trembled.

"That would be showing you mercy." I disarmed her with a smile. "Come. Here." I pointed to the spot between the black Italian leather covering my feet. She followed my finger and then lazily let her gaze travel back to my face. "I'm not going to ask again," I forced through my teeth when she didn't move. I made it to the count of three in my head, and then I watched, feeling my entire body tighten, as she impatiently rose to her feet. "No." She froze and stared back. Confusion clouded her eyes until I ordered, "Crawl."

She stopped breathing, but the fire in her eyes never left. Her attention angrily shifted behind me where I knew Lucas and Z silently watched everything unfold.

"I'll come to you. Isn't that enough?" Pride would cost her everything, but something told me she would happily give pay if it meant not surrendering to me.

"I say when it's enough. I'll spare you the hope now. It will *never* be enough. Now get that ass in the air and *come*."

Damn, that sounded good. The hiss from her lips was sharp and true. "I hate you."

I hungrily watched her sexy lips curl and promised myself I'd taste them again before I killed her. "Like I give a fuck."

After a brief moment of plotting my death in her head and a heart full of hate that shown through her wide green eyes, she finally lowered herself to the ground. But when her knees touched the carpeted floor, she sat in the same position I had found her in and flipped me off before saying, "I'm a Ross and I crawl to no one. If you want me, come and get me."

I heard two sets of breaths expel harshly behind me. Mian Ross had just sealed her fate. "Lucas?"

"Yes?"

"She would like for us to come and get her."

He hesitated before breezing past me and then lifted her in the air before hauling her over her shoulder. "Here?"

I nodded and took a seat in the high-backed, cushioned chair in the corner facing the bed. She remained silent, and I wondered if she finally caught on. We weren't kids bantering anymore. We were enemies trying to out conquer the other.

Z removed his belt while Lucas dropped her on her stomach at the foot of the bed. "How many times has she disobeyed you?" Lucas questioned.

CHAPTER 19

Spare the rod, spoil the child.

MIAN

WHEN I'D WOKEN up, I was still in this hellhole, but at least I'd been alone. I had come so close to being raped a second time, only this time, I would have suffered through it. The only comfort was knowing he would at least kill me afterward, but then I passed out to escape. I feared the worst when I came to, but a quick check between my legs eased my fears. None of the shame and pain I felt from Aaron's violation had lingered.

"How many times as she disobeyed you?"

"Three."

I licked my lips and dug my fingers into the mattress. I was fucking terrified, and now my game face was slipping.

The look in Angel's eyes when I challenged him summoned some common sense. I was out of my league, yet I couldn't find it in me to back down. A part of me was still remembering the

aloof boy from my childhood. He'd been a jerk, but somehow, I still trusted him to keep me safe.

But that boy was gone, and the man who replaced him had left me naked and at the mercy of two men who I didn't know.

The sound of a belt unbuckling drew my attention, so I looked back in time to see Lucas removing his thick leather belt from his pants. "So be it. Three lashes for three offenses."

I exhaled.

I could deal with that.

"Make it your hardest," Angel dictated. "I want her to understand me."

I shuddered involuntarily. Lucas was the most muscular of the three without being bulky. He would no doubt, draw the attention of every female, including mine... and then we would run the other way.

"Tie her hands and feet."

I heard the jangle of another belt, and it occurred to me then that I should fight. With a surge of adrenaline, I was able to lift my upper body and lock my elbows, but then I was pushed back down and eating mattress just as quickly.

"Where would you go?" I felt more than heard the whisper in my ear. I had the perfect retort when he caught the shell of my left ear between his teeth. Strange that my concern was if Angel could see what he was doing. Would he think I seduced him somehow? Would he be jealous?

When I escaped, I needed to get my head examined.

My arms were pulled behind me, and I felt fine leather bind my wrists at the small of my back. My feet were roughly pushed together, and I was tied up with more leather. The cold buckles rested against my heated skin uncomfortably. "Maybe we should use something else to bind her. Or I could use my hand—"

"Use mine."

It took some effort, but I twisted my head enough to bring him into view. He sat as still as death, and his gaze was as hard as stone. I licked my lips again and swallowed hard. It frightened me that he had so much control. God, why won't he move?

My silent plea seemed to awaken him. His hands moved, but his gaze never left me. From his lap, they lifted to his waist, and I watched, spellbound by what would come next. The gold buckle released with a click and his strong hand pulled the smooth black leather through the loops until it was free. He then folded the leather half all the while holding my stare. We were alone in this room. Nothing else existed but us, and nothing else mattered but what he'd do next.

I held my breath.

The hand holding the belt lifted and our spell was broken.

He smirked, and I decided there was nothing that could ever make me not hate him. It was hard to believe I once lov—

"Ahhh!" Burning pain bit into the skin of my ass. I cried and fought against my restraints. The gruff sound of someone calling my name could barely be heard over the screaming pain.

"That was a request for your attention."

I did beg then. "Please let me go."

"Give me what I want."

"I don't have what you want!"

"Then we'll beat you every day until your answer changes. Do you really expect me to believe you sold power to a pawner?"

He nodded to Lucas and the whistle of the belt slicing through the air prepared me in the worst way. My body tensed and I cried into the mattress when it struck.

Fingers threaded through my hair as my head was lifted from the mattress. Bright green eyes stared back at me. "Don't tense," Z advised. "It will only hurt worse."

"Don't touch me."

He cocked his head and stared at me in amazement. "With everything that's going to happen to you... you still want to fight us?" His gaze shifted momentarily and then he focused on me again. "Get ready, sweetheart. Here comes another one."

My body naturally tensed but then something bizarre happened. Z's lips touched mine. Softly. His tongue darted out, licking the seam between my lips. I felt his breath shudder just before he took over completely and kissed me. I was stunned that he would make such a bold move but also terrified at how good he tasted.

I realized it was a distraction when the next blow came. I hadn't fully recovered from the last and the biting pain still proved too much, but at least I had something else to focus on. I cried into his mouth, and he groaned like a starving man.

Why did I enjoy his lips when all he did was hurt me?

He was another criminal.

Another monster.

And he wasn't Angel.

"Come on, sweetheart. Open up that sweet mouth." He bit my lip causing me to gasp and then shoved his tongue as far down my throat as possible. His tongue danced with mine, and I became drunk from the taste of him. It took my mind away from the pain.

When he lifted his head, I chased and was mortified when I heard, "So you like to take amorous liberties with your enemies?"

Z moved away leaving Angel in my line of sight once again. And then the final blow was dealt.

There were no kisses to distract me. I could only concentrate on the pain.

I'd never been beaten—not even by my parents. My mom had preferred talking, and my dad would never raise his hand to me no matter how many times he said I deserved some time over his knee.

"Are you ready to talk?"

My answer was to cry harder. My dignity hadn't returned after I was untied and no longer bent over. I was still very much naked while they were fully dressed. I wanted revenge. I wanted my pride back. But then I reminded myself, it had been three years since I'd seen Angel Knight, and in just a couple of hours, I've been trapped, stripped, and beaten.

Maybe my battle with three powerful men could rest for one night.

"It wasn't rhetorical, Sprite."

I kept my gaze on the floor and nodded. His friends moved for the door, and I almost asked them to stay. Angel and I hadn't been left alone since the summer before my father killed his.

"Where are my clothes?" He still sat upon his throne, making the room seem smaller, and my nakedness more apparent.

"Burned. You won't be needing them."

"I don't have your stupid book so let us go."

"You expect me to believe that you broke into my father's home for a watch?"

"I didn't know it was your father's," I lied. "That's not the same house."

"Lucky coincidence then," he snarled sarcastically. "My father had the house built when business picked up."

"So then you know there's no way I would know the place I was robbing belonged to your dead father."

His eyes darkened, and his body tightened. "Careful, Mian."

As much as I hated him, I regretted my harsh words. I hated any reminder that my mother was dead. I nodded, and he seemed to relax.

"Tell me what you know," he ordered.

"I don't know anything."

"Then tell me what you don't know." The bite in his tone sent a warning chill down my spine. It seems Angel's composure wasn't as airtight as he wanted me to think.

My control, however, snapped. "What I *don't* know is anything about this book you're after. What I *don't* know is why you think I'd want your stupid book. What I don't know," I added smoothly this time, "is why you insist on keeping my son and me here. And what I really don't know is how you've managed to become an even bigger ass than when I actually knew you."

"You never knew me, Sprite." His whisper almost sounded like regret, but his eyes were angry.

"Apparently, not," I whispered back. Could he hear my sorrow?

"Why am I supposed to believe you? You broke into a house intending to steal something that didn't belong to you."

"Wrong. It belonged to my father which meant it belonged to me."

"I thought you said you didn't know whose house it was?" He leaned forward and rested his elbows on his knees. "And I *thought* you said your father didn't know about your little job."

I had been caught in a trap with my back against the corner.

My father never wanted me to be a part of his world, and if mama hadn't died, I never would have. But Angel wouldn't know that. He was too busy hating my relationship with my father to understand it.

"He didn't."

His eyes narrowed dangerously. "I'm counting your lies, Mian, and I intend to pay you back for each of them."

I couldn't help myself. I didn't think about the repercussions. I just exploded. "I haven't spoken to my father since he lost his trial!" It wasn't the truth anymore so I channeled the pain and anger built up over two years. If I wasn't threatened with homelessness, my father's abandonment would still be true.

"What?"

I saw the tick in his jaw, and when I couldn't look at him anymore, I fixed my gaze on the floor and spoke to it. "I have not," I said slowly, "heard my father's voice since they dragged him away."

Even though it wasn't true I still missed him so much. I knew it was the last thing Angel would want to hear. I just needed him to believe it.

I heard him move and the sound drew my gaze to him. He was sitting back, watching me intently. "Why?" Instead of answering, I tried to figure out why his voice was almost tender. "Mian," he snapped, breaking that tenderness.

"He won't take my calls or let me visit."

"Coward."

"Excuse me?"

"Your father is a coward."

"He's trying to protect me. He wants better for me."

He stared at me for a few seconds. "I knew you were spoiled, but I never pegged you for dumb," he scoffed. He looked me up and down with his top lip slightly curled. "He's trying to avoid you, Mian. He wants to cut his losses to make his time easier without having to look in your face every Sunday and feel guilty."

I charged forward, and I couldn't fucking stop. The momentum and angry rush of adrenaline powered my swing, and when I felt my palm connect with his face, it felt good. But then I looked into his eyes and knew I had made a mistake.

He was out of his chair with his hand in my hair, yanking me forward until our faces were closer. I cried out when he pulled harder, and I was forced to stand on the tip of my toes. My body was under his control, and there wasn't a damn thing I could do about it.

Our bodies were flushed.

I could feel his body heat inflaming mine, and the fine fabric of his clothes caressed my naked skin.

"Is this how you want it to be?" he whispered. His voice husky and without even a hint of anger. "I'm willing to hurt you, Mian. Just say the word."

I wouldn't give him the satisfaction. "Let me go."

"You hit me. Give me one good reason why I shouldn't fuck you up."

"You. Beat. Me!"

186

"I had you spanked—something your father should have done a long time ago."

"You had no right."

"You're in my home. Under my hospitality. I'll do to you whatever the fuck pleases me." He released my hair just in time to keep from tearing the strands from its roots but then locked his arms around my body to keep me close. "But I will beat you until you're unrecognizable, even to yourself, if you ever strike me again."

I tried to suck in air and failed. He was holding me too tight. "I can't breathe."

"Am I understood?" he demanded, and I knew he wouldn't let up until I yielded.

"Yes," I squeaked.

I fought to breathe when he finally let me go. My scalp was screaming, and my body was overheated. I pulled myself together and made eye contact. He was watching me strangely.

"What?"

"You're different."

"You are, too." His jaw tightened.

"No, Sprite. You're just finally noticing me."

CHAPTER 20

She's not ready for promises.

MIAN

SEVEN YEARS AGO

"MIAN?"

Oh, no. Go away. Please go away.

My teary gaze snapped from between my thighs to the door. I forgot to lock it in my hurry, so I pulled my knees tighter against my chest, hid my face between my knees, and braced.

Go away. Please go away.

I could hear his irritation when he snapped my name this time. Angel wouldn't hesitate to turn this bad dream into a nightmare. I heard the bathroom door open and forced myself not to move when I wanted to just run away. This could *not* be happening.

"Why are you in here?"

"I just needed to use the bathroom. Jeez."

"So, why are you crying?" I didn't need to see his face to know how angry he was.

"I just am. Please go away."

"Lift your face, tell me the truth, and maybe I'll go away." I couldn't stand the gruffness in his tone. His voice seemed to deepen every day, and I hated how it made me feel. I couldn't put a name to it. "Now, Mian."

I lifted my face from between my knees and gritted my teeth. It was too late for me to take it back. Obeying this cocky, rude asshole was like trying to swallow a mouth full of nails.

"Those tears aren't for nothing."

"You're right, but it's none of your business, so please, please just go away." His perfect eyebrows pulled down and his lips twisted to the side just before he kicked the door close. "What are you doing?"

"Why are you playing this game with me?" he barked. I flinched and retreated further into the corner. "Tell me what's wrong."

"Why do you care?" I screamed suddenly. I choked back the urge to scream again. When he didn't respond, I looked away and studied the paint on the walls. Why couldn't he just go away?

Seconds passed without words spoken. He never made a sound as he moved closer and then crouched to his haunches with his forearms resting on his knees. Muscles that weren't there or quite so defined last summer caught my attention. How could he be this intimidating at only eighteen?

His face suddenly twisted and I realized too late that his gaze was between my thighs. "Are you hurt?"

Oh, God. He *saw*.

A whimper escaped me as I closed my legs again to hide the blood smeared between my thighs. My guard must have dropped while I was staring at him. "Please, *please* just go. I'm not hurt."

He seemed to mull it over before jumping to his feet. I'd already reburied my head between my knees when the door opened and slammed a second later. The dam burst once it did.

Why couldn't he have just left me alone? He's never cared before.

I didn't know how much time had passed when the door opened again. I couldn't move. He ignored me this time and walked past me. I should have left so he could have the bathroom, but fear made my legs weak. It had been so quiet so when the sound of water rushing filled the room, I jumped.

Was he seriously going to shower with me sitting here?

I tore my gaze from the floor and watched as he held his long fingers under the water to test the temperature. When he was satisfied, he poured what looked like salt and smelled sweet from a dark blue and white bag. He then reached inside the large paper bag at his feet and pulled out a small bottle before pouring from the bottle.

He moved from the running water when bubbles started to form and opened the linen closet. After pulling out a thick, white towel, he walked past me again and bent to grab the bag. I almost swallowed my tongue when he turned and caught me staring. The butterflies in my stomach intensified. The only time I ever felt like this was when I had my first crush, only this felt more intense. More real.

Was it possible to have a crush on someone seven years older?

"Did you hear me?" His voice brought me back to awareness.

"What? Huh?"

"I said the water shouldn't be too hot."

"It's for me?"

His face remained expressionless as he answered without emotion, "It's not for me."

"Oh." I didn't move from my spot in the corner. Instead, I tightened my arms around my legs. I couldn't move with him in here anyway. He'd seen enough to disgust him. I was scared and mortified when I used the bathroom and discovered the blood in my panties. I panicked and ripped them off, and when I touched myself, I realized what was happening. I had no idea what to do and no one to turn to so I balled myself in the corner and cried.

He dropped to his haunches in front of me and reached into the paper bag and pulled out a box. "Know how to use these?" My eyes bucked, and I shook my head. Angel holding a box of tampons was not something I ever expected to see. The blue and orange box looked out of place in his hand. It disappeared back into the bag, and then he pulled out a package of pads.

Kill. Me.

He frowned as he ripped open the packaging before pulling out a folded square wrapped in pink paper. "I was told these are easier to use."

"Who told you that?" I blurted. I couldn't believe he'd gotten them much less discussed the advantages of feminine products.

Oh, God. Had he cornered some poor, unsuspecting woman in a store for help?

"Trinity."

His answer brought my musings to a screeching halt. I

watched as he ripped open the pink paper and unfolded the sanitary pad. "I—I can do that."

He didn't respond, but he did toss the pad into the bag and stand. "The water's going to be cold soon."

He made for the door, but my curiosity wouldn't just let him leave. "Who's Trinity?"

The muscles in his back tightened and pulled against his thin t-shirt. He stood silently in the threshold for so long that I figured he wouldn't answer and would tell me it was none of my business. But then he bit out, "My girlfriend," and walked out.

The door slamming swallowed my inhale. I felt as if I'd been punched in the stomach. Fighting my trembling legs, I stood and shed my nightshirt. The water was the perfect temperature. The salt and bubbles caressed my skin and soothed the ache in my muscles the stress had caused. Pretty soon, I was asleep until a knock on the door brought me back to life. The water had gone cold and bumps covered my skin.

"Mian?"

I quickly sat up and stared at the door, hoping he wouldn't open it. "I'm okay!" I yelled to answer his unspoken question. After three years, we were in tune with each other, and it was as if we secretly accepted the connection and silently hated each other for it.

I waited until he left to step out of the freezing water. The large towel was soft and a godsend against the cool air. It wasn't until I finished wrapping the towel that I realized I didn't have a change of clothes.

I'd have to leave the bathroom with only a towel to protect me. He was always disappearing and coming back hours later smelling like weed and looking like trouble. I've never met his friends, but that didn't mean he didn't have them. Maybe if I hid a little longer, he'd leave.

Or he'd realize I was hiding again, come back, and force me out.

I really only had one option.

I put my ear to the door, but it was silent on the other side. Maybe he'd gone to visit Trinity to laugh about what a stupid kid I am. My stomach cramped, but I told myself it was because of my menses and not the thought of him with another girl.

I wouldn't dare have a crush because not only was the thought of *us* forbidden, it was impossible.

It would be a long time before I was old enough for him. I was only twelve, and he would be nineteen in a few months. Our fathers would forbid it, and I was sure Angel thought I was just a dumb kid. I made it to my bedroom and immediately noticed my favorite lime green sheets had been replaced with crisp white sheets. I stood frozen just inside the door until understanding dawn and dread seeped inside.

There must have been blood.

He must have seen it and changed the sheets.

Oh, God.

Could this get any more embarrassing?

"Here."

I inhaled until my lungs were full and pivoted, feeling my heart race. He stood beyond the door holding a napkin and tall glass of water. He shoved it toward me and ordered me with his eyes to take it, so I did and found two pills inside the fold of the napkin. "What's this for?"

"For the pain."

I fingered the pills from the napkin and swallowed them down with half the glass of water. "Did Trinity tell you this?"

"Yes."

"Oh." I felt awkward.

He eyed me, and I could tell he was annoyed when he said, "Problem?"

"You didn't have to do all this," I said even though I knew if he hadn't, I'd still be in a ball on the bathroom floor.

"It was nothing." He noticed me staring and added, "So don't make it into anything."

"You're so confusing."

"How so?"

I shrugged and looked down at my feet. "You're just..." *A walking, talking contradiction.* "Not easy," I finished lamely.

"Then why are you still here?"

"It's not like I have a choice."

"You don't believe that so why do you expect me to?"

"Why would I lie?"

"Because you and I both know if you told your daddy how *not easy* I am, he wouldn't hesitate to bend to your will, would he, princess?"

"What do you have against my father?"

"It's not your father I have a problem with." He stepped closer and his eyes darkened. Suddenly, I was *very* aware of my nakedness beneath the towel. "But I do have a problem with the way you look at him."

"H—how do I look at him?"

"Like he's the only man in the world." I took a step back to escape the heat in his eyes, but he only followed me step for step. "One day, it won't be your father you'll look at that way. One day, it won't be him you belong to."

"I—I don't understand." *God, stop stuttering!*

Suddenly, the brakes were pressed. He stared down at me as if he was finally seeing me, and I watched as the wildness in his eyes dimmed. He started to back up, but I couldn't let him go. I needed to know what tamed him. I started to follow, but the tick in his jaw froze me. He left, and I stood in the same spot long after the front door slammed.

Why did it feel as if he'd just made a promise?

CHAPTER 21

While Angel's away, his friends will play.

MIAN

PRESENT

"RISE, PRINCESS."

I grumbled and fought to stay under. Consciousness chased the friendly voice, but my sore ass begged for me not to trust it.

"And shine, pretty girl." The presence of a second voice rang alarms, and when I felt fingertips trail my spine, they began to blare. I peeked cautiously with one eye open.

Strong legs covered in black denim greeted me. I had both eyes open when I scrambled to sit up, and I very clearly saw Lucas sitting on the windowsill and Z standing by my bedside sporting a grin.

"What are you two doing in here?"

"We need you," Lucas answered. His gaze dropped to my chest, reminding me I was naked. I shivered and told myself it was because I slept in the cold without so much as a sheet or a pillow to keep me warm.

"Why?" I asked warily. His voice had been far too seductive when he expressed his *need* for me.

"It's time for breakfast," Z answered cheerily.

"I'm not hungry."

"But we are." Lucas moved from the window to stand on the side of the bed opposite Z.

"You're grown men. I'm sure you know what you need to do when you're hungry."

"You have a mean mouth for someone so tiny," Lucas said. His gaze pinned me to the center of the bed. "I look forward to putting it to better use."

"Excuse me?"

"Mian," Z interrupted gently. I couldn't tear my glare away from Lucas. "Mian," he repeated, this time with a hand on my chin. Gently, he turned my face up until I had no choice but to meet his gaze. "If you want this to go smoothly, you might consider hearing us out. You deny us as if you have power here."

"I'm not having sex with you," I blurted. His smile was bright as the pad of his thumb caressed my chin softly.

"Let's just have breakfast first, and then we'll talk about it."

Was he not hearing me? What part of me not wanting our genitals to meet needed discussion?

"I don't think so."

He sighed and then climbed on the bed, driving me from the center and closer to Lucas. "Then we'll stay here," he said smoothly.

The bed shifted behind me. Lucas had also climbed in bed. "No reason not to get back in bed since breakfast isn't happening." His lips tilted. His smile made him insanely hot.

I reached out for covers that weren't there and felt the chilly air heat up by at least a hundred degrees. Running meant climbing over one of them or exposing my ass to reach the foot of the bed. I drew into myself to keep from touching them, but they just kept pushing closer.

"Guys, stop." I tried to sound firm, but all I could hear was desperation. Where was Angel?

"Have you reconsidered?"

"You're not going to bully me into doing what you want."

"Why not? It's worked so far." I glared at Lucas.

"What we're trying to say, pretty girl, is that you're still fighting when you've already lost."

"Why do you do that?"

"Do what?"

"Say nice things and threaten me at the same time. I'm not sure if you're worse than this one." I threw my thumb over my shoulder at Lucas.

"Does it matter?" Lucas questioned. "We're both dangerous, and we're not here to protect you. We're not your friends, and we never will be. Does that clear things up for you?"

"It certainly does. Gentleman, I'm naked. I don't know what you want from me, and I don't care. What I want is my son and to be shown to the door. Where's Angel?"

"Business trip to the city," Z answered.

"Why?"

"He left to find answers since he wasn't getting any from you."

"Wait... He left me here? Alone? With you two?" My voice rose with each question.

"Shhh," Z soothed. "He'll be back in two days."

Two days... Angel left my baby and me alone with strangers for two days. The room started to spin. "Oh, God."

Lucas's expression shifted to concern. "Are you alright?"

Fuck no! "Where is my baby?"

"He's fine."

I pounded my fist on the bare mattress and snarled at Z. "He's not safe from you three, so no, he is not *fine*."

"He's safe, Mian. And if you do as you're told and don't try anything idiotic, you will be too."

"Take me to my son." There was no way in hell I would trust anything either of them ever said. I needed to see him and feel his warmth against my skin.

"We can't do that. When we get word from Angel, he'll decide where we go from there."

"Listen to me," I pleaded. "He's not well. I needed cash to pay for a doctor's visit. I don't know how sick he is and I'm worried." When they didn't respond or move, I added, "*Please*." They exchanged looks over my head, and my stomach plummeted.

After another heavy silence, Lucas scratched his head and said, "We thought he might be sick."

"Please, you have to do something." They exchanged another look and my stomach knotted this time. "He could die!"

"Part of Angel's business trip is to arrange for a doctor— one of the best—to look at your son."

I scrambled for the bed and faced off with them. They still sat on the bed wearing shock on their faces. "Are you telling me my son isn't here? He *took* my son?" I roared.

"He's trying to help him, Mian." Lucas's voice deepened.

I was approaching a danger zone but fuck that. My son will always be worth any battle.

"He could help him by letting us go!"

"So you can do what?" Z snapped. "I'm willing to bet you don't even have the money to make it back home, let alone keep you both fed. He would be dead by the end of the week, and you wouldn't be able to live with that. You'd be dead, too."

I tore my gaze away because I couldn't stand to see the truth in his eyes. "I'm going to kill you both." My vow was made quietly and aimed at the ground.

"That may be, but for now, let Angel help him."

I did look up then. "After I'm done with your ring leader, I *will* kill you both." I was sure my promise made its mark this time. They both nodded, seeming to take it in stride. They were men who likely dealt with death threats on a daily basis and still managed to continue breathing.

Not for long.

"Maybe we shouldn't trust you to make us breakfast," Z joked to break the tension.

"Why would I make you breakfast?"

"Angel wanted us to keep you busy while he's away so you'll be seeing to our needs."

My stomach tightened at the thought of their needs. "Like a maid?"

"Titles can be tricky," Lucas said and grinned. I didn't return it.

"Your needs aren't my problem."

Lucas shook his head, took my arm, and steered me toward the door.

"Battles already lost, Mian."

"SO YOU WORKED with my dad and Uncle Art? Why haven't I ever met either of you before?"

After Lucas had led me to the state-of-the-art kitchen with Z trailing behind us, I refused to perform any culinary action. My defiance lasted up until Z calmly worked his belt from the loops of his pants while maintaining eye contact. The threat was clear. I barely knew Z, yet somehow, I was surprised but smart enough to know he meant it.

"Maybe he didn't trust us with you," Z leaned in and whispered.

"Makes sense. My dad didn't really trust anyone with me." He would have told Angel not to bring anyone around.

Lucas chuckled from his perch beside Z at the bar. "He's not talking about your pops, girl."

"Oh..." They were silent but watchful, letting it sink in on its own. "I think you're wrong. Angel didn't even know I existed."

Z rolled his eyes and leaned back. "If you truly believed that, your sexy body wouldn't be so flushed right now."

"It wasn't always tense between us," I admitted.

"You want to fuck him, don't you, pretty girl?"

"No, Zachariah. I do not. I want him to die."

"I call bullshit."

"You can call the press, too, if you'd like. My answer stays the same."

"You like lying to yourself?"

"It's not a lie to say I'm not attracted to the man who kidnapped my son."

"So you feel nothing?"

"Not even a twinge. Eggs are ready." I picked up the hot skillet from the flat top stove and spooned the scrambled eggs onto their waiting plates. Bacon, toast, and fresh fruit were already waiting along with tall glasses of orange juice. "Enjoy," I said, not meaning it.

Lucas smirked and fixed his gaze on mine. "You didn't poison the food, did you?"

"Oh, how I wish I could."

"Ease up, Sprite. Let's have a truce for now and just eat."

"I told you I wasn't hungry." It was a lie, of course. I was starving but eager to get away from them. I was still naked, and the apron Z gave me to cook in didn't preserve much of my modesty.

Lucas's nostrils flared. "And I said to eat."

"There's no food left."

"There's plenty here, princess." Z patted his lap with a grin.

"I'm not sitting on your lap."

"Then you can sit on mine," Lucas offered.

"But there's a seat between you."

"Since you share our food you sit where we want you."

"But I don't want your food!"

"Battle's lost."

I pulled my wild card. "What would Angel say?"

He smirked. "He would insist."

"You're lying."

"Should we call him? He'd be very interested to know that you refuse to eat."

"God, you're both assholes."

"Comes with the job description, babe."

"Yeah, I bet." I grabbed a fork and walked around the counter and because Z was closer and Lucas scared me, I chose his lap. He wasted no time settling me in with an arm around my waist.

"You feel good."

"Yeah, I'm not sitting here so you can sample me." The trill of Lucas's phone sent him away from the bar and into another room. "Can I have some eggs please?"

Z's chuckle was low and deep. "Thought you weren't hungry."

"I guess all this banter has worked up an appetite."

"What's mine is yours," he whispered seductively. "Take what you want."

"Yeah, I'll just take the eggs, buddy."

His sexy chuckle caressed my neck and then we ate in silence until his plate was cleared. "Damn, princess. You can really put it away."

"Do you have any idea how to talk to a girl?"

I felt a fingertip trail down my arm. "To be fair, I don't really do much talking when I interact with women."

"And you're proud of yourself?"

"I've had no complaints. You're welcome to take me for a spin."

"Ok. Breakfast is over." When he didn't unlock his arm from my waist, I added, "May I be excused?"

"You learn quick." I could hear the grin in his tone and gritted my teeth but said nothing. After feeling up my naked hip, he released me from his hold. I wasted no time jumping from his lap and turning my bare ass from his view. Of course, he noticed. "You're making this enjoyable."

"How so?"

"You're hiding yourself from me when I've already seen it all." His gaze drifted to my breasts that were still covered by the apron. "You have nothing to be ashamed of."

"I'm not ashamed of my body. I simply don't want strange men taking my clothes off without my permission."

"You're going to have more things to worry about before this is over."

"But Angel will clear me and let us go." He didn't reply. Z was the easiest to talk to. Maybe I could use it to my advantage and charm him into talking. I leaned toward him and whispered, "What do you know?"

He looked surprised for a moment before his lip curled. "I'm on his side, Mian. Don't take my kindness for weakness." He shoved his empty plate to the end of the bar. My hand flew out to keep it from crashing to the floor. "Clean up."

Shit.

I might have screwed up the only possible ally I had. He didn't talk to me again as I cleaned up. By the time I was finished, his mood hadn't lifted. He wordlessly led me back to my cell and moved to leave once I was inside.

"Wait!" He stopped and lifted his eyebrow but said nothing. "Can I have some clothes?"

"Afraid not."

"Why not?"

He smiled, but it wasn't like the others. It was cold and mocking and meant to unnerve me. "Angel wants you like this."

"Why?" What benefit could Angel possibly get from keeping me like this if he wasn't even here to see it?

"So you can't hide."

"You mean, so he can humiliate me."

"People hide behind dignity... so, yeah."

I'd had enough. "Angel's a creep, Lucas is a creep, and *you're* a creep." I crossed my arms and waited.

He simply shrugged. "A creep with a nice view." He jerked the door close in time to save himself from my fist.

CHAPTER 22

She's a girl you take home to mom.

MIAN

FIVE YEARS AGO

WHY DOES HE have to be so hot?

My secret crush turned his shirtless body from the refrigerator with a Gatorade in one hand and a sandwich in the other. His dark eyes glowed with irritation when his gaze met mine. "What do you want?" he snapped.

"I think you mean *hello*. It's how people *politely* greet one another."

"Where's your father?"

"Why?" I mocked. "Do you need adult supervision?"

He stared at me and then slowly lowered his sandwich and 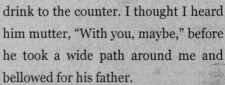 drink to the counter. I thought I heard him mutter, "With you, maybe," before he took a wide path around me and bellowed for his father.

I don't know why, but I followed after him and peeked inside. He was pacing Uncle Art's office with his fists balled and swinging in rhythm with his angry steps. "She can't stay here anymore."

"I don't have time to pacify you. You telling me you can't handle one girl?"

"You know it's not safe for her here with me. Why are you trusting me with this?"

What did he mean it wasn't safe for me here? I pictured the way his jaw would tighten whenever he was close to exploding.

"Because nothing worth having in life is easy. You'll watch over her." Art stood and clapped Angel on the shoulder, but he shrugged his hand off and turned around to storm to the door. I sprinted away before I could be caught eavesdropping, but then ran into my father before I could get far. I nearly toppled over, but his strong hands caught me before I could.

"Why are you running, Mian?"

"A spider?"

He frowned in confusion. "Since when are you afraid of spiders?"

"She's always been afraid of them," I heard behind me.

Shit. Fuck.

Angel always made it a point to show up my father and prove he knew me better. For some reason, he hated the closeness I clung to with my father. He didn't seem all that close to his own father, so I chalked it up to jealousy. Art was hard on him, and Angel was eager to prove himself.

Daddy's eyebrows rose as he stared behind me. I didn't need to see Angel's face to know he was challenging Daddy. My dad rubbed the back of his neck, and when his gaze shifted back to me, he looked guilty.

"Look, baby girl." My body tensed. I knew what came next. It was always the same thing. "I'm sorry I'm not around more."

He'd gotten into the habit of apologizing for not being around and would then promise to do better. After four years, I knew better than to take him seriously, but I never found the heart to call him out on his shit. My father loved me, and that was all that mattered.

"It's oka—"

"You seriously think she believes that shit anymore?" Angel growled over my shoulder. I turned to confront my shadow and smacked into his chest. Why did he have to stand so close?

I shot him a look to stay out of it, which he ignored. This wasn't the first time he toyed with my feelings and heart by implying that my father used excuses to stay away from me. "This isn't your business." My heart fluttered from the emotion in his gaze.

The beating, bleeding part of me wondered if he was defending my honor until he said, "Then why are you still here?"

"Angeles!"

I stepped back. Somehow, I felt more betrayed by him than my father's steady stream of lies. My heart ran away, and the rest of me followed. I ignored our fathers when they shouted my name.

Angel never said a word.

The sunlight blinded me as I took off down the street in flip-flops, shorts, and a tank.

I ended up at the small, neighborhood park. It was still early in the day. Much of the neighborhood was out enjoying the park. Kids were enjoying the summer sun. Their laughter and screams drowned out my cries.

I found an empty swing and kept my gaze locked on the

grass. I didn't have the energy to push myself back and forth through the air, so I rocked instead.

After a few minutes of rocking, I sighed and considered going back. That was until I felt strong hands on my back sending me high into the air. I peeked over my shoulder and caught sight of shirtless Angel. I opened my mouth to scream at him to go away when he pushed me higher in the air.

When he pushed me again, I decided to live in the moment. We became the center of attention. Girls I went to school with giggled as they hurried by, and women watched over their smaller kids who were looking on appreciatively.

Why couldn't he have put on his shirt first?

I dug my feet in the ground before he could push again.

"No," I shouted when he tried to push again. He just stared with no emotion when I turned to face him. "Why did you come here?"

"You took off. I'm supposed to protect you."

"Where's my father?"

"Gone."

I inhaled and turned my head so Angel couldn't see my hurt. How could Daddy leave without saying goodbye? He hadn't cared enough to make sure I was okay before chasing after his next lick.

Maybe Angel was right about him.

That just pissed me off.

"Happy?"

"Pretending to care is worse than not caring at all, Mian. I've never lied to you."

But my father had.

"You have nothing to worry about. I'm safe here." I turned

my back to him, but then I felt his heat against my back as he gripped the chain suspending the swing.

"I can take your mind off your father."

"What?" I tried to stand, but his hand on my shoulder kept me in place. Then I made the mistake of turning my head. His brown eyes captivated me. We were too close, but I couldn't look away. "How?"

Instead of answering, he locked his hands around my waist and lifted me to my feet. He towered over me, and the closeness of our bodies emphasized how large he was compared to my small frame. He intimidated me.

My hands found his shoulders when I swayed, and he gripped me tighter.

"It's the heat," I defended even though he hadn't spoken.

He wouldn't meet my gaze as he looked over my head. "Let's go," he ordered and released me. I took hesitant steps until I could trust my legs and then ran to catch up.

"Where are we going?"

"I need a shirt."

"But I don't want to go home."

"We're going back so I can get a shirt. That's it."

"Then where are you taking me?"

He sighed. "You'll see when we get there."

When we reached the brownstone, he disappeared into his room. I decided I needed a shower and Angel would have to wait, so I grabbed my caddy from my room. After showering, I pulled on another pair of shorts and a t-shirt that was cropped to expose a sliver of my stomach right above my waist. It wasn't something I would ever wear the few times Daddy was around.

I didn't have time to tangle with my hair, so I pulled it up in a messy bun and applied lip-gloss. I was feeling prepared to catch anything Angel pitched when I stepped from my room.

However, my confidence came to a screeching halt when I caught him leaning sexily against the wall. He'd changed, too, into a denim button up with his sleeves rolled up to his elbows and brown cargo shorts. His attention was on his phone, but then he slowly looked up from the screen.

His gaze never made it past my legs.

"Is something wrong?" I asked when his staring grew uncomfortable.

He flinched and when he was finally staring back at me, his eyes held guilt. "Come on," he muttered.

I followed him outside where his white mustang waited. I took my time admiring the clean white paint, double black stripes and blacked out rims. As always, I was nervous to share the small space with him. I was the only one harboring a secret crush, and I was afraid spending too much time in his presence would eventually give me away.

His body was relaxed in his seat when I got in. I stared as he typed fast on his phone.

"Done eye fucking my car?" He never looked up from his phone. His jaw was set telling me he was pissed off, and I wondered who he was messaging.

Maybe it was Trinity.

"Do you still have a girlfriend?"

Please say no. Please say no.

He stopped typing and looked at me. "Why?"

"Why what?"

"Why do you care?"

"I don't," I answered defensively and turned to stare straight ahead. "Just making small talk."

He grunted and turned on the ignition. The powerful engine roared to life, and my body vibrated to match the rhythm of the car. I had only just relaxed when he reached over my legs and opened the glove compartment. I tensed and sucked in air when his scent commandeered my senses.

He smelled like trouble I wanted to get into.

When he drew his hand from the compartment, he held a thin looking cigarette between his fingers. When he lit up the end, and the smell filled the small space, realization dawned.

"Are you addicted?" His glare made me wish I could disappear inside the leather seat.

"I smoke on occasion," he answered. Then he reached out, and I might have squeaked. I breathed out just as his hand passed my face, and he stared at it momentarily before shaking his hand and pulling my seatbelt across. "You should wear a seatbelt."

"You shouldn't smoke weed."

He assaulted me with that intimidating stare of his again. "There are many things I shouldn't do that I may not be able to help, Mian."

I shivered. It was my name and the way he spoke, almost like a caress even when he was threatening or scolding me. I couldn't tell which was happening now.

"Meaning?"

He laughed and shifted his body until he was fully on his side once again and drove off. "Meaning, you aren't ready to know what I mean."

He didn't speak to me again during the two-hour car ride. During the beginning, I was content to watch him slip the blunt between his lips over and over until it was gone.

He never slowed until we pulled into the driveway that belonged to a large white colonial home with black shutters. There was a small balcony above the large porch. It was held up by four white pillars. The neighborhood seemed serene with more two-story homes lining the street on either side.

Angel reached inside the compartment again, but this time, his forearm brushed my knee when he pulled out a can of body spray. He sprayed himself, and I recognized the scent from before, which put my senses back on high alert.

"Come on," he spoke for the first time in two hours.

I followed after him when he left the car and climbed the couple of steps to the porch. "Who lives here?"

"Me." He stuck a key in the door.

"You have a house?" I whispered incredulously. Angel was only twenty-one.

"I live here with my parents," he clarified.

"Why am I here?" I asked warily.

"My mom wants to meet you." I sucked in air and rooted my feet to the porch. There was *no way* I was going in there.

When he opened the door, he grabbed my hand as if he read my thoughts, and pulled me inside. My hands started to sweat, and I felt my heart beating faster. I told myself there was no reason to be nervous. I wasn't his girlfriend. Because of our ages, we might as well have been worlds apart.

"Angeles?" A woman's voice called out.

I dug my feet in.

He tugged me harder.

"It's me," he greeted. Soft footsteps drew closer.

I wanted to run for the door.

A woman around my height appeared. She was modestly dressed in a yellow and white sundress with her blonde hair hanging down her back, teasing her waistline. Her bright, blue eyes were curious as she took me in.

I simply stared back.

"When my son said he was bringing someone home, you were not what I was expecting." I tensed even more and felt Angel squeeze my hand. She smiled and pulled me away from Angel and into a hug. Despite her kind gesture, I couldn't relax. She stepped back to study me, but her expression was troubled. "How old are you?"

"Fourteen."

She regarded her son with disapproval. "She's a little young for you, isn't she, Angeles?" Her welcoming tone was gone and replaced with a hard edge. While I felt sorry for Angel, he didn't appear bothered.

"This is Mian," he answered as if that explained everything.

Her eyes watered as her hand covered her mouth. "I should have recognized the resemblance. Oh, my... You look just like your mother."

I sucked in air. I used to beam with pride whenever someone compared me to my mother, which was often. Now, it just hurt.

"You knew my mother?"

"Knew her? She was my best friend."

My stomach twisted in knots.

I heard her ordering Angel to bring water. I felt her hand on my arm and the plush cushion beneath me as I sunk into it. Through it all, I couldn't find my voice. So many questions fought for dominance.

"I didn't mean to shock you. Are you okay?"

"She never mentioned you," I blurted.

Regret was evident in her features when she sighed and took my hand. "I don't doubt it. We fell out our senior year of high school, and I never saw her again."

"Why?"

"Because we were in love with the same man."

I snatched my hand from hers and moved away. "Excuse me?"

She didn't seem surprised by my rejection. "Arturo was every girl's dream come true. He was older, popular, and the apple of every girl's eye." Her gaze lost focus as she became caught up in the memories. "Your mother was the one who had more than a crush on him. She was in love."

She fell silent, and I watched a tear stream down her cheek. "And you?"

"I couldn't stand him," she answered dryly and then laughed. "I thought he was arrogant and overrated." Angel chose that moment to reappear, and it was like déjà vu as he set down a tall glass of ice water. I quickly picked it up and took a healthy sip.

"What changed?"

"For the life of me, I couldn't see what she saw in him, but she was sure he was the one... So, one day, I cornered him. I thought if I talked her up to him, then maybe he'd notice her."

"Except he noticed you."

"I talked and talked and talked about your mother and he just listened. I had his undivided attention. I thought he was interested. I can still remember how much he unnerved me when he never looked away." She looked down at her manicured fingers as her shoulders trembled. "I suppose I should have known. I didn't want to see until he forced me to."

"What did he do?"

"He kissed me."

"So you fell in love from a single kiss and decided it was worth my mother's heart?"

She whimpered. "I—I kissed him back. I lost myself in him for so long that she caught us. It was horrible. She wouldn't talk to me for weeks. Art chased me the entire time. I tried to get Ceci to forgive me. Word spread around school that Art was pursuing me. I think it only made it worse. Some time after, it became clear she would never forgive me, so I gave in to him." She looked over my shoulder at Angel whose presence I felt. "I became pregnant with Angel shortly after. I was too young, and many people assumed he was a mistake, but that wasn't the case. Art eventually knew that if Ceci decided to forgive me, I would have chosen her."

Suddenly, I began to see Art in an entirely different light.

"He trapped you?" When she nodded, I was tempted to look over my shoulder. "But you loved him."

"I still do," she said. "Art is manipulative and calculating, but he's mine. I just wished it hadn't cost so much to keep him."

"So, if you never saw each other again, how did my dad and mom meet?"

Her gaze was steady as she looked me in the eye. "I have no idea."

CHAPTER 23

Friends are there for better or worse...
and then some friends just make it worse.

ANGEL

PRESENT

I WATCHED THE small man in a white lab coat squirm in his high back leather chair.

"How can I help you, Mr. Knight?" The good doctor tried to sound in control and failed miserably. His gaze nervously swept from me to the infant in my arms.

"I need your discretion."

"Of course."

"The kid is sick. Run some tests. Make him better. Do it quietly."

His gaze flitted back to the kid. "I—I wasn't aware you had a child."

"I don't."

He flinched. "A—and where are his parents?"

He'd already figured out the answer. "His father is MIA, and his mother is unavailable."

"Why, may I ask—"

"You may not ask. I'm sure your wife's trips to Paris and your kid's private schools aren't paid for with questions. If your morals are getting the better of you..." I pulled out my gun with a silencer and laid it on my lap. "I can take care of that."

He paled at the sight of the gun. "I can assure you my morals remain corrupted by your money. I'll just need something viable to tell my staff."

Mian's kid wheezed and coughed causing my patience to evaporate. "I don't care what you have to tell them, just get it done. If this kid dies, I'll consider *you* responsible."

I stuck around for the diagnosis, and when the Doc told me the baby would need a close watch for a few days, I kept one of my men on guard in case the Doc's conscience got any ideas.

Lucas called as I pulled up to my next stop. I was nervous as I answered the phone and wondered what trouble Mian might have found in the few hours I'd been gone. "Is she behaving?"

"Like a tigress in captivity for the first time," Lucas muttered. "How's the kid?"

"Doc says it's an infection called respiratory syncytial virus."

"Is it as bad as it sounds?"

"Doc wants to keep him for a few days, so I'll be here longer than expected. They have him on a fucking ventilator."

"Son of a bitch..."

"Doc isn't taking chances, and neither am I."

"What do I tell his mother?"

"Nothing."

"You don't think she has a right to know?"

Lucas had been questioning me more often than normal since the day we found Mian in my father's house, and sometimes, it took more patience than I possessed not to lose my shit. For the sake of brotherhood, I decided to focus on the other half of my business trip.

"I paid another visit to Jonny. Ross has been moving quietly, but Jonny thinks something's up."

If Ross put her up to robbing me, then he'd know the buyer. Even if Mian was as innocent as she claimed, it still meant that either Ross had someone on the outside who could get their hands on the book, or he knew someone he could sell the information to. I intended to find out.

There was one question that bugged me the most?

Why would Mian bother pawning a watch when she had so much to gain from selling the book? Theo had never moved so carelessly before to not collect at least half the money upfront. There were too many holes that shed light on Mian's innocence, but I couldn't ignore the evidence that made her look guilty either.

"So we're not setting her free?"

"The book is still missing, and as long as it is, she's still a suspect. If we find the book, and if she's not behind it, we let her go."

"She's not going to take that well."

"She's not in control here."

"Right. Because you have a handle on your feelings for her," he said sarcastically.

"You have something you'd like to say?"

"Nothing that you'd listen to."

"Try me."

"You're too soft on this girl. If you really feel nothing—if you really want to find your family's book—then remember what she did to your family by stealing your legacy. Remember what her *father* did to yours. Fuck man, this isn't just about you. Art was the only pops Z, and I had ever known, and that motherfucker took him... from *all of us*."

"What do you suggest I do, Lucas?"

"Find something else to motivate her because I can't and won't hurt a fucking infant. I don't even feel right insinuating that I will."

I took a deep breath, but when the ice in my veins failed to thaw, I embraced it. "I'm sitting outside her apartment building."

"What the fuck? Why? I told you I already checked it."

"I thought I'd check again and maybe find a clue on how to motivate her. I know her better than either of you do. If there's something there, I'll find it." Silence filled the line. "Don't question me again. Ever. If you do, I'll begin to wonder if I can trust *you*."

I had nothing more to say. I hung up and moved toward the front door. Getting my head back in the game, I examined the piece of shit building. It didn't even have a security system to keep dangerous men like me out.

I walked right into the darkened lobby. The only two working light bulbs flickered, and the smell that met my nose was pungent. An out of order sign was taped to the elevator doors, so I made my way to the stairs. I hesitated at the bottom. The boards didn't appear as if they could even support my weight. Slowly, I climbed the steps to Mian's floor. Her apartment was the second on the right.

It was locked, but the door was flimsy, so I stood back, lifted my foot, and kicked in the door with ease. The door swung back and forth on its hinges as I walked in. One look revealed that Lucas hadn't been laying it on thick when he described her situation. It was hard to believe that she even wanted to come back to this piece of shit.

As I invaded her space, the floorboards creaked and groaned. The walls were stained and cracked. The living space was tiny as fuck. The furniture was a fucking joke. I could tell after only thirty seconds in her space that Mian had nothing. I wasn't even sure it was better than being homeless. She had no security or comfort in a place like this.

The hall leading to the back of the apartment was short, and with only a few steps, I was standing in the only bedroom. In the far corner was a small crib that looked well used. The bed was just a mattress and box spring. The lime green sheets on her bed were familiar. The pillowcases were black as well as the thin blanket that looked handed down a few times over.

I expected pleasure over witnessing how far the spoiled princess was knocked from her throne, but all I felt was anger and shame. She shouldn't be living like this. It wasn't the life her father wanted for her.

She shouldn't be a mother.

She should be studying liberal arts in college, drinking caramel frappe, pulling late night study sessions, and dating some pretty frat.

I moved through the run down yet clean apartment. There wasn't much of the usual furniture or comfort items like a dresser or television. She kept clothes for herself and Caylen in bins. The closet was completely empty. The bathroom was clean but only held the necessities. There were tears in the white shower liner and tattered rugs to keep her from slipping.

The kitchen was just as depressing. On the counter decorated with chipped paint were a stack of bills. The first envelope was a notice from the electric company threatening termination if the bill wasn't paid.

I picked up the stack, stuck them in my back pocket, and made my way to the door. I'd seen enough.

As soon as the door closed behind me, a door down the hall opened, and a girl of average height with blonde hair stepped out. She was wearing a shirt that didn't cover much and shorts that were so short she might as well have gone without them. When her head turned toward me, I noticed how young she was. She couldn't be more than sixteen years old.

"Can I help you find something?" She was frowning as she looked from me to Mian's door. Her gaze narrowed when it landed on the broken frame. Her attention shot back up to me when I moved.

I sensed a protective streak in her and a thought formed. I donned my friendly face. "Do you know the girl who lives in this apartment?"

"Of course, I do. I'm her best friend."

"Then *you* are exactly what I'm looking for."

CHAPTER 24

He wields a mother's love like a weapon...and that makes him evil.

MIAN

ANGEL DIDN'T RETURN in two days and worry for my son broke me. Lucas and Z weren't talking, and other than the occasional meals I was forced to make them, I was kept confined.

When Lucas showed up on day three with a black silk kimono that didn't even look long enough to cover my ass, I lost it. I calmly took it from him, and then pulled at the thin material until I heard it tear. I then threw it to the ground and wiped my feet on it before handing it back to him as calmly as I had taken it.

"Bad move, girl."

"Where is my son?"

"He's safe. You should worry about yourself." He walked away with the kimono, and when the door slammed, I broke down.

That was four days ago.

On day seven, I woke up to Angel leaning a shoulder against the door as he watched me. Angel in control was a panty melting sight to see. Especially, when paired with a three-piece suit. Too bad my pussy had to get in line for a piece of him.

I didn't think.

I just reacted.

"Where's my son?" I bawled the lapels of his suit jacket in my fist. I threw my weight into him causing his body to collide with the door. Nothing fazed him as he gripped my waist and swung our bodies until I was pinned against the door. His voice was rough as he spoke.

"You're forgetting yourself, Mian."

"I don't care," I growled back. "Do what you want to me just give him back!"

"He's safe."

"That's not enough!"

He didn't react. He simply stared.

"I need to know he's okay," I pleaded this time. Fear that he was hiding something seized my emotions. "I need to see him." His gaze never wavered, and doubt seeped in.

I may never get through to him.

I closed my eyes and took a deep breath. I didn't let go until I heard him speak.

"Bring the kid," he ordered. He shoved his phone in his pocket, stood back, and fixed his jacket. When he caught me staring, he pointed toward the bathroom. "Go pull yourself together. Your son doesn't need to see you like this."

I didn't move. I was afraid it could be a trick.

"It was not a request."

I didn't hesitate that time. I closed myself in the bathroom and washed the tracks from my face only for new ones to appear. It took me a few extra minutes to pull myself together.

I haven't seen my son in a week. I would finally get to hold him close and smell his hair.

The unmistakable sound of my baby's laughter drove me from the bathroom. I stood in the doorway and watched Z interact with my son. He made silly faces at Caylen who ate it up.

Angel's gaze was fixed on the baby, but his expression was unreadable. I was nervous about what he was thinking. His mercy was likely holding on by a thread.

I held my breath as I closed the distance between Caylen and me. What I really wanted was to take my son and run as fast as I could. "May I hold him?"

Two sets of eyes immediately fell on me. Caylen was a little slower to take notice. With his fist now in his mouth, he finally noticed me and smiled.

He looked healthy and happy as he kicked his feet and made spit bubbles.

They hadn't hurt him.

I got choked up as I reached out for him.

"Wait," Angel ordered. "Put this on." It was the robe Lucas tried to dress me in before. I hesitated, but the retribution in his eyes made me take it and slip it on. The material was soft and fine, and most of all, didn't leave me so exposed even though I had been right about the length.

Z finally handed him to me, and when my arms closed around him, my heart folded in, and my body threatened to collapse.

"Jesus..." Angel had sworn a millisecond before his hand

closed around my trembling arm and he led me toward the chair. "Sit before you drop him."

I sat and immediately leaned in to smell Caylen's scent. He smelled clean, and his skin was no longer pale. It was a while before I noticed the silence. Z was gone, but Angel stood near the door again where he watched us.

"Who has been taking care of him?"

"I've been personally seeing to it."

"You think you're capable of caring for *my son*?"

"You should know the rules of this game by now. He belongs to me until I have my property back."

"Have you lost your mind?" I hissed. It was a struggle not to keep my voice level. I didn't want to scare Caylen. "He's not property to be bartered. He's a human being, and he's my son."

"That's your opinion," he answered smoothly.

"It's fact. We are not yours."

"You're both guests in my home until I decide otherwise. You have nowhere to go unless I say so. You will not eat or drink unless I say so. You will do what I say when I say. I think that does make you mine. If you want the best for your son, I suggest you make do with that."

"And if I refuse?"

"I'll take your son from you, and you'll never see him again. That includes anyone you care for."

Suspicion crept down my spine. "There's no one else."

"So you say."

"My dad is in prison. You can't touch him."

"We'll see about that."

"What do you want from me? My story checked out, didn't it? Why are we still here?"

"You know why. You were the last person in my home before the book that ensures my family's legacy continues went missing."

"But you know I didn't take it."

"If that's true, you have nothing to worry about. When it's recovered, you'll be free to go."

"But that's what you said about the watch!"

"Things changed."

"Like hell."

"In the meantime," he continued, "what we want from you, you won't fight it, will you?"

"*We*?"

"Will. You?"

I studied him—the evil in his eyes and the confident way he held himself. I needed to protect my son from him. Maybe that meant losing a few battles to win the war.

I nodded and swallowed back the bile that rushed up.

Just then, Caylen started to fuss until his fussing turned into a cry. Soon he was screaming at the top of his lungs. My attention had already turned to him, so I missed the concern etched on Angel's face, but I heard it when he asked, "What's wrong with him?"

I ignored him and felt Caylen's diaper. "He's probably hungry." The last thing I wanted was to ask him for anything but my hand was forced. "I need his food."

He was focused on his phone, so I questioned if he heard him until he cleared his throat and said, "He had a virus called respiratory syncytial."

"What?" It wasn't the response I was expecting.

"I thought you might want to know what was making him sick."

I glanced down at Caylen who didn't look ill anymore. I was so happy to see him alive that I hadn't noticed. "Oh, God. Why didn't I see? The doctor... he warned me RSV was common. I should have known. I should have—" I stopped. Breaking apart wouldn't cure my baby. "I need to get him help. My voice shuddered so I took a deep breath and begged for the sake of my son. "I know your heart is cold, but you still have one—"

"It's been taken care of."

"It's been taken care of..." I repeated slowly.

"The doctor said these things normally cure themselves, but for babies, it's much more sensitive. He would have been at risk for lung failure."

"Are there antibiotics..." He was already shaking his head.

"He kept him on a ventilator to make breathing easier, but within a few days, he was already getting better." The door opened, and Z stepped through. Angel's gaze never left us as he said, "Take him."

"What? No!"

"I can't let you be with him. The virus was contagious and until I'm sure you don't have it—"

"But I'm not sick!"

"You could be."

I shot up from the chair and backed away. Caylen sensed my distress and released a heart-piercing cry. "Please, Angel."

"Mian." His voice was surprisingly tender. "I am not doing this to hurt you. I am *telling* you to do what's best for him."

"He needs me."

"Right now, he needs his health." I shook my head and backed away until the wall stopped me. "Don't make me take him from you by force." He stepped forward to back up his claim.

Caylen's face was completely red now. His cries grew, and my heart broke into little pieces when I realized *I* was the one doing this to him.

The rational part of me knew Angel was right. Viruses usually carried an incubation period before symptoms showed and the host became contagious. It was quite possible that I could be infected which meant, right now, the only person who was a threat to my son's health was *me*.

My body relaxed with defeat and Z swooped in to take the baby. I wanted to kiss him goodbye. Instead, I watched him go. When the door closed, my legs gave out, but unfortunately, Angel was there to catch me.

As soon as his arms closed around me, I screamed and beat at his chest. He didn't fight me or threaten. He simply held me tighter until all the fight I had drained out of me. My head unconsciously settled against his chest and my body sunk into his warmth.

I hurt enough to seek comfort from my enemy.

Did it make me broken?

"Look at me." It was the last thing I wanted, so I ignored his command. "Look at me, Mian," he demanded more forcefully.

I did. Reluctantly. Slowly.

My gaze first landed on his chin and his neatly trimmed scruff. Slowly, my gaze traveled up to thick lips. I wondered what his kiss tasted like, and the betrayal of my body was like a punch to the gut. His arms crushed me until I finally gave him what he wanted.

The cold in his brown gaze reflected the ice in his heart. "One way or another, I'm going to get what I want from you. So you can either give it to me..." He brushed his thumb down my cheek. "Or I can take it."

A teardrop rested on the tip of his thumb. I grabbed his wrist and slowly slipped my lips over his thumb, taking my tear back. His next breath didn't come, but I could feel his heart pounding harder in his chest.

"Promise?" My fearlessness was an illusion, but he didn't need to know that. When I broke into hell, I thought I knew what would happen if I were caught. Angel proved me wrong at every turn.

"It's already carved in your headstone."

CHAPTER 25

She's still too young.

MIAN

FIVE YEARS AGO

MY MOTHER ALWAYS told me there were two sides to every story, but I don't think she knew her side would be buried with her. I had every reason to distrust Bea after what she did to my mother. But she also seemed genuinely distraught over the loss of my mother. What could it hurt to suspend judgment and get to know her for one afternoon?

She showed me mementos of her and my mother, and I repaid her by crying all over them. She wrapped me up in her arms, and it didn't feel wrong. When the tears were dry on my cheek, she patted my back and told me story after story belonging to her favorite memories.

"This picture was from the year your mother and I won a talent contest together. I'm not much of a dancer, but your mother made sure the routine was as natural to me as breathing. After fighting about it, I convinced her

that the trophy belonged with her. She wanted it more than I did." I recalled a trophy my mother kept in the family room. I remember asking her about it, and she would only say it was a long time ago. "Ceci was quite the dancer," Bea continued. "She could dance to any tune and captivate her audience with just the switch of her hips."

"Did you truly love my mother?"

"I did, Mian. I know you're wondering whether you can trust me after what I did, but a day hasn't gone by that I haven't thought about her."

"You didn't come to her funeral." *You never came around after either.*

"No." She placed the pictures back in the box and ran her hand over the top before setting it aside and taking my hands. "I wasn't sure she'd want me there, and I know it was silly, but even after she died, I still hoped to win her back by respecting her wishes." I felt her hand tremble in mine, letting me feel her emotions. "That meant never meeting you."

"I don't think that's what she would have wanted at all," I argued. Bea was one of the last connections I had with my mother. Mom may not have forgiven her before she died, but I was selfish enough to do what she couldn't. "My mother can't hold a grudge in her grave."

"You may be right. We both lost Ceci, and though no one will ever replace her, I'd like to get to know you. I lost fourteen years with you because of your mother's stubbornness and my cowardice."

"I'd like that." I had to force the words from my throat even though I felt them in my heart.

She embraced me, and I found it natural to return her

affection. Did I feel I was betraying my mom by accepting the love of a friend who betrayed her?

I wasn't sure.

I could only hope that maybe I was giving my mom the chance to make it right.

After promising to visit again, I let Angel lead me away from Bea Knight and away from Crecia. We weren't long into our drive back to Chicago when I whispered, "Thank you."

"For what?"

"For what you did."

"And what did I do?"

I should have known he wouldn't make this easy. "You gave me a piece of my mom back. Your mother is nice."

"But?"

"But she seemed..." I struggled, but it seemed he knew exactly what I was searching for.

"Lost?"

"Yes. Why?"

He shrugged, but the clenching of his jaw told me he had an idea. He glanced at me but then turned away just as quickly when he found me watching.

I was fixated on the blur of asphalt and yellow lines as I spoke. "My mother was sad too until she became too sick for anyone to tell the difference." The reminder of my mother's fight with cancer and depression left me feeling low, but I couldn't stop talking because I knew he was listening. "I would draw her pictures to try to cheer her up. At first, they would be true things like our house and our family and my friends at school." I released a dry laugh. "But then I drew a picture of our dog." I can still remember the smile that stretched my face at the promise of her laugh. It had been so long. "His name was Danger. He had a golden coat and was the biggest and smartest dog in the neighborhood." When I handed her the picture of him, she barely glanced at it and told me it looked just like him.

"So? What's so funny about that?"

"We didn't have a dog."

"Maybe she didn't want to hurt your feelings."

"Or maybe she stopped caring."

He looked at me then but only for a moment, and then his eyes were back on the road. "Do you really believe your mother didn't care about you?" His doubt annoyed me, so I returned the favor and shrugged. "Symptoms don't only show when the person afflicted is aware they are sick. She may not have been herself, but I'm sure your drawings did more for her than you realize."

"You could be right." I dug my fingernails into my thigh to keep from saying more but then found the physical pain insufficient to ignore emotional suffering. "But it still hurt."

"Because you rely too much on others for affection."

"So I should be more like you?" I couldn't keep the indignation from my voice if I tried.

"You can never be anything like me. I wouldn't let you."

"What makes you think you could have any say in who I am or what I do?" He didn't answer, and that just pissed me off. "Maybe I'll get a boyfriend who is bigger than you to kick your ass for thinking you can boss me around." I wanted to force a response from him, but when he jerked the wheel, taking us off the road, fear pooled in the pit of my stomach.

He slammed on the brakes, threw the car in park, and then shoved his face in mine. He was foaming at the mouth, and smoke billowed from his ears as his eyes flashed red. I bet ol' Lucifer never mastered the art of looking as pissed off as Angel Knight clearly had.

I heard the click of my seatbelt releasing just as common sense flooded and the warning to run blared loud and clear. I reached for the door, but a steel band wrapped around my waist and hauled me over the console.

"What are you doing?" I shrieked when I realized I was kneeling over his lap. My hands had fallen to his chest while he arranged my knees to rest on either side of his legs. My ass in the air was the only thing keeping me from sitting in his lap. He dodged just in time to miss my fist connecting with his face. I tried again, and he captured my wrist, pressing down his thumb until I cried out.

"Do you think it's wise to continue pissing me off?" he asked in a quiet, almost patient voice. If I hadn't seen the torturously sexy features of his face, I wouldn't have known he was upset.

"You're hurting me." He maintained pressure until a tear rolled down my cheek. Only then did he let me go. "I can't believe you did that."

His hand glided down the column of my throat. I didn't know whether it was a caress or a threat. "You tried to hit me, brat."

"Guys aren't supposed to hurt girls."

"Not only are you spoiled, but you live a double standard, too."

I didn't appreciate being called spoiled, but arguing with him wouldn't get me off his lap any faster. "Why am I on your lap?"

"Because I enjoy seeing the fear in your eyes every time you're close to me."

"I'm not afraid of you."

"So your pretty pink lips say."

I felt something hot and painful stir deep in my belly. "You think my lips are pretty?" When his gaze fell to my lips and darkened, that feeling in my stomach exploded.

"I think..." I held my breath when his fingers wrapped around the side of my neck and squeezed. "...there isn't anything about you I don't like." His throat worked up and down as he swallowed hard.

"That's not true."

"Oh?"

I lowered my gaze and somehow found my fingers on the button of his shirt. I wanted nothing more than to slide one after the other through and unwrap what was underneath, but I settled for fiddling with the center one.

"You don't like me at all. You're always mean to me."

He made a sound in his throat, and then his hands were on my waist, pulling me closer. Our bodies together felt like a furnace. "This is wrong," I heard him whisper as he clenched his eyes closed tight as if in pain.

"Sorry?"

His eyes popped open. "I said you're wrong," he answered louder.

He's lying. That's not what he said. I ignored the flutters low in my gut anyway and said, "Should you be holding me like this?"

More painful throat sounds. "No."

"Then why?"

"Would you like the answer to your first question?" I glanced up in time to catch his lips twitch with amusement even while I was freaking out inside.

"Um... can you remind me?"

"You wanted to know if I thought your lips were pretty."

"I thought we covered the answer to that." I kept my gaze on his buttons. Buttons were safe. Angel Knight was not.

"Not really. You made an assumption before I could explain."

"Ok, so, explain."

"I will." I nodded but then he said, "But to you. Not the top of your head."

I looked up all the while debating if it was smart and at the same time, unable to ignore his subtle demand. The single moment that followed our gazes meeting was all it took for me to understand that more than just our gazes had connected.

"Yes?" I prompted when he said nothing. He freaked me out in ways that made me tingle and soar, and others that made me feel like I would crash and burn.

"I think you're beautiful."

I gasped, but his finger falling on my lips didn't allow me to do or say anything more.

"Sometimes I don't know how to handle that." He paused but his eyes searched mine before he whispered, "and I'm sorry."

"You're sorry?"

"Yeah. I am."

"Oh."

Silence.

We were too busy not saying everything we wanted to.

"So am I forgiven?" he asked after the silence grew to be too obvious.

"Do you really want to be forgiven?"

"I wouldn't apologize if I didn't, Sprite."

"Sprite?"

"You're so fucking tiny," he growled. I could feel his frustration vibrating off him.

"I'm sorry?" I said because I didn't have a clue of how else to react.

"Don't apologize. I love your body." I sucked in a breath, and he cursed and then cursed some more. "I need you to return to your to seat. Please," he begged when I didn't move.

"Why?" I wasn't experienced with boys and sex, but I knew that sitting in his lap wasn't right. Lines had been crossed, but since they had already been crossed, why not explore?

"Fuck, Sprite. You don't—" His Adam's apple bobbed. "You're only fourteen."

"So?"

He jerked as if I hit him. "So? So?" His voice rose on the last. "So I'm fucking *twenty*."

"Why do you care?"

"Why do I—" He stopped and barked out a laugh. "Do you have any clue what guys like me would like to do with little girls like you?"

"Um..."

"The guilty flush on your cheeks say you do," he snapped. "Some wouldn't hesitate to take what you don't even know you're offering."

"What am I offering?"

He closed his eyes and leaned his head back. "I'm not having this conversation with you," he answered more calmly than he had ten seconds ago. "Get off my lap."

"Not until you make me understand why you're mad at me again."

"For fuck sake." He gripped my waist and lifted. I found myself dumped into the passenger seat, and before I could right myself, the engine roared and tires spun as he took off. "Seatbelt," he ordered.

It was the last thing he said to me during the ride. When he pulled up to the brownstone, he watched me go up it. I didn't see him for two days. I was worried something had happened to him and was tempted to call Daddy, but I knew our fathers would be furious that he took off.

On day two, I learned from one of my classmates that he had spent the last two nights locked in her older sister's bedroom.

CHAPTER 26

A deal she can't refuse.

MIAN

PRESENT

IT RAINED HARD the next day.

When the lights went, I ran to a corner and hid. I hated storms. They scared the shit out of me. There was nothing beautiful or poetic about a storm. With each flash and thundering boom, I imagined a new kind of freak accident. The house would split down the middle. A tornado would sweep the house from the foundation and toss it into outer space. A large ship would come crashing through, wiping us all out in one swoop.

I had my head between my thighs when the door opened. If terror had a sound, it was what escaped my throat. This was it.

Arms closed around me and lifted me, but I still couldn't open my eyes. I didn't need to. When he pulled me tight against the warm wall of his chest, his scent surrounded me. "You remembered."

He didn't reply, but arms tightened around me as he walked. When I finally found the courage to open my eyes, I saw candles. Lots of them lit the way to wherever he was carrying me.

"The lights will be on soon. You're safe."

I almost snorted. He needed a reminder of our roles and why I was here, but since he rescued me from the storm, I wouldn't bait him.

He entered a huge room with a large cream sectional spanning the entire left side of the room. Mounted on the opposite wall was the largest flat screen TV I'd ever seen. Candles covered nearly every surface lighting the space and creating a warm ambiance. He carried me to the couch in front of the large bay windows. It gave me a front row seat of the storm. Lightning chose that moment to light the sky. I crawled into Angel's side and buried my face in his chest. My head rested right about his heart so the increase in tempo couldn't be missed. He pried my fingers from his shirt to free himself and walked away. I stared after him feeling rejected until he pressed a button that lowered a shade over the windows and shut out the storm. Angel turned and regarded me with mocking eyes. "Better?"

"Much." It took every ounce of discipline I possessed not to sneer.

"I got dibs on first movie pick!" Z interrupted our stare down with a huge bowl of popcorn while juggling four cans of soda.

"But there's no power."

"Lucas went to turn on the generator."

"Oh." Angel had already seen my fear, but for some reason, I hid my relief. The candles made the space we were forced

241

to share too intimate. I'd felt his gaze on me while I watch Z looking through a tall stack of DVDs. The lights suddenly flickered on, and the house went through the motions of coming back to life.

"Why don't we let Mian choose?" I gripped the cushions and refused to look at him. He was baiting me. He sat down next to me despite the enormous space and slouched with his legs spread. I flinched when he threw his arm closest to me along the top of the couch. The side of his leg brushed mine, and I jerked as if electrocuted.

He was definitely overindulging in testing the limits of my comfort zone.

"Because dibs still means dibs, dude. Besides, she'll pick a chick flick, and I'm not sitting through one of those if there is zero possibility I get pussy after." He suddenly spun and cocked his head, appearing too hopeful. "Is there?"

"Zero chance," I confirmed with a firm head nod.

"Don't knock it until you try it," Lucas greeted. He swaggered into the center of the room. "I've witnessed firsthand how good Z is at making girls scream."

"And you witnessed this how?"

Lucas smirked but didn't answer my question. Angel, of course, obliged. "Because they rarely fuck without a woman between them."

"I see. So the woman would be the excuse to get each other naked then?"

Angel snorted. Lucas looked pissed. And Z's laughter echoed around the room.

"I've got a warm bed ready," Z said with a grin. "Would you like to test that theory, princess?"

"You might be surprised to find what comes once we get *you* naked," Lucas added.

Angel shifted beside me and leaned close until I could feel him breathing on my neck. "And I'll watch."

I swallowed hard. The idea of Angel watching while his brothers took turns with me made my body burn. *Or maybe they wouldn't take turns.*

The image of our naked bodies, hot and sweaty and tangled caused me to shift in my seat and press my thighs together. They looked completely serious about making it happen.

"She's fidgeting," Lucas observed out loud. "Maybe that's exactly what she wants."

"We'd have no issues satisfying your curiosity."

I looked down when I felt tugging at my waist. Angel was pulling the ribbon that kept the robe closed. I gripped his wrist even though we both knew he could easily break free. "What are you doing?"

He pulled at the tie causing my robe to fall open. "Stand up."

"Why?"

"Because I said so."

"That's not a reason." I didn't see Lucas move until his hands closed around my waist. He lifted me from the couch and set me on my feet against his chest. I pushed against the hard plane of muscle, but he wouldn't budge. "Let me the fuck go."

I didn't notice him turning our bodies until I felt another against my back. Unwillingly, I looked to Angel for help, but he seemed content with watching his brothers feel me up.

"When we get a woman alone, we close in on her just like this," Z's husky tone whispered.

243

"Most women like to be chased." Lucas hands shifted as he spoke, moving from my waist to my sides, and then sliding up. "They want to be hunted."

"It makes them feel special. Like we'd do anything to have them."

"And it's only been for one that it was true."

"I'm sure she's a lucky girl," I returned sarcastically.

"We'll see soon enough," Z answered. His lips pressed against my nape.

The mind-blowing assault came again. This time, it was Lucas who pressed a hot kiss on my throat. "Yeah," he growled low.

With their help, my robe fell from my body leaving me naked between two of my abductors. They stayed close, but their bodies weren't fully pressed against mine. I didn't trust their control, though because I couldn't even trust my own. It was impossible not to find either man sexy, but they were not who my body truly burned for.

I felt him watching me even now. He kept as still and silent as a statue. His energy surrounded us and pulled at my ties, daring me to let go. In a weird twist of fate, he was the one that had bound me, and now it seemed he was the one desperate to free me.

Maybe I was the one truly in control.

Maybe I could play this game better than any of them could.

I ran my hands up Lucas's chest to test that theory and watched his eyes flare with surprise. He stalled, so I played harder and rose to the tips of my toes. Lips parted, head slanted, I leaned in for a kiss.

"Enough." Angel's voice was thick with boredom, but when I gave him my eyes again, I found jealous eyes watching me in return. "I think she gets your point."

Z and Lucas moved away immediately while I celebrated the victory in my head.

"Sit down." He stabbed the cushion next to him and stared past me.

What a sore loser.

I picked up my robe and pulled it on. I could feel his eyes on me as I did. When I collapsed on the couch next to him, he finally relaxed again.

Z was searching through the movies again. His face was tight and so was the bulge in his sweats. Besides their hands and lips, their erections were the only part of them they had freely let me feel.

Lucas had taken a seat on the far end of the couch, and when my gaze traveled to his, I found he was already watching me. He nodded slowly as if he'd figured out my game. I stared back as he smirked and took a drink from his soda.

Z finally chose a movie and popped it into the DVD player. He didn't choose the couch and instead, stretched out on the plush carpet, but not before removing his t-shirt and winking at me when it cleared his head.

I blushed and then peeked over at Angel scared that he might notice. His attention was also on Z, and the angry scowl made me look away. That did me no good since my gaze landed in his lap. My pussy wept at the subtle tent in his sweats and the thick length stretching along his thigh. His size made me curious.

In a perfect world if I could let him fuck me... would he even fit?

Suddenly, my pussy had a pulse.

It was shamelessly seeking out the feeling of him inside me even though I didn't want it.

Right?

Thirty minutes into the movie, Z and Lucas were arguing the merits of purging. That was when I heard him cry. My body tensed along with everyone else in the room, Z and Lucas's debate forgotten.

Instinctively, I rose to see to him until Angel's grasp on my wrist reminded me that it wasn't allowed.

"Let me go," I gritted. "I need to see to him."

"That's not what we discussed."

"You discussed. I wasn't given a choice."

"Sit down, Mian." When I hesitated, he squeezed my wrist until I cried out. I didn't give in, though. I couldn't. Caylen's cries grew more intense as we stared into each other's eyes. His were screaming to obey, and mine were screaming to understand.

My knees buckled when I couldn't take the sound of his distress any longer, and I collapsed to the floor with my knees pressed into my chest. Angel stood, so I braced for a fight. He surprised me when he stepped around me and left the room. Minutes later, Caylen's cries could no longer be heard, but it didn't lessen my urge to go to him. One quick glance at Lucas and Z told me they wouldn't hesitate to stop me.

When Angel reappeared, the t-shirt he was wearing before was gone. "Where's your shirt?"

"He threw up on it after I burped him."

"*You* fed him?"

"Yeah."

"You have experience feeding infants?"

"Doesn't require a degree to figure out how to feed a baby."

"But apparently you fed him too much if he threw up on you."

"I fed him until he stopped reaching for the bottle, Mian. It's not my fault his eyes are bigger than his stomach."

"So now you're calling my baby fat?"

"What I'm saying is that he has a healthy appetite and that his mother is a lunatic."

"Oh, right. You kidnap a mother and child and keep them apart, yet I'm the lunatic."

He had the nerve to shrug his shoulders. "Just calling it like I see it."

I started to curse him out when I heard, "You two fight like you're already married." Z grinned from his position on the floor.

"Pardon?"

"Cut it," Angel warned.

Z shrugged his shoulders and lay back down. The movie resumed, and everyone returned their attention to the screen, but my mind was still racing.

"Was he feeling okay?" I whispered. "Did he feel too warm or fussy?"

"He's good, Mian. He was just hungry, and now he's asleep."

"You sure he's asleep? Because he's not like most babies. He won't fall right to sleep. It—"

"I know." Finally, he turned his full attention on me, and I was struck by the warm brown of his gaze. There was no trace of irritation in them, though his tone didn't change when he said, "He didn't fall asleep right away, so I rocked him, and that was it."

"Oh... Thank you."

He didn't bother to reply and turned his attention back to the television.

"I think her baby did a Jedi mind trick on you," Lucas said after a few moments of tense silence.

"What the fuck does that mean?"

"Well," he shrugged with a grin, "he's got you playing Daddy, and you're none the wiser of who his father even is."

Angel's jaw clenched while Lucas and Z laughed at his expense. These were one of the moments when I believed it was wise to keep quiet. The last thing I wanted to do was discuss Caylen's father.

The movie played, and I pretended not to notice Angel's stare.

"SO YOU'RE A mother... How did that happen?" Angel had me brought to him the next day. I watched him sit confident and strong behind his father's desk, unbroken by the decisions of our fathers.

"Oh, you know... the natural way. If you want to know the positions we used—"

"You still haven't learned a damn thing, have you?"

"Such as?"

"Your mouth will get you in trouble."

"Sorry. I'm not much of an actor."

"You had no trouble pretending you wanted Lucas and Z's cocks last night."

I quirked an eyebrow and smirked. "Who said I was pretending?"

"Would you like to fuck them?" he asked quietly. He was calling my bluff.

"I wouldn't want you to be jealous." I winked.

He stared at me for a beat and then closed his eyes. When he opened them again, I wasn't prepared for the heat within them. "I'm going to ask you again, and this time, I want you to think about what comes from your mouth. If I don't like it, I'm going to walk to the other side of this desk and do something to it. Are we clear?"

I nodded.

"How. Did. Caylen. Happen?"

"I went on a date with a college frat, decided to give it up on the first date, it didn't go as well as I liked so I decided not to continue our relationship. Does that satisfy your question?"

"So he's not involved in Caylen's life?"

"Never told him about him," I lied. Aaron could be the only person able to do something about our abduction. Anna would have already noticed I was missing. The police wouldn't do much without signs of foul play. I knew Anna. She would become desperate enough to go to him. I thanked my lucky stars that I told her about him. I just hoped Caylen's father was human enough to give a shit about his missing son. If Angel were to ever know about him, there was no doubt in my mind that Aaron would come face to face with him.

I hadn't noticed Angel had moved until it was too late. He leaned against the desk in front of me. Angel in my personal space meant all I could breathe was *him*.

"I have a proposition for you."

I did not like the sound of that, but I was curious. "Yes?"

"Despite how I feel about you, my brothers don't feel the same. They like you."

"I can't say the same."

"It's not necessary that you do."

I definitely didn't like where this was going. "What is this proposition, Angel?"

"They want to fuck you, Mian."

They hadn't exactly been subtle about it considering their insinuations over the past week, but it still came as a shock to hear Angel admit it so freely. "What does that have to do with me?"

I had known his answer before he spoke it. "You're going to let them."

"No, Angel. I will not." My virginity was stolen from me, and I promised myself that the next time would be because I wanted it. Sure, I thought Z and Lucas were hot, but they weren't what I wanted.

I want freedom.

I swallowed down the guilt of the other half of the truth and stood up.

Angel didn't make requests, but this... I closed my eyes and breathed deep. *Not this.*

"In a few more days, when I'm confident you aren't sick, you can see your son." I was already feeling the fight inside me wither to dust. "I know you can barely sleep from the cold. I know you want clothes that will cover your body. I know you want a towel to wrap around yourself when you step from a warm shower rather than the cold air. I know you want to be free..."

I sneered at him when he finished. "And if I fuck your brothers, you're going to give me all that?"

"If you please them."

"Fuck you."

"I'm the only man in this house you'll never have to worry about spreading your legs for."

"What's wrong? You can dish it, but you can't take it?"

He reached out and took a strand of my hair between his fingers. "You have no idea how bad it can get for you if I take you."

I almost did something insane by challenging him to try. I made a note to have my head examined when I made it back to Chicago.

"My father is going to kill you."

A mocking grin spread his sexy lips. "Don't tell me you actually believe your father can save you?" He laughed, and I wanted nothing more than to kill him myself. "I know you're missing your father, and I'm a kind man when I want to be. I'll be willing to play the part." His gaze blackened as he snidely whispered, "All you have to do is call me daddy."

I swung, but he caught my fist and yanked me forward. "You'll never be anything to me but a dead man," I hissed.

He smirked. He fucking smirked! "Until then, I'm the man with the only say."

"Well, *man*... you have the misconception that you can loan my body out to your friends, and I'm just supposed to fuck on command."

"The only misconception is how you refuse to accept the inevitable."

"I'm not fucking your friends. You can't just snap your fingers and expect me to open my legs."

He gripped the lower half of my face. His hand covered my mouth entirely to keep me from screaming as he shoved me across the room until my back was against the wall. When we collided, an unlit candle resting on a scone crashed to the floor beside us.

"For now, and until I say otherwise, you belong to them, so when they command it, you smile and offer your pussy for fucking. Are we clear on that?"

I heard the door open. Angel's grimace was now for whoever interrupted. "We need to talk," Lucas explained. Angel didn't respond. He lifted his chin and the door closed. He turned his head to face me again. I blinked hard when I realized his face was closer and continued getting even closer.

Then he completely turned my world upside down and set the pit of my stomach on fire.

He kissed my lips.

Softly.

And I swore my lips would never feel the same again.

"Let's not have this conversation again."

I'VE BEEN SKIRTING the edge of sanity since my talk with Angel that afternoon. I kept my eye on the door for hours, but no one came—not even to demand a cooked meal or to offer me one, for that matter. Maybe he decided to starve me until I gave in to his friends.

The rest of the day passed, and no one came. I decided to take a shower before bed. I used to love showers until Angel used it as a way to torture me. The water was freezing cold, and I couldn't bear to spend more than two minutes inside. Stepping out into the equally cold air without a towel to dry myself or keep me covered also made me dread them.

But this time, I stepped inside of the private bath and found a towel waiting on top of the vanity. I longingly ran my fingers over the thick white cloth but was smart enough to know Angel had made his move. He thought he could pay me to slut for his friends with a towel. I lifted my fingers and entered the shower, and this time, I welcomed the cold spray. I just hoped it froze over my heart this time.

When I was done with my bath, I ignored the towel and stepped back into the room.

"Mian."

I screamed my surprise, but it was quickly cut off by a strong hand lightly clamped over my lips. "Shh. It's just me." I recognized the playful sound of Z's voice and tensed even more.

He finally let go of my face, and I sputtered, "Is that supposed to comfort me?"

"I'm sorry if I frightened you."

"No, you're not."

"I am. I won't argue with you," he added when I started to tell him off. Instinct warned me that underneath the boyish smirks and mischievous eyes lurked someone who dominated as easily as he played.

"What are you doing in here?"

"I have a proposition for you."

"Oh, great," I replied sarcastically. "Another one."

"You have a wicked sharp tongue, you know that?"

"I'm usually a delight. It's the assholes and child abductors I have trouble holding back for." He didn't get angry like Angel or annoyed like Lucas. He laughed and nodded his head in agreement.

"I can understand the temptation." The look in his eyes said he was talking about a different temptation. I needed to change the subject fast.

"What's your proposition?"

"All business. I respect that." He grinned, and I swear if I had panties, they'd melt.

"Zachariah."

"No one calls me Zachariah."

"I do."

"You are a mother," he whispered with admiration. I tapped my foot letting him know I was becoming impatient. "I know you want him." Before I could deny what we both knew was the truth, he added, "But you want to withstand him more."

I struggled to find the denial that would make the most sense. The one that would sound the most believable when uttered.

"Yes." I instantly regretted giving him even that much. I shouldn't trust him since we both knew whose side he was on.

"I could help you."

"Why would you do that?" *How would he do that?* He didn't answer right away. Instead, he lifted me in his arms and carried me to the bed. "What are you doing?" I squeaked when he followed me down.

"Isn't this where you were headed?" He leaned over my prone body. His hands were planted on each side of me, keeping me caged in. *God, he smelled good.* Like citrus and smoke.

"Yes, but without you."

"Relax."

"Get out and I will."

"He kissed you, didn't he?"

I wasn't even surprised by the abrupt change of subject. "How do you know that?'

"Lucas said you two were pretty cozy this afternoon." Damn, Lucas and his big mouth. "So?"

I nodded.

"Did you enjoy it?"

"Of course, I didn't."

"Don't lie to me, Mian. I'll know."

"Why do you care? Did he send you in here to find out how good of a kisser he is? I'm nineteen, and even I find that completely juvenile."

"What upsets you more? That he kissed you and left you wanting more, or that he didn't come back for more?"

"You're full of yourself."

"I wish you were full of me right now."

"God! You're so—"

"Hot?"

"Looks don't win over every girl. Sometimes a little chivalry is needed."

"Let me get this straight." I didn't like how his hot gaze traveled from my eyes. Down they went until they settled between my thighs and rested. "The idea of Angel kissing you again while you are full of me," he spread my thighs apart until I was bared completely for him, "doesn't make you wet?"

"Z, don't—"

"You need relief," he guessed. "I could give that to you." Without permission, he moved his fingers between my legs. I moved to close them, but he was too quick. His fingers settled over my lips, stroking, and teasing my arousal higher.

"I wish you wouldn't do that." The moan that followed didn't help me sound convincing.

"I could help you, princess."

I hated how my body grew warm all over when he called me that, and how the ache between my legs intensified under his command.

What an asshole.

"Why would you do that?" I gasped when he strung the right cord over my clit.

"Because it would be fun for me." I wasn't surprised. Someone like Z was always looking for fun. "I won't fuck you if you don't beg me to. I'll just get you off... I know you're in need."

"I won't help you betray him." I shrunk back when his eyes narrowed to fiery slits. Chill bumps that had nothing to do with the temperature of the room lined my skin even as my entire body flushed from the rush of heat.

"I'd never betray my brothers."

"Then what do you call going behind his back by keeping me sane?" Insanity was the only word to describe why I wanted my captor's touch.

"Helping him." I almost missed his words and the vehement way he spoke them.

"How could getting me off help him?"

Instead of answering, the corner of his lips lifted and his eyes lit with mischief. "You'll see, and you'll both thank me. All I'll require is his first son named after me."

"Excuse me?" I successfully yanked his hand from between

my legs and told myself I didn't mind the loss. "Why would I have any say in that?"

His gaze lit up and then I felt his fingers pushed through my hair. His hand cupped my face perfectly, making the moment intimate. "Damn, you're naive," he whispered, ruining the moment.

"I'm not naive. I want to *kill him*."

I gasped when he stole my lips with his and sighed. His lips didn't taste like that of a serpent. His kiss was warm and gentle. He skillfully coaxed me into kissing him back, but he didn't stop there. I accepted his tongue when he offered it, and he seduced away any doubt I had.

I felt his hand on my thigh, but I didn't care about it. I only cared for what came next. When his lips left mine to trail to my neck, I didn't fight him. It took every bit of fortitude and dignity he hadn't already seduced away not to beg for more. Finally, he took pity on me and lifted his lips from my throat. A groan followed when his gaze settled between my thighs.

"You have a pretty pussy," he praised. "Maybe even the prettiest I've ever seen." Without warning, he slid his teasing finger deep, and I arched my back against the shocking pleasure of it. "You didn't have to go hungry with a cunt like this."

"Please don't say that word."

"What word?"

"Cunt. I don't like it."

"Why?" He looked genuinely interested in the answer just before he shed his shirt. My mouth fell open, and I could have sworn my tongue swelled. Maybe all the moisture seeped inside because my mouth was dry as hell.

"It makes me feel dirty."

"But you are dirty." He leaned down until his hard chest was flush against my needy breasts. "You're our dirty, little girl."

"It's crass."

He swiped a finger through the lips of my pussy. "Is crass the reason your cunt is so wet?"

"Don't." He continued to caress me.

"Don't what? Touch your cunt?" He leaned closer until his lips brushed mine. "Make it wetter?"

"Stop it."

"No." He stroked faster. My hips began to move of their own accord. "Such a greedy puss." I couldn't fight where my body was taking me. Effortlessly, he shoved me over the edge and watched me fall but not before pressing a finger inside me. The walls of my pussy gripped the digit as I fell down, down, down...

I was paralyzed once I finally stopped falling. The violent tremors had ceased, and my moans had fallen silent. Only the sound of his throaty chuckle signaled that I was alive. He then kissed me on my forehead and smirked when his gaze met mine.

"Sleep tight, kid."

CHAPTER 27

Father knows best.

ANGEL

THREE YEARS AGO

"WHERE ARE YOU, Angeles? You should have been back a week ago."

"And why is that?" I questioned when I knew the reason for his call. Business was usually high this time of year with jobs that took him away for a long time.

"You said you needed a break so I gave you one. Now it's time to resume your duty."

"She's sixteen fucking years old. Why does she still need a babysitter?"

"Watch your fucking mouth," he cursed back. "If you want to work for me, you take orders just like anyone else."

"Yeah? How many babysitting jobs did you do for granddad?"

"Don't question me, son. I earned my place just as you will. Get here." The call disconnected, and I crushed my phone in my fist rather than chuck it across the room.

Mian fucking Ross. That little girl has owned me since she was ten. Every day for six years, I kept her, protected her, and grew a little more obsessed with her each day. My father knew of my obsession with her but didn't have the good judgment to keep her away from me. He preached control but seemed to do everything he could to try to make me lose it.

Hours later, I walked into the quiet brownstone. For a moment, I wondered if anyone was even home until I heard the musical lilt of her laugh. I stopped when my dick stirred to life and swore.

She's sixteen.

She's fucking sixteen.

The knowledge didn't abate my hard dick, and as painful as the effort was, I kept moving until I found her.

She was splashing around in the pool in the dick tease she called a swimsuit. She was hard to miss or ignore in the lime green and black two-piece.

I swallowed a groan and scrubbed the palms of my hands over my eyes in a desperate attempt to erase the images of what I'd like to do to her from my mind.

I was sick for wanting her the way I did.

"I know that look in your eyes, son." I never even heard my father approach. "I haven't stopped looking at your mother that way since the day I met her."

"I don't know what you mean."

"Mian."

I reluctantly ripped my gaze away from her playing in the pool with her slutty ass friend, Erin. She'd been giving me the eye ever since the first time she stepped through the door. "The kid?" Saying her name would leave me exposed.

"The kid you'd fuck six ways to Sunday as soon as her father's back was turned."

"Jesus, pops. She's sixteen! I'm. Not. A Fucking. Pedophile."

"I never said you were, but I also know firsthand how someone like her can be hard to resist. She'd make you throw away your morals and your goddamn soul for just a little taste and all she'd have to do is whisper, *yes*."

"Bullshit."

"So you don't want her?" The knowing glow in his eyes didn't need an answer. "You're only twenty-two and still a kid yourself. I know what you're thinking."

He watched me, dangling the bait. He was a lot more calculating and patient than I was. I sighed and gave in. "What am I thinking?"

"You're wondering just how far you could push the boundaries that keep you separated before your conscience gets the better of you."

"Wrong."

"How so?"

"Because I'm wondering how many of her boundaries I could push before I destroy her." He swore and shoved his hand through his hair when I gave him the answer he sought.

I wanted her.

My mind was made up, and I wasn't changing it. Not for him, her father... or her.

"You can't have her, son."

"It's too late to stop me."

"You are not going to pursue her, Angeles." He used my full name to let me know he was serious.

"Maybe not today." I met his stare. "But she's mine, pops."

He sighed. "At least allow her to grow up. She's got years before she'll be ready to be a lady of this life. Even then, Theo may kill you before he allows you to take her."

"When I take her," I said, letting him know I would take her with or without Theo's approval, "the first thing I'm exorcising from her mind is her father."

"Meaning?"

"She's too dependent on him."

"She's sixteen," he reminded me unnecessarily. I was well aware of her age. It was the only thing that has held me back.

"I meant her emotional dependence on him. The only man she'll need to take orders from is me."

My father left knowing he couldn't persuade me onto some righteous path. I holed myself in my room until the sound of her laughter drew me out again. Erin left hours ago. She should have been alone.

I was drawn to the guest room she had turned into her own since everything in that room belonged to her... right down to the racy boy shorts and tiny tops she liked to wear when her father wasn't around.

I didn't bother to knock. I twisted the knob and pushed open the door. If the door had been locked, I would have broken the fucking thing down.

She watched with wide eyes as I entered. After a brief glance her way, I searched the room. If I had taken in the sight of her half-naked in tiny shorts and tank in the middle of her ruffled lime green and black sheets, I would have lost it.

"What are you doing here?"

"I live here."

"Well, why are you barging in *my* room?"

"It's a guest room, which means it belongs to whatever person who temporarily inhabits the room. Spreading your shit around does not make it yours," I lied.

Pain appeared in her sensual green eyes. "Get out."

"In a minute." I ventured deeper inside as she pressed her thighs together and eyed me. She wasn't even aware of the cues she gave off. She wanted me. Maybe even as much as I needed her. The thought had me wanting to climb right into that bed with her and do things that were illegal. "Who is in here with you?"

"Excuse me?"

"I heard you laughing."

"And that means someone is in here with me?"

I'd had enough of her games. I stalked her, which made her scramble to get away from me. I was too quick for the Sprite. With one hand, I grabbed the front of her pathetic excuse for a shirt and lifted her in the air. I held her safely out of the way as I used my other arm to rip the mattress and box springs beneath it away.

There was nothing underneath it but dust.

"Have you lost your mind?" She struggled to free herself from my hold. She even growled, and I found it to be the cutest sound. I set her down on her feet and ignored her as she cursed. I searched her closet full of clothes and even knocked some from the hangers. "Satisfied?"

"Why were you laughing?"

She gestured to the TV she hadn't had before I left and smirked. She'd been using the TV in the living room since she didn't have a personal one. She must have convinced her father to install one while I was gone. I was still high off being angry, so I pushed my body into her smaller one. I wasn't above intimidation to get the reaction I wanted.

"Move," she warned.

"What will you do?"

She cocked her head and snorted just before she brought her knee up. Lucky for me, I was quicker. I gripped her underneath the offending knee and wrapped her leg around my waist. Because we were standing in the middle of the fucking room, the only leverage I had to offer her was my hand.

"What are you doing?"

"You were going to knee me, Sprite. Not a very good idea."

"Then why did you teach me how to do it?" she challenged.

"So you can fight off horny teenaged boys who can't keep their hands to themselves."

As opposed to a grown man who damn well should keep his hands to himself?

Her mouth twisted and her eyes debated. I tightened my grip on her leg but then decided to test the waters and let go. Holding my breath, I waited to see if she would make the sane choice for the both of us and lower her leg.

She didn't.

I don't even think she noticed my hand was gone. She was too busy staring at my lips. I leaned forward, drawn by a will that was not mine. The hitch in her breath brought me back to my fucking senses.

She was just a child, and at this age, there was no chance in hell she was in control of her own body yet. Not enough to resist me if I pursued her.

My other hand fell from her as if I'd been scalded, and I quickly stepped back. She looked startled. The arousal in her eyes rapidly dimming.

"I need to get the fuck out of here."

I needed to talk to my father. There was no way I could keep this shit up and not take her. It wasn't just about her age. I had been warned away from Mian Ross. I knew my father would never let me take my rightful place as The Bandit if I didn't heed his warning.

Nothing short of her whispering the words, "Fuck me," would make me give in.

CHAPTER 28

Enemies don't flash each other their playbook.

ANGEL

PRESENT

SEDUCING MIAN WASN'T as easy as I had assumed. Each day in her presence, I was finding less of the spoiled girl who had her daddy catering to her every whim, and more of the guarded woman she had become since I had last seen her.

"How'd it go?"

"She has a beautiful face when she comes. And the sound... None of that over the top, porn shit. It was... sweet."

I played it cool as if the thought of him touching what I had made mine didn't make me want to murder them both. "Is she on board?"

"Not yet but she will be."

"So you didn't fuck her?"

"Nope." His nonchalance was getting on my last nerve. "She could be on to us."

"Bullshit. I've seen you two seduce happily married women, twice her age, out of their panties within a week."

"She's young, but she's not dumb," Lucas corrected. He'd been silent for most of the meeting, but he took a deeper interest when the subject turned to Mian.

"And we don't get to fuck a married woman if she's happy," Z clarified. "We get to fuck married women who can't admit they're unhappy until we send them on their way and they come back for more."

"I don't care how you do it. Just do it."

Lucas's eyebrows reached for his hairline. "You saying we should rape her?"

"Of course not. Use her, but do not hurt her."

"You two were childhood friends..."

"You could say that..."

"You don't think you're hurting her by giving her to us? Blind men could tell the only man she cares to spread her legs for is you."

I turned to Z who looked deep in thought. "How long did it take before you made her come?"

"A few minutes... why?"

It only took her a few minutes to yield to another man, yet they expected me to believe I was the key to cracking Mian?

"Could you please tell Lucas that spreading her legs for any man but me won't be a problem?"

His bark of laughter as he sat back surprised me. "You're fucked if you think that's true."

"Meaning?"

"She didn't stop fighting me until I mentioned your secret kiss. Yeah, we know about that. I seduced her with thoughts of you coming into her room and finding her waiting so you could give her more of what you're denying yourself. She couldn't get enough of my hand between her thighs after that."

I stood and paced the room. "You're playing a dangerous game, Z."

"No more than you."

"You were supposed to seduce her, not unearth her secrets."

"It's the same thing. You don't get close to a girl like Mian and not want to know more."

"So what? You have a crush on her?"

"I'm too old for crushes. I like her. She's innocent."

"She's dangerous," Lucas added.

"She's just a nineteen-year-old girl," I groaned.

"Then why are you still avoiding her?"

"Because I'm still planning to kill her father. I think that would put a damper on our *relationship.*"

"You sure it not's because once you've had her, you won't be able to kill her?"

Sometimes I would forget that Z and Lucas weren't henchman collecting a paycheck. They were my brothers, and they knew me better than anyone did. Including my father.

"I'm not sticking my dick in someone whose father killed mine."

"And after he's dead and the score is settled? Theo won't be out for a long time. Too long for 'what ifs.'"

"I'm not waiting until he's released."

They both sat up at the same time. "Come again?"

"Yeah. What changed?"

"If Theo is behind me getting robbed, then how much more does he know? If Mian isn't involved, then he obviously has connections outside those prison bars. We cannot allow him to reach too far."

"He already has."

"Then we cut off his arm as payment."

"How exactly do we do that?" Z questioned.

I pinned Lucas with my stare. He didn't fidget like most men. He stared back, which is one of the reasons I trusted him. "You said you have a guy inside, right?"

"Yeah. He's looking to get out in a year with good behavior, and he needs money quick."

"Tell him to *stay* ready, but warn him I don't pay for sloppy work."

"On it."

"I want this message sent personally. No paper trails. No loose ends. Establish contact and pay him a visit."

"You want me to go back to Chicago for *this*?"

"Not just for this. There's something I want you to steal."

LUCAS LEFT THE next day, and I was faced with a difficult decision. Mian wasn't going to be moved by force, which only left gaining her trust. I pushed inside the nursery and found Caylen awake in his crib and kicking his feet contentedly. I stood over the crib and gazed down at the child whose happy personality had yet to waver despite everything I put his mother through.

It's been two weeks since I discovered she had a kid. I'd lie awake at night wondering about the man she gave her body to. I told myself his father didn't matter, but then jealousy forced my hand. She lied about Caylen's conception. Sometimes we forget how those years together made us know one another better than we knew ourselves. When the time was right, I'd finally uncover her secrets.

I guess Z had been right.

Mian made it impossible not to want to know more.

I was pulled from my thoughts when I felt a light touch on my hand. The baby stood with his little fists grasping the edge in between my hands. When my gaze met his shiny blues, his gummy grin shone bright.

"What are you up to?" He made a high-pitched squeal of excitement, and he bounced up and down in place. "Showing off?" His grip slid closer to mine until his fist touched my much bigger one. I flinched and lifted my hand to move it away but froze when his smile dropped.

I told myself it was a trick of my own mind.

My hand lowered anyway and closed over his fist. His smile returned brighter than before.

I ignored the stabbing pain in my chest and took a deep breath. "All right, kid. Let's go see your mother."

He did that squealing shit again when I lifted him from the crib. I held him to my chest while he stuck his fist in his mouth. My heart stopped beating for a moment as if to disguise itself when he laid his head against my chest.

I was reminded of Mian. While she guarded her emotions with others, she let them free with Caylen. Keeping them apart had been my only weapon, but last night, I'd begun to wonder if there was a different way to yield it.

I kept my arm locked around him to keep him secure and unlocked the door. She stood with her back turned, gazing out the window.

"I get this chill down my spine whenever you enter the

room. It's how I know you're there even when you don't want me to."

Caylen chose that moment to babble in my arms. Mian spun around. Fear and surprise seized her when her gaze landed on Caylen in my arms.

"What are you doing with him?"

We moved at the same time. She looked ready to defend her child against me, and for one insane moment, it made me want to protect them both against me, too.

"I thought he would like a visit with his mother."

"So you're satisfied I won't infect my own child?"

"The continuation of this visit is contingent on whether or not you can behave."

She glanced down at her son and her hard exterior softened. Caylen's head moved excitedly, and I wondered if he recognized his mother's voice.

"I can behave." She'd whispered so softly it was a wonder I'd heard her at all. I handed her the baby. She spoke to him softly in a way she had never spoken to me and held him close in a way she would never offer me.

Come on, Knight. You're not actually jealous of the baby.

I stood back and watched them interact. I kept as still and silent as possible so as to not taint the scene playing out in front of me. She leaned down and rubbed her nose with his, and he returned her affection with a toothless grin.

"Have these bad men mistreated you?" Though her tone was light, I noticed how she subtly checked him for signs of abuse as soon as he was in her arms.

"Mian."

"It never hurts to ask," she grumbled. She looked up and met my gaze, which had turned hard and cold again. "Why are you hanging around anyway? You don't trust me with my own baby?"

"Just satisfying a curiosity."

"I see." She lowered her head again to stare at her son. "And whatever business you have waiting for you isn't more important?"

"Business doesn't happen without my say so."

"Fascinating."

"What is?"

"How proud you are to be a criminal."

I felt my gaze narrow. "I thought you said you were going to behave."

A tiny smile spread her lips, but she turned away before I could see it form into a full-blown smile. She had no idea her smiles weakened me or else she would never deny me them. Mian had never been the type to tempt, but I was sure she was willing to do just about anything to rescue her son.

"Can I ask you something? It requires honesty."

She faced me with suspicion in her gaze. "Okay," she conceded with hesitation.

"Your father's eyes are green. Yours are green."

"Where is the question?"

"Does Caylen's father have blue eyes?" She looked alarmed confirming only half of what I knew about the father.

"Why do you ask?"

"Answer me."

She thought it over before she answered. "Yes."

"I'll leave you two alone then." I caught her frown before I turned and headed for the door.

"Angel."

I turned at the sound of her call.

"Yes, Mian?"

She seemed to struggle with something before she moved to the chair and took a seat. "Nothing."

THE SUN WAS starting to set when I returned to Mian's room. I found her stretched on her side next to a sleeping Caylen.

"He fell asleep."

"Babies do that."

"Maybe he'd be more comfortable in his crib."

She snorted. "Come on, Angel. Be a man. You're taking him from me."

"Yes, Mian. I am."

She was silent for a while but then she said, "Can I see?"

"See what?"

"I want to see where you're keeping him."

I started to ask why, but then it occurred to me that, as his mother, it was important to her. "Sure."

Her eyebrows shot up. "Really?"

"Yeah. Really." I held the door open and waited. She watched me for a few seconds longer and then scooped the baby in her arms.

I led the way to the other side of the house with her close on my heels. When we reached the nursery, I let her pass and tried to ignore the guard Lucas insisted we put in place. His attention was locked on Mian. "It's the door right in front of you."

"You aren't coming in?"

"No." She must have sensed my anger because she entered the nursery without a smart retort. Once the door closed, I pushed into the guard's space. "Something wrong with your focus?"

"Sir?"

"I know an eye fuck when I see one. Do I pay you to eye fuck?"

"No, sir."

"So next time, what will happen?"

"I... uh—"

"You'll keep those thoughts to yourself, or I'll take care of your eye problem with my favorite knife. Get me?"

He gulped and wouldn't meet my gaze for shit. "Yes, sir."

I made a mental note to send him packing in the morning and entered the nursery. Mian already had Caylen in his crib where she stood over him. Her attention, though, was shifting around the room. She looked confused.

I tried to see what she saw but couldn't see past the comfortable crib, soft lighting, and changing table stocked with pampers and wipes. On the shelves I had brought in were onesies and caps, bibs and binkies, and blankets. Her precious Caylen wanted for nothing.

"Something wrong?"

Her gaze finally locked with mine and there was nothing but disdain in her green eyes. "It's not what I expected."

"Meaning?"

"You're going through a lot of trouble to pretend you aren't a monster."

My gaze narrowed. "Would you rather I dangle him over a tank of hungry sharks?"

"I'd rather you let us go, but since that isn't happening, then yes," she hissed. "I'd like you to stop playing games, but by no means do I want you to hurt my son."

I moved in until she had no choice but to retreat. "If you're looking to be hurt, I can accommodate you."

"I want to know what game you're playing."

"We're at war, Mian. Enemies don't flash each other their playbook."

"What does it matter if you're already dead? It's just a matter of time." The venom in her tone was chilling, but I had years of conditioning and wouldn't tremble so easily even if I did believe she meant it.

"I could say the same for you." She bared her teeth, and I could almost feel them sinking into me as I drove into her.

Damn.

"Have dinner with me."

Instantly, she changed from angry tigress to scared doe. "What?"

"I want us to have dinner together."

"Why would I do that?"

"Because I'll starve you if you don't." I considered if it was smart to show her my hand, but she made it necessary to remind her why she should be afraid.

She glared, and I pretended I hadn't noticed the way her chest rose and fell with each deep breath she took. Besides, it was the fight in her eyes that captivated me. Like she could keep me from starving her if I wished.

"Golly gee, but they are both such equally repulsive choices." She lifted her gaze to the ceiling and stuck her finger to her chin. "However, starving does not agree with me, so I guess I'll have to accept your invitation."

"You do me an honor," I returned with equal sarcasm.

She opened those pouty pink lips to one up me, but I grabbed her around the waist, stealing her chance. She stiffened when I slid my hand across the small of her spine. My fingers tingled just as she shivered, and then our gazes met.

She felt it, too. She had to.

With her face upturned, I couldn't ignore how she licked her lips. Everything—dinner, seduction, revenge—it all fled, leaving only one thing behind...

I pulled her into me.

She had nowhere else to go.

Lust had already clouded her judgment.

She was mine.

"Angel?" She sounded uncertain.

My shirt shifted under her fingers as she clenched the material. Her breathing was no longer steady. It shook along with her body, and I wondered how fast I could melt Mian's ice.

"Angel," she groaned.

This time, I answered. My lips took hers, and I swallowed the surprised gasp that escaped. My little bandit pushed to get away until I growled. Her whimper of defeat was muffled, but my dick still felt it.

Slowing the kiss down, I nudged gently at her lips until they parted and then I waited. Her nails dug into my chest now, urging me on.

Perhaps she was confused.

I fought my smile and took pity. Licking slowly across her plump bottom lip, hinting at what I wanted and waiting for her to take the bait.

She stiffened. But just as quickly, she softened, gave in, and timidly she offered her tongue. I felt it brush my lips briefly as it sought out mine.

Check fucking mate.

I pushed her away. "Did you learn that in the strip club or spreading your legs for money?"

"Excuse me?"

"I know you work for Caesar?"

"Who the hell…" she trailed off. "You think I'm a stripper?"

"And a prostitute. You saying you aren't?"

"That's exactly what I'm saying. I don't work for Caesar."

'Then why were you in his club? I know it wasn't for the entertainment."

"How did you know I was in his club?"

"You didn't think I'd let you go without keeping an eye on you, did you?"

"Stalker," she hissed.

"Why were you in his club?" She crossed her arms and stared. "It wasn't a rhetorical question."

"If you must know, I was looking for work."

"And you thought fucking was constructive?"

"I didn't know that was part of the job description."

"Bullshit."

"I didn't!"

"You have ears, don't you? Even I've heard of Caesar's back door dealings."

"Well, it doesn't matter because I didn't get the job. I blew it."

"Literally or figuratively?"

She shook her head with disgust. "I hate you."

CHAPTER 29

When death is knocking at your door, do you ignore it even if it has a key?

ANGEL

I STEPPED FROM the black town car that arrived without warning and made my way up the steps. I knew the call would come, but I was hoping I'd have more time and more answers. I had an hour car ride to prepare myself for this meeting and spent the last twenty minutes smoking when my mental pep talk failed.

Grey, the Knight butler, stood by the doors waiting to open them on my arrival. The Knight estate was a massive symbol of the wealth my family had stolen over generations. It was three times the size of my father's home and a century's worth

 of our family's dark history. Only with the death of The Bandit was the estate inherited by the next in line. Since my father died before his time, it never passed from my grandfather.

Grey escorted me to my grandfather's bedside. Alon Knight

was seventy-five years old and required formality as a sign of respect. The butler announced my presence before bowing and taking his leave. I stared at the man who rejected weakness even as his body grew old for all to see. He sat ramrod straight, his white hair meticulously brushed, and his aging face relaxed with the impression that control was still his.

"I'm disappointed, Grandson. You should know better than to keep me in the dark." He stirred his tea and took a sip. "The book is missing."

"It is." I wasn't surprised he knew. He had eyes and ears everywhere, and I didn't doubt one of his sources was among my men. He should only hope I never identify him because not even grandfather could protect him.

"Do you know who is responsible?"

"I'm working on it."

He continued to sip his tea without sparing me a glance. "I assume you mean Theo's daughter?"

It was a struggle to remain impassive. Grandfather knowing she was the one to steal from us sealed her fate. Mian's death was as sure as if God personally commanded it. "She's a person of interest."

"Meaning?"

"I have her, and she'll be dealt with when I have answers."

"You've had her for nearly two weeks now. You haven't recovered the book, and she isn't dead. What *are* you doing with her?"

"I've interrogated her. Her story remains the same."

"I see. And how many times have you satisfied your cock while you were interrogating her?"

"I haven't fucked her, Grandfather."

"Maybe you should. With your cock's needs out of the way, maybe you'll focus on the fact that six generations and our future could be in the hands of the highest bidder as we speak."

"I'm not fucking her," I growled. He finally looked me in the eye.

"The anniversary is in two weeks."

"I'm aware."

"You have until then."

"Pardon?"

"Mian will die the night of the celebration, book or no. How painful her death will depend on her."

THE FRONT DOOR crashed into the wall, but I didn't stop. I heard the loud echo of my hard footsteps, but I didn't stop. Lucas and Z emerged from the kitchen with shocked expressions, but I didn't stop. Nothing but answers would stop me.

I could barely muster enough calm to get the key in the lock, but when it gave, I pushed open the door and was surprised to find her waiting. She looked ready to do battle, and I wouldn't keep her waiting.

"No more fucking around. Where. Is. The. Book?"

"For the last time, I don't—"

Her voice trailed off with each foot of space I closed between us. With her throat in my grip, I backed her up until her knees hit the end of the bed and gave out. I followed her down and covered her body with my own. My hips settled between her legs as if they belonged, and I could feel my heart pound in rhythm with hers. We are both so fucked.

"Do you understand what's going to happen here? You're dead if we don't recover my family's book... you may be dead even if we do." The truth of my words strangled me.

"What's the matter, Angel? Are you so eager to kill me or afraid you might have to?" I stared into the jade of her eyes and found myself wondering about the answer. "Be a man and kill me already so you can move the fuck on. I don't have your book," she sneered, "and even if I did, there's no hurt you can unleash, no pain you can cause, no threat that will shake me." Her head rose from the bare bed and when our lips were in danger of meeting she stopped. "So fuck off."

The smile I bared snuck up on me, and I could tell it took her by surprise, too. Her shiver shook me all the way down to my cock. I was already moving before I could stop myself. Upon her perfect pink lips, I delivered a kiss of death.

"Then let the games begin."

CHAPTER 30

She may be Cinderella, but he's no Prince Charming.

MIAN

"I'VE BEEN SEARCHING for your waistline ever since I stitched my first dress. You could use a little more hips, however..." Madame Torre roughly palmed one of my breasts. "And a little less here."

I fought myself from prying her fingers from my body. Not when Angel watched me so closely.

"Or I can just love my body the way it is."

She scoffed and continued to take my measurements. I was sick of being turned and prodded. I woke up that day to Angel's threats heavy on my mind. His threats weren't new.

I'd even come to expect them, but this time felt different. The control Angel normally possessed was gone.

Even more unusual was when I was taken downstairs where a tall, flame-haired woman, who was dressed for the runway, waited with her two assistants,

Ricardo and Ricardo. The first Ricardo was tall and thin with light brown hair styled in a Mohawk. The second man was short and muscular with a thick goatee. Lucas whispered to me when she dismissed me to fawn over Angel, that she never kept assistants long enough to learn their name, so she named them all after her ex-husband. I didn't know whether to hate her or feel sorry for her.

"Angel, my dove." I coughed to cover up my laugh. Angel was no dove. "May I see the dress?" She spoke to him, but his attention never left me. He probably heard me laugh. I shrugged and looked away. It wasn't like he appreciated the name, either. "Ahhh, yes," Madame Torre cooed. I hadn't even noticed Z carrying a stunning black gown. "I remember this dress well. This is your mother's, no?"

Angel nodded and took a sip from his glass. The robe slipped off my shoulders. His eyes finally left mine to watch it fall to the floor. I was the center of attention as I stood naked in the center of the room.

Suddenly, it was dark but only for a second, and then my body was covered in layers of organza silk. The low cut bodice molded to me, pushing up my breasts while the rest of the dress fell a little baggy around my waist and hips.

"I'll need to make some alterations."

"How soon can you get it done?"

"A few days. She'll be the belle of the ball."

Ball? I was going to a ball? I stared at Angel for answers but found none. I didn't know how I felt about wearing his mother's dress or going to a ball for that matter. Once again, he strayed from the script. I was his prisoner, and he was my captor. Music, dancing, and glass slippers didn't fit into our world.

CHAPTER 31

Shotgun!

ANGEL

THREE YEARS AGO

I NEEDED MORE than just a cold shower after what had happened. I pulled on basketball shorts and left my damp chest bare after stepping from the bathroom. The hall was clear, and there was not a sound to be heard, but I knew Mian was nearby. She wasn't allowed to leave without me unless she was heading to school. In my room, I turned up Korn's 'Coming Undone' and lit up. Smoke billowed and the scent of a bad habit permeated the air. It only took a couple of pulls for me to mellow into a safe zone.

I almost kissed her.

I had been willing to welcome insanity just for one taste of her.

Damn.

She wanted to bust my balls, and in retaliation, I practically molested her. I wasn't proud of myself but damn if I didn't want to do it again.

My dick was already on the rise thinking about it, so I took another hard pull and exhaled sharply through my nose. A knock on the door had the rest of my body stiffening along with my dick. It could only be one person.

"What?"

"Can I come in?"

I hesitated. Her voice was low and light. She at my door tempted me, but I wasn't eager to poke the beast. She never came to my room. Even when we stopped snapping at each other, we still avoided each other.

"Why the fuck not?" I growled. The door pushed open, and her eyes found me lounging against my headboard. "What?"

"I wanted to talk to you." She licked her lips—her signature sign that she was nervous—before wrinkling her nose at the thick smoke. "You really shouldn't smoke weed."

"Because it's bad for me?" I mocked. She rolled her eyes.

"Because you're bad enough," she countered.

"Not true. I can always do worse." I winked.

Such a simple gesture made her freeze like a baby deer caught in a truck's headlights yet my intimidation tactics that folded grown men didn't faze her.

She huffed and mumbled, "I wanted to apologize."

My eyebrow lifted. "For what?"

"For trying to knee you in the balls." I stopped myself from laughing. It was undeniable that I deserved it. I had no business touching her the way I had. Why couldn't she see that? I know she's only sixteen, but innocence only stretched so far.

"It's cool, Sprite. You couldn't hurt a fly." I fit the blunt between my lips, watching her as she watched me inhale.

"Is it really worth it?"

"What?" I knew what.

"Smoking weed. Getting high?"

I stared, and she stared back. Making a decision, I sat up against my headboard and while holding her gaze, patted the bed beside me. "Come here." She took a step closer to the door, and I bit back a curse. "Come here, girl. I don't bite."

But I might if you beg me.

She looked like she was having the same thought because her head tilted warily.

"I want to show you something."

I knew the exact moment she gave in. Her eyes were so damn expressive. I wondered what side of Mian I'd see when her guard was down.

She crawled to the spot I designated for her, and she watched me take a pull. Without warning, I turned my face and blew the smoke in hers. She coughed and sputtered and waved her hands furiously to fight the thin cloud of smoke.

"Why," she coughed, "did you do that?"

I smiled, and she seemed to forget all about her coughing fit. "Open your mouth."

"Why?"

"Because I want you to."

She frowned. Deeply. And then she did as I asked and parted her lips and I knew... I just knew... if I licked, and kissed, and sucked them between my own, they would taste sweet.

I pulled on the blunt again, and this time, I exhaled slowly and blew the smoke between her lips. She coughed again, but this time, her eyes watered as she stared at me alarmed.

"Again?" She looked unsure, so I decided for her. "Again." Surprisingly, she opened her lips without direction. I leaned in closer until our lips almost touched. "This time I want you to inhale," I spoke directly in her mouth. "Ready?" Her eyes widened, but she nodded, closed her eyes, and waited expectantly.

I inhaled from the blunt and moved closer until my left hip touched her right, and my top lip brushed hers. When she shivered, I exhaled. She inhaled and coughed, but it wasn't violent like before. Her eyes were glassy and dilated when they opened, and she seemed to sway.

"Feel good?" I whispered against her lips. She nodded, her forehead rubbing against mine. "Want another?"

She hesitated even though I had already seen the curiosity in her eyes. "Yes, please."

I smiled to keep her focus from my dick growing in my shorts. I wanted another brush of her lips. "Good girl." I took another pull, and she opened up for me. She took the shotgun more smoothly this time, and I gave her two more shots before deciding she'd had enough. I stubbed out the lit end and placed the rest of the blunt on my nightstand.

"We aren't going to finish it?"

I chuckled and turned back to face her. "Look who's addicted." She giggled and swayed into my chest, so the only natural thing was for me to run my fingers through her hair... *Right?*

"You have really pretty eyes."

I jerked and blinked. "What?"

"Your eyes... they're really pretty. *You're* pretty." She laughed some more, sighed like she was relieved she'd said it, and then froze... with her gaze on my lips.

"Sprite?" She leaned in closer and rested her hand on my chest that I now remembered was bare. I liked how it felt. Her

287

hand was small and warm on my hard chest, and I wondered if she could feel my heart fighting to free itself from its cage.

"Your skin is so hot."

Her attention had been on my chest, but when she looked up with wide, bright eyes, I was hit with the force of her innocence. I couldn't do this. I threw myself away from her and exploded. "Damn it, Sprite!"

"What?" She genuinely appeared confused which only pissed me off more. "What's wrong?"

"You're *sixteen*." I stressed her age for my benefit as well as hers.

"I know." She scooted closer and rose up to her knees.

"I'm twenty-two goddamn years old."

Again... for my benefit.

"I know."

"I'm a grown man. You're a child."

"I know."

"You know? *You know*?" She flinched when my volume rose. I didn't let up. I needed to scare her to stay away from me. Getting close had been a mistake that I was now forced to rectify. She nodded but didn't lose the look in her eyes, and I felt the grip on my will slip. "So what would it make me?"

She whimpered. "It doesn't matter."

"It fucking does, so say it? What does it make me if I gave you what you're begging for and kissed you right now?"

She was reluctant, but she knew the truth, so I waited. "A...A...A pervert." Her eyes flowed when she admitted it as if the thought of my perverseness turned her on more.

Fuck no.

"That's right, but more than that, it would make me a goddamn pedophile."

She blinked, and I watched her process it, but then she did something that fucked my whole world up. She slipped her arms around me and whispered in my ear, "I don't care."

I pulled back, but that was a mistake because it only gave her access. Her lips touched mine, and she sighed again. "I've never been kissed." She moved closer until she was practically on my lap. "Kiss me."

I opened my mouth to deny her, but she didn't wait around to hear it. Pressing her lips against mine, she explored by brushing her lips against mine. "Baby... no."

I wrapped my arms around her waist to move her away. I really did. But then I felt her tongue shyly prying for entrance and I was screwed.

With a groan she swallowed, I gave up the fight. Gripping the back of her neck, I pressed my lips against hers and had my first taste of Mian Ross. It lasted only a second because we both froze at the sound of our fathers calling our names.

CHAPTER 32

Blood looks good on you.

MIAN

PRESENT

NO ONE CAME or went for three days.

I figured out his intention the very first day and laughed. It was clear Angel hadn't done his homework. Starvation became a close friend of mine months ago. Sometimes ensuring Caylen was clothed, fed, and in perfect health meant having nothing left after. Most of my meals came from the mercy of the restaurants where I waitressed.

My body jerked from the cold, but I had little energy to shake it free. My prison became a winter wonderland without the wonder. The temperature in my room dropped steadily

every day until I had only the chatter of my teeth to keep me company. There were no clothes to ward off the chill and no blankets to bundle under. He didn't even leave behind the damn curtains. Angel had thought of everything it seemed.

Curled on top of the plush carpet, I plotted my revenge. I pushed aside everything I loved and filled my heart with hate. The ball, the gown, legacies, and Knights consumed me. He'd be back.

He always came back.

I WAS BREAKING free.

Two days ago, I started to hear my son's cries. The lucid part of my brain argued that it was a hallucination. The desperate part of me only cared that he was close.

Squeezing my eyes closed, I sent the chair flying. It bounced, anticlimactically, off the window and fell to the floor. The sound it made when it hit the window was loud. I picked it up again and ignoring the double vision and trembling muscles, sent it forward with a little more force. The window cracked, but it was the noise I cared about. Even if I broke the window, it was at least a thirty-foot drop to a stone bed.

I gripped the arms of the heavy chair, but my ears perked when I heard the sound of footsteps rushing closer. I waited, timing the footsteps. I listened to the lock turn. As soon as the door flew open, I hoisted the chair in the air, but before I could send it flying, I felt his harsh grip on my arm.

He tore the chair from my grip, which sent me spilling forward. The chair crashed to the ground, and then he growled. "What are you—"

I didn't give him the chance to finish. The path to the door was clear. Jumping to my feet, I sprinted for the door. I expected his hands on me any second. I expected to be dragged back by my hair and threatened. When I made it through the door, I ran *faster*.

I fell into the first door and tried the knob. I couldn't leave without him even if it meant getting caught. When the knob twisted, I threw it open.

Empty.

There was no sign of Angel when I glanced behind me. Hairs on the back of my neck stood up. Where was he?

I tried another handle, which turned out to be Angel's old bedroom and found it empty.

I knew from when I robbed the place there were only three rooms on this wing.

Maybe I had been hallucinating...

I fought a wave of nausea and rushed for the east wing.

Make a sound, baby boy.

"You're making this fun for me."

I stopped cold at the sound of his voice. I expected to see him standing behind me when I turned, but I was still alone. Taking a deep breath, I ran to the room I knew Angel kept Caylen. It was locked.

"Breaking someone already weak isn't much of a challenge." His voice was back to send chills down my spine. "You're giving me a reason to do my best."

This time, I noticed his voice seemed omnipresent and realized he must have been speaking through an intercom. "I got out, and I'm leaving with my son. You're not exactly winning awards." I threw my shoulder into the door, but it was weak. Suddenly, Caylen's cry broke from the other side.

Angel's chuckle was chilling, but I made myself ignore it. "You haven't eaten in five days. You couldn't even break that door down at full strength."

He was watching me?

I looked around for a camera but found none. I threw my shoulder into the door again but had to grip the handle to keep from crumbling to the floor when my legs gave out. Caylen's cries were louder now and my desperation to get to him grew.

"Return to your room, and I'll forgive you."

I chuckled and then blinked to clear another wave of double vision. "And if I don't?" I tried to sound strong, but five days without food had taken a bigger toll on me than I had expected.

"I'll punish you. Personally and painfully." His voice was deeper. His mood was pitch black.

"As exciting as that sounds, I'll have to decline." I pushed myself up from the floor and took slow, shaky steps to the stairs. My body was fighting to give up, but my mind wouldn't take the hint.

Downstairs, I searched the kitchen for something useful to pick the lock or pry the door open. I grabbed the biggest kitchen knife I could find and then stumbled my way down a short, dark hallway. I found a single door and quickly pushed it open before I lost my nerve. I blindly slid my hand along the side wall in search of a light switch. When my fingers moved over the panel, I hurriedly switched it on.

The room turned out to be a garage, and after a quick search in the corners, I found no boogeyman lurking. A black Suburban, black BMW, and sick looking red and black bike filled up three of the spaces, leaving an empty space near the furthest wall. On the far wall was a red, metal chest that stood as tall as I was. I stepped onto the cold concrete and ignored the chill and roughness on my bare feet. Searching through the treasure chest of tools, I found a tension wrench and pick. I peeked around every corner as I made my way back upstairs.

Angel could have stopped me at any time. Instead, he once again used me for his amusement.

When I broke out of here, the joke would be on him.

I laid the knife close to me and set to work picking the lock. When the lock gave, I picked the knife from the floor and rushed inside. Like before the room was clean and simple. I was relieved to find the room warm. I only hoped he hadn't chosen to starve him, too.

Caylen looked healthy with the rail under his tiny fists to hold him up while fat tears rolled down his face. My heart was pounding fast when I surged forward. I had my hands out ready to grab him from his prison when I was suddenly lifted into the air and drawn away.

"No!" My scream of frustration would have been heard by neighbors if the fucker had any. Caylen was screaming at the tops of his lungs, but his cries were broken now from overuse. I fought and kicked and even bit Angel's fingers when he made the mistake of trying to silence me with a hand over my mouth. When he didn't release me, I remembered the knife and awkwardly slashed at his forearm. Angel grunted from the pain, and after ripping the knife from my hand, he flung me across the room. I hit the wall hard and fell to the ground. When my body settled, I rejected the beckon of unconsciousness and found Angel standing a few feet away. His chest heaved up and down as he stared down at me with malice in his eyes. Blood trailed down his muscular arm and stained the plush carpet beneath us.

He didn't seem to notice as he glared down at me. He looked ready to kill me. I searched for the knife and found the stained blade lying on the other side of the room. I would have to get past him, which would never happen, so I eyed the distance to the open door and realized I could make it out. I could run.

Of all the chances, it was the only one I really had.

But I couldn't leave my son.

"Now would be the time to beg."

I pushed myself up to sit on my ass and curled my knees against my chest. I fought, and I lost, but that didn't mean I wouldn't fight again. Next time, I wouldn't stop until he was dead. A smile crept up on my face, and I finally met his gaze. He was the one that fucked up.

"I won't beg. I will never beg."

"We'll see about that."

He stalked forward, and I discreetly moved to back away, but the unmoving wall he'd thrown me into earlier stopped me from going far. When he leaned down to grab me, I ducked his hand, but he caught me anyway and tugged me up by my hair instead of my throat where he first aimed. I cried out, but it was cut short when he swiped a finger through the blood on his arm. He held up his bloodied fingers for me to see.

"How does it feel to draw my blood?"

"Like I wouldn't hesitate to do it again."

He chuckled. "Would it be wise for me to believe you?"

"Give me the knife back and let's find out." *I'll cut your throat this time.*

"Hmm," he quietly said while staring into my eyes. God, I hated when he did that.

"Well?" I prompted. My eyebrow lifted when he didn't answer immediately.

"Well..." he said and then brought his finger closer to my face. I cringed when he lightly trailed his bloody finger across my cheek. "...I think my blood looks better on you."

CHAPTER 33

Because bad ideas are what I'm good at.

ANGEL

"WE LEAVE FOR a few hours, and you start World War Three," Lucas accused. Z laughed while he bandaged my arm.

I look up from pouring the much-needed whiskey to meet Lucas's angry gaze. "I didn't start it."

"Then how did she get out or even far enough to get a goddamn kitchen knife?"

I drank the whiskey down in one gulp and reached for a second serving. "I got bored."

"You're fucking with me, right? She could have escaped."

"From the looks of it, she could have killed you while she was at it," Z joked.

 I ignored Lucas's anger and Z's ribbing and focused instead on the naked wildcat who had cut me up. She sat gagged and tied to the chair I placed between my father's desk and the couch. Lucas and Z had found us in

the nursery moments after I smeared my blood on her cheek. She actually looked grateful to see them, or maybe she figured she'd been spared. Lucas and Z had tied her to the chair, and I pretended I wasn't jealous of their hands on her body. She was naked except for the thin, short robe.

"We should lock her back up."

"She's fine here." The anger in her eyes told me she didn't agree. Tough. She wanted an out, and I gave it to her.

"What are you going to do about her little escape attempt?"

"More than she bargained for." I stared into her eyes while I said it and smirked when she looked away. "Mian will be spending the night with me, and I want no interference." She met my gaze again with panicked eyes. "No matter what you hear," I added.

Z finished bandaging my arm and moved back. "Are you sure that's a good idea?"

"I know it's not."

"Then why are you doing this?"

Mian looked all too interested in the answer, as well.

"Because bad ideas are what I'm good at."

CHAPTER 34

Trick of the light.

MIAN

"SHE'S GOING TO need her strength."

I *felt* the promise behind his words. Surely, he didn't think I'd actually sleep with him? A vivid flash of my first night here reminded me that Angel had been all too willing to take me without my permission.

Lucas sat me at the table while Z disappeared into the kitchen. He came back carrying a plate of grilled chicken, zucchini, salad, and a large roll of baked bread. The glint from a sharp blade was my only warning before Lucas cut through my ties. I rubbed my wrists to relieve the ache and then dug  in without waiting to be told. A full meal wasn't a part of my diet even before Angel decided to starve me, so I had plenty of time to build up an appetite. When the food was gone, and my stomach didn't feel any closer to feeling full, Z offered a second helping.

The only sound in the room was me savagely tearing into the food. A tall glass of ice-cold water suddenly appeared courtesy of Lucas.

"You should slow down before you choke," he advised. I heeded it long enough to take a long sip of water.

"What were you thinking, princess?"

"Stop calling me princess. Princesses aren't starved and beaten."

"We didn't beat you, princess. We *spanked* you." He leaned in and whispered, "You were a *very* naughty girl.

I clutched the fork tight in my fist and slowly forced the excess air from my lungs. "You shouldn't get too close." I leaned forward and closed the distance between us until we were practically smooching. When his eyes lit up with delight, I added, "A fork could land in your eye." I spanked his hand with the back of the fork, winked, and sat upright to finish my chicken.

"I knew we should have given her plastic," Lucas muttered. I finished eating and was led back to the east wing. Lucas pulled me by my arm when I dug my toes into the carpet.

He was heading straight for the master suite.

I resisted harder, but then Z gripped my shoulder and spun me around. When he bent, I tried to knee him in the face, but he was too quick. With his shoulder in my stomach, he lifted me over his shoulder and carried me the rest of the way.

Lucas entered without knocking, and Z followed him to the master bath. Z let me go, and the sudden sound of rushing water caught my attention. I stared at the large white garden tub in the center of the room as it filled up with water. Lucas poured from a bottle and sweet scented bubbles sprouted from the water. "Let me guess. We're all going to climb inside and play a round of rubber ducky?"

"Are you offering?" Lucas smiled, but it felt dangerous.

"Because we wouldn't mind."

I looked behind me to see Z lifting his shirt and flashing drool-worthy abs.

Out of the corner of my eye, I noticed Lucas reaching for his belt. They moved in closer from both sides. I panicked and planted one hand on Z's naked chest and the other on Lucas's covered one.

"She thinks she can stop us." Z chuckled and pushed his chest into my hand in a test of strength. His skin was way too hot not to combust.

"Angel—"

"Won't stop us. He won't care to."

"So you'd better be careful how carelessly you tease us," Lucas added. "Because the next time," his tone dropped to a whisper, "we might not stop."

I WAS BATHED, gagged, on my stomach, and tied to the large bed. The room had changed since the first time I was here. It smelled different. Less like death and dust and more like men's cologne and smoke.

So I guess he still smokes.

It was a dirty habit, but somehow Angel made it alluring.

My arms began to ache by the time night fell. Angel still hadn't made an appearance, and I wondered if he was off kidnapping more women and children. Had his father ever been so ruthless or was Angel still craving to make a point to dear ole dad?

I never heard the door open.

It was a woman's husky moan that alerted me I was no longer alone. I craned my neck to see but didn't get far. Two bodies stumbled through the dark into my view. The larger body lowered into the chair facing the bed while the one the sounds were coming from eagerly sunk into their lap.

The window curtains were left open, allowing the moon to illuminate the writhing figures. Their faces were hidden in the shadows, but I knew it could only be one person.

How could he not remember I was here?

I was too deeply ensnared by confusing thoughts to realize I was being watched. It wasn't until the woman he had in his lap lowered to the floor that I noticed his eyes fixed on me. They seemed brighter, and I figured it was the moonlight highlighting them. I heard the jingle of his belt being removed, but his gaze wouldn't let me go. I couldn't believe he was getting his dick blown while I was naked and tied in his bed.

His whore must have been paid a lot of money. If she'd noticed me, she didn't even blink. By the sounds coming from her throat, she was enjoying herself. Then again, maybe it was for his benefit. I watched her head move up and down and gritted my teeth when he gripped her hair to control her movements. He moved her head lower, and I completely stopped breathing when his hips lifted from the chair to aid in fucking her mouth. His slacks were lowered around his hips and the loose belt buckle jingled with each movement.

His groan of satisfaction vibrated down my spine, and at the same time, made my blood run cold. I closed my eyes only to open them again when I heard movement. The woman sat in his lap once again, but this time, she worked her body on him like a pro.

I hated her.

I hated him.

Was I jealous?

Fuck no.

I simply wanted them both dead.

She moaned loudly and dramatically. It might have been convincing if Angel moved or paid attention. He sat unmoving and uninterested in anything but me.

Gagged, I had no way to wish him a happy trip to hell. Bound, I had no option but to wait it out. But even though I wasn't blindfolded, it didn't mean I had to watch.

I snapped my eyes closed and thought I had won.

Until I heard everything. Every slap of their skin and ecstatic moan. I could even smell the thick scent of their sex.

Her moans suddenly turned to surprised gasps, and I realized it was because he was *participating*.

Rat bastard.

But I didn't care, right?

I wasn't supposed to care.

They sped up, grew louder, and more frenzied until they crashed. I just wished they'd burn while they were at it.

He slapped her ass, and she giggled before removing her long legs from around his waist. Angel bent to wrestle his pants back over his ass when the moonlight caught his hair. I froze and studied the strands a little harder.

They weren't dark locks.

They were blonde. And longer.

It wasn't Angel who shamelessly fucked and made me watch. Hands suddenly closed around my hips and yanked me by my lower half. I screamed against my gag, but the sound was too muffled to mean anything.

The man, who was clearly Z, sat back and watched with a smile. His pearly white teeth shone through the dark, mocking me at the same time I felt hips press into my ass. I yelled against my gag, but it didn't make him stop. He pulled me into him and pressed his hips hard. I felt him again and again and realized I was being fucked.

It felt so real.

The only free movement I had was my head. I thrashed it about wildly until a hand shoved my face into the bed, all the while the phantom hips moved against my ass, and I felt his cock through the fabric of his pants. My body came alive while my brain screamed to fight a second before I heard him groan. Silence followed. He stopped moving, but I could still feel his body pressed against mine. Suddenly, I felt his breath tickling my ear and then a long, slow lick up the shell of my ear. "Enjoy the show?"

Angel.

CHAPTER 35

Maybe she needs you.

ANGEL

I NEVER INTENDED to touch her. Her body fell once she didn't have my hands to hold her up.

"Damn..." Z spoke from my right. I glared at him when I noticed his attention fixated on Mian. The whore I hired was gone, so he must have sent her away. "That was hot as fuck."

My stomach turned with regret and desire.

I fucked up.

But even knowing the truth, I still wanted more.

Touching her wasn't part of the plan, but touching her against her will? That made me afraid to face myself.

 Just what the fuck was she doing to me and why was I allowing her?

"I know what's going through your head right now, but she asked for this when she escaped." Z clapped his hand on my shoulder, and it took everything not to shove it off. I was disgusted with myself, but I wouldn't show it by snubbing my best friend. I continued to watch Mian, whose breathing turned even and deep. She must have passed out from exhaustion. I hired the whore to fuck with Mian's head and ended up fucking with my own. I couldn't keep my eyes off her. Bound and gagged, she still found a way to fight. It made my dick harder than any live show. Each time I saw her body was like the first time, but seeing her naked and bound made me want to convince her to forget we were enemies for just one night. She still wanted me even though she didn't want to. How hard could it be to convince her? I've owned her desire since the moment she first knew what it felt like coursing through her veins.

"What are you going to do now?" Z questioned when I didn't respond. I scrubbed my hand down my face and forced my gaze away from her.

"I'm going to go to sleep."

"Next to her?"

I answered by stripping off my clothes. Mian wasn't the only one who deserved punishment.

I WOKE UP just as she was slipping from the bed, and I grinned. It seemed we were starting early. Reaching out, I caught her ankle and held on when she kicked out to dislodge my hand.

"Let me go," she growled.

"Not a chance."

She gave up trying to kick my hand away and snatched the lamp from the night table. Her swing was swift and missed my head by a hair. Wildly, she swung again, but I lunged and took her down.

"You have a lot of anger toward me even though it's my bed you slept in last night."

"Which is exactly why I'm going to kill you." We tore up the bed fighting for dominance. I won, of course, but she made winning fun. I pinned her arms to the bed and fit my hips between thighs. She was still trying to catch her breath, and I enjoyed the sight of her chest heaving up and down as she panted.

"You done yet?"

"You dead yet?"

I thrust my hips against her and lowered my head. "Does it feel like I'm dead?" My dick was hard enough to break a brick and was only getting harder. I shifted my grip to one hand and brought the other to her face, but the sight of blood stopped me. A quick glance over her revealed it wasn't her bleeding. My hand was bleeding at the juncture between my pointer and thumb. Without thinking, I sucked at the wound and looked down to see her watching me bleed without even a hint of remorse.

"This is the second time you've made me bleed."

She quirked an eyebrow. "You don't expect me to feel sorry, do you?"

Normally, her defiance amused me, but this time, I needed to see her yield. "You like my blood then?" Wisely, she chose to remain silent probably from the change in my tone, but it was too late to back down. I pulled the torn skin between my teeth until I tasted blood, and without warning, I closed the distance between us and stole her lips with mine.

She squealed and fought to dislodge me so I deepened the kiss until I was sure she tasted nothing but me... and my blood.

Only when I had no choice but to let her up for air did I end the kiss.

She stared up at me in shock, but it was her dilated pupils that stole my interest, and I was willing to put my legacy and life on the wager that her pussy was wet. Even with my blood smeared at the corner of her lip...

"I want you."

She looked as shocked as I felt but recovered quickly.

"Good luck with that," she panted.

I smiled, but I could tell she didn't trust it by the suspicious look in her eyes. "I could have you if I wanted."

"Your stomach's too weak for rape. Pussy."

"For once, those sweet lips speak the truth." I ran my nose down her neck and inhaled as much of her as I could. "When I have you, I want you willing and eager."

She froze. "When?"

Her tone said there would never be a when, but her eyes said she was past ready. A knock on my door saved me from responding. I rolled off her just as Lucas and Z rushed through the door. They looked prepared to do battle as their gazes flitted from me to Mian to the bed.

"Gentlemen," she said when the silence stretched too long.

"What the hell happened in here?" Z gestured to the lamp tossed on the floor.

"I tried to bash his head in."

Their faces showed surprise and then they burst out laughing. Mian flinched, and quickly, her entire body stiffened when Lucas said, "Damn, girl. I bet you're a firecracker in the sack."

"You'll never know."

"You know better than to make promises you can't keep," he flirted.

She scoffed and turned away, but her entire body flushed red. She should have learned she couldn't hide from us when she was naked. Lucas and Z snickered while I stood from the bed. "Return our guest to her room. She's overstayed her welcome here."

I HAD TO force last night and this morning from my head. Having her sleep so close to me was an amazing test of control that I passed until this morning.

Now, I stood with Lucas and Z in one of the guest rooms surrounding the girl we took from her bed while she was sleeping.

"So how do you know Mian?"

"I told you we're friends."

"And neighbors," I added.

"Obviously." She rolled her eyes but then sat up straight at the look in mine. "Why am I here?"

"You're here because of Mian. She took something from me, and I intend to get it back."

"Mian wouldn't do that."

"Apparently, she would, or we wouldn't be standing here right now."

"What does this have to do with me?" She flinched, and I could tell by the regret in her eyes that she felt guilty.

"You're incentive."

"For what?"

"To give me back what belongs to me."

"And what belongs to you?" she asked warily.

"My legacy." I could see her confusion but didn't bother to elaborate. The fewer people who knew about the book, the better. Those pages were power and the only rightful heir to that power was me.

"So what will you do with me?"

"In due time."

"And until then?"

I looked to Lucas and nodded. He left and came back moments later carrying Caylen. She didn't hesitate to rush forward and to take him carefully from Lucas's arms.

"Why do you have him?" she cried and clutched Caylen closer. She backed away while her frantic gaze moved between us, probably to determine the most dangerous threat.

Lucas swore. "How old is this girl? She barely looks old enough to take care of herself."

"He's right," Z added. "I don't think we should trust her with him. She'll run first chance she gets. Mian did."

I stared at Mian's friend and weighed my options. The kid had been fussy the past few days even though he'd been kept warm, fed, and clothed. The thought that maybe he missed his mother entered my mind, so I set him up in a temporary room in the west wing with Mian. I knew she could hear his cries when she began beating at the door and walls and yelling threats. I had no doubt he was the reason she pulled her little escape attempt.

Lucas stared hard at the girl until she began to fidget. "What do you think, little one? You gonna run?"

"Probably," she answered honestly.

"Even if it means he'll slit your friend's throat the moment you do?" She gasped, took another step back, and pulled Caylen closer to her chest.

Her frightened eyes turned to me. "You wouldn't really do that, would you?" Fuck... How old *was* this girl? Innocence was written all over her.

I took a step toward her. "Do you really want to find out?" Her blonde locks tossed about as she vigorously shook her head. "Then we have an arrangement?"

"Yes," she replied instantly.

My gaze narrowed as I inspected her. "How old are you?"

She glanced in Z's direction before moving to Lucas. Her gaze rested on him for a fraction longer before flitting back to me.

"I'm twenty-one."

I gazed into her big brown innocent eyes and knew she was lying.

I decided to see how it would all play out and had Lucas and Z set her up in the nursery. I escaped to my father's office to think. I had only a few days left to get Mian to talk, but a part of me was beginning to believe her. I practically raised her myself and knew her like the back of my hand. She would put her son before money.

"Penny for your thoughts?" Lucas cracked.

"We need to find a way to get her to talk. I'm starting to think..." I stopped because once I said the words, I couldn't take them back.

"What?" Z questioned. I could detect a little hostility in his tone. "That she didn't do it? Of course, she did."

"You don't know her."

"But I know how far a woman with a kid to feed is willing to go."

"She's not your mother." The words were out before I could swallow them back. Z didn't ever talk about his mother, but the little we did get out of him was so ugly that no one blamed him. He was taken in by the state at the age of thirteen and placed in foster care when it was discovered that he had become the caretaker of his drug-addicted mother after her pimp—his father—abandoned them both for a less broken model. She fucked, sucked, and stole to keep him fed and alive until the drugs completely took over and she faded into nothing.

"I'm well aware my mother is dead," he snarled.

Behind Z's easy smile was a temper that not even I dared to test. His father was a tool, but his mother screwed him over real good after he vanished.

"Fuck." I blew out a breath and ran my fingers through my hair. "I'm sorry, man. I'm just—"

"Forget about it," he said and waved me off.

"Let me suggest something," Lucas cut in.

"What's that?"

"You."

"Me?"

"As pleasant as we find Mian's company, maybe she needs someone closer to convince her. As you've said, you know her. We don't. You know how far and hard to push and what makes her tick. Mian's weakness is her son, sure, but she knows you aren't willing to go that far. She's already called your bluff by not talking."

"So we're at a stalemate."

"Not even close. Her kid isn't her only soft spot. The girl loves her father, does she not?"

I was already turning him down. "I'm not ready to kill Theo."

"We don't need to kill him. We just need to push her into a corner with no way out."

CHAPTER 36

No way out.

MIAN

I SPENT TWO days watching the door. Even in my sleep, I dreamed of him walking through that door. It wasn't desire that made me anxious for his presence. It was the growing sense of doom that kept me awake at night. When the door finally opened, and he sauntered through, I knew instantly the bad feeling deep in my stomach wasn't unfounded.

He shut the door and helped himself to a seat on the bare mattress. He was dressed in a burgundy waistcoat and tailored black slacks. "How are you, Mian?"

"Sick to my stomach and having this feeling that you have something to do with that."

"Ah."

"So?"

"So..."

"Why are you here?"

He rubbed the trimmed scruff adorning his lower jaw and looked at

me with something akin to compassion in his eyes. "I wanted to show you one last mercy. Tell me where the book is."

"I don't—" I started to deny when he held up his hand, effectively silencing me.

"Before you answer, know, this time, your lies will cost you more than you're willing to pay."

"What does that mean?"

"Pray you won't have to find out. Now, tell me where the book is."

"I told you before. I don't know what you're talking about."

Instead of threatening or crowding me to intimidate me into giving up answers I didn't have, he hung his head, exhaled, and then spoke into his phone. "Do it."

Tears poured from my eyes and my heart stopped and plummeted from my chest to my feet. *What did I do?* I heard faint words that sounded something like, "My baby," and realized it was me who spoke the words brokenly.

"No, not your son." He held out his hand to me. "Come and see."

I went. I didn't take his hand, and he didn't seem to care. He simply curled it around my waist and tugged me down onto his lap. He held the phone away from me and as soon as I was settled, he locked his arm around me so I couldn't move and held up his phone. There was a live video feed and the story it told had me drawing back in horror. There was no sound, and I was grateful for small favors as I watched a man be savagely kicked and punched into an unrecognizable pulp.

"What is this?" I looked away, but he grabbed my chin and forced my gaze back.

"This is the price you pay." I squinted when the camera stopped jostling enough to bring it to focus, and I studied the broken man leaning against the dull gray wall. Blood covered almost every inch of his face, and as I studied him, closer recognition dawned.

"Daddy?" My heart raced, and the funny feeling in my stomach must have been fear. They continued to beat him even when he stopped fighting back. "Stop them!"

"You haven't paid in full."

"Angel, please! They'll kill him."

"If that's what it takes," he coldly answered.

I struggled to free myself and then to look away, but he held my face steady. "I don't have your book! Just please stop! Please!"

"Do you know what happens after your father dies? You'll be next. My grandfather wants your head, and he'll take it, book or no book. Do you want to leave your son an orphan?"

"Don't touch my son." My voice was a lot calmer than the rage that stormed free inside of me.

"I won't kill him. I'll leave him to a far worse fate. My family will expect nothing less."

"Then I'll destroy your entire line."

"Time's ticking, Sprite. You'll be dead in a week."

I turned my body enough to bring him into view. I wanted him to see just how much I meant my next words.

"And I'll haunt you from the moment I take my last breath to the moment you take yours."

I glimpsed in his eyes and saw something more telling than fear.

Emptiness.

CHAPTER 37

Plan B.

ANGEL

MIAN WAS OUT of time.

Tonight was the night of the ball, and my grandfather was expecting her head. She might have been innocent, but without the book, there was nothing I could do to save her. Her death wasn't only about the book. It also meant vengeance for Grandfather for his son's death. I wanted the same, but the eagerness to take her life had faded.

I stared at my mother's gown. She had an impressive collection, but this one was by far the plainest. The gown was simple, and the color made it a perfect choice for Mian to die

 in. My mother wouldn't appreciate one of her expensive pieces being ruined, but she chose to leave it behind along with my father's memory.

I spent the day holed up in my father's office trying to come to terms with what would happen tonight.

Mian's insistence that she didn't steal the book didn't add up. I threatened her life, her son's, and her father's, but she didn't budge. It was not like her to put self-gain before someone she cared deeply for... even if they were undeserving. My decision to leave her father alive didn't come easily when I could have so easily had him killed, but it wasn't the right time. I wanted to look into his eyes when he died so it would be the memory of me that tortured him in hell.

When I couldn't settle the sense that I was making a mistake, I left my office in search of Z. Lucas had already left to escort my mom from the airport. Even though Victor flew in with her, my mother would expect my interference. In Florida, she was Victor's wife, but here in Chicago, she was still my father's widow.

I found Z in the den sitting in complete darkness. The only light came from the laptop he worked on. He looked up when I entered, closed his computer, and set it away with ease. I picked up on his subtle attempt to hide what he was working on and made a mental note to ask him about it later.

"I need a favor from you, brother. Off the record."

"What's up?"

I took a seat and stared off into the distance before coming to a decision. "I need your skills to find another answer. I need to know that we've ruled out every possibility."

He was silent for several long moments, and I wondered if he was piecing together what we were asking. When he finally spoke, it was low and hesitant. "Do you know what you're asking me to do?" I waited for him to explain because I really didn't understand. "You're asking me to try to save Mian's life. Is that really what you want?"

His question all but stopped my beating heart.

Was he right?

Was this one last desperate attempt to spare the life of the girl I could never have? Her death was more than just retribution for a stolen legacy and loss of power. It was retaliation against the man who took my father's life. It was a score to settle, not just for me, but for Z and Lucas, as well. Art became a father to them the day he took them off the streets.

But looking in Z's eyes, I didn't see anger or accusation. I saw understanding I didn't deserve. I wasn't Mian's knight in shining armor. I was her executioner.

Z cleared his throat and turned his laptop toward me. He gestured to the screen that was littered with windows I didn't understand.

"I was already looking," he said simply.

CHAPTER 38

When the hour strikes...

MIAN

I WAS PRIMPED and painted, and this time, when I wore the dress, it hugged my body perfectly. The beading adorning the gown was exquisite. I ran my fingers over the intricate design while Madame Torre fussed and barked orders at the Ricardos. I dreaded what the evening could bring, but was grateful to finally have my body covered, with the exception of my shoulders. The gown was truly beautiful. Black wouldn't have been my first choice of color, but oddly it didn't detract.

"Do you like it?" I didn't turn around to greet the man behind the sinfully deep voice. I wasn't ready to face him after what he did. "It was my mother's."

"It's beautiful," I admitted reluctantly.

"I want to see all of you," he said after Madame Torre and the Ricardos had left, and I kept my back to him. If he were anyone else, I would have

blushed at the request, but he wasn't anyone else, and I knew better. He didn't seduce. He commanded. I turned carefully in the high black and silver stems and rested my hands on my waist for balance when I caught sight of him looking debonair in a black tux. His hair was perfectly gelled and combed into a fashionable design and the hair on his jaw and chin were freshly trimmed to accentuate his strong jaw.

He took his time inspecting me, too. My hair was pulled back so the curls Mohawk Ricardo had skillfully created fell down my back. My makeup was applied sparingly. Goatee Ricardo had focused on accentuating my eyes, which he complimented repeatedly. Even covered in layers of silk, he still managed to make me feel naked. It was as if the heat in his eyes seared away the layers.

"So? Do I satisfy your taste for arm candy?"

He smiled a feral smile. "What makes you think you'll be my date?"

No sane part of me wanted to be his date, but it didn't make the rejection hurt any less. "Then what am I?"

"You're the final act." He closed the distance between us and then flipped open a royal blue box. The most beautiful diamond choker rested on a velvet bed before he plucked it from the case and tossed it away. I didn't move as he stepped around me and wrapped it around my neck. It was so heavy and cold against my skin. When I heard the clasp click, I fingered the necklace and wondered if it was real. It seemed too extravagant, even for the Knights.

I was surprised when something settled over my face. He quickly secured it and then stepped away while I fingered what must have been a mask. It was hard but bearable since it didn't weigh much. I wanted a mirror so I could see and thought about stepping inside the bathroom for a peek, but the jerk held out his arm, offering me the crook of his elbow, and waited for me to accept with a quirk of his eyebrow. I cupped the muscle underneath his finery and stared ahead in horror when my pussy reacted to the feel of his muscles bunched beneath the tux. It had to be a natural response—like drowning when water fills your lungs. I did *not* desire this man.

Outside, there was a limo waiting. Lucas flashed me a sexy smile while I admired him in the black tux. He held a thick black box in his hand, and I was curious about what was inside.

"You look good enough to eat, pretty girl." He bit his bottom lip and eyed me. I had the feeling he was imagining doing just that. Lucas opened the back door, and I ducked inside. He then followed and took a seat on the bench across from me. Angel sat next to me, forcing me to curl up against the opposite door. I heard the locks engage as if I were really going to jump from a moving vehicle.

"So, Mian, why aren't you in college?" Lucas questioned after we'd been riding for some time. He reached for the chilled champagne and poured a glass.

"I had a kid," I answered coolly.

He shrugged. "Single mothers can still attend school. There are programs, aren't there?"

"It's so easy to assume anyone can still conquer the world with a baby on their hip. The world is full of failures and rejects. Programs can't save us all. If they could, the world would be a much more colorful place."

"Didn't you have relatives to help you?"

I noticed Angel's head cock slightly. He must have been interested in my answer. If he knew about my aunt and uncle, he wouldn't hesitate to use them against me. I pressed a hand to my stomach. When they turned their backs on me, there was no love lost, but that didn't mean I wanted to see them dead.

"My grandparents are dead."

"Theo had to leave you with someone since you weren't in the system."

Damn. "I never had family other than my father's brother and his wife. My mother was an only child."

"So he left you with them?"

I nodded not really wanting to talk about them but found the words spilling out anyway. "He had to pay them to accept me but, yeah... they were my guardians before Caylen was born."

"Before?"

I took a deep breath slowly released. I could feel Angel watching my every move. "They kicked me out after they found out I was pregnant." Angel made a sound I couldn't describe. I found his eyes black and spitting fire. "You thought I ran away, didn't you?" He didn't answer. He didn't have to. Before he turned his head to stare out the window, I saw guilt in his eyes.

Why would Angel feel guilty? He stopped being responsible for me when his father convinced mine to send me home. I thought the day Daddy left me with him was the worst thing he could ever do to me, but it couldn't compare to the day he took him away from me. How hormones and a little kindness changes things...

We spent the rest of the ride in silence. I looked out the window in amazement when the house came into view. The lush green land stretched far and wide around the castle. It made Arturo Knight's home seem like a trailer home.

"What is this place," I heard myself asking.

"It's home," Angel answered.

He was staring when I looked away to face him. "Home?"

"The Knight Estate. It was built over a century ago by the second Knight."

"Aren't there more of you in your family?"

He shook his head. "*The* Knight not a Knight."

"I'm not following."

"The Knight is the head of the family. The head of the family will only ever be The Bandit." It sounded like a riddle, which I strangely got. The real legacy must be his place as The Bandit. The book he thinks I stole was just a shiny crown.

"So why don't you live here?" He didn't claim his father's home, and I knew now it was because it never truly felt like home to him.

"Because the house can only be inherited after the death of The Knight."

"And since your father died before your grandfather could—" When our gazes met, words were lost.

"Something else your father took from mine... *and me.*"

His hate was my truth. I could feel it as if it coursed through my veins. I turned away to admire the house as much as I could from the limited vantage point of the car. When the car slowly stopped, Angel took the box from Lucas. I watched, feeling my heart race, as he opened the box. He lifted a black leather mask from the box and secured it onto his face. When he turned to me, the top half of his face was covered by large wings that extended away from his face. The feathers were captured in amazing detail.

His eyes, lips, and jaw were the only visible parts of his face now. He looked sexy and scary all at once, and I was grateful my body was hidden under so many layers. He would have used my reaction as a weapon to take what he wanted.

The car was uncomfortably silent as we stared at one another. My face was hidden by a mask I had yet to see, and now, so was he. Suddenly, Angel's door was opened, breaking our moment. He took my hand and helped me from the car. Nervously, I glanced around. The circular driveway was full as women in gowns and men in tux's poured from their limos and made their way inside.

Light shone from the white terra-cotta home through the spacious windows while music I didn't recognize, and hoped I didn't have to dance to, played through the open doorways.

Suddenly, the unexplained meaning of my presence here turned my legs to jelly. Prisoners didn't go to balls. Angel said I was the final act. What had he meant?

"Don't be scared, girl."

I turned to Lucas who grinned down at me. "Why would I be scared?" I was totally scared.

"Because you stopped walking and gave Angel no choice but to stop, too, or drag you." Angel's expression was curious as he stared down at me. I lifted my chin and walked ahead while ignoring the stares. It was then I noticed that no one else wore masks. Not even Lucas.

I was stopped from entering when we reached one of the three entryways and was asked my name. "She's with me," Angel answered. The man must not have noticed him standing just behind me. He sputtered to correct himself and lifted the red velvet rope.

Angel's hand fell on the small of my back. I couldn't feel anything else but the place where his hand and my back met.

As he led me through the grand foyer and mingling guests, his thumb caressed me.

We eventually made it past the stairs and through another set of open doors into a ballroom. Guests danced under the chandeliers to the soft music. The ballroom floor looked bigger than my entire apartment. There were people mingling on the sidelines with drinks in their hands as they talked and laughed. A stunning blonde in blue gossamer caught Lucas's attention. He broke off to pull her onto the dance floor.

"Where's Z?" I'd only just noticed a member of their trio had been missing.

Angel selected a champagne flute from a passing waiter and handed it to me. "Why?" His gaze was steady as he ignored the guests around us and waited for my answer. I shrugged after noticing how tense he became. "He'll be joining us later."

"Why am I here?"

"I told you."

"That isn't an answer."

"It's the only one you're going to get." He nodded to the untouched glass in my hand. "Drink."

"Why should I?" I didn't feel right enjoying a party with the man who held my son's life and mine in his control.

"Because it could be your last." He watched me from behind his mask. I didn't get the feeling he was playing a game, so I tipped the glass back and let the cool liquid caress my tongue and throat.

Suddenly, a man with thick white hair and beard appeared at Angel's side and clapped him on the back. "Nice of you to join us, son."

"I had last-minute business to attend," he answered back without warmth, and I wondered how he knew him.

"You're the guest of honor. It doesn't do well to be late to your own party."

This was a party for Angel?

"I'm here, aren't I?"

Rather than answer, the man's gaze slid to me, and suddenly, I felt like I was under a microscope. "Hello, Mian."

I was taken aback. "You know who I am?"

"Of course, my dear. You caused quite an upheaval for my family. Not to mention, your father killed my son." He spoke dispassionately—and that scared me more than if he had yelled. Alon Knight's eyes were blank and without feeling. I searched for the right response, but really, what was one to say at a party when the host accused you of crimes you didn't commit?

Thankfully, Lucas saved me from responding. He sauntered into our circle with the blonde.

"Mr. Knight," he respectfully greeted.

"Lucas..." Alon's gaze coldly assessed the woman on his arm. "I see once again you do not hesitate at indulging in all the party has to offer."

"You know me. I never miss an opportunity to spend the night between a beautiful pair of legs."

"It's good my grandson does not share your sentiments."

Lucas didn't react, but I was willing to bet if he wasn't Angel's grandfather, and we weren't standing in a room full of people, that he would have been a dead man. "Always a pleasure, Alon."

Alon didn't seem to appreciate either one of our presence, but Lucas was still my enemy so I didn't want to laugh, but a smile snuck up on me anyway. I ducked my head, but when I lifted it again, Lucas caught my eyes. There was a twinkle in his as he winked.

"Mian, may I have this dance?"

He didn't wait for me to deny him. He took my hand and guided me onto the dance floor away from Angel and Alon. When we reached the center of the room, he tugged me close and wrapped his arm around my waist.

I looked back in time to see Angel and Alon leaving the ballroom. "So I take it he's not your favorite person?"

He snorted and twirled me before bringing me close again. "He's a prick, girl. Stay away from him."

My eyebrows shot for my hairline. "You're warning me?"

His face settled into a blank mask, and we continued to dance. Suddenly, he pulled me even closer. His arm tightened until I gasped.

"Why are you doing this?"

I frowned. "I'm not doing anything. I *haven't done* anything.

"Just tell him where the book is. No amount of money is worth your life, girl."

"I don't. Have. The book. I don't even know what the book is."

His face said he didn't believe me as his eyes searched mine. He seemed to decide something and relaxed his arm.

"No shit?"

"Why is this book so important to him? What makes it a legacy?"

"Because it's not just a book. It's a contract."

"A contract," I repeated. "How's that?"

"The book contains a record of every job, client, and contact since Alexander Knight."

"The first Knight," I guessed. He nodded. "Why would they keep something like that? It's a criminal justice wet dream."

"That's one way of looking at it, but the book has been untouched by anyone who wasn't the Knight for almost two-hundred years. Until you."

"That still doesn't tell me why his family would keep something so incriminating."

"Because it's power. It can start wars, break allegiances, and cripple empires. The entries will incriminate anyone who's every laid in bed with a Knight."

"It imprisons them."

"Yeah, girl. It does."

"But that includes you, doesn't it?" He shrugged and moved his hand down to cup my ass. I didn't welcome his touch, but I didn't fight it either. He ran his lips down my neck until it reached my shoulder. "You'll never be able to walk away."

"I have no intentions of walking away. I owe Art my life."

"But not Angel?"

He lifted his head and pinned me with his stare. "He's my best friend. His father gave me a job when everyone else overlooked Z and me like trash. *I'd die for him.*"

"It doesn't sound like friendship. It sounds like servitude to me."

"I'm no one's slave, girl. If I ever wanted to walk away, Angel couldn't stop me, and I know for a fact that he wouldn't try. *That* is why I'm loyal."

We danced some more in silence and by the end of the third song, I'd had enough. "Where's the bathroom?" I asked as an excuse to get away.

"I'll escort you."

"So I'm still in shackles," I said as he guided me through the dancing crowd.

"Afraid so." His hand didn't leave the small of my back until we reached a quiet corner. There was a single door, and I assumed it led to a bathroom. "Sure you don't need any help?"

I started to respond, but the words were caught in my throat. Three men dressed in black suits rushed for Lucas. He couldn't see them, but he could see me. His grin disappeared just as I went to shout a warning. Two of them jumped him.

"Don't!" I screamed as they savagely beat him. I didn't even see the third lunge for me until my scream was cut off by his hand covering my mouth. I fought him, which loosened my mask until it fell from my face. I stared at the black feathers detailed into the leather and realized I was staring at a replica of Angel's. I was too stunned to fight and was dragged away. The last thing I saw before being pulled around a corner was Lucas sending the head of one of the attackers into the wall.

CHAPTER 39

...will she live?

ANGEL

THE BAD FEELING in the pit of my stomach wouldn't go away. My grandfather insisted on talking to me in his office. I had been reluctant to let Mian out of my sight, but then reminded myself that my protection was not hers to have. She wasn't leaving this party alive. I needed to remember that.

"What did you need to talk about?"

"I take it you have not recovered the book."

"She's not talking."

"I see. And do you have any other leads?"

"Not even a crumble."

"Then you're prepared to do your duty tonight?"

"She's not dressed in black because I like the color."

He nodded and clapped me on the shoulder. "Good. Now I have a speech to give. Join me."

I followed him back to the party, but as we passed the entrance, I noticed Z arguing with security. He had the man's shirt in his fists and lifted him off the ground just as we passed. Z's hair was standing on end like he'd tried to pull it from the roots. He even still wore his jeans and t-shirt.

When Z saw me approach, he shoved the guard away. Time was running out, so I cut to the chase. "Did you find something?"

"Where is she?" He looked around frantically, and his skin went pale.

"She's with Lucas." I caught the relief in his eyes as some of his color returned to his skin.

"What did you find?"

"She didn't do it. She *couldn't* have done it."

"What—"

The music suddenly cut, plunging the party into silence, and stealing my attention.

Fuck. The speech.

"Later," I said to Z and gestured for him to follow me. We made our way to the top of the stairs where my grandfather presided over his guests. I stood by his side like the dutiful grandson. Even though I was the Knight, I paid grandfather respect as my elder and was willing to let him take the lead when I didn't need to.

"Many of you are Knights, and many of you are friends," Grandfather began. "Nonetheless, we are all here to celebrate the year which marks two hundred years of prosperity. My grandson, as you know, has taken his rightful place as The Bandit and The Knight, but I am thankful to still be alive to deliver this speech..."

I drowned my grandfather out and searched the crowd for Mian and Lucas. I couldn't see them anywhere even though everyone in attendance had gathered in the foyer and on the stairs for the speech.

That feeling in my stomach intensified, but the hairs on my skin stood up when I tuned into my grandfather's next words.

"I hope even after my death, the next two hundred years are as successful as the first, and that responsibility starts with my grandson who recognizes that *family*," his gaze met mine, "will always mean sacrifice."

I heard the gunshot and recognized the satisfaction in my grandfather's gaze.

I was already running by the time the screams started.

CHAPTER 40

Everything's different now.

MIAN

I STARED AT the hole in the man's head while his face froze from death just before he dropped to the floor.

He tried to shoot me.

He *would* have shot me.

Lucas rushed forward and picked me up from the floor. I couldn't believe he just saved me. "What just happened?"

"He was going to kill you, so I stopped him," he answered gruffly. He looked down at me as he walked swiftly for the door of the room I'd been dragged into. "You got a problem with that?"

"Why did you save me?"

"It didn't feel right to let you die."

"It didn't *feel* right?" He grunted his response. Lucas saving me didn't make sense. The moment I looked into Alon's eyes, I could feel my mother surrounding me. Her arms pulled me in as she welcomed me home.

I knew then that Angel planned my death that night.

Without Caylen, I might have accepted death, but I remembered Angel's promise regarding my son's fate. I couldn't give up and leave him to his mercy. I'd hoped the bathroom would allow me time and space to plot an escape. But then Lucas was beaten, I was dragged away, and a gun was pointed at my head.

And then I was saved.

By Lucas.

He ran with me still in his arms. The closer we made it back to the party, the more vivid the screams became, and I realized they weren't in my head. The gunshot must have frightened the guests, and I wondered if Alon would blame me for ruining his celebration.

Then again, those men had attacked Lucas, which meant the attack couldn't have been Angel's doing...

Without warning, I was roughly pulled from Lucas's arms. I was wary of everyone, and so I fought even when I realized the arms I had been pulled into belonged to Angel. My gaze swept over his uncovered face. With the mask gone, his anger was palpable. But it was the fear I saw that made me stop fighting him.

What reason would Angel have to be afraid?

"Are you hurt?" he demanded. His voice was so hoarse and thick that if I wasn't so in tune with him, I wouldn't have understood him.

"You sent that man to kill me," I accused. Even though I suspected Angel's intention, a part of me had believed he would never actually go through with it. A part of me believed he was still the boy who made me fight my battles.

"No, Sprite. I didn't."

"Why should I believe you?" His heart was beating fast. I could feel it under my palm.

He ran his hand through my hair and rested his forehead on mine. "You just have to," he whispered softly.

"What is going on here?" I unconsciously pulled Angel closer at the sound of Alon's voice. Unfortunately, Angel chose to set me on my feet just before facing off with his grandfather. It didn't escape my notice that he moved his body to block me from Alon's view. I felt Lucas's presence close in behind me. I didn't notice Z until he moved to stand close by my side. I was completely surrounded by them.

What was happening?

"You went behind my back?" Angel spoke calmly, but I could hear the chill in his tone. Men also dressed in suits surrounded Alon with their guns pointed. There were too many of them for even Angel to outmatch.

"Of course, I did. I couldn't trust you to pull the plug given your feelings for the girl."

I stiffened. Angel didn't have feelings for me. In the place where his heart should have been was an organ that only understood power and revenge.

"That wasn't your call." He didn't bother to correct his grandfather regarding his feelings.

"It is my job to protect this family."

"No, old man. I respect you because you are my grandfather, but *I* am the Knight. Your reign has ended."

"And yours will too if you let this girl come between your senses of duty."

"She didn't do it," he growled. I gasped and felt my fingers tremble against my lips.

"Ten minutes ago, you weren't so sure."

"Some information was recently brought to my attention. I'll bring you up to speed, but regardless of what I decide, you *will* fall back in line."

The authority in Angel's tone caused the heat in my belly to spread to my legs. More words were exchanged, but I didn't catch any of it.

Angel believed me.

Did this mean he would finally let us go?

THE BEDROOM DOOR opening woke me from my sleep. Even with my newfound innocence, finding sleep hadn't come easy. Maybe it was the strange house I was forced to sleep in or my near death experience. Angel had Lucas lock me in one of the many bedrooms while Angel, Z, and Alon disappeared to discuss my life. I remember being angry before I fell asleep. My fate would be decided in a meeting between men who should have never had that power.

"I know you're awake."

"And the award for the creepiest moment goes to..." I could feel him standing over me, so I sat up. My dress shifted and tangled around my legs as I moved.

"Almost dying hasn't affected your mouth." His gaze sexily dropped to my lips. I picked at the silk and tried to guess why he was here. When I couldn't stand the silence anymore, I just asked.

"Why are you here?"

He sat on the side of the bed, and I noticed he was still dressed in his tux. He ran his fingers through his hair, and I wanted, at least once, to follow the tracks he made with my own fingers.

"Don't you want to know what happened?" I was too busy staring at his stupid, gorgeous hair to notice he was staring.

"What happened?"

"Z saved your life." His frown was troubled as he stared deep into my eyes. Did he not like the idea of not having a reason to kill me?

"Sorry to spoil your fun," I mumbled. The look he gave me was impatient even though he had done nothing but assure me I would die. I cleared my throat when his stare became uncomfortable. "So what changed?"

"I never considered that I had been outsmarted."

"I'm not following."

"There's a silent alarm that's routed to Lucas, Z, or myself whenever triggered. You tripped that alarm the day you broke in."

"And?"

"The alarm was disarmed and reactivated the day before you broke in."

Which meant he'd been betrayed.

"Why didn't you pick this up before?"

"We missed it."

"And so you kidnapped my son."

He rolled his eyes. "Well, you did break into my house."

I decided to ignore that. "Even so... what makes you so sure that I'm innocent?"

"Because whoever deactivated the alarm wouldn't take the time to reactivate it unless they were trying to hide something... and whoever knew about the alarm had to know about the book."

"So does this mean you're going to let us go?" He avoided my gaze when he didn't answer. "Angel?"

"Why didn't you come to me?"

I was caught off guard. "Pardon?"

"When you were in trouble. Why didn't you come to me?" My mouth opened to speak, but words didn't come. "I wouldn't have abandoned you like your aunt and uncle did."

"But isn't that what you did long before I got pregnant?"

"My father had just been murdered by your father. What did you expect?"

"Friendship." He flinched. I knew he didn't expect my answer, but it was the truth. "I know you were hurt, but I wasn't the one to pull the trigger."

"I know."

"Then how could you expect me to run to you at the first sign of trouble?"

"Because you should have known me better than that," he gritted.

"Yeah? Then where were you?"

"Grieving." He moved closer to me and in a desperate attempt to keep space between us, my back hit the mattress. He caged me in by leaning over and resting his hand on the other side of my body. "My father wasn't winning any awards, but he was the only one I had."

"I know. I lost my mother too, remember?"

"You loved your mother," he pointed out as if there was a difference.

"Didn't you love your father?"

He frowned, and I sensed he was sincerely confused. "I'm not sure."

Art was never cruel, but he had a lot of rough edges. He was a formidable man, and even dead, I could see some of him living through his son.

"You can't blame your father for the bad decisions you made after he died."

"Why can't I?" I could have sworn his mouth moved closer when he spoke. My heart stuttered before picking up speed.

"Because I'm not buying it."

"Then what will you buy?"

I saw it then. He was closing the distance between us. I could feel the beginning of panic rising in my chest.

"My freedom," I whispered truthfully. I needed to get away from him. Formidable Angel couldn't break me, but sweet Angel would wreck me.

"And how much are you willing to pay?" His hand clutched the layers of silk and pushed them up my legs. We were riding fast with no brakes with a dangerous cliff up ahead.

He wanted my body as payment for freedom?

Haven't I already paid enough?

I pushed against his chest, and since he wasn't expecting it, he fell back enough for me to scramble from underneath him.

"What—"

"What the hell do you think you're doing?"

"Something I should have done a long time ago."

"You're insane if you think I'll let you touch me and I'll kill you if you try."

"Fall apart with me, and maybe I'll let you." If his promise didn't tempt me, then it was definitely the way he watched me as he stood from the bed. "Come here." When I didn't move, he removed his phone from his pocket and set it on the nightstand.

"I'm not leaving, and neither are you. I told Lucas to lock the door behind me."

"Why would you do that?"

"Because I wanted to be alone with you."

"You and I both know that's not a good idea."

His grin was wide and bright. "Because you can't resist me?"

Yes. "Don't flatter yourself."

He didn't respond and walked around the bed. I was tempted to crawl to the other side to keep my distance, but running would only amuse him. So, stupidly, I stood my ground, and when he got close, I held my breath.

"Never a dull moment with you, Sprite."

"I assure you I don't want to be entertaining."

"Nevertheless..." He reached behind me and tugged free the tiny buttons holding the dress together. Soon I was naked with nothing but my hands to cover me. When he took them and placed them on his chest, I knew I was screwed. "Now undress *me*."

"Why would I do that?" I questioned. My hands wouldn't move from his chest, so did it really matter?

"I don't want anything between us."

"But captors don't sleep with their prisoners." He took my chin in his hand and gently lifted my face. There was no regret in his gaze. Only desire.

He pressed his lips against mine, and I got a taste of the alcohol on his tongue before he pulled back. "Things are different now." His gaze dropped to my hard nipples. "Much different."

CHAPTER 41

It's over.

MIAN

THREE YEARS AGO

WE SNATCHED APART.

I felt my cheeks flush with embarrassment and guilt. Angel turned away so I couldn't see his face, but I noticed him adjust his shorts. I could blame what I had almost done on the shotguns, but I knew it wouldn't be true. I started to feel something foreign for Angel the day he made me beat up my bully. It took me months to admit I was crushing on him.

I was surprised when he took my hand and led me downstairs. I didn't think it was a good idea for our fathers to see us like this. He must have thought the same because he dropped my hand when we entered the living room where Daddy and Uncle Art waited. Daddy was busy looking out the window, but Art's attention was fixed on where our joined hands had been. Had he seen?

My skin prickled with that feeling of being watched and realized it was Art who was now watching me. Being

the center of his attention was too intimidating, so I looked away. I wasn't all that sure the guilt of what we'd almost done upstairs wasn't visible.

"Son."

"Dad."

The air was cold as father and son faced off. They never seemed to be close, and I had a feeling Art's constant absence was to blame. Even so, Angel was more like his father than anyone would have guessed.

"Baby girl," my father warmly greeted. His arms were open as he moved away from the window. Like a true father's girl, I rushed into them like I hadn't just seen him hours ago. My anger over him leaving again was forgotten. Over the last two weeks, I became the center of his world again while Angel took a break. I didn't doubt that it was me he needed a break from. He was only supposed to be gone a week, but much to Art's irritation, he was gone for two.

"I thought you had to leave? Are you staying longer?" I asked with hope in my voice. The pain in his eyes told me my answer before he spoke. "It's okay if you can't. I know—"

A mocking laugh cut short the excuse I was willing to make for my father. Angel watched our exchange with his face twisted from disgust.

"This isn't your business," Daddy growled.

Angel didn't appear fazed. "Mian is my business. She certainly isn't yours."

"Angeles!" His father roared. I drew back, but Angel didn't even flinch. He never took his hard gaze from my dad. "Come with me to the kitchen." Angel didn't budge at first, but one look at me had him retreating to the kitchen with his father.

I was fighting back the tears even though I wasn't surprised. Over the years, Angel had become increasingly hostile toward Daddy. I didn't know if he truly cared about my father's absence in my life or if he was holding a grudge for being stuck with me.

"Baby girl." I didn't realize I was staring even after Angel disappeared until I heard my father call my name.

"Yes, Daddy?"

"You know I would stay if I could."

You can. You just don't want to. "I know." I smiled, but I didn't feel it. My father would leave me no matter what I said or felt, so I chose to be silent and numb.

"I enjoyed these last couple of weeks. You've grown into a young woman so fast." *Or maybe it's because I can count on one hand how many times a year I get to see you.* "You're old enough to take care of yourself now. Maybe better than I or anyone can."

I frowned and stared into my father's troubled eyes. What was he saying?

I didn't get to ask. That feeling whenever Angel was near had returned, and I found him hovering in the doorway. His glare was filled with hate and fixed on Daddy. I tore my attention away from Angel and found Daddy staring back. There was worry etched in his features.

"What's going on?" I directed to my father.

"Sprite." Angel wouldn't speak again until he had my full attention. "Let's go."

"What?"

"I want to get out of here. You coming?" The doorway was empty before I could even form a response. I stared at the empty space wondering what was happening. In minutes, it felt as if my entire world had shifted.

"You should go."

I faced my father again and let my disbelief shine through. "I should go?"

"He looks like he could use the company." When I continued to stare, he added, "Don't worry, baby girl. I'll be here when you get back."

"Uh... okay."

He smiled, but it was sad. "I love you."

"I love you, too." He kissed my forehead and then he was gone. The house was too silent. I took slow steps out of the house and found Angel standing by his car. His head hung, and his hands were shoved in his pockets. Suddenly, his head lifted, and I was surprised to find his eyes blank.

What the hell was going on? I slowly repeated to myself.

"Where are we going?"

"Pete's," he simply said and started down the block on foot. I fell in step next to him. Pete's had the best burgers in all of Chicago. It was only a couple of blocks away, and on weekends, you could find most of the neighborhood hanging around the restaurant since there was a skating rink next door.

Halfway there, memories of our kiss seeped into my mind. For a moment, he was almost mine.

I touched my lips and peeked up at him. He looked deep in thought, his body tense as he led us with long strides. When we got to Pete's, he chose our seats. We ordered as soon as the waiter came since we both always got the same thing. An extra cheesy bacon burger with a side of fries and a strawberry milkshake.

"Is everything okay?"

"Your father is a prick," he said through a french fry he was chewing.

"Do you hate him because of me?"

He shook his head and stuffed more fries in his mouth. If he wasn't so hot, I would be turned off by his lack of table manners. "I hate him because he's a prick."

"Your father ain't a peach either."

"I know, but the difference is, I don't care. You do."

"He's your father. Of course, you care."

"You don't know me, Sprite."

"I know you're a jerk," I muttered and sipped at my shake. When I looked up, I found him watching me... or rather, watching my lips around the straw. I don't know what made me do it, but I sucked a little harder and kept eye contact. The disgust on his face was not the reaction I was looking for. He threw down his napkin and sat back.

"You've got to be fucking kidding me."

I immediately let go of the straw. "What's wrong?"

"You're looking at me that way again."

I gulped. *Again?* Was he talking about today or every single day during the last five years? It started out as an innocent crush, which slowly turned into something that ached in my lower stomach. "I don't know what you're talking about."

"Oh, yes, you do."

"Ok then. How am I looking at you?"

"Like you want what I got, and I'm not talking about the food."

"I'm not sure I—"

He leaned over the table. "Listen to me," he growled. "It will never fucking happen. Do you know why?"

Stupidly, I shook my head.

"Because I do not *fuck* little girls." My gasp of embarrassment fell on deaf ears. "Jesus, I thought you were

345

cool." He stood up quickly, and his chair scraped across the floor, drawing attention and adding to my pain. "I'm in love with someone else. Stay away from me."

As soon as he pushed through the doors, I flew out of my seat for the bathroom and burst into the nearest stall to empty my guts.

He *was* capable of love.

Just not for me.

CHAPTER 42

Branded.

MIAN

PRESENT

I WOKE UP alone the next morning. I pulled the blanket tighter around me and willed myself to go back under when last night came rushing back. Memories of almost being killed and Angel's vow that everything was different now left me with a hangover worse than a night of drinking.

Angel's grandfather tried to kill me.

Lucas saved me.

Angel believed I was innocent.

Angel slept with me. And he didn't just sleep with me. He held me the entire night.

And I liked it.

I stretched and gazed at the sunlight coming through the window. I didn't hear the door open, and my back was turned so I couldn't see, but I felt him like I always did.

He came into view, and the first thing I noticed was the jeans he wore.

My body reacted involuntarily. It's been years since I've seen him in jeans, and it was no argument that he filled them out even better now. The second thing I noticed was the shopping bag he held in his hand.

He sat down in the space between the edge of the bed and me as he set the bag on the floor. "Good morning."

"Morning." I inwardly groaned at the deep, raspy sound of my voice. I sounded like a bear whose honey just got stolen.

"I had clothes brought for you."

I perked up. "Clothes?"

"And shampoo."

"Conditioner, too?"

God, were we actually rhyming? I groaned and covered my eyes with my hands. I peeked through my fingers and caught him staring at my chest. The blanket had slid down to reveal my bare breasts.

"What's the catch?" I asked because I wanted his eyes off my chest and because I didn't trust him.

"I'm happy to continue parading you around naked."

"Or you could just let me go."

He broke eye contact and rose from the bed. "Get dressed. You have an hour."

As soon as the door closed, I peeked inside the bag and pulled out a simple sky blue dress. It was strapless and short but not fitting enough to make it slutty. It looked like those skater dresses I saw girls wearing lately. There was a smaller pharmacy bag inside the shopping bag. I found shampoo, conditioner, lotion, shaving cream, a razor, shower gel, and a loofah. I finally felt excitement again at the thought of showering.

Now, the only thing I needed was a pair of underwear and a bra. I stuck my hand in the bag, and then my face—but found it empty. Once again, Angel had found a way to keep me prisoner.

I spent most of my time in the shower when I found the water warm. I even took the time to shave every nook and cranny. When I was almost out of time, I forced myself out. The bedroom door opened just as the dress skimmed past my hips and fell to mid-thigh.

"I see you do follow orders," he simply said before leading me downstairs. I expected him to lead me out the door and was surprised when he stopped inside the foyer. We weren't alone.

An attractive man, sporting a blonde Mohawk and covered in tattoos checked me out as Angel made the introductions. "Mian, this is Josh. He's a friend of Z." He then gave me a look warning me to be on my best behavior.

Yeah, we'll see.

"Nice to meet you, Mian." He stroked his chin while eye fucking me. He didn't give me the same hot and gripping feeling Angel did whenever his eyes took liberties with my body. Even Lucas and Z managed to flirt with my desire, though the feeling was never as powerful as the one Angel created. I looked away only to find Angel staring. When I didn't look away, he smirked as if he knew my secret.

Was I so transparent?

Josh finally got the hint and focused his attention on my captor. I cringed when I noticed the gigantic hole in his lobe where skin should be. "Where should I set up?" It was then I noticed the two black cases he held.

"Dining room." He led Josh away. Just when I thought

I would be left alone to hide, his voice boomed through the foyer. "Mian, come."

A sharp whistle followed his command, but when Angel's back stiffened, I knew it hadn't come from him. Josh laughed at his own joke. I held my breath waiting for what Angel would do, but he kept walking.

Once in the dining room, the men sat while I stood and waited by his side. Josh had implied I was a pet, and at that moment, I felt like one.

"So, what can I do for you, Mr. Knight?"

"I want this," he slid a sketch across the table. I only caught a glimpse, but I recognized it as his family crest: A kneeling knight piercing the spine of an open book with his sword. I'd only seen it once, and it hadn't made sense until now.

This Knight, though, had wings instead of armor.

"Where do you want it?"

"On her right hip."

Josh nodded and set to work. My throat desperately worked to push out words. I willed my feet to move or my hands to reach out and strangle him.

What right did he think he had to permanently mark my body? Since the day we met, he tormented me simply because he could, and I had let him. But *this* was too far.

"I'm not letting you do this."

Josh pulled out more materials as if he hadn't heard. Angel didn't even acknowledge me. The only evidence that he had heard was the tick in his jaw. I was breaking rule number one. They continued to discuss exactly what Angel wanted to have done to *my* body.

"It's going to take a few hours to really capture the detail. I assume you want it finished today?"

Angel nodded, and I could practically feel anger seeping from his pores. Josh kept stealing glances, and I pretended not to notice.

"Sweet. Let's get started." He smiled at me behind Angel's shoulder.

"Mian," Angel called. His attention was still focused on the creep who didn't realize he should keep his smiles to himself.

"Yes?"

"On the table."

I shook my head as if he could see. "I didn't consent to this."

"Do I need to strap you down?"

"It's the only way he's going to touch me." I stared at his profile until he rose from his seat and invaded my space. I wasn't expecting him to sink his hand in my hair and grab my waist with his other.

"Wha—"

It was all I could manage before he kissed me. His lips were soft as he patiently coaxed me to give in. I sunk so deep into the kiss that I had no way out until his lips left mine.

"That was to remember you by."

Confusion replaced desire. "What?"

"The only way you're walking out of here alive is with my mark. No games, Mian. There's no coming back if you test me."

He didn't put a gun to my head and threaten to blow my brains out like most villains would have done. He didn't need to. With a grace I didn't normally possess, I climbed onto the tabletop.

"She'll need to remove her panties," Josh said excitedly as he licked his lips.

"She's not wearing any." He then ordered me to lift my dress. I closed my eyes and pushed up the dress I had been so happy to wear only moments ago. The more Angel took from me, the more I accepted that spilling his blood would never be enough to heal the scars he had created.

"I'll be in my office if you need me." My eyes popped open and found Angel's staring back at me. Was that meant for Josh or me? He was the one making me do this. If I needed rescuing from anyone, it was he.

"I'm sure we'll be fine," Josh replied. Angel didn't move. He was waiting for something.

I nodded and then turned my head to stare at the chandelier directly above me. I listened to his footsteps, which eventually faded as he walked further away.

"Pretty intense guy, huh?"

I shivered. "He's a monster."

"You shouldn't be afraid of him."

"Why shouldn't I?"

"Because even monsters have a weakness and something tells me he's discovered his."

I turned my head to face him. He was unwinding his power supply cable and staring at me with a grin. "Angel doesn't have weaknesses. His power is in making you believe whatever he wants."

"Not weaknesses. Just one."

"Care to share?"

His look was skeptical. "You don't see it?"

"Should I?"

"It's you, beautiful. You're his weakness."

"Me?" It took me three tries to speak the simple word.

He continued to set up as if he didn't just make a lie out of everything I knew to be true about Angel.

"We men can be simple minded creatures so I can tell you, we don't act possessive over pussy unless the pussy was attached to something we wanted even more."

"That makes no sense."

"It's like I told you. We're simple minded." I didn't give him a response, and he didn't wait around for one. He finished setting up, and I held my breath, waiting for the first moment the needle would corrupt my skin. When it finally did, I closed my eyes and zoned out. I felt the first pinch, but not the second or third or even the hundredth. Hours had passed before it was over and the silence broke.

"There. All done. That wasn't so bad, was it?"

"I just had my skin permanently marked against my will to satisfy a man's ego."

"Are we done here?" Angel's voice interrupted his response and simultaneously penetrated all my senses.

"We're done. Would you like to take a look before I apply the wrap?"

Wordlessly, he moved across the room, and I bit down on the inside of my cheek to keep from running away. He'd catch me before my feet even touched the ground. His intoxicating scent teased me when he finally stood over me. I waited for his next move. Craved it even. It was addicting, our song and dance. Our tempo was one only we could hear.

His fingers lightly skated over my hip as he studied his barbaric idea of marking as Knight property. I studied the wings where the armor should have been. *Or maybe he thought of me as just his...*

"So you like?"

"It will do," he answered when our eyes met. Something told me he had other ideas of how to mark me as his. He moved away again so Josh could wrap my hip, but he hadn't moved far away. He stood behind Josh, but instead of watching him apply the wrap, he watched me.

"All right, man. Leave this covered for a few hours, make sure you keep it clean and apply anti-bacterial ointment for a few days." He started to rise, but Angel gripped the back of his head and slammed it down on the tabletop. Josh's groan as his head rose was the only sound in the room. Just as quickly as the first, Angel repeated the violent act. This time, I scrambled backward as quick as I could, using my hands and feet to propel me. Blood smeared his nose and lips and dripped onto his white shirt. "What the fuck, man?"

"If I ever hear you whistle again, it will be your last." He tossed a thin stack of neatly wrapped hundreds on the table and growled, "Get out."

He quickly snatched up the money and threw his equipment in his cases before slamming them shut and running away. I stood in silence with Angel and considered what to do or say. He stood up for me like he had all those years ago, and while it didn't erase the last two weeks, it confused me.

The sound of the front door opening and slamming shut couldn't even break the invisible cord that bound us. Any moment, it could snap, and I knew it wouldn't be cruelty and pain he unleashed, but something much more powerful than I could handle.

He turned to walk away, but I couldn't let him go. Not when he continued to play the game with my mind and heart.

"Do you always beat up your friends because they were rude?"

He made a quick turn on his heel and held out his hand. I slipped my hand in his after hesitating long enough to feel his impatience grow. My fingers trembled, but I managed to force them still until he swept his thumb across my knuckles. My legs were the ones to tremble this time as he helped me down from the table.

"You didn't have to do that for me."

"Do what?" he sighed and pulled my dress back down. He walked away before I could answer, so I followed him.

"Defend my honor. Because of you, I'm not even sure there is any left to defend."

His chuckle was rich and dark and mocking. "Your honor is mine to take as well as it is to defend. I do what the fuck pleases me, Mian. Don't you know that by now?"

"But you don't. Not really."

"Come again?"

"Well..." I'd ask myself later what the hell I was thinking. He'd already stopped walking and turned to face me. His deep brown eyes were becoming darker by the second. "You want to fuck me, but you're afraid."

He blinked once. Slowly. "And why would I be afraid to fuck you, Mian? Do you think you scare me?" He bared his teeth, gripped the back of my neck, leaning down. "That's incredibly cute."

"Then why won't you?" I challenged. Was I begging for it or truly hoping to prove a point? The lines blurred when he put his hand on me and invaded my space.

"Are you that hot for my dick inside you? You'd be dead before I came inside those tight walls of your cunt." His hand slid from my nape to my throat. I wasn't expecting the pressure that followed and instinctively, wrapped my hand around his wrist to stop him. "I didn't say you could touch me." His hand tightening around my throat ensured I couldn't. "I'll give you more than just a rough touch with your pleasure. Sex with me would be deadly, Mian. Are you ready to dance in the dark with me?" I suddenly felt the press of his fingers between my thighs. "Say the word, and I'll fuck you right here."

I was supposed to hate his touch. But my body's needs betrayed me once again, and he was very soon, going to discover it. What would stop him then from taking me?

Angel has had a lifetime of taking what he wanted. Including my son. I closed my eyes so the picture of his smile would be more vivid. He trusted and depended on me to keep him safe. I *had* to find a way.

I had no hope of controlling what my body waned, so I would follow my heart instead. It was the one place I could truly be safe from Angel.

Confidence allowed my body to relax, which Angel noticed immediately. "You think shutting me out will stop me?" I didn't respond, but I could feel him watching closely. He kept his grip, and my body began to slack even more from lack of oxygen. "Very well," he finally said and let me go. I coughed, drew in large gulps of air, and rubbed the sore spot on my throat. "Go upstairs."

He walked away from me, but I couldn't let him get the last word. "And then?" I said between sucking in air.

He stopped and turned back to face me. "You test me, Mian." He shook his head. Then he said as he walked away again, "And then you wait for me."

CHAPTER 43

The world is small for men with power.

ANGEL

I BURST THROUGH the doors like I owned the place, which I pretty much did. It was also why I was so annoyed my presence had been demanded. I may have been the hired hand, but I did not take orders. My clients knew, with a single entry from my family's black book, I could have them killed or imprisoned. The Knights took the soul of anyone who made a deal with us for power, fortune, or prosperity. For six generations, The Bandit never failed a job, which made the cost of their soul well spent.

The high back brown leather chair spun around and revealed dull brown hair, sharp eyes, and an expensive suit.

"What can I do for you, Senator?" My tone held a bite in it that I knew he wouldn't miss. Senator Staten was as corrupt as the rumor mill accused. It just so happened that he gained his seat because of my father and was due for reelection soon.

"I need a job done, and I want it to be top priority."

It wasn't new for clients to demand priority. They all felt their problems were paramount, and with endless money to throw around, they were more than willing to pay for that illusion.

"That's going to cost you."

"I'm well aware of the costs, young man." If this wasn't a business meeting, I'd laugh at his attempt to make me feel small by pointing out my age, and then I'd slit his throat and sleep like a baby tonight.

My attention shifted to his excuse for a son sitting in the corner wearing a smug smile. He wore khaki shorts and a mint colored polo shirt with loafers. His pansy ass barely had hair on his legs but had the nerve to think he had some control.

"Eye problem?"

His smile dropped, and for a moment, he looked uncertain. "Excuse me?"

"You got something to say to me? You're staring like you do."

His chin lifted, thrusting his nose in the air as he turned to the senator. "Father, do we really need the help of a common criminal?"

His father started to respond when I cut him off. "Considering the reason he called me here is undoubtedly a crime, I'd say so." I stalked forward and balled the front of his shirt in my fist before either one could know what I intended to do. I lifted him from his cozy spot on the couch until his feet dangled in the air. "But there's nothing common about what I'll do to you if you try to insult me again."

"D—Dad," he squeaked.

358

"Please, Mr. Knight." *Oh, now I'm Mr. Knight?* "Unhand my son. I need him." He regarded his son coldly. "At least, until the next election."

A feral smile spread my lips, and I swear, another second, and he would have pissed himself. I set him on his feet gently and smoothed the front of his shirt. When I got bored with taunting him, I turned back to his father.

"You were saying?"

"Yes, well, I'm prepared to pay the cost... extra in fact... if you can do this quickly and quietly."

"Don't I always?"

He cleared his throat—probably to wash away an apology rather than his pride. "This is a sensitive matter. I need your absolute discretion."

My gaze narrowed. "By discretion you mean—"

"This cannot go in that *book*," his lips curled, "your family keeps."

"Not happening."

"I'll pay extra."

"Not. Happening." Everything went into the book. Everything. It was our insurance as well as our destruction and no amount of money would buy exception.

Some have even gone as far as to offer money to destroy it.

No one needed to know that the single piece of evidence that could destroy families, careers, and end lives were no longer in our control.

"I do this job with a ten percent increase. Take it or leave it."

He didn't respond. The door opened behind me, and I immediately moved to protect my back even though I was unarmed. Three of his personal guards walked in—one carrying a briefcase—and formed a circle around me.

"I'm afraid I'll have to insist, son."

My fists curled hearing him call me son, but otherwise, I didn't move. I didn't need to. The tension in the room spiked and his twerp of a son was back to smirking. I winked, and his face paled. I was outnumbered, sure, but I was still in control.

As much was proven when red dots appeared on every man's head.

I made a mockery of their attempt to strong-arm me. Fear was palpable, and I basked in it.

"Let's make that a fifty percent increase."

He sputtered and stumbled to collect himself while trying to evade the target on the back of his skull. He couldn't see it, of course, but he was smart enough to know it was there. His son did the same while his guard remained in place. They eventually figured out there was no escape.

"Call them off."

"Give me the name and all the money upfront." Before his stupidity got the best of him, he would have only needed to pay half up front.

"But that's ridiculous!"

"Not as ridiculous as you thinking you can threaten me. You'll be lucky if I don't decide to kill you even after you pay me."

"But—"

The picture of his wife suddenly flew off his desk and landed a few feet away from my feet. Her face was completely obliterated from the shot.

"My money," I warned.

He stumbled to the phone and spoke harshly and quickly to the poor bastard on the other line. Not five minutes later, a man in a gray suit with thinning hair and specks bustled in with another briefcase. The senator nodded to one of his guards who was holding his briefcase, and they immediately sat them at my feet.

"The name."

"Mian Ross."

Time stood still as I replayed the name he spat in my head. It couldn't be. What would Mian have to do with the senator? I begin to consider that I was being set up until I reasoned that the senator might know Theo, but *no one* knew of Mian. Theo made sure of that.

"You want her dead, I assume?"

"The sooner, the better."

"Why?" I couldn't stop myself from asking the million dollar question.

He paused and shrewdly studied me. "You never cared before."

"You never threatened to kill me before," I answered smoothly. "Any pretense of trust is gone."

He seemed to accept my answer and said, "My son couldn't keep his dick in his pants. At least for girls of legal fucking age."

My heart ceased to beat, and the blood in my veins froze. It took every ounce of willpower to keep my gaze calm.

"He got her pregnant, and now she's causing problems."

"You want me to off a pregnant chick?" I played stupid even when I'd already pieced together every piece of the goddamn puzzle.

"She's already had the bastard."

Don't kill him.

Don't kill him.

"She wants money even though my son denies paternity."

"So. What's the big deal? Get a DNA test." I bit the inside of my cheek until I tasted blood. He cut his eyes at the little fucker lounging without a care in the world.

He was definitely hiding something.

"I don't believe my son *didn't* father that child no matter what he tells me."

"So because she's telling the truth, you want her dead?"

Don't kill him.

Don't kill him.

"She's threatening to go public. I can't have some girl and her bastard son messing up my campaign. Besides, she was underage and still in high school. Even if she was old enough to consent, it would still hurt our image."

"And what happens to the kid?"

"I told you... I want this clean."

Meaning no loose ends.

Son of a bitch...

I TOOK LUCAS by surprise when I returned from the meeting. I stood still while he avoided my gaze and buttoned the jeans he hadn't bothered to remove. Unwillingly, my gaze slid to the bed and the girl he'd just been balls deep in. I tried to keep my irritation under lock and key but failed.

"Fucking seriously?" I spat when she whimpered and scrambled up against the headboard while pulling the sheets up to cover her body. I looked away to give her privacy and regarded my best friend.

"You were supposed to be watching her, not fucking her," I forced through my teeth.

A sneaky smile tugged up the corner of his lips as he shrugged. "I couldn't help myself."

A small gasp wiped the smile off his face. She watched him with tears in her eyes while his avoided her. I jerked my head toward the door, and he followed.

"Do you know what you're doing?" I questioned as soon as the door was closed.

"No," he answered honestly.

"Are you even sure she's legal?" He looked back at the door with a wary look, and I could tell he had doubted his answer before he shrugged again.

"What's up?" he said by way of changing the subject. I hesitated for a half a second before leading him to my father's office and launching into a recap of the meeting. I had Z hang back with some of the men to keep an eye on the senator while I figured out my next move.

"Fucking hell..." He blew out a breath and roughly shoved his fingers through his hair. "So the contract on her head—"

"I'm not going to do it."

"You took the money."

"He threatened to kill me." He nodded, satisfied with my answer. "We need to take care of him."

Lucas's head jerked back in surprise. "Take care of him? He's a fucking senator!"

"He may be a blue blood, but he bleeds red just like the rest of us." Lucas didn't appear convinced. "If it's not me, he'll hire someone else."

"You care about her." He said it as if he had just realized it for the first time.

"I'm *responsible* for her."

"Your father's dead. You're the head of the family, which means your babysitting days are over."

"It's not that simple."

"Just admit it, man." He smiled like he'd just uncovered my dirtiest secret. "She makes your dick hard, and you *like* it."

"I'm not talking about my dick right now. Maybe after I kill the senator."

His playful mood shifted into business as he leaned forward. "What's the move?"

"I need you to pay a visit to Jonny. It's time we brought Theo up to speed."

CHAPTER 44

Happy Birthday.

ANGEL

THREE YEARS AGO

SHE WOULDN'T CALL.

I wouldn't call me either.

Mian had this corny tradition of telling me happy birthday at exactly midnight. Birthdays were her favorite, she'd explained with a shrug when I asked the second year she'd done it. It was strange because I was sure she hated me. Since my father was never around, and my mother refused to come to the city, I figured she did it out of pity. I tried not to be angry that she pitied me at all.

It was hard to be upset when she was being so fucking sweet.

But this year, she wouldn't say it.

Those three words sweetly whispered from her lips had become the one thing about my birthday I looked forward to. I stared at the time on my phone and watched the minute hand change to midnight.

I dropped my phone face down on my chest and waited.

Four months ago, my father made the decision that I couldn't be trusted with Mian. Taking her from me was the smartest decision he ever made, but that didn't stop me from resenting myself. Two weeks prior, I convinced my father I needed time away, but the truth was, I needed distance from Mian. It had become impossible to resist her. Had I known the day I came back would have been our last, I never would have left.

My father made Theo believe she could take care of herself. He had been reluctant to uproot her from another home and decided to leave the decision to Mian. He figured Mian still hated me and that would make the decision easier on him. My father, however, knew my feelings weren't one-sided.

That's where I came in.

She could have returned home where she could feel closer to her mother, but she was more than just a girl with a crush... and she had no business being in love with me. So I was supposed to ride in like a black-hearted knight and break her heart so she would *want* to leave.

Unfortunately, it worked like a charm.

Theo was kept in the dark, Mian went home, and my father was happy that his heir was free to toe the line once again.

He had warned me to stay away, but I didn't listen.

Because I was a man falling for a goddamn teenager.

I didn't understand it at first. We barely spoke, and when we did, it was to spew insults, yet somehow, I looked forward to each encounter. I even started a few just so I could see the fire that raged in her eyes whenever I got under her skin.

My heart sped up when my phone finally rang. I couldn't pick up the phone fast enough.

MOM.

My jaw clenched as I hit ignore. The minute changed to one minute past twelve, and I found myself dialing a number I knew from memory. The seconds it took for her to pick up the phone seemed like an eternity.

"Angel?" Her whisper was full of surprise.

"You didn't call." I was even angrier that she actually picked up. Mian wasn't a night owl. She was usually dead to the world by nine and up before the sun rose each morning.

She *remembered*.

"Should I have?" There was ice in her tone, and my jaw was bound to break at this rate.

"Say it."

"Say what?"

"You know." She sucked in air and then there was nothing. "Do it, Sprite. I want to hear the words."

I counted to three in my head and made it only to two when she breathed, "Happy Birthday, Angel." My eyes closed and I held them tight. "Angel?" she called when minutes ticked by.

"Yeah?"

"Why did you have to hurt me?" She was on the verge of crying. I could hear it in her voice. If she had stabbed me in the heart, it would have hurt less.

"Because it was the right thing to do."

"Hurting me was right?"

"I would have never let you go if you didn't want me to. We both know that."

"I just don't understand why my father wanted me back here in the first place."

"He didn't." I forced the air from my lungs. "It was my father."

She was silent for so long that I checked to see if she'd hung up. "He knows, doesn't he?"

We had never even spoken about it to each other, yet somehow, it was so easy for my father to see. If Theo would stop keeping Mian at arm's length, maybe he would have seen it, too.

"Yeah."

"Angel?"

"Yeah?"

"Did you know?"

"Not until I thought I lost you." I heard her sigh and pictured her smile. It would be sweet and soft like her. "My father is throwing a party tonight, and I want you there." *I need you there.* "You'll be my guest of honor." Birthday parties haven't been the norm since before I grew my first pube, and even then, it was my mother who put it together. This year it had been my father's idea, and I wondered if it had to do with business and I had finally earned my place.

"But our fathers—"

"Fuck our fathers." I heard her inhale and waited for her to release, but she never did. She was holding her breath, waiting for what I would say next. "One day, you won't belong to him."

"Then who will I belong to?"

So fucking innocent.

"Me."

CHAPTER 45

A father's love—means nothing.

PRESENT

"YOU LOOK LIKE you've seen a ghost."

I gazed across the table at the man who took what was left of my humanity. He looked two seconds away from lunging across the table and killing me too. I've waited for this moment for three years and spent the last two weeks in anticipation.

"What the fuck have you done to my daughter? Where is she?"

"She's safe. Which is more than I can say you've done for her."

"I've kept her safe."

"You avoided her. That's not the same thing."

"I was grieving," he whispered loudly.

"For six goddamn years?"

"One day, when you're in love and that love is gone forever, you'll understand true pain has no timetable."

"Until then, you're still a shitty father."

"Where's my daughter?"

"I told you she's safe. That's more than you deserve to know."

"You better not harm a hair on her head."

"If I had, the only one who would be to blame is you. What the hell were you thinking sending her after me?"

"I didn't send her after you. She was going whether I wanted it or not."

My gaze narrowed. "So you're telling me she took the book?"

"Of course not. I never told her about the book."

"Then why did you send her to my father's home?"

"The night your father died—"

"The night you killed him. Be a fucking man and own that shit."

He looked ready to argue but something in him gave up the fight. "I was going after the book that night and planned to hand it over to someone I owed."

"Who?"

He shook his head. "Not important."

I gritted my teeth and forced myself to move past his secrets while praying he wasn't lying to me. "So you sent Mian to finish the job without even telling her exactly what she was getting herself into?"

"It's like I told you. She would have found a way with or without my help. She thought I was going after money."

"And you didn't bother to tell her different."

"She was in a bad way and needed cash. Mian's a smart girl. Even if she didn't find a safe full of cash, I knew she'd take something worth some value."

"So you sent her in blind and you call *that* protecting her?"

"Mian has no skills as a thief. She's a good girl. The chances of her getting caught were high, but there was nothing I could do to stop her behind bars. Her safest bet was you. I knew you wouldn't hurt her."

"That's where you're wrong. I *did* hurt her." I kept my smile at bay when his face paled.

"What did you do?" he urged through his shaken voice.

"Nothing that will scar."

His fist slammed on the table top as he leaned close. "I trusted you," he spat.

"Like my father trusted you?"

"You *know* why he died that night," he gritted. I wanted to kill him on the spot. He was still excusing himself from blame. "Let my daughter go. She doesn't deserve your wrath."

"I'm not sure about that, but it doesn't matter anymore. Mian is in even bigger trouble, and I'm going to get her out of it. I just came to warn you that once I do, I'll be keeping her."

"Trouble? What kind of trouble?"

"Did you know that her son's father is Aaron Staten?"

"Impossible."

"Why not? Your daughter is a beautiful girl." He looked as if he wanted to kill me for noticing.

"Because she'd never go for that prick, much less—" He stopped and looked away. He was clearly having a hard time accepting the thought of a cock between his daughter's legs. The thought made me want to put a bullet in someone so I could only imagine how he felt. I decided to change the subject for both of our sakes.

"The senator wants her dead." I dropped the bomb in his

lap but didn't wait for the explosion. "I'm not going to let that happen."

His eyes were rimmed with red as he stared at me in disbelief. "You would do that for her? Why?"

"You were supposed to protect her, and at the very least, love her enough to keep her from doing something stupid."

"I *tried.*"

"And you failed." I rubbed my chin as we locked gazes. "But that doesn't matter now. You had your chance, and you won't get another one. She's no longer yours."

"What the hell is that supposed to mean?" He spoke so harshly spit flew from his mouth.

I leaned forward so there was no mistake. "It means, I'm her daddy now," I growled.

CHAPTER 46

Old habits die hard.

MIAN

I FELT LIKE a dog that had been let off the chain for the first time. The first place I went sniffing was after my son. After Angel had scarred me for life, he didn't bother to lock me up. At first, I figured he was too pissed off to realize his blunder until Z passed me in the hall with a bright smile and one of his chin lifts.

After searching the house from top to bottom, I couldn't find a trace of my baby or Angel. I did, however, find Lucas lounging in the den.

"Where's Angel?"

He looked up from drinking milk from the bowl of cereal he had just eaten, and reluctantly, I had to admit to myself how cute he looked with his milk mustache.

"Out."

"Fine. Where is my son?"

He set the bowl down on the coffee table in front of him and leaned back, resting his arms along the back casually.

"He's out, too."

God, I wanted to kill him. "Where did he take my son?"

"To get some fresh air."

"You mean, keeping him from me."

He shrugged. "You can't be trusted, girl."

"That is not for any of you to decide. He is *my* son."

"And you're Angel's prisoner, which means your son belongs to him unless he lets you both go."

"You mean *when* he lets us go," I corrected with suspicion in my gut.

"Sure." His lips tilted.

I stalked to the back of the couch and placed my hands on his powerful shoulders. I leaned down to whisper in his ear. "I'm free now," I reminded him. "You should watch your back."

I felt the muscles in his shoulders stiffen, but I didn't stick around for the aftermath. Without Caylen to find or a working phone to call for help, I retreated upstairs in defeat. It was my intention to return to my cell, but somehow, I stood in front of the door to Angel's old bedroom.

He spent six years of his life babysitting me. This room hadn't been his space in all that time. There was nothing in here that would give me answers. I accepted that, but it didn't stop me from being curious. The last time I'd been here, I was preoccupied looking for a place to hide.

I pushed open the door, and the first thing I noticed were the bare walls. There were no posters of buxom beauties or angry rock bands. The floors weren't littered with discarded white t-shirts and sneakers. The bed wasn't made, but I had a feeling that was because of Lucas uncovering my hiding spot weeks ago.

I laid down and found the mattress soft. The sheets smelled too clean. They didn't hold his scent.

"You have no idea how many times I've pictured getting you in my bed."

I jackknifed from his bed and found Angel's muscular body filling the space in the doorway. His long arms were stretched over his head gripping the frame. The position put his impressive muscles on display under the white t-shirt that was damp with his sweat.

"I was looking for my son. Where did you take him?"

"I thought he might need a change of scenery."

"You're lying. You were making sure I couldn't get to him. Why not just keep me locked up?"

"If that is what you wish, I can make it happen. But this time, it will be to my bed."

I ignored the hot ache in my gut. "I told you before. I'm not getting into bed with the man who kidnapped my son."

"So, if I gave him back to you...?"

My heart raced. "What are you saying?"

He walked inside and shut the door behind him. I held my breath as I watched him slowly turn the lock. "You used to follow me with your eyes," he said without turning around.

"That was a long time ago."

"Old habits die hard," he countered. He turned and leaned against the door to watch me under lowered lids. He bit his lip, and my pussy sang a song of rejoicing.

"I don't watch you."

"But you want to. You're more in control of your emotions now."

"And?"

"I don't like it."

"Because it's not so easy to take advantage of me anymore?"

I pictured hate to be cold and dark, but his burned bright and hot. "I never took advantage of you."

"I was young—"

"So was I," he said through clenched teeth.

"You were old enough to know better."

"So were you." He pushed from the door and stalked me. "Despite what you think, you weren't innocent about what almost happened between us. You wanted it. Perhaps even more than I did," he taunted. He was back to being cruel again. Within his eyes, I caught a glimpse of a younger Angel—the one who let his emotions rule him.

"I guess it doesn't matter anymore. I'm over you." He stood at the foot of the bed gazing down at me.

"I bet you won't taste as sweet with a lie on your lips." The way he spoke made me believe him.

"I. Don't. Want. You."

"Prove it."

"H—how?" It was official... I was the masochist to his sadist.

"Pull your dress up and spread your legs. I want to see what's not mine."

My fingers twitched and my legs trembled to do his bidding, but I held back. "So this is how you get girls? You coerce them?"

"Only you." He jerked his chin toward my hands which were already at the hem. I just couldn't bring myself to follow through unless I had control.

Maybe it meant making him lose it first.

My fingers curled under and then I slowly lifted it until I couldn't anymore. He stood as still as a statue, and if it weren't for the heat wave coming from his body, I wouldn't have believed he was real.

I knew what he would find once my legs were spread. My desire threatened to consume me the moment I saw him standing in the door. I knew how much he wanted me. It was time I exploited his desire.

I was willing to do anything to have my son back, and Angel was willing to give anything to have me.

"No," he said when I started to move my thighs apart. He crawled on the bed, his shoulders bunching and rolling until he sat beside me against the headboard. "Let me." His hand touched my knee. I braced for him to expose me and when he didn't, I met his gaze. "May I?"

Damn him.

He didn't ask for permission because he was a gentleman.

The son of a bitch wanted me to admit that I wanted it.

The corner of his lips tipped up when I nodded. His attention was between my legs, but I couldn't bring myself to look anywhere but his face as he gently pushed my legs open. He was sitting so close, my knee had no choice but to fall in his lap. When he leaned forward to get a better look, I found myself inhaling the scent of his hair before I could rethink it. If he noticed, he didn't make it known. His fingers softly and slowly skated from my knee. I tensed the closer he got to my pussy and sung the alphabet to keep from bolting.

By the letter G, his fingers found my pussy, and I forgot what fucking letter came next.

"Damn, baby." His voice was low, husky, and filled with sex.

I expected him to stop there, but his fingers continued to heighten my arousal until I was unable to deny what this really was. My head fell back against the headboard, and my hips rose from the bed.

"You said you only wanted to see," I moaned.

"But what do *you* want, Mian?" I didn't answer him. I couldn't. Torture felt damn good. "Goddammit, tell me," he urged. I bit my lip and gazed into the dark brown pools that guarded his soul. I was bound by loyalty to my father and son but tormented by the demands of my body. He must have sensed my uncertainty because his hand threaded through my hair and he lowered his forehead to rest against mine. "I'll do it. I swear." He sounded as desperate as I felt.

"I want your mouth," I gasped.

His eyes clouded, and it seemed his gaze completely lost focus when he growled, "Where?"

Everywhere?

"Angel..."

He groaned and hid his face in my neck. "Say the words. I need them, or I won't touch you. Not until then." He was barely coherent, but somehow, I understood.

I slid my hand between my legs and rested it on top of his larger one. His head lifted from my neck and our gazes connected as I helped him stroke me. "There."

"God, baby. I will, but I need you to do something for me first." I would have lost touch with reality if I hadn't craved more.

"What?" *Anything.*

I felt a thick finger slide up my hungry slit. "Tell me..." I gasped when his finger circled my clit. "...who daddy is?"

I halted mid moan and stared. "What?"

His voice was so thick I thought maybe I'd misheard him. How could he be thinking of my father at a time like this?

He went on, the passion still in his tone as if he couldn't sense the change in my tune. "Sweet fucking Mian. You think you're still his spoiled little girl." He took my bottom lip between his teeth and let go. "But you're mine now."

"A-a-are you high?" I didn't know how far he'd taken me until I came crashing back down. I inhaled, trying to catch the scent of smoke on his clothing, but all I could smell was male. Pure, hard, unadulterated *male.*

His body shook against mine as he laughed soundlessly. "No, I'm not high, Mian. I need you to realize who you belong to."

"I don't belong to anyone," I said with enough venom that he should have been dead at my feet.

"You don't belong to Lucas. You don't belong to Z." *Where was he going with this?* "You don't belong to your dead mother." I gasped and shoved against him. He had no right to talk about my mother. He locked his arm around my waist to keep me at his side. "And you sure as fuck don't belong to your disloyal and soon-to-be *dead* father."

I was enraged.

"Wanting my father dead won't stop yours from pushing up daisies." I was uncomfortably aware of my dress bunched around my waist and my bare bottom open to him. The passionate look on his face had long been replaced by hatred. "Let me go." I needed time to regroup and to figure out when

I'd fallen this stupid. His free hand shifted to my calf and yanked until I was on my back. He then spread me and settled his body between my shaking thighs.

I hated myself for not only letting him touch me but also for giving in. I fooled myself into believing I could take control for a few, guiltless moments of pleasure.

"Haven't you figured it out yet?"

"Let me go," I repeated. I didn't care about puzzles, or legacies, or even the past. I simply wanted to get away from him.

"That's *exactly* what you're missing," he spat impatiently. "I'll *never* let you go. You and your son are here to stay."

I hardened myself to withstand his threats and claim of possession. Angel Knight was neither my guardian angel or knight in shining armor. He was my enemy.

"Know this..." I witnessed his flinch and was also surprised by how cold and hard my voice had become. I didn't let it show and instead, clung to the wall I'd built in a matter of seconds. "No matter how long it takes—weeks, months, years... I'll kill you before I let you keep us."

CHAPTER 47

Fear is an unbreakable chain.

ANGEL

SHE THOUGHT LEAVING me meant she'd go on with her life, raising her son, and working dead-end jobs she couldn't keep long enough to keep them fed. It was dangerous and rash, but I decided to show her just how fucked life would be without me.

Little Mian Ross did things to me I wasn't proud of, but she had a way of making me not care. I didn't know what came over me when I finally had her in my hands on the brink of release. The words spilled from my lips and just like that, I lost her.

"You sure it's a good idea taking her with us?" Lucas grilled for the fifth fucking time.

"She needs to see for herself what she's up against," I answered the same as before.

"She could get hurt."

"She'll be killed if she's not convinced leaving isn't in her best interest."

He was silent, but I knew it wouldn't last. "What if you're just looking for a reason to keep her around?"

My jaw worked, and I forced my response—the only response—through my teeth. "I don't need to." Why did I need a reason to keep someone who was already mine?

I had clothes sent up to Mian with the order to show her face in five minutes, or I'd drag her down naked. She came down mere seconds before the five-minute mark. She didn't question or bother to look me in the eye.

WHEN WE ARRIVED, the guards at the gate were reluctant to allow us entry but a few guns to their heads and the promise to visit their families while they slept in their beds changed their minds. I had my entire security team flanking us as we made our way inside. Mian remained silent through it all, and Z guided her inside by her arm. We were shown to the senator's office after forcing submission from the rest of his security team. They would all be out of a job by morning anyway, so all they had left to lose was their life.

"Knight," the senator greeted after I pushed my way inside and closed the door. "Your visit is unexpected."

"I'm not the type to make an appointment."

"Or wait for an invitation for that matter." I shrugged and took a seat without him offering, and his eyes narrowed at the slight. "What brings you by?"

"The job's not going to happen."

"But you took the money."

"And I intend to give it to your grandson for child support.

It's not enough for what your punk ass son did by abandoning him before he was even born, but it will do."

"You'll do no such thing. We don't even know if that baby is really his."

"You and I both know if he wasn't your son's kid, we wouldn't be having this discussion."

"What makes you think I'll just *let* you take my money and give it to her bastard?"

Most of my control evaporated, but I managed to keep my fists tight around the arms of the chair rather than pummeling them into his face. "Call him a bastard again, and you won't live to see me take all your money and give it to *Caylen*." He looked confused, and it dawned on me that he didn't even know his grandson's name. "Your illegitimate grandson's name is Caylen. Now, be a good boy and say his name so I'll know you get me."

He hesitated, so I pulled my gun and sat it on my lap. I wasn't the least bit concerned about the guards standing on the other side of the door.

His faced paled as he looked from me to the gun. I didn't remove my finger from the trigger until he said his name. I told myself it was guilt for what I had done to his mother that made me want to protect him so fiercely. No one knew that I spent the nights sitting with him to make sure he slept well. They didn't know I talked to him when no one was around. I told him stories of how she'd been a pain in the ass since she was ten years old. If I had a heart, I'm sure he would have stolen a place in it. But since I didn't, taking down the senator was merely restitution.

"So we are in agreement then." He was smart enough to know I wasn't asking and kept his mouth shut. "I'll give her the money you've already paid me, and she stays away forever. With the amount of money you paid to off them, she won't need to bother you again." My lips curled as I stared down the senator. It would have been cheaper for him to simply pay her off, but the pussy had zero honor.

Mian wasn't money hungry.

She had no aspirations of wealth or prestige and would have been content just being able to give Caylen a healthy life. She's sacrificed her entire life to give him one, and she would have continued to do so long after he was old enough to take the wheel.

"We have an arrangement," he agreed slowly.

"Good. Now where's your son? There's someone you should meet." The senator's sat stoic. His refusal to answer didn't deter me, however, from going to the door and opening it. Mian stood between Lucas and Z with our guard surrounding them. Her wide-eyed gaze met mine and in them were questions she was about to get the answers to. I crooked my finger and for the first time she came without coercion. "Bring his son to me," I directed to Lucas and Z before hauling her in and shutting the door.

Not long after, I heard shouting and then the door was ripped open. A struggling Aaron was thrown inside the room and landed on his stomach. Lucas and Z entered and closed the door behind them while the senator stood from his chair and slammed his fists on the desk.

"What is this?" he shouted.

I saw Mian tense in my peripheral, so I used my body to shield her from the senator's anger. Aaron was righting his clothes and had yet to see her, but I knew the moment Mian recognized him. She gasped and something inside my chest shifted when she moved closer to me. I wasn't naive enough to believe she trusted me to protect her. I was just the lesser of two evils... in *her* book.

Aaron finally noticed me standing in the corner but then his attention shifted behind me, and he leaned over to try to get a better look. "Is that..." The room fell silent as we waited for the other shoe to fall. "Mian?"

"This is preposterous," the senator blubbered. "Why is that lying harlot in my home?"

Mian made another sound, but this one was filled with pain. My finger moved back to the trigger, though my gun remained at my side. Lucas and Z were staring down the senator looking only seconds away from ending him.

"Senator," I called to get his attention. He was busy trying to glare a hole through me to reach the innocent girl who'd asked for none of this. "I would say the same rule applies to her, but I don't want to taint her name by letting you speak it. You don't talk to her, and you for damn sure won't talk *at* her."

"What makes you think you can come into *my* house and give orders?"

"The bullet I can put into your son's skull before your security team can even have a chance to pull their head from their asses. Shall we continue?"

Wisely, he reclaimed his seat, so I reached behind me and pulled Mian to my front. She fought me, but like always, I won. Her gaze was fixed on Aaron as I brought her back against my chest to share my strength. He was already leering at her, and I seriously wanted to pull my blade and carve his eyes out.

"Why did you bring her here," the senator asked more cordially.

Because I need to scare her from leaving me. "So your son can tell her in person why he shunned his responsibilities." The truth was I had no interest in why he was a prick, and I doubt Mian would ever have the courage to confront him if her trembling was anything to go by. It made me wonder what happened between them. I expected anger, not fear.

"She spread her legs and got herself in trouble, so she screams rape and my son is just supposed to pay?" As soon as the last word left the senator's lips, his son spat blood onto the carpet and regarded Mian with disgust. It wasn't just the way he was looking at her that made me want to rip his heart out and make his father eat it, but *what* his father had said.

I must have done something because all eyes were suddenly on me, but I only had eyes for one person. One look in his eyes told me the truth.

That motherfucker raped her.

I didn't think after that.

I just reacted.

I lifted my gun and aimed it between his eyes. My finger squeezed the trigger without hesitation or remorse. He should have been dead, but my aim was compromised when my hand had been knocked away at the last moment. The bullet killed the wall and not the bitch I was aiming for. Enraged, I turned on the fucker who dared and stared into frightened green eyes while the senator's men tried to break the door down.

My fury only heightened when I found the culprit was Mian. Was she actually protecting that cunt?

I sent her my most menacing expression, but she didn't flinch. In fact, there was no emotion in her eyes to be found. Anger turned into worry, and suddenly, we were the only two people in the room. After a few tense moments, she finally spoke, but it wasn't the words I wanted to hear.

"You can't kill him."

"And why is that?" Did she love him?

I'll kill them both and bury them in the same hole where they could be together.

Forever.

"Because he's the son of a senator."

I was not moved.

"I can always kill the good senator, too." Both of those bitches gasped like women making my trigger finger itch to put them out of their misery for good. "Give me one good reason why I shouldn't."

She started to speak but immediately snapped her mouth close.

Like I thought.

"You have something you want to say to me?"

She gripped my shirt under her fingers, and finally, there was life staring back at me. "I don't want anything from him. Not even his blood."

"Well, that's too bad."

Her frown deepened. "The senator has agreed that you and your son deserve more." I looked up to meet the senator's gaze. "Isn't that right, Senator?" Her head turned in the senator's direction, and her body tightened even more.

"That's right. One hundred and fifty grand in cash to you and Caylen."

"I—I don't know what to say."

"The senator doesn't deserve your gratitude." She looked uncertain and ready to thank that asshole anyway until I promised death with a glare.

"I assure you it's not necessary," he rushed to agree. He slid his gaze back to me. "You have your money now leave my home."

I almost put a bullet in his skull just because.

CHAPTER 48

You need me.

MIAN

WHAT THE HELL just happened?

We were back in his father's home where I watched Angel take a drink while I sat on the couch in his father's office next to Z. Lucas disappeared somewhere in the house as soon as we arrived, and I worried over who had been watching Caylen all this time.

I was surprised when Angel pushed his glass away and then slammed two briefcases down on the desk. His strong fingers deftly popped opened the cases and lifted the tops. Stacks of money filled both briefcases to capacity.

"What is this?" I asked when he stared at me expectantly. I needed to react. I just didn't know how.

"Child support."

I gaped. A part of me didn't believe the senator had really offered me so much money and it was all because of Angel.

Instead of grateful, I felt trapped. "Am I supposed to thank you?"

"I don't want your gratitude." I nodded and relaxed until he said, "But you should know this money was originally payment to kill you." I gasped. "*Both* of you," he corrected, sending my heart to my stomach.

"I don't understand."

"The senator paid me to make you and Caylen disappear, and since neither of us like loose ends, which took making you simply leave the city off the table."

It was scary to know my life had a price on it. There were many questions running through my mind, but only one spilled forth. "You were going to kill me, anyway. Why not just take the money?"

His face looked like I'd just ripped out his gut at the thought of taking my last breath when he'd been so eager just days before. "That was before I knew you were innocent."

It was an answer, but it wasn't good enough.

"If you believe that, why haven't you let us go?" I felt the pinch from my nails digging into my thighs. "Why haven't I been able to see or hold my son?"

"Believe it or not, I'm protecting you."

"I don't believe it," I confirmed. "What do you think you're protecting me from?"

"The bounty on your head?" he answered as if I was dimwitted. I was well aware of the bounty, but what he didn't realize was that *he* was the only danger to me.

"Who will protect me from you?"

"Angel may not be many things, but he is loyal," Z answered when Angel couldn't. It was the first time I'd seen him speechless. I'd forgotten Z was even in the room. "He'll protect you because you need it, and he owes you. It's as simple as that."

"I'm supposed to trust the man who had my son ripped from my arms while he slept?"

"Like I said... he owes you."

"That's not loyalty. That's guilt."

"I may be guilty, but I'm still in control," he growled. "And you aren't leaving until I say it's safe."

"I know the senator only agreed to pay me the money instead so I'd disappear. What makes you think I'm still in danger?"

"Because as long as you're breathing, you're a threat to his position and name. He'll just pay someone double what he gave me to kill you."

"What about the book? Isn't the purpose to keep your clients under control?" His gaze slid to Z accusingly, but Z shrugged in an "it wasn't me" gesture.

"The book holds power, but it doesn't stop bullets."

"I can leave Chicago." I refused to accept that Angel was my only hope.

He was already shaking his head before I finished. "If I let you go, he'll find you. One hundred and fifty stacks isn't enough to get you out of his reach."

I continued to argue, but he backed me into a corner at every turn until I was too mentally exhausted to keep up.

"Promise me you'll stay, and I'll give you back your son."

No. Never. "I can't do that."

"Then I can't trust you with him."

"He's *my* son."

"You say that, but you aren't putting his safety first like a mother should."

"How the fuck would you know? Your mother was too busy hiding, and your father was too busy stealing livelihoods and getting blood on his hands."

"And your father was right there with him."

We both seemed to back down at the same time knowing our parents left lasting damage on both of us. Pointing fingers didn't change our past, and it sure as fuck didn't make our present easier to swallow.

At that moment, I made the decision to accept Angel's protection. I wouldn't do to Caylen what my parents did to me.

"I'm the one who was raped, yet I get imprisoned," I muttered to myself.

His eyes flashed with something. Jealousy? Anger? I couldn't put a finger on it, but I did not want to be on the other side of it.

"What did you just say?"

I swallowed even though my mouth and throat had long dried out. "Which part?"

"You know damn well which part, Mian."

"I was raped, Angel. Is that what you would like to hear? I was slipped a drug after a party and woke up the next day with his come on my thighs and no memory of how it happened." I didn't mean to be so upfront, but the way he looked at me made me defensive. Reliving that night wasn't exactly good for my mood either. But it was more than two years ago, and I was dealing with it.

Sort of.

"You were a virgin." Z's striking green eyes were troubled as he stared into mine. "Weren't you?" He spoke softly. Maybe that was why I found myself nodding. "Jesus Christ..." He shoved his hands in his hair and met Angel's hard gaze. "You need to erase that memory from her mind. Fucking destroy it."

Just like that, the vibe in the room changed to something warmer and more dangerous. Before I could ask what he meant, I was pulled into his lap.

"What he did to you..." He wrapped his hand around my neck and tilted my head back to rest on his shoulder. "That isn't the way a man should touch you." I sucked in air when I felt his other arm wrap around my waist. "You should want it." His fingertips skimmed my lips. "You should crave it." I felt his hot breath on my neck. "And if he's really good, you should beg for it."

What was happening? One moment, I was arguing against staying with the man who had kidnapped my son, and the next, I was sitting in his partner's lap as his husky voice did things I wasn't proud of to my body.

"Am I scaring you?" I twisted my head enough to see genuine concern in Z's green eyes. Once again, I found myself nodding. He didn't scare me. He *terrified* me. "Do you like it?"

I didn't know if the torturous feeling low in my stomach was right or wrong. It was akin to how Angel made me feel back when I was just a kid with a crush though it didn't burn as hot.

Z was right.

If I wanted to be touched, I'd beg for it, and it didn't always come with words. My body knew what it wanted even when my brain boycotted. I lifted my head and saw Angel watching. His dark, burning gaze never left me, but I knew he was clocking every move Z made.

"What do you say we put on a show?" Z whispered so only I could hear. "Let him see how much you really want it?"

It was too late to pretend. Z knew who and what I wanted, which meant Angel would too.

"How?"

"We'll make him jealous, princess." I felt his hands leave my waist. The breath I almost took was caught in my throat when his hand slipped beneath my shirt. He caressed the spot, low on my stomach, where I felt my urges. "You in?"

If sex had a voice, it would have been Z's. He waited while I finally exhaled. There was nothing I could do without my racing heart, though.

Gratifying sex with a man who helped kidnap my son?

Why would I say yes?

I met Angel's darkening glare, and wondered why I couldn't say no either.

"You control the pace and how far this goes." He paused to kiss my shoulder through my shirt and said, "But don't worry. He'll give in before you do."

My nod was barely complete when he lifted my shirt over my head. I was still coming to grips with my answer when he tossed it on the empty seat beside us. I should have felt shy and shameful for being exposed, but we were past that, weren't we?

"You have beautiful tits, princess. Did you know Angel was a tit man?"

I saw Angel's surprise when I nodded. "All the girls used to talk about it... He'd go crazy for them and make them come just by sucking on them." I could still feel the devastation and misplaced sense of betrayal whenever I heard about Angel with other girls. And I always heard about him. When girls weren't whispering about Angel, they were interrogating me.

I was hurtled back to the present when Z flicked my nipple and growled. "Yeah, but it's *you* who drives him crazy. Never forget that, princess." He repeated the assault on my other nipple before moving his hands down to my jeans and flicking open the button.

Angel didn't take his eyes off of us, so I waited for him to make his next move. I was confused when he pulled his hands away. "If you want more, show him. He can't resist you if you command it." I felt him wrap his hands around my waist and lift me from his lap.

What did he want from me?

I wanted Angel, but our past wouldn't allow me to speak the words.

Angel sat so still behind his father's desk, but I could sense the struggle within him to hold back and win this round. Years ago, my age kept a barrier between us, but now that I was of age, there was nothing but his restraint keeping him contained.

I could return the favor, push his boundaries until they collapsed, and push him away like he did to me. Z promised I controlled how far this would go, and for some reason, I believed him.

"Remember, Mian... you're in control," Z reminded as if on cue.

My hands moved to my open jeans and pushed them down my legs. I had to force my gaze away from Angel to step out of my jeans. It would be a definite mood killer if I were to fall on my face.

I stood up and forced my hands to hang by my sides. I was completely naked since, once again, I wasn't given a pair of panties.

"Damn, princess. I've missed you naked for us." I watched Angel for a reaction. His jaw ticked but other than that? Nothing.

God, why won't you say something?

"Come here," Z commanded. I didn't move. I couldn't. I wanted to scream. It should be Angel touching me. It should be him showing me that sex isn't something you take, it's something you give. Instead, he was determined to resist me.

For a moment, I was desperate enough to believe he'd read my mind and knew I intended to leave him high and dry the moment he gave in.

Maybe he just knows you well enough.

I ignored the voice and made the decision to try harder. I didn't doubt Angel's desire, but he obviously questioned mine. I turned my back on Angel and climbed gracefully onto Z's lap. I moved to wrap my arms around his neck, willing to give this my all, when he suddenly lifted me up and turned me, so my back was against his chest once more.

Shit.

I wanted to provoke his possessive nature by shutting him out, but Z had other plans. I hadn't realized his intent when he slid his palms over my knees until he cupped them underneath to lift and spread my legs apart enough to qualify as obscene. I was spread open like an offering and Angel had a front row seat.

My heart hammered against my chest. I felt trapped. If I panicked, it would scare them both off, and I'd never get this chance to make Angel lose control again. Angel's gaze lowered, but I couldn't stop watching him. If I had, I would have missed the first slip of his control. It was so fleeting that, had I blinked, I would have missed it.

I would have moved in for the kill, but Z's hands on my thighs destroyed the little control I had. He may not have been Angel, but I wasn't oblivious to his touch either. "Don't let him fool you, princess." His hands caressed my skin as he moved closer to my center. "He would have fucked you a long time ago if he thought you could handle him."

"I can handle him," I gasped. Z's fingers skimming my pussy erased reason from my mind.

"Then what do you say we kick this up a notch?" Z whispered. It was too late when I realized what was happening. At some point, while he was driving me crazy to torture his best friend, he'd released his cock. When I felt the hard length of Z's cock slide between my legs, an electric shock ran through me. With his hands on my hips, he lifted and lowered me, moving my sex along the length of his cock all the while Angel watched. I was spread open like an offering.

His voice was thick with barely restrained lust when Angel finally spoke. "I know what you're doing."

"But is it working?" Z whispered to me. I cried out when he lifted me again. This time, he shifted his hips and positioned his cock at my entrance. Angel's eyes blackened. "That's it," Z encouraged. "He's almost ready." He lowered me and at the same time, lifted his hips from the couch. The head of his cock pushed inside and when the sensation proved too much, I screamed as my orgasm unexpectedly rocked through me.

"Goddamn it!" Angel roared and surged to his feet. His chair toppled over when he charged for us. I expected Z to pull away, but I had the feeling he was still trying to push Angel's buttons. "You won't break me before I break you," he said as he slid to his knees. Z lifted me, breaking our meager connection, and sat me in his lap. His cock was now hidden as it pressed hot against my spine.

Angel's eyes were wild, but I saw the intent in them just before he lowered his head and destroyed me completely. His tongue swept my pussy lips, and he groaned like a starving man just before he devoured me.

"I told you he wanted it. He needs it," Z taunted over my cries. He pinched my nipples while Angel ate my pussy as if it were his last meal on earth. I don't remember sliding my fingers through his hair, but I tugged him closer anyway and demanded everything he had denied me since I knew what desire was. "How does she taste?"

I moaned despite my confusion.

"She tastes exactly how I thought she would." Angel's voice was rough like gravel.

"Like you'd kill to have more?"

"Precisely."

Oh, God. They were talking about killing just to have me, and I was growing wetter at the possibility. How much more twisted could we get before we completely snapped and destroyed each other?

I came apart again without the answer, and when my cries died, I slumped back against Z's chest. However, before I could fully recover, I was lifted into Angel's arms and carried away...

CHAPTER 49

They combust.

ANGEL

FINALLY.

I carried her upstairs, and instead of my parent's old bedroom where I'd been sleeping, I took her to my old bedroom. The rare times I visited home, I had fantasized about getting her in this bed, and then I'd fall asleep disgusted with myself for lusting after a kid. Sure, we'd known each other since we were both kids, but the age gap was always there, and when I became an adult, everything changed.

No other girl ever did more than turn my head. They didn't follow me in my dreams or keep me awake at night.

I was Adam, and she was forbidden fruit.

She always would be.

I lowered her to my bed and stood back to watch her. I realized I would never have my fill, so I removed my clothes and climbed on top of her. Her

eyes were closed, and she wasn't moving. A gentleman would let her rest, but I was neither gentle or patient. I was a man who needed her.

"Angel?" Her voice was soft and sleepy from two orgasms. "Baby?"

Her eyes peeked open, and she stared at me through narrow slits. "What are we doing?"

I nudged her legs apart and settled between them. "We're finally combusting." My cock wasted little time finding her pussy and hardened, even more, when it felt how wet she was, and I knew damn well it was all for me. I pushed my hips and reveled in the sounds she made as I slowly began to slip inside her. Her breath caught in her throat, and her gaze lost focus as her body welcomed me.

"What if I don't want to combust?" I looked deep into her eyes and saw only longing, desire, and something else that pulled at something deep inside me. There was no fear.

She wanted this.

So I gave it to her.

I slid deep and hard and watched the breath leave her lungs. Her head fell back, exposing her neck as she cried out.

She was tight.

So damn tight.

I bent low and whispered in her ear, "Don't you?"

All the breath left her body in one long exhale and ended with a whimper. The sound was tortured, and when she didn't move, I had a moment of regret for not taking more care. Her first time was traumatic, and she was still very much a virgin. But then she did something to remind me she wasn't made of glass.

She dug her nails deep enough in my back to return the pain I had caused her.

Her devious smile when I grunted tempted me to ignore the rules and take her with the little mercy I'd shown her since she came back into my life. I pushed deeper, testing the waters. She slid her hands down my back and gripped my ass. I didn't miss the subtle way she pulled me deeper and lifted her hips.

When I pulled my hips back, she dug her nails into my ass and moaned, "No." Smiling, I gave her what she wanted and thrust inside her, harder and deeper than before. Her lips parted when she groaned. The sight was so sexy, I considered pulling out so I could fuck them. Her pussy tightened around me as if to protest.

"I'm not going anywhere," I promised her.

She lowered her head and met my gaze. "Stop talking," she ordered.

Grinning, I gave her what she wanted. Mian didn't want to be wooed. She wanted to be fucked. She shuddered beneath me as I pounded inside her. I couldn't look into her face twisted with pleasure without wanting to explode, so I shoved my face in her neck and inhaled her scent instead. God, she smelled as sweet as she tasted. Just when I didn't think I could hold back much longer, I felt her pussy grip my dick. I lifted my face from her neck to watch her come and decided Z had been right. Mian coming was fucking sweet. When she settled, I managed to hold back my need to come and flipped her on her stomach.

No way in hell was I done with her.

I leaned over and slid deep again. "Stay with me, baby. We're not done." When she didn't move, I rose to my knees and lifted her ass against my hips. She moaned when my cock reached even deeper. "Wake the fuck up." My voice was thick with lust.

"Angel," she whined.

I wasn't having any of that shit. I'd waited too damn long for her. "Move your hips and fuck me," I ordered without mercy.

I needed her to show me how much she wanted me. Obediently, she pushed her ass against me, her rhythm gaining speed with each thrust. I was momentarily dazed by the sight of my cock entering her. Her come coated my dick making everything wetter and hotter.

When the beast inside me broke free, I lifted her upper body from the bed and rested her back against my chest. My hand found it's way to her neck and tightened slowly, cutting off her air little by little. She struggled and whined, so I fucked her harder. The only thing that moved was our hips. Even as she fought, she never stopped fucking me back.

"I told you, sex with me could be deadly," I whispered just as her consciousness began to slip away.

Her pussy gripped my dick, and she fell again. Her pussy sucked me dry until I was weak in the knees. This time, I flew over the edge with her, but she was already gone. I finished coming inside her, laid her down on her stomach, and gently slid from her body.

"What are you doing here?" I said without turning around. I'd known the moment they entered the room but had been too far gone to stop.

"Watching," they said at the same time.

"That was fucking intense," Z groaned.

"Why were you watching?" It wasn't the first time they've watched me fuck, but this was different. This was Mian.

"Because we want our turn," Lucas answered.

I finally turned on my back to face them. "That's not going to happen unless she wants it," I answered confidently. She'd never want it.

They broke out in smiles at the same time. "We figured you'd say that." Lucas laughed.

"So," Z drawled. "You and her?"

I looked down at her comatose form. The sharp pain in my chest was answer enough. "It's not possible."

"Says king of making the impossible possible," Lucas argued.

I shook my head and fell back against the headboard. "Not this time."

A heavy silence descended, making the atmosphere uncomfortable. "We'll leave you to it then." Z walked out first while Lucas hung back.

"What's on your mind, man?"

I didn't expect him to crack a smile. "Z told me he got to stick the tip in. Don't I get to play?" He feigned hurt, and if I had my gun, I would have shot him. He must have read my mind because he quickly pulled the door closed behind him. I could hear them laughing as they walked away. As soon as the sound of their footsteps disappeared, I didn't hesitate to pull my troublesome bandit in my arms.

CHAPTER 50

You shouldn't be here.

MIAN

"FUCKING SAY IT, Sprite."

There was no way in hell. I was holding out, although it was costing me a lot. The need to come built, and each time I was ready to throw myself off the ledge, his hand tightened around my neck, stealing my breath and pulling me back.

He was fucking me deep and hard when he told me I'd never see my father again and that I was his. To my disgust, I tightened around him and begged him to make me come.

"Tell me who daddy is."

I couldn't.

It was degrading and weird, and I wished my pussy would get the memo and stop getting wetter every time he said.

"I can't."

My legs tightened around him when his pounding cock drove me up the shower wall. The sound of the running water drowned out my cries. I didn't know which kink was worse, choking me until I lost consciousness or withholding my orgasm until I gave in to his degradation.

"You want to come, don't you?"

So fucking much.

"Don't you?" he roared.

"Yes!"

"Then give me what I want. Tell me you're mine."

Saying I was his would never be enough for him. For me to truly be Angel's, I had to be broken. If that were true, why wasn't I sure I didn't want to belong to him?

As if he'd read my thoughts, Angel sunk his teeth in my cheek. It was cruel and hurt enough to bring tears to my eyes, and when he didn't let go, I found myself screaming, "Daddy, stop!"

His teeth released my cheek only for him to steal my lips in a savage kiss. "Fuck yeah, I am," he growled. His hips crashed into mine increasing our tempo.

I came screaming his fucking name and didn't care how weird it was. I was too weak to clean myself, so he took over and dragged me from the shower. I was silent as he toweled me off and led me back to bed since the sun hadn't even risen yet.

He wouldn't let me have my space and wrapped my leg around his waist and then pushed my head on his chest. I let my thoughts torture me until I couldn't take the silence anymore.

"Do you enjoy degrading me?"

"Yeah, Mian. I do."

"Why? I didn't take you for the kinky type."

"Because if your father walked through that door right

now, you'd still look at him like he was the only man in the world." I peeked up at him and saw his stony expression.

"You're jealous."

"Yes," he growled without hesitation.

My smile snuck up on me, and I couldn't stop it from spreading. I kept my chin tucked down so he couldn't see. I definitely think calling him daddy during sex crossed too many lines, but I'd be lying if I said I didn't like knowing he was jealous.

I was a daddy's girl. It was true, but I never understood why Angel hated the closeness I felt with my father. He barely tolerated it before, but now he sought to destroy it.

"Why don't you like my father?"

"Because he killed mine," he said without emotion. I shook my head and felt him stiffen. "If you try to convince me of his innocence," he snarled, "I swear, I'll fuck you so hard you'll forget how to speak."

"I..." Words were lost as I imagined his body over mine, thrusting so hard, he'd do as he promised. "I wasn't going to." Something warned me to just end talk of my father, but I asked anyway, "Why do you care that I'm close to my father?"

He was silent for so long that I didn't think he would answer. "Because he hurts you."

"You hurt me, and you still think I belong to you."

"But at least I know I don't deserve you."

I shook my head and said nothing. He wasn't making sense, and I had the feeling I wouldn't be able to make him see reason. He's hated the thought of me loving my father since I was dropped on his shoulders nine years ago. It was becoming apparent that nothing would change that.

ANGEL FED ME breakfast and announced he had business to tend to. He left and came back minutes later holding my son in his arms. I wept when his blue eyes found mine, and he smiled. He looked healthy and had even gained weight. When I reached for him, Angel's dark look stopped me, and then he made me promise him I wouldn't run.

Standing so near to my son, it was easy to forget pride and my hate for him, so the promise slipped from my lips with ease.

I was so caught up with my son, I hadn't realized the entire day had passed until my stomach growled. I fed and then laid Caylen down for a nap and made a sandwich since it was quick. I hadn't seen Angel since this morning. The house seemed empty after I finished eating so I searched for him. Lucas and Z were nowhere to be found either. I neared one of the guest rooms when I finally heard the first sound I had heard in hours.

As I got closer, the sounds became familiar. A feminine moan and a masculine groan mingled and together, filled the hall outside the door.

It could have only been one of three men behind that door. Jealousy and insecurity needed to know who. As silently as I could, I pushed open the door enough to see the bed which was at the perfect angle.

I was confused by what I was witnessing. For one, there were too many limbs tangled together. With the door opened, the sounds were heightened, and I realized there weren't just two people moving on that bed.

There were three.

Lucas and Z kneeled on each side of the woman in their arms. Their mouths sucked at each of her nipples while their fingers worked together to pleasure her—Lucas at her clit while Z's fingers plunged inside her. Her head was tilted back so all I could make out was her blonde hair and slim body as she writhed with pleasure.

"Anna... baby... come for me." Lucas's passionate demand sent my world spiraling. I told myself she could have been anyone. I looked closer and studied the woman as much as I could with her head tipped back.

"Please," she moaned. My knees weakened, and a gasp of horror escaped my lips. I knew that voice. My gaze lost focus. I could no longer hear what went on around me. I couldn't even tell if I still stood on two feet.

It can't be her.

I hadn't realized the world had stopped moving or noticed the silence until I heard, "Mian?" Z ripped the door open and stared down at me in shock. My eyes traveled back to the bed like a moth to a flame. She gasped when our eyes connected.

"Mian?" I couldn't tell if the flush of her body was from heat or guilt, so I forced myself to focus on answers.

"What are you doing here?"

"They took me."

Anger and hurt washed over me. He made me promise not to run even though he'd taken my only friend and let them have her. Rationality was replaced by the beckon of violence. I needed to cause pain so mine didn't consume me.

So I did.

Z clutched his nose where I punched him and roared his rage. I wondered if I'd broken his nose, but then he dropped his hand and stared at me as if I had betrayed him. There was a bruise already forming, but his nose didn't appear to be broken. "What the hell did you do that for, princess?"

"Because she's seventeen!"

My outburst caused Z to forget his nose, and when my gaze found Lucas, he stood way too still. Anna pulled her knees up to her chest and wrapped her arms around them. She wouldn't look at anyone.

"What the hell are you talking about?" Lucas's frown deepened. "She's twenty-one."

"Is that what you tell yourself to assuage the guilt?"

"No," he said and bared his teeth. "That's what *she* told us."

I looked to Anna who flushed a deep red. She lied to them? She saw the question in my eyes and jumped from the bed. "I'm so sorry, but it was the only way to protect Caylen."

What would her age have to do with Caylen?

"Mian—" She scrambled from the bed, but her first step toward the door was blocked by Lucas. I watched as he wrapped a possessive hand around her jaw to keep her from moving.

"You lied to me?" I tensed when his voice and his eyes held no emotion as he regarded her. He appeared calm to someone who wouldn't know better, but I knew he was holding in his anger for the right moment to strike. Lucas had a temper that he wielded like a secret weapon.

"Yes."

"You're seventeen," he said unnecessarily. I could tell he didn't want to believe it and would only accept the truth from her.

She squeezed her eyes closed tight and nodded. No sooner had she opened them did he suddenly shove her hard enough to send her flying a few feet. She landed on her hands and knees and cried out. I pushed past the door and past Z and didn't stop until I was toe to toe with Lucas.

"What the hell is your problem?"

"I don't fuck children," he snarled.

"You've tried to fuck me on numerous occasions, and I'm only two years older than she is." I agreed that he never should have touched her, but I couldn't allow him to play the victim. Anna was well developed for her age, but he was a sharp man. He had to have known she was younger than she claimed.

"Yeah? Well, there's a big difference between jailbait and a legal fuck." Fire was burning in his eyes so I made the decision to get Anna far away before he consumed us all.

I turned away from him and helped her from the floor where she stared up at Lucas like a kicked puppy.

"Come on, Anna."

"She's not going anywhere."

I made sure Anna was steady on her feet before turning to face off Lucas again. "She's not staying here either."

"She's a prisoner and so are you. You don't get to decide."

"I'm not a prisoner anymore. I'm a guest."

He glanced at Z who leaned against the door silently. His eyes narrowed when they moved back to my face. "When was this decided?"

"This morning. Right after I fucked Angel's brains out," I gloated.

To my surprise, he smirked and took a step back. "Well done, then," he smartly retorted and moved for the door. "She stays here. You're welcome to do the same." With that, he grabbed Z's shoulder and stormed out. The door slammed, and the lock turned to keep us inside.

"I'm so stupid," she cried as soon as it did.

"Oh, Anna." My anger dissipated as I witnessed my only friend lose control of her emotions. "What were you thinking?"

"Angel wanted me to look after Caylen, but Lucas kept talking about my age. He thought I was too young and stupid, apparently, to look after a baby. I could tell he was convincing Angel, so I lied. I didn't want to leave Caylen at the mercy of those monsters."

Her tears spilled faster, and she looked ready to collapse at any moment so I led her to the bed. She continued to cry, and I searched for words to say to make it all go away. I came up empty, so I went with the truth that was heavy on my heart, especially since she admitted why she lied. "I don't know how I will ever thank you for what you did."

She sniffled and lifted her head. Her cheeks and eyes were puffy with red. "You would have done it for me."

I would have. Faster than a heart could beat. Unfortunately, I didn't feel any better about the sacrifice she made for me. I had no idea how much pain my actions caused the day I broke into my dead godfather's home.

"Did they force you?" I had to force the words out. It was hard to believe given their response to my own rape, but what if they hadn't given her a choice?

She looked horrified when she gasped. "No!"

We sat in silence until the questions tormenting me spilled out. "Which one?"

She blushed and stared at her fingers. "Lucas."

It was worse than I thought. At least with Z, he would have been nice. Anna never understood the type of men she tempted with her body. "Was he gentle?"

"Yes... at first." Her smile held a secret I wasn't sure I wanted to know. "But then it started to feel so good," she rushed out, letting me in on the secret.

I listened to her tell me about her first time with Lucas. It seemed that not only was he's God's gift to bed play, but I underestimated him as well. He wooed her before bedding her, and it was clear Anna was falling for him.

Instead of feeling lighter, I wanted to scream. I knew he wouldn't feel the same. Especially, not after this.

Z returned with a fussy Caylen, and I forced myself to leave Anna. "He stinks." Z's nose was turned up as he held my baby out like a bomb about to detonate.

"You could have changed his diaper."

He appeared sheepish when he said, "I don't know how."

"It's easy really. It's just like wiping your own ass after it explodes."

He bent over to laugh and just like that, the tension between us eased. Z was sweet and funny. He wasn't intense like Angel or temperamental like Lucas. He was easy.

I stopped walking, and he did the same, though he looked confused. "I'm sorry I punched you in the nose." I wasn't completely sorry, but for some reason, I apologized anyway.

"It's cool, princess. I'll take anything to get your hands on me."

I laughed and started walking again when I heard him say, "By the way... it would have hurt more if you'd slapped me with a feather." He guffawed and held my son up as a shield when I faced him with a menacing expression.

"Really? You're going to use my son?" I took Caylen from him, and he followed me to the nursery where I demonstrated how to change a diaper.

"Ever think you'll have little Zs running around?" I asked after I tossed the diaper.

His eyes were blank when he answered, "No."

"Why not? You don't like kids?" He seemed pretty comfortable with Caylen.

"I like them, just not enough to give them my blood or my name."

"I'm sure that's not true."

"That I don't like kids?"

"That you don't deserve them." What was I saying? This man kidnapped my child.

"Trust me, princess. There's not a sane woman alive who would take my seed." He walked out before I could respond, and I felt more than just a twinge of sadness for him. My heart actually broke. I always had the feeling his easy smiles were a mask to hide the broken man underneath.

After I had put Caylen down for another nap, I headed back to Anna's room. I didn't want to leave her alone for too long. It seemed I came not a moment too soon when I found Lucas outside her door pacing like an angry cat. "What are you doing here?"

He stopped pacing and leaned his forehead against her door. "I don't know," he croaked.

"Are you okay?"

"Of course, I'm not okay. I stuck my dick inside of a goddamn child."

"You shouldn't blame her."

"Ok." He lifted his head and turned to lean his shoulder against the door. "Give me a good reason why I shouldn't and maybe I won't." His voice was calm, but his eyes were impatient as he waited.

"She didn't know."

"She didn't know that she was only seventeen? Try again."

"She didn't understand the magnitude of what she'd done by lying."

He rolled his eyes. "Now you're pushing it. She's seventeen not seven."

"She did it for me. If you're going to be mad at someone, be mad at me." I stalked forward until my forehead was almost touching his chest and poked him there. "I dare you."

He smiled, and I tried not to get caught up in how much sexier he was in these rare moments. "You never cease to push me, girl."

Then he did something completely unexpected. He shoved his fingers in my hair, pulled me against his chest, and kissed me. I pushed against his chest, but he only wrapped his arm around my waist and tried to coax my lips open. When I wouldn't budge, he finally pulled back. "You can pretend I'm Angel if it helps."

My mouth opened to call him insane, but the words died when he stole my lips again. His tongue swept inside. I swallowed his groan and allowed him to kiss me since it was clear he wasn't going to let me go until I did.

When he finally broke the kiss, he stared in my eyes. I grew uncomfortable while wondering what he was thinking.

"The things I did to her..."

If it was any girl but my friend I would have been insulted that he'd been kissing me and thinking about another. "Is she the real reason you kissed me?"

"Yeah," he croaked.

"You're insane."

"Maybe." I stepped away from him before he got any more ideas. Lucas was incredibly hot and a damn good kisser, but we both knew I wasn't going to be the outlet he used to erase Anna. "Tell me something."

"What?"

"Is she turning eighteen soon? Like maybe tomorrow?"

I shook my head. "'Afraid not. She turned seventeen three months ago."

"Fuck!" He shoved his hands in his hair and stormed past me.

I WAITED UP for him in his bed. I knew he would come looking for me, to ensure himself I kept my promise, before coming to bed. I gave Caylen to Anna for the night to keep her mind off Lucas. From the look on Lucas's face when he stormed away from her room, he wouldn't have trouble staying away. I spent the rest of the day hoping to uncover secrets while Angel was away. I needed something to tip the balance in my favor. I promised Angel I'd stick around and accept his protection, but that didn't mean I had to trust him completely.

After an hour of snooping, I found something better.

I found a gun.

CHAPTER 51

She plays well.

ANGEL

I GRITTED MY teeth to keep from tearing the entire house apart.

She was gone.

I came home weary, pissed, and horny after a long, stressful day knocking heads. Now, I was just pissed and horny. I went to her room with the intention to climb in bed and pull her under me so I could fuck her long and hard. But she was not in bed waiting for me. It didn't help that when I checked the nursery, I found the crib empty.

She played me.

I wasn't even as pissed at her as I was at myself. One taste of her pussy and I crumbled. I found Lucas in the den, lying on his back, and staring at the ceiling. It pissed me off that he allowed her to slip through his fingers and then appear so laid back.

I had his shirt in my hands and lifted him off the couch before he even knew I was there.

"What the fuck, man?" He easily dislodged my grip on his shirt and shoved me back.

"Mian's gone, asshole!"

"What?"

"She's gone," I repeated impatiently. "Her bed is empty and so is Caylen's crib."

I wanted to break his jaw when he laughed and shook his head. "Dude... you're fucking whipped."

"What are you talking about?"

"She isn't in her bed because she's in *yours*." He shook his head as if it should have been obvious.

"Then why is Caylen's crib empty?"

"He's sleeping with Anna."

"Why?"

"Because your girl is using him as a repellent to keep me away." I ignored his reference to Mian being mine and focused on the part where Mian knew about Anna.

"She knows?"

He sighed, grabbed two beers from the mini cooler, popped the tops and then handed me one. He had already downed half of his by the time I could lift mine to my lips. "She knows," he finally confirmed and then dropped down on the couch.

"How?"

"I forgot to lock the door so she walked in on Z and me with Anna."

I did punch him then.

His head flew to the side, and I watched his jaw work as his fists bunched in his lap. Despite it, he remained seated, but the look in his eyes told me I was pushing it.

After a few moments of tense silence, he blurted, "She's seventeen."

"Who?" I was distracted by the fight I had waiting on me upstairs.

"Anna."

I knew she'd been lying, but I was too focused on keeping my dick down and one finger on the trigger. I fucked up.

"You okay?"

He scoffed. "Fuck no. I'm twenty-seven years old and was sticking it to a kid still in high school." He tipped the bottle back and rested his head against the back of the couch. "The worst part is... I still want her."

I nodded. If anyone could understand the torment Lucas was going through wanting someone he shouldn't have, it was me. At least Anna was closer to the legal age limit.

I topped off my beer and tossed it into the trash. "I wouldn't be your friend if I wasn't completely honest with you about your predicament."

"And what's that?"

"It doesn't get easier."

"Thanks, man," he replied dryly.

I left him alone because it seemed like he needed it and headed upstairs. When I opened the door to my old bedroom, I found her exactly where Lucas said she'd be. She was lying in a ball on top of the covers with her knees to her chest. I recognized the shirt she wore as one of mine, and I admitted that I liked it. I quickly stripped down to nothing without taking my eyes off her, pulling her into my arms. Once I had her where she belonged, fatigue hit me like a ten-ton truck, and I fell under.

I slowly drifted back to consciousness when I felt a tight pinch around my wrist.

What the hell?

My arms were pulled over my head. I tried to lower them, but they wouldn't budge. Awareness slammed into me hard enough to fully wake me.

"You won't get free. Before my mom died, I was a dedicated camp scout and can tie a hell of a knot." Mian was lying on her side with her head resting in her hand and a smug smile on her face.

"Untie me."

"No." Her smile grew brighter.

"Damn it, Mian. What the hell are you playing at?"

"Why did you kidnap Anna and bring her here?"

I pulled at my bonds again, and when I couldn't break free, I answered her. "She was leverage."

"She's my *friend*."

"Exactly why she made the perfect leverage."

"Why didn't you tell me? Even after everything—" She seemed to lose her composure, but I was still surprised when she shoved her hand under one of the pillows. I tugged at my bonds a little more desperately when I realized what she held. "I found this, and I have to admit I was shocked. A revolver doesn't really seem like your choice of weapon." Her eyes twinkled as she smiled down at me.

"What the fuck?"

"I know. I thought to keep it for a rainy day." She studied the gun and said, "But it looks like it already rained."

"Untie me," I ordered when my tugging didn't set me free.

"I didn't give you permission to play."

"I don't need your permission." She spun the cylinder with a grin, and I swear I felt my balls tighten. "And I'm not done yet." I was searching for a way to bring her to heel with my hands tied when the cold steel was suddenly pressed under my chin. "What's *my* name?"

Did she just...? My anger was so palpable I couldn't finish my train of thought. I schooled my face into one that I knew made even grown men three times her size cower, and I growled, "Mian." It wasn't an answer. It was a warning.

"Good." She ignored the warning and leaned down until our faces nearly brushed. "Now say it like you mean it."

"I'm not playing this game. You'll lose. You always do."

She seemed to be processing this but then gave a careless shrug. "Hmm... maybe. But not before I win." She tore her gaze from mine and gently, despite the malice she displayed, worked my dick from my shorts. My dick was far from hard, but it didn't deter her. She further amazed me by shooting a wad of her saliva on my dick. It twitched to life, and her knowing eyes flashed to mine. I looked away, but when her soft hand began to work me, I was drawn again by the sight of her dainty hand working my cock. The part of me that was hornier than pissed wanted to work my hips in her tiny fucking hand until I came. I'd gladly hand over my claim as a man just for a few more moments of her touching me.

"You really are magnificent," she whispered distractedly. Her gaze was unfocused, and I wondered if she knew what she had confessed. She didn't leave me guessing long. Her gaze was once again focused and trained on me when she said, "And tonight, *I'm* going to fuck magnificent." She straddled me without warning.

"Fuck, Mian!"

She shifted her hips and I found—or rather my dick found—that she was now bare beneath my shirt. "Goddamn," I muttered. She was drenched, and I hadn't even touched her. Did she get off on power? Or just power over me?

"You know there will be consequences," I warned when she lifted and positioned herself over my now rock hard cock. I wanted to deny her at the same time I wanted to shove myself so far inside her, I'd breach her fucking throat. Then she'd be at *my* mercy once again.

She didn't respond. She slid down my length and didn't stop until she was fully seated. Her moan mingled with my groan, and I wrestled with the need to pound. My head was tilted back as I sucked in air so I didn't see her lean closer until I felt her breath on my skin when she moaned, "Worth it."

We'd see about that.

She rose and plunged over and over. Slowly—too slowly—until she drove us both crazy. I needed more. She knew this, and she refused me. I pulled at my bonds again—not to escape, but to *take*. My muscles strained to overpower the ties.

"You won't escape." I stopped fighting to watch her tight, little body release me from the confines of her cunt. "I was a damn good camp scout." She slammed down and trapped my dick, sucking in large gulps of air at the same time. I was big—almost too big for her tight cunt, so I knew she was feeling the effects of how well I filled her. I kept the grin off my lips and locked my gaze on her tits. Her rosy colored nipples were the stuff of dreams, and I wanted my mouth on them.

I could have only the taste of her body as sustenance for the rest of my life and never suffer.

Her whimper drew my attention back to her face and saw her face drawn tight with anguish. She wanted to come.

"Christ." I was no longer fighting it. "You're going to ruin us both." I dug my heels in the sheet, used all my lower body strength to fuck her back as much as I could—as hard as I could—from beneath. Her expression was no longer drawn tight. It was soft again, but her body was still searching.

"You want to come? Untie me." I punctuated my demand with a hard upward drive of my hips. She gasped her surprise but maintained her stride.

Fuck yeah.

"I want my name. Say it," she growled.

"Fuck," I grunted. I needed my hands free, so I could take her hips in my hand and guide her. Her rhythm was now erratic. Uncontrolled. *Mindless.*

Did I mention she never removed her aim of the gun? She had been on the ride of her life, but now she'd lost control.

"Daddy, please," she'd cried out, and that was when I knew I had her as much as she had me.

"Baby..." My tone was soft and still she wouldn't open her eyes. She just kept riding. So I gave her the out she sought to give us—what we both wanted. "Mian..." Her eyes were suddenly bared to me. I drank in the sight and tasted the need in them. "Come on my dick. *Please.*"

"Send Anna home."

"Come. On. My. Dick."

"Send Anna home!"

"Damn, baby. I will. Now please—"

Her eyes were once again hidden from me when she threw back her head. I watched her body jerk and spasm as she screamed and very soon after, she sucked my own release deep inside her.

She fell on top of my chest, leaving me tied and aching to hold her closer. The gun had fallen from her hands and rested near my shoulder. It took a while but our breaths caught and the silence that followed had eventually become too loud. "Mian," I barked. Drowsily, she lifted her head and gazed at me with sleepy eyes. "Untie me."

She nodded and lifted her hands to the knot, easily slipping the rope through and moving to the next. Once free, she dropped her head to my chest again. I felt her body settle into sleep and her breathing evening out.

"Well played," I whispered in her hair. I settled my arms around her and joined her.

CHAPTER 52

You fucked up.

MIAN

"MERCY!" I RECEIVED a stinging slap to my thigh and corrected. "Mercy, Daddy!" My well spent, well-used body jerked for a third time after I came. I had no idea how much time had passed since my punishment started.

I really should have thought last night through.

I not only challenged Angel, but I did it with a gun after I tied him to the bed while he slept. He must have been drained because he'd slept through it until it was too late. This morning, I'd woken up to a ringing pain in my ass delivered by his palm. When I tried to turn, to protect my ass from further assault, I

 was held down as he delivered another blow. "Worth it," he'd said, low and sinister.

"Wha—what?"

"Last night, while you held a gun to my face, I warned you of the consequences, and you said it would be *worth it.*"

Oh, *God*. Did I?

I was brought back to the present when I became aware of him covering my body with his. "I can't." My legs were spread wider. "Tired." I felt his cock positioned at my entrance. "No more." He entered me hard and deep.

My cry was swallowed.

He didn't listen.

He didn't stop.

But he did remind me, sometime during another orgasm, that we were better off enemies. Each time we get too close we nearly destroy each other.

After my orgasm stole the last of my strength I slumped against the bedsheets and pillows and didn't fight it when my eyes closed. I heard him walk away and seconds later, the shower run.

I felt his hands sometime later through the fog of post-orgasmic sleep. I pried my eyes open just enough to see him now dressed in blue jeans. They were left open to show the mouthwatering V-shaped cut just below his hard abs. His chest was bare with the exception of the shower watering dripping from his muscles. I cursed my body for responding as he gently lifted my hips from the bed and spread my knees apart. My heart pounded against my chest that remained flush against the mattress while my sex was already preparing for him. I was too sore to take him again, but it didn't mean anything when I saw he was still impressively hard.

His fingertips grazed up from my knee and I held my breath as I waited for him to touch me. "Are you sore?" he asked when his fingers stopped an inch away. I quickly shook my head. Seeing his erection must have short-circuited my brain. I heard him chuckle, which meant he knew I was lying, but then it didn't matter when his fingers moved. This time he didn't stop. The shock of his first touch kept me in place, but then the continuous caress of his fingers as he toyed with my pussy made me come alive. My clit pulsed against his fingers as they circled gently. I thought I would come. I needed to come. "So, you can you walk then?"

Walking away from this bed was the last thing I wanted to do so I didn't answer him this time. But then his fingers moved away and he might as well have thrown me into a frozen lake with an anchor tied to my ankle.

"Why did you stop?" I heard myself say. My voice sounded sleepy and full of sex.

"Because you came. Many times. It's my turn." I eyed his cock near to bursting from his jeans and didn't realize I'd licked my lips until his gaze narrowed in on them. I felt the moisture on them and when my gaze returned to his cock, I wondered how he'd taste. "You're eyeing my dick like it's your last meal." He pulled me from the bed and brought my naked body against his barely clothed one. "If you ever hold a gun on me, it will be." So we were back to threats it seems. Before I could retort, he yanked his shirt I'd worn from the floor and shoved it over my head. "Come on," he ordered. His mouth was set in an impenetrable line.

"Where are we going?" I questioned as he took my hand.

"I keep my promises."

I DIDN'T UNDERSTAND until I witnessed Anna standing between Lucas and Z near the front door. *He's sending her home.*

"Mian?" Anna's voice shook with fear. I immediately figured Lucas was the culprit. His face was blank as he leaned against the door with his hands shoved in his pockets. Z moved away to speak with Angel so I took the opportunity to go to Anna. "I don't know what's going on. They came and took Caylen and—"

"You're going home," I interrupted, hoping to calm her. She was trembling when I pulled her into my arms.

She gasped and pulled away. "Why would Angel let me go?"

"Because I asked him to," I answered truthfully. I left out the part where I had to hold a gun to his head for him to agree. I didn't need Anna more freaked out than she already was.

"But what about you and Caylen?"

"We have to stay here. For now," I clarified when horror filled her eyes. "It was my choice," I lied. The truth was I didn't have a choice. Our death certificates would be written the moment we leave.

Doubt replaced fear in her gaze. She pulled me away and just as I expected Angel, Lucas, and Z's attention shifted our way. Anna hadn't noticed, but thankfully, she lowered her voice when she spoke again. "What aren't you telling me, Mian?" Her stern tone let me know I wouldn't be able to just blow her off, but I couldn't tell her the truth either.

427

"It's not safe for me to leave."

Her gaze narrowed. "But you're innocent. He said so himself."

"It's more complicated than that."

"How so?"

"It's not safe for me to tell you everything yet. It doesn't matter anyway because you shouldn't be here. School's starting soon and your mother will be worried."

"That's a bullshit answer, Mian and you know it. My mother probably didn't notice I was even gone until she ran out of cigarettes." I didn't have a response because it was sadly true. Brandi had even gone as far as to get Anna a fake ID so she can fetch her booze and cigarettes whenever she needed which was often. "How am I supposed to just go home and act normal knowing my best friend and nephew are in trouble? I was worried sick about you when you disappeared. I didn't know what to do or think. I even started to think you just left." Her voice teetered between anger and sadness as she broke my heart in two.

"I'm sorry I worried you, Anna, but I didn't have a choice. He took my son and then he kept us."

"I don't blame you." Her voice was thick from the tears she didn't shed. "I blame him. He'll never break you from your chains... and you don't even see it."

"Anna—" I was so focused on her that I hadn't noticed Angel until he was pulling me away. "What are you doing?" I hissed. "I'm not done!"

"The time to say goodbye is over." He paused from dragging me away, gripped my arms, and leaned low. For a moment, I thought he would kiss me. "You and I have business to finish."

The promise was there, and for once, I wished it weren't a promise he kept.

"Mian!" I turned to see Lucas hauling Anna to the door over his shoulder. Anna fought harder when he opened the door. I couldn't just let him take her away. Not like this. As if reading my mind, Angel pulled me into his body with a death grip around my waist that I fought as hard as I could. Just then, a feral growl ripped through the air, shifting my attention back to the door. I realized it had come from Anna when she savagely sunk her teeth into his shoulder. I heard him grunt just before he slapped her ass. Hard. Even I flinched.

Anna's scream of outrage was cut off by the door slamming closed.

CHAPTER 53

Sooner or later trouble knocks.

ANGEL

I HELD THE ice pack to Mian's jaw, and pretended I didn't feel like an asshole for what I did to her as soon as Lucas carried Anna out the door.

"I want your mouth."

"Wel,l you're not going to get it." It was amusing to watch her backing away at the same time trying to sound in control.

"All right, I feel like playing. This one is a classic. You're going to hide. If I don't find you in five minutes, I'll consider the consequence of last night paid."

She didn't look like she was buying it. "What's the catch?"

My smile disarmed her completely.

"If I do find you, I get your mouth... and the rest of you."

"What if I don't want to play?" she challenged.

I shook my head because she knew better. "Time's already ticking, Sprite."

When I woke up this morning and felt her ass nuzzled against my cock, I couldn't help wanting to do things to her that would make a God fearing lady clutch her pearls. But then I remembered what had happened hours before, and I couldn't stop my hand from flying. I slapped her ass hard enough to wake her and then put her on her knees.

Now that I wasn't thinking with my dick and controlled by my need to dominate her, I needed answers. Starting with where she'd gotten my mother's gun. The doorbell rang while I switched the ice pack to her other jaw. I peppered kisses down her available neck and ignored the doorbell when it rang again. "We need to talk."

"Aren't you going to get that?" She sounded horny and nervous at the same time, and I resisted the urge to smile.

"No."

"I think my jaw is fine now. I'm moving my mouth, and words are coming out." I leaned down to kiss her when I felt movement on my right. Lucas stood in the doorway watching us. He'd been quiet since I told him we were freeing Anna. I expected him to fight me on it, but he didn't. He even volunteered to take her. His eyes have been vacant ever since, and at the same time, I think he was relieved she wasn't around to tempt him anymore.

"What's up, man?"

"Cops."

CHAPTER 54

Everyone dies.

MIAN

ANGEL'S LOOK OF betrayal before I was sent to my room like a child was all I could think about. That had been two days ago.

I was back to being locked in my room, but lucky for Angel, he didn't try to keep me from my son. He had Lucas and Z bring the crib and his supplies to my room. They also took turns checking on us while he stayed away.

When the police showed up, and Angel turned cold, I knew it was because he thought I tipped the police somehow. I would have, but I was never able to find a working phone. Besides, it wasn't as if the police didn't have more than enough reason to show on his doorstep.

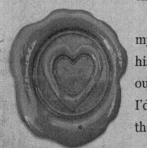

Caylen tugged at my hair, stealing my attention. He stared up at me with his bright blue eyes. "We've got to get out of here, baby boy. We're not safe." I'd been kidding myself because of all the sex he used to cloud my judgment.

His answer was to stick my hair in his mouth. Clearly, he wasn't going to contribute to the plan to bust out of here.

The door opened while I tried to wrangle my hair from his fist and mouth. He had such a strong grip for a baby. I didn't look up to see who graced my doorway this time because the odds it was someone I didn't care to see were too high for me to bother.

"How are you?"

Ok, I wasn't expecting him.

I finally dislodged my hair from Caylen's mouth and looked up. I expected him to look as formidable as always but the jeans and shirt he wore two days ago were wrinkled, his eyes were weary, and his hair was beyond his normal bed hair. His left hand was also bandaged.

"What happened to you?"

"My grandfather died."

Suddenly, the burning anger I held over my two-day stint went up in smoke. I didn't say anything as I placed Caylen carefully in his crib. Angel continued to stand unmoving just inside the door. I walked up to him and wrapped my arms around his neck.

"I'm sorry." He buried his face in my neck, and I felt him nod. When he didn't respond, I pulled back and stared until he lifted his eyes from the floor. "How did he die?"

"A gunshot to the heart." I gasped and grabbed him again so I wouldn't collapse.

Alon had died the same way his son had, and once again, Angel was left without a father.

CHAPTER 55

When it rains, it pours.

ANGEL

I DON'T KNOW how I ended up here, but when she pressed her body against me and wrapped me in her arms, I knew there was nowhere else I would rather be.

I missed her, but I would never tell her.

When the police showed up at my door, I thought Anna ignored my threats and went to the police. Mian may have got to me through my dick, but I wasn't stupid enough to set Anna free without putting the fear of God in her first.

As it turned out, my grandfather was murdered that morning, and the shooter fled. I spent the last forty-eight hours searching for him nonstop.

Until this morning.

Lucas received a phone call from Anna to warn him that some Joey kid had gone to the police when Mian disappeared. The police wrote her off when the landlord reported that she skipped rent. She had so little, leaving her apartment bare, that it was easy for them to deduce she took what she could and move. When Anna disappeared almost two weeks later and her mother showed no concern about her daughter's disappearance, this Joey kid reported it to the police. Fortunately for me, her mother's shitty parenting made her a primary suspect in her underage daughter's disappearance. Anna, it seems, showed up just in time to offer the same story Brandi gave them about running away to spite her.

It was the phone call that reminded me that I had more than one problem. I promised to keep Mian and Caylen safe from the senator, but I left them alone for two days.

"Angel." I didn't realize I was hiding my gaze from her again until she lifted my chin. I didn't want her to see my pain. When my father died, I broke down, and the only thing that pieced me back together was punishing Theo. I wanted to kill Theo for what he took from me, and because I spent the time sulking, I missed my opportunity. It was a mistake I wouldn't make again, but it seemed all I did was make new ones.

"I'm sorry," I found myself saying.

I was more surprised when I felt her press a gentle kiss to my lips as she whispered, "Me, too."

CHAPTER 56

It wasn't lost. Only forgotten.

MIAN

I HAD NO idea how large the Knight family was. Every member, no matter how far down the line, were spread out over the estate.

And Angel was the head of them all.

I also learned that day that the Knights had their own personal graveyard.

At the estate.

And now that Alon was dead, Angel inherited the estate and was expected to live with a bunch of dead people in his backyard. The estate was vast, I was told, which allowed them to keep the graveyard out of sight but *definitely* not out of mind.

I brushed my feelings about it aside since I wasn't the one who had to live there. I'd definitely be afraid of waking up and finding one of Angel's dead relatives watching me from the foot of my bed.

The funeral had been sad, even for me when my sole memory of Alon was him trying to kill me. That certainly had been memorable. Especially, the part when Angel stood up to his grandfather for me.

My gaze was drawn to him against my will. He stood across the room talking with two men. I noticed how he was never far away even though he never got too close either. He had been distant since he came to my room and announced his grandfather was killed.

"Mian?"

I turned at the sound of the familiar voice and was shocked to come face to face with a blast from the past. "Bea?" I asked with surprise blatant in my tone. There were too many emotions involved with seeing Bea again.

"Yes, dear. How are you? I didn't expect to see you here. I didn't even know you knew Alon."

"Oh, um... I didn't really. I only met him once."

She stared, and I had the feeling Angel's mother was reading me like a book. Someone should have warned her my ending was tragic.

"Recently?"

"Mian," Lucas interrupted before I could answer. He was staring at Bea as he said, "Caylen's awake."

"Caylen?" Bea questioned.

"My son," I simply said. I stuck around only long enough to see her surprise and hurried upstairs. I entered the room where he had been sleeping and found him still soundly sleeping.

"I want you to stay here." I turned and found Angel in the doorway watching me from under his shell.

"Why?"

"Because I said so."

I stiffened as irritation took over. "Try again."

He moved inside and threw the door closed as he kept coming for me. "Because people are asking questions I don't care to answer."

"You could tell them the truth. This is a crime family, is it not?"

He laughed. "Most of my family turn the other cheek and pretend the money they enjoy spending is not ill-gotten."

"Which means they're using you."

"No, baby. It means I don't owe them an explanation."

"Don't call me that."

"Call you what?" His voice didn't hold any confusion. Only challenge.

"Baby. You and I both know I'm still around because I don't have a choice."

"You're no longer my hostage. You're my guest."

"And without you, I'm dead." My laugh was dry. "I bet that makes your dick hard."

"There are many things you do that make my dick hard. Being dead isn't one of them. Well... not anymore."

He grinned and it was such a sexy look on him. It was too bad his smile wasn't enough to thaw the cold reminder of death that he once planned for me. I shoved him, but he caught my waist and threw me on the bed before climbing on top of me.

"You're upset." He didn't appear the least bit apologetic.

"What was your first clue?"

"The frown on your face. It's sexy, don't get me wrong, but you're beautiful when you smile."

"You running games on me, Knight?"

"Yes," he growled. "My dick made plans with your pussy tonight, and I screwed it up by being an ass."

I patted his cheek. "No, sweetie." My voice dripped sweet sugary venom. "You screwed it up when you opened your mouth." He looked confused so I threw him a bone. "You're grieving. I got that."

"But?"

"But you reminded me of everything you did to my son and me when you admitted you wanted me dead once upon a time."

"So what are you saying?"

The promise of sex evaporated from his eyes. Instead, he stared down at me as if I just kicked his puppy. It still didn't compare to all he'd done to me. He'd somehow made me admit I still wanted him, but that didn't mean he could make me forgive him. My heart and body wanted different things from him.

"I'm saying, I can't forgive you."

His eyes moved over my face, and I had the feeling he was searching for a way in. My heart? My soul? He didn't know that he already found his way into both. The path he used, though, was too ugly and broken to makeover with pretty words.

"Ever?"

I answered only when I was sure my voice was strong. "Ever."

A KNOCK ON the door came a few minutes after Angel stormed out. "Come in."

The door opened, and Bea slipped inside. I had the feeling she didn't want her son to know she was with me.

"Hi, honey." Her smile was warm, but I could see the sadness she attempted to hide within her eyes.

"Hey." She glanced toward the crib where Caylen played with his toes. He was ten months in a few days and getting more limber by the day. Pretty soon, he'd be walking, talking, and running. I only hoped I could keep up. Bea walked over to the crib and cooed when she got a better look at him. "He's so handsome. Maybe even more so than Angel when he was his age."

My blood ran cold.

She thought Caylen was Angel's.

"Unfortunately, I think he looks more like his *father* every day." When she turned to regard me, her frown was deep. "He's not Angel's son."

She didn't bother to deny what I had picked up from her comment and looked back down at Caylen. "Nevertheless. He is a handsome one." She smiled, and it seemed genuine. "The girls won't stand a chance."

"Thank you," I forced out, not feeling as genuine.

"So, how have you been? It's been a while."

"More than just a while, Bea." *Try five years.*

She had the decency to look contrite. "It seems I have a lot to apologize for."

Don't bother. "Don't worry about it." I tried to remind myself that her husband was murdered, which meant she wasn't obligated to reach out to the daughter of his killer. Even if my mother had been her best friend, and I was just a kid left with no one.

"I care about you, Mian. I know I haven't shown it well, but I do." I nodded since I had nothing to say. "I have something for you," she said when the silence became awkward. I watched her reach into her purse and felt uneasy. She had no idea she'd be seeing me. How could she know to bring something?

I thought I was hallucinating when she pulled out a doll I hadn't seen in three years and haven't played with even longer. "When Angel sold the brownstone, he put your things in storage." *He did what?* "Anyway, I couldn't bear to see this locked away to collect dust. My husband gave this to you as a gift, didn't he?"

My lungs felt like a boa constrictor was wrapped around it while my heart threatened to burst. I couldn't breathe.

Once upon a time this doll lost her head.

And I lost a memory...

CHAPTER 57

One dangerous secret.

MIAN

THIRTEEN YEARS AGO

STUPID TEARS.

They were always around when I broke the head off my dolls. I sniffled and wiped my face and then got up to find my mommy. She always knew how to fix Suzy. Uncle Art came over to visit again. He mostly came over when Daddy was around, but he came over a lot when he wasn't, too. I liked his visits since he always bought me new toys, even though Mommy would send me to my room right after. When she'd finally come to get me, he was already gone.

Downstairs, I went straight to the kitchen. Whenever the hand on the clock was at seven, I knew it was time for dinner just

like my Daddy taught me. I got closer and didn't smell the yummy smells when my mommy cooked, or hear her humming a happy tune. I peeked inside the empty kitchen. The living room was empty too when I checked.

"Mommy?"

She didn't answer.

She *always* answered.

Upstairs, I called her name again and again until I heard a sound. I listened real hard, and the sound came again. It sounded like Mommy was crying. I was scared to know why, but since my daddy was gone, it was up to me to rescue her. I rushed to the door when I heard her cry again, but stopped when another sound, this time, harder and louder, drowned out her cries.

My eyes grew wide when I realized someone was in there hurting her. The door creaked when I opened it, and before I could peek inside, I remembered Daddy's instructions to call him if someone was ever trying to hurt us.

I knew he would make the bad person go away, so I rushed for the stairs. I heard the door open before I could make it to the stairs. I kept running so they didn't get me, but my mother's voice calling my name stopped me. I turned around and found her rushing to tie her favorite blue robe. Her hands moved too fast so it took her three tries.

She looked so scared, but I didn't see cuts or scrapes or blood like I got when I fell down and hurt. "Mommy! Are you hurt?"

Her bedroom door creaked again, and a tall man stepped out behind her. His jeans were unfastened, and he didn't wear a shirt. When I finally looked at his face, I gasped and stepped back.

It was Uncle Art. I didn't understand what was happening. Why would he hurt her? He was daddy's best friend, and he always brought me toys.

"Sweetheart... honey... look at me," my mother pleaded. I

slowly did as she asked and found my mother's eyes watering. "Have you called your father?"

I shook my head.

"Good. I know this looks bad, and I'm so sorry you had to see this."

Should I tell her I didn't see anything? She seemed so upset. Had I done something wrong by wanting to rescue her? "He was hurting you," I blurted. I didn't want to, but my gaze slid back up to Uncle Art. He stood behind my mother watching me silently. His gaze wasn't cruel or scared, though. He just looked worried.

"No, baby. He wasn't. He would never do that, do you understand?"

"But I heard you crying." She flinched, and out of the corner of my eye, I saw Uncle Art stiffen and then run his fingers through his hair.

"Listen to me, sweetie. I just need you to not say a word to your father about this. It would hurt him, and we don't want that, do we?"

I shook my head so hard my pigtails hit my cheek and stung.

"Good, baby. Now Mommy just needs for you to forget. Can you do that?" I nodded, even though I wasn't really sure I could.

Mommy sent me to my room. Tears spilled onto my pillow, and my chest hurt as I listened to them arguing downstairs. She was pleading with him that nothing had changed. The last thing I had heard before the door slammed was Uncle Art telling Mommy it was over. He never came back to visit.

Not even for Daddy.

CHAPTER 58

One cannot steal what's already stolen.

ANGEL

PRESENT

I SENT MIAN and Caylen home with Lucas and Z while I met with family lawyers to settle the estate.

Home.

It was easy to think Mian's home was with me and hard to remember it wasn't.

"Per the will, you are the sole heir of the Knight estate..." I tuned the lawyers out as they droned on with their legal garble. I would inherit a whole bunch of money, a big house, produce an heir, and not fuck it up. Yada yada...

My mind was stuck on my stepfather. Victor couldn't keep his eyes off of Mian during the funeral and reception. I wanted to confront him, but there were too many eyes and ears around. I was confident the confrontation would have led to death. Instead, I hid Mian before Victor could get to her and decided against telling

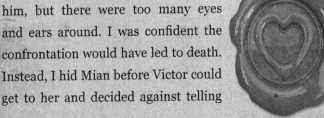

her anything to keep her from freaking out. It didn't help that my mom had chosen that moment to discover Mian's attendance. Luckily, Lucas had intercepted before I could.

Time dragged. but when the jargon finally stopped, I signed some papers, and they promised to be in touch. I didn't waste time leaving the offices. My struggle to not put a bullet in Victor didn't keep from me sensing Mian's uneasiness when I sent her home. During the meeting, I had to force myself to ignore the demand in the pit of my stomach to go to her. As I jogged down the steps, I replayed what had happened between us upstairs. Nothing we said could have completely drained the color from her face. Something was up.

I got a phone call from Z the moment my feet touched the pavement. "Where are you?" he questioned as soon as I picked up. The urgency in his tone made me tense.

"Leaving the lawyers. What's up?"

"Dude," Z blew out. "It's way more fucked than we thought."

I stopped dead on the sidewalk and forced the people walking by to move around me. "Tell me."

"I know who disabled the system and took the book."

"Well, don't keep me in unnecessary suspense. Fucking tell me."

I FORCED MYSELF not to go to Mian when I walked through my father's door and up his stairs. Lucas and Z were in his office bent over Z's laptop with expressions to kill.

"Are you fucking sure?" I demanded without preamble. Their surprise at my sudden presence was evident.

"I'm sure, man. The IP address belonging to the public library was just a mask. The real IP address was buried among over a million existing addresses. It's a coded system I don't recognize. It's designed so if I figured out the first was a fluke, I'd have to weed through too many to find the real one in time."

"How did you figure this out?"

"You."

"Me," I repeated.

"When Lucas asked why Mian needed a mask for the ball you said—"

"So no one can see what I'm hiding underneath," I finished.

"When I realized our system had been hacked, I checked the IP address. Using a public computer made enough sense for me not to question it. The person who checked out the computer was a ten-year-old kid in a wheelchair. His parents are dead from the crash that crushed his legs and the grandmother that takes care of him can barely see ten feet in front of her."

"There's just one thing that doesn't make sense. Why would my mom steal the book? She hates the life my father led and between her new husband and me, she's a well-kept woman."

My phone rang. I was tempted not to answer it until I saw it was my mother calling.

"Son," she breathed. "How did the meeting with the lawyers go?"

"I inherited everything, Mother." I couldn't keep the ice from my tone. "I'm a very rich man."

"I'm happy to hear it. Shame you won't be able to spend all that blood money," a voice that didn't belong to my mother's said.

It was Victor's daughter, Eliana. I knew immediately what this was.

"You made a big mistake taking her."

"She's not all I took," she cackled. "Or don't you know?"

"What the hell are you talking about?"

There was shuffling and then I heard, "Angel?"

No.

There was no fucking way.

I stormed out of the office with Lucas and Z already on my heels. "Don't bother looking," Eliana boasted. "You heard for yourself."

"The only thing I hear is the sound of you screaming while I kill you."

"I want to make a trade," she stated confidently. "You can have your mom and girlfriend back alive if you come alone and die like all Knights should."

CHAPTER 59

Three can keep a secret...

MIAN

MY HEAD CONTINUED to throb long after I came to. The last thing I remember before everything went black was the look in my mother's eyes when she begged me to forget her affair with my father's best friend.

But that was thirteen years ago.

I stared at the concrete beneath my bound feet and willed myself to remember the moments before I was knocked unconscious. Lucas and Z had disappeared upstairs, leaving me alone, after they claimed my pacing after we returned to Crecia were making them dizzy.

The here and now came back into focus, but then I figured I must have been hallucinating when I heard Bea's voice. Her voice sounded addled as she asked about a meeting, and then the same feminine voice spoke that I had heard seconds before I was knocked

unconscious and brought here. The conversation was one-sided, so I figured out she was on the phone just before said phone was shoved against my ear.

"What the hell are you talking about?" an enraged voice spoke, which I recognized.

"Angel?" The phone was gone before I could say more. Had he set this whole thing up? I tried to lift my head, but it felt too heavy. I was little more than a tomb—dead and hollow.

Had Angel changed his mind about keeping me alive? I needed to tell him what I remembered before it was too late. I knew in my gut my dad didn't betray and kill Art for his legacy. He killed him for fucking his wife. Art had been the one to betray my dad. Angel would have to see that.

"I'm sorry the accommodations are grossly unpleasant," she whispered in my ear. "I'm afraid this was your boyfriend's doing."

Fear allowed me to finally lift my head. I took in the concrete walls with small windows too high to do me any good. The space was large and mostly empty except the chains that hung from the ceiling. It creeped me out enough to send a chill down my spine.

"What is this place?"

"This, I'm told, is where he keeps people on ice until the client who pays for them comes to collect or where he makes them disappear altogether. These bleak walls closing in on them are the last thing his victims' eyes see before he closes them forever."

"Who told you this?"

"I did, dear girl." A voice I didn't recognize echoed around the room. I heard footsteps as a man who resembled Emiliano

Diez, only shorter, approached. Bea, who I noticed was also tied, shrunk in her chair.

"Who are you?"

"I'm Victor Castro. Eliana's father."

I may not have recognized his face but his name instantly resonated. "You were my dad and Uncle Art's friend and Bea's husband after he died."

"Yes, well, I had many titles. Too many in fact. I was first Art's best friend, and then merely his bookkeeper when your father came along. You can understand why I felt the need to shed the dead weight."

"No. I can't."

"Well, let me enlighten you. I was Art's only friend for fifteen years. I did as he asked, when he asked, and never questioned him. Your father rescues him once, and the years I put in are simply forgotten. Loyalty means nothing to a man with so much power. He would never have given that power up without death."

"And you made that happen."

"It wasn't hard. A man's wife... and her pussy... is something to kill for."

"Has it ever occurred to you that Art didn't respect you because you were weak? He treated you like an errand boy because... well... if it quacks..."

"So you think your father was better than me?"

"No," I answered confidently. "He was a criminal the same as you. He was just better and stronger at it."

"And where are two of Chicago's *strongest* criminals now?"

"One is rotting in a grave and the other behind bars," I answered, feigning indifference. "What's your point?"

"My point is that *I* put them there."

"What makes you think you put my father behind bars?" My heart beat faster when I witnessed the pride in his eyes.

"Who do you think told him about Art and Ceci's illicit affair?"

It was impossible to keep a hold on my composure. Bea wept next to me, but the sound of her cries were muffled by her gag.

"Why?"

"Art was planning to announce his retirement the night of Angel's birthday party. But that's not all that was planned."

"What else was there?"

His smile was cruel. "Your betrothal to his son."

I repeated his words in my head, but they refused to make sense. I was *never* engaged to Angel. "What the hell are you talking about?"

"Art convinced your father to save you for his son with the promise of you always having the protection of the Knight name and fortune. This was his way of ensuring Angel produced a suitable heir. Art was growing concerned over Angel's insistence to stick his cock in every girl in Chicago. They signed a contract that only death could break. On your eighteenth birthday, you both would have married, and Angel would have assumed the throne."

Suddenly, I was replaying Angel's phone call on his birthday and his invitation to be by his side. It wasn't because he wanted me. It had been a front for something he wanted more.

I was his ticket to power.

"Why would that make you betray them?"

"Because I was the one who put the idea of an arranged marriage in his head when he complained to me about his son's whoring."

My gaze was drawn to Eliana standing beside her father appearing just as enraged, and suddenly, it all pieced together.

"You expected him to marry your daughter. Not me."

"My Eliana is closer in age and far more beautiful, yet he completely overlooked her."

"How did you convince my father my mother cheated on him?"

"Seeing is believing." Suddenly, my head was grabbed from behind to keep me still. I hadn't realized there was anyone else in the room. I should have known. Eliana's voice may have been what I heard before I was knocked over the head, but she looked like she hadn't lifted more than a hair brush in her entire life. She approached with her phone and thrust the screen in my face.

The video played clear footage of a naked couple going at it on a red cushioned settee I didn't recognize. The woman was mostly hidden by the strong body of the man. His back faced the camera, and I could see the muscles in his ass bunch as he thrust deep. Her legs were wrapped around him, and the only thing she wore were her heels. Their clothes were scattered on the floor around the chair they were fucking on. It was clear they didn't know they were being recorded. It was impossible to see faces, but I closed my eyes anyway knowing who it was.

"Now open your eyes, dear. This part is important."

I was repeatedly slapped until I complied, and when my eyes flew open, my heart cracked, letting every horrible feeling imaginable inside.

"Why are you showing me this?"

"You need to know what a whore your mother was."

I wanted to burst his bubble and confess that I'd known about the affair for years, but at my mother's pleading, I had filed it away and forgotten. Bea giving me the doll I broke the day I found out triggered the memory and everything after poured out. Art never visited my mother again, and my mother became distant. I told myself it was because she was sick, but I now knew it was because she blamed me for taking away what she truly wanted.

Art.

Not Daddy.

And not me.

I chose not to give Victor the satisfaction and kept silent.

"I think that's enough story time. Don't you?"

"What are you going to do with us?"

"I'm going to kill both of you. Bea's death will make me a very rich man and yours will just give me the satisfaction."

"Why haven't you already killed us then?"

"Oh, but temptation does pour from your sweet lips, doesn't it? Alas, I have to wait until the guest of honor arrives. He dies last."

"Do you really believe you can kill him?" Victor may have been capable of murder and manipulation, but Angel made the devil want to step his game up.

"Certainly, dear. I have you to convince him. He'll die because of a woman, the same as his father. It's oddly poetic."

"He's here, Father." I snorted. Her formality would have made her a good wife for Angel. He wouldn't have felt the need to compete with her father like he did with mine. I loved my dad, and I wasn't willing to give him up for Angel. Just then, the doors opened, sunlight poured in, and Angel casually walked through them promising death with every step.

CHAPTER 60

...if two of them are dead. — Benjamin Franklin

ANGEL

I TOOK ONE look at my gagged and bound mother and wanted to cut down everyone involved. "That's far enough, and you can drop your gun."

I stopped walking but didn't lower my gun. "Not a chance."

"Then I'll shoot her now, and your mother can join her in hell." He aimed his gun at Mian's head. The true test of control was ignoring my rage. Reacting in anger would be stupid and fatal. I needed him to think I was calm inside and out. It meant control.

"If you shoot her, what will stop me from killing you?" I rationalized.

The fucker pursed his lips as if he hadn't thought about it. I almost snorted. He thought he could actually kill me. "It seems we are at an impasse."

"What do you want, Castro?" There was only irritation in my tone, but the

truth was, I was scared as fuck. This was the first time I was the one with something to lose besides my life.

"Revenge before I take your family's empire."

"Not going to happen."

"When you're finally dead, I'll inherit your power."

"Not. Going. To. Happen."

"I have your book. It will happen."

"Then why do you need me dead? Why do I still sit on my throne while you hide and creep among my court like a coward?"

"Because fear creates a false sense of loyalty. Having the book isn't enough. No one is willing to believe you aren't smart enough to keep a copy. It seems I can't do business unless you're dead."

"Whispers can ruin you."

"What the hell does that mean?"

"I don't have a copy. I guess I'm not as smart as people think."

"You're lying."

"Maybe. I would be smart to lie. But since I'm not..."

He exploded. "Enough with the mind games! Do you have a copy or not?"

"If you're going to kill me, will it matter? Without me to refute it, you can make them believe anything you want."

"Is that the same thing you told your mother the night your father died?" I watched his gaze move to Mian while he continued to speak to me. "Isn't that why you want Theo dead?"

I felt the first crack in my control. "Shut up, Castro." But it was too late. Mian's ears were already wide open.

"A dead man can't talk," he continued. He had a death

wish. I started to pull the trigger and unload on Castro until he was as dead as my father, but her voice stopped me.

"What is he talking about?" I didn't answer. I didn't look at her. She would never forgive me if I did.

"My dear, your father didn't kill Art." His cold gaze watched me as he delivered the final blow. "His mother did."

I did pull the trigger then. Just as he glanced away to smile at Mian, my bullet pierced his skull, shutting him up forever. His lone henchman fired a shot, but before he could fire a second, I sent him to hell.

Eliana stared down at her father as blood poured from his head onto the concrete. I aimed and whistled to get her attention.

"Any last words?"

She dropped her gun and threw her hands up pleadingly. "Plea—" I shot her before she could finish.

Through it all, Mian kept her head down, and I knew it wasn't fear that made her curl into herself. Even now, I could feel her pain. Her shoulders trembled, and I knew when I looked in her eyes there would be tears. I cut through the tape binding her and dropped the knife to pull her into my arms.

"Mian?"

She wobbled when I stood her up so I held her tighter. "Is it true?" Her voice was so small.

Suddenly, I was falling from a cliff and reaching for anything that would keep me from hitting rock bottom.

"Fuck." My voice was shaking too. "We can't talk about this here. Let me untie my mom and get you two somewhere safe." It was hard letting her go, but I managed and turned to remove my mom's gag when I stopped short. I couldn't move, speak, or think. My mom's eyes were open and staring down at the ground as her head hung, but there was no life in them. Blood poured from the side of her head. "Mom?" It was my turn to sound small. I barely recognized my own voice as I called out to her again.

"Victor's guard killed her," Mian answered when my mother didn't. I couldn't stop staring and waiting for her to move. She couldn't be dead. "Angel," Mian called more forcefully. I answered her demand by facing her. Tears poured down her face as she moved into my body, but I couldn't bring myself to hold her. I was too numb.

"I know how you're feeling," she said into my chest. "I know how it feels to lose a mom and even a dad. I know how it feels to lose everything. That's how you're feeling, aren't you?" I didn't answer. "Everything I had lost was because of you and your family and your *lie*."

A sharp pain in my stomach punctuated her claim. We both stared down, mesmerized by the sight of my knife in my stomach. "That was for my son." I parted my lips, I heard the words in my head, but nothing came out. "I couldn't fall out of love with you, Angel. Even when you refused to love me back." I watched a lone tear trail down her face just as she drove the knife deeper into my gut. I struggled again to speak, but a pain filled gasp was all I could manage. She was tearing me apart inside in more ways than one. "But the man you hate is my father, and since the moment I was born, I also promised him I'd love him. *This* is for him."

She let go of the knife as if it burned her and stepped back. I tried to keep my eyes from closing so I could see her one last time, but then she turned and ran before I could force more words past my pain.

"Sprite," I whispered too late.

CHAPTER 61

Your secrets will eventually betray you.

ANGEL

THREE YEARS AGO

I WALKED INTO my parent's home and caught the weight of my mother after she flew into my chest and broke down. "I killed him. Oh, God. I killed your father, Angel."

My father told me the day might one day come when I'd have to avenge his death. He even prepared me for it. He just hadn't prepared me for my mother being the one to off him.

"Where is he?"

"Upstairs." She hiccupped and burrowed her face back in my chest. I wanted to console my mother, but I needed answers. I knew I wouldn't get any from her so I picked her up and carried her into the living room where I laid her down on the couch. She curled into the cushions and repeated, "I killed him." Her eyes were empty as she stared up at me.

I forced my feet to move and headed for the stairs with heavy steps.

For the first time in my life, I would meet death. I knew this wouldn't be the last it came for me.

AUTHOR'S NOTE

FOR THOSE WHO missed the announcement and were still expecting a standalone, The Bandit was planned as a standalone. When it was time to write the ending, I realized how much I'd unsaid and unresolved with little time to unveil the rest of their story. When you sit down to write a story, it's not always easy to predict where the characters will lead you. Even more so, life doesn't care about deadlines. Some of you may be angry with me, and I won't blame you. Some will just find excitement in getting more story. Whichever way you choose to swing, I am grateful you took a chance on The Bandit.

Please stay tuned for the second part of their story coming as soon as I can get it written.

ACKNOWLEDGMENTS

FAMILY & FRIENDS – Once again I've brushed you aside to get through another deadline, and through it all, you've been understanding and had my back faithfully. I couldn't ask for better people to share my blood or know me better than anyone.

ROGENA & AMI – Thank you for once again putting up with missed deadlines, dramatic breakdowns, and overall nuttiness. You must really love me. Just know I love you both back.

AMANDA SIMPSON – For once again making such an amazing cover and being so great about redoing it because I have issues.

SUNNY B. – I don't think there is anyone I bugged more often about this book than you. My whiny, half-finished voice messages must have annoyed you a time or two.... Honestly, I don't know why you're still friends with me. What's wrong with you, dude?

LISA P. KANE – You're my voice of reason, and I love how you go with the flow no matter what nonsense or fuckery I throw at you.

LJ SHEN – Thank you for not being afraid to tell me to get a grip.

PENELOPE DOUGLAS – God, I don't know how many times I've cried in your inbox, but thanks for patting me on the back when I needed it.

STREET MASTERS – We're small, but we kick ass anyway. Thank you, ladies, for all the constant love. Long ago, I stopped thinking of you all as a team to promote for me and as a group of friends who are always around to give me the support, a hand, or the kick I need. I LOVE YOU!

To the handful of special ladies who are not a part of my street team but promote me daily, THANK YOU! You know exactly who you are.

REIDERS – You are, without a doubt, my most loyal group of readers. You all keep me going and put up with my need to tease like champs. You even continue to read my words and stick around even though I'm a train wreck, and I love each and every one of you for it.

BLOGGERS – There are so many of you that I could never thank you all individually but never think I don't know who you are and what you do. Without you, no one would know my name or read my books. I never have to bribe or beg for your support, and I love that most about the bloggers in this community.

5-1-4 – The support I've found in this company amazes me. Without the support of my leadership, this book wouldn't have made it out on time. I'll never forget it. Thank you!

ALSO BY B.B. REID

CONTACT THE AUTHOR

Email: authorbbreid@gmail.com

Twitter: _BBREID

Instagram: _BBREID

Website: www.bbreid.com

ABOUT B.B. REID

B.B., ALSO KNOWN as Bebe, found her passion for romance when she read her first romance novel by Susan Johnson at a young age. She would sneak into her mother's closet for books and even sometimes the attic. When she finally decided to pick up a metaphorical pen and start writing, she found a new way to embrace her passion.

She favors a romance that isn't always easy on the eyes or heart and loves to see characters grow—characters who are seemingly doomed from the start but find love anyway.

Made in the USA
Charleston, SC
20 January 2017